ALL THE DEVILS ARE HERE

LOUISE PENNY

ALL THE
DEVILS
ARE HERE

MINOTAUR BOOKS
NEW YORK

First published in the United States by Minotaur Books,
an imprint of St. Martin's Publishing Group

ALL THE DEVILS ARE HERE. Copyright © 2020 by Three Pines Creations, Inc.
All rights reserved. Printed in the United States of America. For information,
address St. Martin's Publishing Group, 120 Broadway, New York, NY 10271.

www.minotaurbooks.com

Endpaper art by MaryAnna Coleman / www.maryannacolemandesign.com

Excerpts from "Sekhmet, the Lion-Headed Goddess of War, Violent Storms,
Pestilence & Recovery from Illness, Contemplates the Desert in the
Metrop" from *Morning in the Burned House: New Poems* by Margaret Atwood.
Copyright © 1995 by Margaret Atwood. Reprinted by permission of
Houghton Mifflin Harcourt Publishing Company. All rights reserved.
In Canada: Copyright © 1995 by O. W. Toad. Reprinted by permission of
McClelland & Stewart, a division of Penguin Random House
Canada Limited. All rights reserved.

Excerpts from *Vapour Trails* by Marylyn Plessner (2000).
Used by permission of Stephen Jarislowsky.

Library of Congress Cataloging-in-Publication Data

Names: Penny, Louise, author.
Title: All the devils are here / Louise Penny.
Description: First U.S. edition. | New York : Minotaur Books, 2020. |
Series: Chief Inspector Gamache novel ; 16
Identifiers: LCCN 2020017253 | ISBN 9781250145239 (hardcover) |
ISBN 9781250785541 (international, sold outside the U.S., subjects to
rights availability) | ISBN 9781250145253 (ebook)
Subjects: LCSH: Gamache, Armand (Fictitious character)—
Fiction. | GSAFD: Mystery fiction.
Classification: LCC PR9199.4.P464 A79 2020 | DDC 813/.6—dc23
LC record available at https://lccn.loc.gov/2020017253

Our books may be purchased in bulk for promotional, educational, or
business use. Please contact your local bookseller or the Macmillan Corporate
and Premium Sales Department at 1-800-221-7945, extension 5442,
or by email at MacmillanSpecialMarkets@macmillan.com.

First U.S. Edition: 2020
First International Edition: 2020

10 9 8 7 6 5 4 3 2 1

To Hope Dellon,
a great editor, an even better friend.
Goodness Exists

ALL THE DEVILS ARE HERE

CHAPTER 1

H ell is empty, Armand," said Stephen Horowitz.
  "You've mentioned that. And all the devils are here?" asked
Armand Gamache.

"Well, maybe not here, here"—Stephen spread his expressive
hands—"exactly."

"Here, here" was the garden of the Musée Rodin, in Paris, where
Armand and his godfather were enjoying a quiet few minutes. Outside the walls they could hear the traffic, the hustle and the tussle of
the great city.

But here, here, there was peace. The deep peace that comes not just
with quiet, but with familiarity.

With knowing they were safe. In the garden. In each other's
company.

Armand passed his companion a *tartelette au citron* and glanced casually around. It was a warm and pleasant late-September afternoon.
Shadows were distancing themselves from the trees, the statues, the
people. Elongating. Straining away.

The light was winning.

Children ran free, laughing and racing down the long lawn in front
of the château. Young parents watched from wooden benches, their
planks turned gray over the years. As would they, eventually. But for
now they relaxed, grateful for their children, and very grateful for the
few minutes away from them in this safe place.

A less likely setting for the devil would be hard to imagine.

But then, Armand Gamache thought, where else would you find darkness but right up against the light? What greater triumph for evil than to ruin a garden?

It wouldn't be the first time.

"Do you remember," Stephen began, and Armand turned back to the elderly man beside him. He knew exactly what he was about to say. "When you decided to propose to Reine-Marie?" Stephen patted their own bench. "Here? In front of that."

Armand followed the gesture and smiled.

It was a familiar story. One Stephen told every chance he got, and certainly every time godfather and godson made their pilgrimage here.

It was their best-loved place in all of Paris.

The garden on the grounds of the Musée Rodin.

Where better, the young Armand had thought many years earlier, to ask Reine-Marie to marry him? He had the ring. He'd rehearsed the words. He'd saved up six months of his measly salary as a lowly agent with the Sûreté du Québec for the trip.

He'd bring the woman he loved best, to the place he loved best. And ask her to spend the rest of her life with him.

His budget wouldn't stretch to a hotel, so they'd have to stay in a hostel. But he knew Reine-Marie wouldn't mind.

They were in love and they were in Paris. And soon, they'd be engaged.

But once again, Stephen had come to the rescue, lending the young couple his splendid apartment in the Seventh Arrondissement.

It wasn't the first time Armand had stayed there.

He'd practically grown up in that gracious Haussmann building, with its floor-to-ceiling windows looking out over the Hôtel Lutetia. The vast apartment had herringbone wood floors and marble fireplaces and tall, tall ceilings, making each room light and airy.

It was an inquisitive child's paradise, with its nooks and crannies. The armoire with the fake drawers made, he was sure, just for a little boy to hide in. There were assorted treasures to play with, when Stephen wasn't looking.

And furniture perfect for jumping on.

Until it broke.

Stephen collected art, and each day he'd choose one piece and tell his godson about the artists and the work. Cézanne. Riopelle and Lemieux. Kenojuak Ashevak.

With one exception.

The tiny watercolor that hung at the level of a nine-year-old's eye. Stephen never talked about it, mostly because, he'd once told Armand, there wasn't much to say. It wasn't exactly a masterpiece, like the others. Yet there was something about this particular work.

After a day out in the great city, they'd return exhausted, and while Stephen made *chocolat chaud* in the cramped kitchen, young Armand would drift over to the paintings.

Inevitably, Stephen would find the boy standing in front of the small watercolor, looking into the frame as though it was a window. At the tranquil village in the valley.

"That's worthless," Stephen had said.

But worthless or not, it was young Armand's favorite. He was drawn back to it on every visit. He knew in his heart that anything that offered such peace had great value.

And he suspected his godfather thought so, too. Otherwise he'd never have hung it with all the other masterpieces.

At the age of nine, just months after both Armand's parents had been killed in a car accident, Stephen had brought the boy to Paris for the first time. They'd walked together around the city. Not talking, but letting the silent little boy think his thoughts.

Eventually, Armand had lifted his head and begun to notice his surroundings. The wide boulevards, the bridges. Notre-Dame, the Tour Eiffel, the Seine. The brasseries, with Parisians sitting at round marble-topped tables on the sidewalks, drinking espresso or beer or wine.

At each corner, Stephen took his hand. Holding it firmly. Until they were safe on the other side.

And slowly young Armand realized he was safe, would always be safe, with this man. And that he would get to the other side.

And slowly, slowly, he'd returned to life.

Here. In Paris.

Then one morning his godfather had said, "Today, *garçon*, we're going to my very favorite place in all of Paris. And then we'll have an ice cream at the Hôtel Lutetia."

They'd strolled up boulevard Raspail and turned left onto rue de Varenne. Past the shops and patisseries. Armand lingered at the windows, looking at the mille-feuilles and madeleines and *pains aux raisins*.

They stopped at one, and Stephen bought them each a *tartelette au citron*, giving Armand the small paper bag to carry.

And then they were there. At an opening in a wall.

After paying the admission, they went in.

Armand, his mind on the treat in the bag, barely registered his surroundings. This felt like duty, before the reward.

He opened the bag and looked in.

Stephen put his hand on the boy's arm and said, "Patience. Patience. With patience comes choice, and with choice comes power."

The words meant nothing to the hungry little boy, except to say that he couldn't yet have the pastry.

Reluctantly, Armand closed the bag, then looked around.

"What do you think?" Stephen asked when he saw his godson's eyes widening.

He could read the boy's mind. It wasn't, in all honesty, all that difficult.

Who'd have thought such a place existed anywhere, never mind tucked, essentially hidden, behind tall walls, in the middle of the city? It was a world unto itself. A magic garden.

Had he been alone, Armand would have walked right by, mind on the uneaten pastry, never discovering what lay inside. Never seeing the beautiful château with its tall windows and sweeping terrace.

While not at all jaded, the child was by now used to magnificent buildings in Paris. The city was thick with them. What astonished him were the grounds.

The manicured lawns, the trees shaped like cones. The fountains.

But unlike the huge jardin du Luxembourg, created to impress, this garden was almost intimate.

And then there were the statues. Come upon here and there among the greenery. As though they'd been waiting patiently. For them.

Now and then the wail of a siren could be heard, coming from the world outside. The blast of a horn. A shout.

But all that did was intensify, for Armand, the sense of extreme peace he'd found, he felt, in the garden. A peace he hadn't known since that quiet knock on the door.

They walked slowly around, Stephen, for the first time, not leading but following, as Armand stopped in front of each of Rodin's statues.

But the boy kept glancing over his shoulder. To the cluster of men at the entrance, and exit, to the garden.

Eventually, Armand led them back there, and stood transfixed in front of the statue.

"*The Burghers of Calais,*" Stephen had said, his voice hushed, soothing. "In the Hundred Years' War, the English King, Edward, laid siege to the French port of Calais."

He looked at Armand to see if he was listening, but there was no indication either way.

"It was a crisis for the citizens. No food, no provisions could get past the English blockade. The French King, Philip, could have parleyed. Could have negotiated, to relieve the city. But he did nothing. He left them to starve. And they did. Men, women, children began to die."

Now Armand turned and looked up at Stephen. The boy might not really understand war. But death he understood.

"The King did that? He could've done something, but he let them die?"

"Both kings did. Yes. In order to win. Wars are like that." He could see the confusion, the upset, in the boy's deep brown eyes. "Do you want me to go on?" Stephen asked.

"*Oui, s'il vous plaît.*" And Armand turned back to the statue and the men frozen in time.

5

"Just as complete catastrophe threatened, King Edward did something no one expected. He decided to have mercy on the people of Calais. But he asked one thing. He'd spare the town if the six most prominent citizens would surrender. He didn't say it exactly, but everyone knew they'd be executed. As a warning to anyone else who might oppose him. They'd die so that the rest could live."

Stephen saw Armand's shoulders rise, then fall.

"The most prominent citizen, Eustache de Saint-Pierre, volunteered first. That's him, there." He pointed to one of the statues. A thin, grim man. "Then five others joined him. They were told to strip to their undergarments, put nooses around their necks, and carry the keys to the city and castle to the great gates. Which they did. The Burghers of Calais."

Armand raised his head and stared up into the eyes of Eustache. Unlike all the other statues he'd seen around Paris, here he didn't see glory. There were no angels ready to lift these men to Paradise. This was no fearless sacrifice. They were not marching, heads high, into splendid martyrdom.

What the boy saw was anguish. Despair. Resignation.

The burghers of this seaside town were afraid.

But they did it anyway.

Armand's lower lip began to tremble and his chin pucker, and Stephen wondered if he'd gone far too far in telling this boy this story.

He touched his godson's shoulder, and Armand swung around and buried his face in Stephen's sweater, throwing his arms around him, not in an embrace but in a grip. As one might cling to a pillar, to stop from being swept away.

"They were saved, Armand," said Stephen quickly, dropping to his knees and holding on to the sobbing boy. "They weren't executed. The King spared their lives."

It took Armand a few moments to absorb that. Finally pulling away, he dragged his sleeve across his face and looked at Stephen.

"Really?"

"*Oui.*"

"Really truly?" Armand gulped, his breath coming in fits as it caught in his throat.

"Really truly, *garçon*. They all lived."

The little boy thought, looking down at his sneakers, then up into Stephen's clear blue eyes. "Would you?"

Stephen, who knew what he was asking, almost said, *Yes, of course.* But stopped himself. This boy deserved the truth.

"Give up my life? For people I love, yes." He squeezed the thin shoulders and smiled.

"For strangers?"

Stephen, just getting to know his godson, was realizing that he would not be satisfied with the easy answer. There was something quietly relentless about this child.

"I hope so, but honestly? I don't know."

Armand nodded, then turning to the statue, he squared his shoulders.

"It was cruel." He spoke to the burghers. "What the King did. Letting them think they'd die."

His godfather nodded. "But it was compassionate to spare them. Life can be cruel, as you know. But it can also be kind. Filled with wonders. You need to remember that. You have your own choice to make, Armand. What're you going to focus on? What's unfair, or all the wonderful things that happen? Both are true, both are real. Both need to be accepted. But which carries more weight with you?" Stephen tapped the boy's chest. "The terrible or the wonderful? The goodness or the cruelty? Your life will be decided by that choice."

"And patience?" asked Armand, and Stephen caught something he hadn't noticed before. A hint of the mischievous.

The boy listened after all. Took everything in. And Stephen Horowitz realized he'd have to be careful.

There was no bench in front of the burghers, so Stephen had taken Armand over to his own favorite work by Rodin.

They opened the brown paper bag and ate their *tartelettes au citron* in front of *The Gates of Hell*. Stephen talked about the remarkable work while brushing powdery icing sugar off Armand's sweater.

"I still can't believe," Stephen said fifty years later as they sat in front of the same statue, and ate their *tartelettes au citron*, "that you decided to propose to Reine-Marie in front of *The Gates of Hell*. But then the idea did spring from the same mind that thought it was a good idea to take her mother a toilet plunger as a hostess gift the first time you were introduced."

"You remember that."

But of course he did. Stephen Horowitz forgot nothing.

"Thank God you came to me for advice before proposing, *garçon*."

Armand smiled. He hadn't actually gone up to Stephen's office, high above Montréal, that spring day thirty-five years ago, for advice. He went there to simply tell his godfather that he'd decided to ask his girlfriend of two years to marry him.

On hearing the news, Stephen had come around his desk and pulled the young man to him, holding him tight. Then Stephen gave a brusque nod and turned away. Bringing out a handkerchief, he glanced, for just a moment, out the window. Over Mount Royal, which dominated the city. And into the cloudless sky.

Then he turned back and considered the man he'd known since birth.

Taller than him now. Sturdy. Clean-shaven, with wavy dark hair, and deep brown eyes, both solemn and kind. With, yes, still that hint of the mischievous.

Armand had been to Cambridge to learn English, but instead of taking law, or business, as his godfather had advised, young Armand had, upon his return to Québec, entered the Sûreté academy.

He'd made his choice.

And he'd found wonderment. It came in the form of a junior librarian at the Bibliothèque et Archives nationales in Montréal named Reine-Marie Cloutier.

Stephen had taken his godson out for lunch at the nearby Ritz, to celebrate.

"Where will you propose?" Stephen had asked.

"Can you guess?"

"Paris."

"*Oui*. She's never been."

Armand and his godfather had returned to Paris every year. Exploring the city, discovering new haunts. Then ending the day eating ice cream at the Hôtel Lutetia, which was just across the street from Stephen's apartment. The waiters always made a fuss of the boy, even when he grew into a man.

Armand's adopted grandmother, Zora, who raised him, didn't approve of his going to the hotel, though it would be years before Armand understood why.

"It'll be our little secret," Stephen had said.

Zora also did not approve of Stephen. Though, again, it would be many years before Armand learned the reason. And learned that *crème glacée* at the Lutetia was the least of his godfather's secrets.

Over a glass of champagne in the Ritz in Montréal, Armand had told Stephen his plans for the proposal.

When he'd finished, his godfather stared at him.

"Jesus, *garçon*," Stephen had said. "*The Gates of Hell*? Dear God, and they gave you a gun?"

Stephen had been in his late fifties by then and at the height of his powers. The business magnate intimidated all around him. Armand suspected even the furniture cowered when Stephen Horowitz entered a room.

It wasn't simply the force of his personality and the immense wealth he was busy acquiring and wielding, but his willingness to use both power and money to destroy those he felt were crooks.

Sometimes it took him years, but eventually, he brought them down. Power. And patience. Stephen Horowitz had command of both.

He was genuinely kind and openly ruthless. And when he turned those intense blue eyes on a quarry, they quaked.

But not Armand.

Not because he'd never been in the crosshairs, but because what Armand was most afraid of wasn't being hurt by Stephen. He was afraid of hurting him. Disappointing him.

He'd argued with Stephen. Explaining that he loved Reine-Marie, and loved the tranquil garden in the middle of Paris.

"Where better to propose?"

"I don't know," Stephen had said, the clear blue eyes challenging Armand. "The métro? The catacombs? The morgue? For God's sake, *garçon*, anywhere but *The Gates of Hell*."

And after a moment's pause, Armand had chuckled. Seeing Stephen's point.

He hadn't actually thought of that bench as being in front of *The Gates of Hell*. He thought of it as the place where he'd found a measure of freedom from crushing grief. Where he'd found the possibility of peace. Where he'd found happiness, with lemon curd on his chin and icing sugar down his sweater.

He'd found sanctuary with his godfather just outside *The Gates of Hell*.

"I'll tell you where you need to do it," said Stephen. And did.

That had been thirty-five years earlier.

Armand and Reine-Marie had two grown children now. Daniel and Annie. Three grandchildren. The imminent arrival of Annie's second child was what had brought them to Paris.

Armand was now the same age Stephen had been when they'd had that conversation about the proposal. Over six feet tall, and stolidly built, Armand now had mostly gray hair, and his face was lined from the passage of time and the weight of difficult choices.

A deep scar at his temple spoke of the toll his job had taken. The wages of being a senior officer in the Sûreté du Québec.

But there were other lines. Deeper lines. That radiated from his eyes and mouth. Laugh lines.

They, too, spoke of the choices Armand had made. And the weight he gave them.

Stephen was now ninety-three and, while growing frailer, was still formidable. Still going in to work every day, and terrorizing those who needed the fear of, if not God, then this godfather put into them.

It would come as no surprise to his business rivals that Stephen Horowitz's favorite statue was Rodin's *Gates of Hell*. With the famous image of *The Thinker*. And, below it, the souls tumbling into the abyss.

Once again, godfather and godson sat side by side on the bench and ate their pastries in the sunshine.

· "Thank God I convinced you to propose in the jardin du Luxembourg," said Stephen.

Armand was about to correct him. It hadn't actually been that garden, but another.

Instead, he stopped and regarded his godfather.

Was he slowing down after all? It would be natural, at the age of ninety-three, and yet for Armand it was inconceivable. He reached out and brushed icing sugar off Stephen's vest.

"How's Daniel?" Stephen asked as he batted away Armand's hand.

"He's doing well. Roslyn's gone back to work in the design firm, now that the girls are in school."

"Daniel's happy in his job here in Paris, at the bank? He plans to stay?"

"*Oui.* He even got a promotion."

"Yes, I know."

"How do you know that?"

"I have dealings with the bank. I believe Daniel's in the venture capital department now."

"Yes. Did you—"

"Get him the promotion? No. But he and I get together every now and then, when I'm in Paris. We talk. He's a good man."

"Yes, I know." It seemed curious to Armand that Stephen felt the need to tell him that. As though he didn't know his own son.

And the next thing Stephen said went beyond curious. "Speak to Daniel. Make it up with him."

The words shocked Armand and he turned to Stephen. "*Pardon?*"

"Daniel. You need to make peace."

"But we have. Years ago. Everything's okay between us."

The sharp blue eyes turned on Armand. "Are you so sure?"

"What do you know, Stephen?"

"I know what you know, that old wounds run deep. They can fester. You see it in others, but miss it in your own son."

Armand felt a spike of anger, but recognized it for what it was.

Pain. And below that, fear. He'd mended the wounds with his oldest child. Years ago. He was sure of it. Hadn't he? "What're you saying?"

"Why do you think Daniel moved to Paris?"

"For the same reason Jean-Guy and Annie moved here. They got great job offers."

"And everything's been fine between you since?"

"With a few bumps, but yes."

"I'm glad."

But Stephen looked neither glad nor convinced. Before Armand could pursue it further, Stephen asked, "So that's your son. How about your daughter and Jean-Guy? Are they settling into their new lives in Paris all right?"

"Yes. A transition, of course. Annie's on maternity leave from her law firm, and Jean-Guy's adjusting to life in the private sector. Been a bit of a challenge."

"Not surprised. Since he's no longer your second-in-command at the Sûreté, he can't arrest people anymore," Stephen, who knew Jean-Guy Beauvoir well, said with a smile. "That can't have been easy."

"He did try to arrest a colleague who cut into the lunch line, but he learns quickly. No damage done. Thankfully, he told her his name is Stephen Horowitz."

Stephen laughed.

To say going from being Chief Inspector Beauvoir in the Sûreté du Québec to running a department in a multinational engineering firm in Paris was an adjustment would have been a vast understatement.

Having to do it without a gun was even more difficult.

"Daniel and Roslyn being here has helped a lot." As Armand spoke, he examined his godfather, to see his reaction to those words.

As a senior officer in the Sûreté du Québec, and Jean-Guy's boss for many years, Gamache was used to reading faces.

Less a hunter than an explorer, Armand Gamache delved into what people thought, but mostly how they felt. Because that was where actions were conceived.

Noble acts. And acts of the greatest cruelty.

But try as he might, Armand had difficulty reading his godfather.

For a time, he'd thought he was in a position of privilege, and had unique insight into this remarkable man. But as the years went by, he began to wonder if maybe the opposite was true. Maybe he was too close. Maybe others saw Stephen more clearly, more completely, than he could.

He still saw the man who had taken his hand and kept him safe.

Others, like his grandmother Zora, saw something else.

"How's Annie?" asked Stephen. "Are they ready for the baby?"

"As ready as anyone can be, I think."

"It was a big decision."

"*Oui.*" No use denying that. "She's due any day now. You'll see them tonight at dinner. I've made reservations for all of us at Juveniles. Eight o'clock."

"Terrific." Stephen unzipped his inner pocket and showed Armand the note in his slender agenda. "I assumed."

Already written there was *family*, then *Juveniles*.

"Reine-Marie and I will swing by and pick you up."

"*Non, non.* I'm having drinks with someone first. I'll meet you there." Stephen looked ahead of him. Staring at *The Thinker*.

"What're you thinking?" Armand asked.

"That I'm not afraid to die. I am a little afraid of going to Hell."

"Why do you say that?" asked Armand, shaken by the words.

"Just the natural fear of a ninety-three-year-old reviewing his life."

"What do you see?"

"I see far too much ice cream."

"Impossible." Armand paused for a moment, before speaking. "I see a good man. A brave man. This's a better world because you're in it."

Stephen smiled. "That's kind of you to say, but you don't know everything."

"Are you trying to tell me something?"

"*Non*, not at all." He reached out and gripped Armand's wrist. His laser-blue eyes holding Armand's. "I've always told the truth."

"I know you have." Armand placed his warm hand over Stephen's cool one and squeezed gently. "When we first sat down, you said that Hell is empty and all the devils are here. What did you mean?"

"It's one of my favorite quotes, you know that," said Stephen.

And Armand did. Stephen loved to use the lines from *The Tempest* to unnerve business rivals, colleagues. Friends. Strangers on planes.

But this time was different. This time Stephen had added something. Something Armand had never heard from him before.

A specificity.

"You said the devils aren't here, here." Armand lifted his hands in imitation of Stephen's gesture. "Why did you say that?"

"Who the hell knows? I'm an old man. Stop badgering me."

"If they aren't here, then where are they?"

The shadows had reached them now, and it was growing chilly in the shade.

"You should know." Stephen turned to him. But not on him. It was a slow, considered movement. "You've met them often enough. You hunt devils for a living." His blue eyes held Armand's brown. "I'm very proud of you, son."

Son.

Stephen had never called him that. Not once in fifty years.

Garçon, yes. Boy. It was said with great affection. But it wasn't the same. As son.

Armand knew Stephen had been careful never to use that word. To not step on his late father's memory and place in Armand's life.

But now he had. Was it a slip? An indication of age and frailty? The defenses worn down, allowing his true feelings to escape? On that one, small, word.

"Don't you worry about the devils, Armand. It's a beautiful September afternoon, we're in Paris, and your granddaughter is about to be born. Life is good." Stephen patted Armand's knee, then used it to push himself upright. "Come along, *garçon*. You can take me home."

They paused, as they always did, at *The Burghers*. To look into those grim, determined faces.

"Just remember." Stephen turned to look at his godson.

Armand held his eyes and nodded.

Then the two men walked slowly down rue de Varenne. Armand took Stephen's arm as they crossed the streets. They ambled past antique shops and stopped at a patisserie, where Armand bought a *pain aux raisins escargot* for Reine-Marie, her favorite. And a croissant for Stephen to have with his breakfast.

At the large red-lacquered double door into Stephen's building, the elderly man said, "Leave me here. I might just go across to the Hôtel Lutetia for an aperitif."

"And by 'aperitif' you mean ice cream?"

It was only when Armand was crossing the Pont d'Arcole, on his way to their apartment in the Marais, that he realized he hadn't pursued the question with Stephen. Or maybe Stephen had managed to divert his attention.

Away from the devils. That were somewhere here, here. In Paris.

CHAPTER 2

⸺

Jean-Guy Beauvoir could almost feel the chill enter the room, despite the sun streaming through his office window.

He looked up from his screen, but already knew who he'd see. Along with the lowered temperature, a slight aroma always accompanied his deputy department head. And while Beauvoir knew the chill was his imagination, the smell was not.

Sure enough, Séverine Arbour was at his door. She wore her usual delicately condescending smile. It seemed to complement, like a silk scarf, her designer outfit. Beauvoir wasn't aware enough of fashion to say if Madame Arbour was wearing Chanel, or Yves Saint Laurent, or maybe Givenchy. But since arriving in Paris he'd come to at least know the names. And to recognize *haute couture* when he saw it.

And he saw it now.

In her forties, elegant and polished, Madame Arbour was the definition of *soignée*. A Parisienne through and through.

The only thing she wore that he could name was her scent.

Sauvage by Dior. A man's cologne.

He wondered if it was a message and considered changing his cologne from Brut to Boss. But decided against it. Things were complex enough between them without entering into a war of fragrances with his number two.

"Lots of women wear men's cologne," Annie explained when he

told her about it. "And men wear women's scents. It's all just marketing. If you like the smell, why not?"

She'd then dared him ten euros to wear her *eau de toilette* into work the next day. A dare he took up. As fate would have it, his own boss, Carole Gossette, chose that very day to invite him out for lunch. For the first time.

He went to her private club, the Cercle de l'Union Interalliée, smelling of Clinique's Aromatics Elixir. The exact same scent the senior VP at the engineering giant was herself wearing.

It actually seemed to endear him to her.

In a *quid pro quo*, Annie went into her law offices smelling of Brut. Her male colleagues had, up to then, been cordial but distant. Waiting for the *avocate* from Québec to prove herself. But that day they seemed to relax. To even pay her more respect. She, and her musk, were welcomed into the fold.

Like her father, Annie Gamache was not one to turn her back on an unexpected advantage. She continued to wear the *eau de Cologne* until the day she took maternity leave.

Jean-Guy, on the other hand, did not put on the perfume again, despite the fact he actually preferred the warm scent to his Brut. It smelled of Annie, and that always calmed and gladdened him.

Séverine Arbour stood at the door, her face set in a pleasant smile with a base note of smoky resentment and a hint of smug.

Was she biding her time, waiting for her chance to knife him in the back? Beauvoir thought so. But he also knew that compared to the brutal culture in the Sûreté du Québec, the internal politics of this multinational corporation were nothing.

This knifing would, at least, be figurative.

Beauvoir had hoped that, with the passage of time, Madame Arbour would come to accept him as head of the department. But all that had happened, in the almost five months he'd been there, was that they'd developed a mutual suspicion.

He suspected she was trying to undermine him.

She suspected he was incompetent.

Part of Jean-Guy Beauvoir recognized they both might be right.

Madame Arbour took the chair across from him and looked on, patiently.

It was, Beauvoir knew, meant to annoy him. But it wouldn't work. Nothing could upset him that day.

His second child was due any time now.

Annie was healthy, as was their young son, Honoré.

He had a job he enjoyed, if didn't as yet completely understand.

They were in Paris. Paris, for God's sake.

How a snot-nosed kid went from playing ball hockey in the alleys of East End Montréal to being an executive in Paris was frankly still a bit of a mystery to him.

To add to Jean-Guy's buoyant mood, it was Friday afternoon. Armand and Reine-Marie Gamache had arrived from Montréal, and tonight they'd all be having dinner together at one of their favorite bistros.

"*Oui?*" he said.

"You wanted to see me?" Madame Arbour asked.

"No. What gave you that idea, Séverine?"

She nodded toward his laptop. "I sent you a document. About the funicular project in Luxembourg."

"Yes. I'm just reading it." He did not say it was, in fact, the second time through, and he still didn't understand what he was looking at. Except that it was an elevator up a cliff. In Luxembourg.

"Is there something you want to say about it?" He removed his glasses.

It was the end of the day and his eyes were tired, but he'd be damned if he'd pass his hand over them.

Instinctively, Jean-Guy Beauvoir understood it would be a mistake to show this woman any weakness. Physical, emotional, intellectual.

"I just thought you might have some questions," she said. And waited. Expectantly.

Beauvoir had to admit, she was beginning to dull his sense of well-being.

He was used to dealing with criminals. And not petty thieves or knuckleheads who got into drunken brawls, but the worst of the worst. Killers. And one mad poet with a duck.

He'd learned how not to let them into his head. Except, of course, the duck.

And yet somehow Séverine Arbour managed to get under his skin. If not, as yet, into his skull.

But it wasn't for lack of trying.

And he knew why. Even the brawling knuckleheads could figure it out.

She wanted his job. Felt she should have it.

He could almost sympathize with her. It was, after all, a great job.

Beauvoir had had his regular Friday lunch with his own boss, Carole Gossette, in a nearby brasserie. But the previous lunch had been at thirty thousand feet, on the corporate jet, as they flew to Singapore.

Two weeks before that, he'd gone to Dubai.

His first trip had been to the Maldives to look at the reef-protection system they were installing on the tiny atoll in the Indian Ocean. He'd had to look it up, and finally found the cluster of islands hanging off the southern tip of India.

A month earlier he'd been rolling around in the ice-encrusted muck in Québec, trying to arrest a murderer and fighting for his life. Now he was eating langoustine off fine china, and approaching a tropical island in a private jet.

On the flight, Madame Gossette, in her fifties, small, round, good-humored, filled him in on the corporate philosophy. On why they chose to do certain projects and not others.

A mechanical engineer herself, with a postdoc degree from the École polytechnique in Lausanne, she explained, in simple terms, the engineering, avoiding the infantile tone Madame Arbour used.

Beauvoir found himself turning to Madame Gossette more and more, for guidance, for information. To explain certain projects. Where perhaps he'd normally be expected to talk to his deputy head, he found he was avoiding Arbour and going straight to Madame Gossette. And she seemed to enjoy the role of mentor to the executive she'd personally recruited.

Though she did gently suggest he lean more on his number two.

"Don't be put off by her attitude," said Madame Gossette. "Séverine Arbour is very good. We were lucky to get her."

"Didn't her previous company go bust?"

"Declared bankruptcy, yes. Overextended."

"Then she's the lucky one, to find another job," said Beauvoir.

Madame Gossette had simply shrugged, in an eloquent Gallic manner. Meant to convey a lot. And nothing.

Jean-Guy lapsed into silence, and went back to reading the documents Madame Gossette had given him when they'd boarded. About coral, and currents, and buoys. About shipping lanes and something called anthropogenic disturbance.

Finally, nine hours into the ten-hour flight to the Maldives, he'd asked the question he'd been dying to pose but was a little afraid of the answer.

"Why did you hire me? I'm not an engineer. You must've known that I can barely read these."

He held up the sheaf of paper. Part of him suspected they'd hired the wrong Jean-Guy Beauvoir. That somewhere in Québec there was a highly trained engineer wondering why he hadn't gotten the job with GHS Engineering.

"I was wondering when you'd ask," said Madame Gossette, with a hearty laugh. Then, still smiling, she looked at him, her eyes keen. Intelligent. "Why do you think?"

"I think you think there's something wrong in the company."

That, of course, was the other possibility. That she had hired the right Jean-Guy Beauvoir. The senior investigator with the Sûreté du Québec. Skilled, trained. Not in engineering, but in finding criminals.

Madame Gossette sat back in her seat. Examining him. "Why do you say that? Has something come up?"

"*Non,*" he said, careful now. "It's just a thought."

To be fair, it wasn't something that had occurred to him until he'd said it. But once it was out, he could see that it might be true.

"Why else would you hire a cop to fill a senior management job when clearly it should be taken by an engineer?"

"You undervalue yourself, Monsieur Beauvoir. We have plenty of engineers already. They're thick on the ground. *Eh bien*, another engineer was the last thing we needed."

"What did you need?"

"A skill set. An attitude. A leader. You convinced men and women to follow you into life-and-death situations. I've read the reports. I've seen the online videos."

Beauvoir bristled at that. Those stolen videos should never have been posted. But they had been, and there was no undoing the damage.

"You're not expecting me to do the same for you," he said, managing a smile.

"Lead us into battle? I hope not. I'd make quite a target." She laughed and put her hands on her substantial body. "No. You're heading up a new department, created to provide another level of scrutiny. Each project is carefully evaluated before we choose to bid on it. It must be both profitable and have some benefit to the larger population."

He had noticed that. It was one of the reasons he'd accepted to work for GHS. As the father of one child with another on the way, he was waking up to certain frightening truths about the state of the world.

GHS designed dams and highways, bridges and planes.

But at least half of its projects were water treatment plants, anti-erosion methods, reforestation. Alternatives to fossil fuels. Disaster relief modules.

"But," said Madame Gossette, breaking into his thoughts, and leaning forward, "it's always wise to have disinterested observers making sure all is going according to plan. That's your department."

"Then nothing's wrong?" he asked.

"I didn't exactly say that." She was choosing her words carefully now. "It's one thing to have a philosophy. It's another thing to follow through. That's what we expect from you. Not to come up with the plan, others will do that, but to make sure it doesn't . . . what's the word? Corrupt."

"You suspect corruption?"

"No, no, not that sort of corrupt. Our concern is that, with all good intentions, some project managers might start cutting corners. It's easily done. Don't be fooled by the trappings." She glanced around the cabin of the corporate jet. "This sort of success comes with a lot of pressure. There're deadlines, penalties, bank loans, violent regime changes. And our people are stuck in the middle. Priorities can become muddy. It would be natural for some to feel that pressure and choose speed over quality. And try to hide it when something goes wrong. Not because they're bad people, but because they're people. That way lies tragedy."

"Which isn't good for business," he said.

She spread her hands. It was a simple truth. She reached for her tea. Then, after taking a sip, she said, "Are you familiar with the poet Auden?"

Oh, shit, Beauvoir thought. *Not another one.* And here he was, trapped at thirty thousand feet. What was it about bosses?

"I've heard of him." *Her?*

"And the crack in the tea-cup opens / A lane to the land of the dead."

"Is there a crack in your cup?" he asked.

She smiled and put it down. "Not that I know of. If one occurs, it's your job to find it."

He understood then what she meant. And, miraculously, what Auden meant.

"But how can I tell if something's wrong if I don't even know what's 'right'?"

"That's why you have a department full of engineers, including Séverine Arbour. She's a first-rate engineer. Use her." Madame Gossette's eyes held his. "Trust her."

Beauvoir nodded, but quietly wondered why, if Arbour was such a great engineer, she was in his department instead of working on actual projects.

"So 'Quality Control' is a bit misleading. It's really policing. I'm an enforcer?" asked Beauvoir, cutting into his profiterole.

"You must've suspected that when we gave you those brass knuckles in your welcome basket."

He laughed then.

"No, you're not an enforcer," she said. "You're our safety net. Our last hope if things go wrong, to stop something horrible from happening." She held his eyes, deadly serious. "I don't expect it, don't suspect it. But I need to be sure."

It was interesting, thought Beauvoir, that she said "I," not "we."

"I've told you why I hired you, now you tell me why you took the job. You turned it down a number of times."

She was right. He'd declined it twice, but finally relented. And the reason?

He was worn down, worn out by his work in the Sûreté du Québec. He'd headed up the homicide department after his mentor and chief, and father-in-law, Armand Gamache, had been suspended.

Beauvoir had watched the humiliation Gamache had been put through. The insinuations of wrongdoing. The failure by politicians to protect and defend Gamache. Though they knew he'd only acted in the service's, in the citizens', best interest.

Chief Inspector Beauvoir himself had been reinstated after an almost equally humiliating series of investigations.

Each day they tracked down killers. Each day they put their own lives on the line.

And in return they were scapegoated. Chained to the ground, food for politicians looking for reelection.

The salary was modest compared to private industry, the risks incalculable, the rewards harder and harder to find. Jean-Guy had a young family, who he hoped to see grow up. He had a daughter arriving who'd need both her parents.

And so the third time GHS Engineering had approached him, shown him the salary they were offering, told him the job was in Paris, he'd discussed it with Annie. And they'd agreed.

So Jean-Guy Beauvoir had left the Sûreté, just as Chief Inspector Gamache had returned. Beauvoir handed the job back to the once and future head of homicide.

But he wouldn't tell Madame Gossette all that.

"It was time for a change," he simply said as the flight attendant cleared their plates.

And change it certainly was proving. Though perhaps not quite as much of a change as he'd thought.

"What happens if I find something's wrong?"

"You come to me."

"How do I know the—how did you put it?—crack in the teacup didn't come from higher up? It often does, you know. Start there."

"*Oui*. I guess that's where your investigative skills come in." Once again she leaned forward, as the plane banked and prepared to land on the tiny island in the middle of the vast and impossibly blue ocean. "*Voyons*, I have absolutely no reason to suspect anything's wrong. If I did, I'd direct you to it. You're here to make sure we don't, intentionally or not, *open a lane to the land of the dead*." Her gaze now was hard. Almost fierce. "We design things that improve quality of life. But that, if they fall apart, take lives. We need to make absolutely sure. You understand?"

She stared at him so intently, he was taken aback. Until that moment he'd seen the job from his perspective.

A soft landing after the harsh realities of the Sûreté. A salary far in excess of anything he ever thought he'd make. They'd be safe. They'd be comfortable. They'd be in Paris.

Now he saw it from Madame Gossette's perspective.

Lives were at stake. And his job was to make sure none were lost.

"I can't possibly keep an eye on all the projects," he said. "There are hundreds."

"Which is why you have a staff. Don't worry, once you get comfortable, you'll be able to get a sense when something's off. To sniff it out."

Sniff? he almost said. What exactly did she think investigating was? And yet he had to admit when something went corrupt, there was a certain odor.

Jean-Guy Beauvoir had thought about that conversation a lot in the following weeks and months. And he thought about it again as he looked at his deputy head of department, radiating Dior and resentment.

"I think I can muddle through the Luxembourg plans, Séverine. *Merci.* How's work going on the Patagonia project?"

A part of him sympathized with Madame Arbour. But if she hadn't accepted him by now, hadn't gotten on board with his leadership, then one of them would have to go.

And it won't be me, thought Beauvoir.

"Patagonia? I know nothing about Patagonia." She got to her feet. "I'm sorry. I was under the impression you'd want to talk about the Luxembourg project."

"Why would you think that?"

"Well, the final safety tests are next week. Maybe you'd like to be there for that?"

"I don't see why. Would you like to go? Is that why you're here?"

"No, no. That's okay."

It was, even by Séverine Arbour standards, an odd and off-putting exchange.

"Is there something you want to say, Séverine, about Luxembourg?"

"No."

As she left his office, Jean-Guy considered looking at the Luxembourg report. Again. But it was past five. He had to get home and help feed Honoré, let Annie nap before their dinner out.

Luxembourg would wait.

Grabbing his jacket from the back of his chair, he walked next door to Arbour's office and said, "I'm going home. Have a good weekend."

She glanced up, then back down to her screen. Without a word.

When she was alone in the office, Arbour looked around. She was about, she knew, to pass what pilots called the point of no return. One more keystroke and she'd be totally committed to this course of action.

Through the window she could see the Tour Eiffel in the distance.

A marvel of French engineering. A monument to innovation and audacity. Something to be proud of.

Then, returning to her laptop, she pressed send.

Gathering her Chanel handbag, she left, pausing only to sign out.

"*Bon weekend*," said the guard, after he'd searched her bag.

She smiled, wished him a good weekend, too. Then headed to the métro.

There was no turning back now.

CHAPTER 3

⁓

Reine-Marie Gamache slipped her arm through her husband's as they walked along rue des Archives to the bus stop on rue des Quatre-Fils.

Armand had suggested he flag down a taxi to take them from their apartment in the Marais to the restaurant, but Reine-Marie preferred the bus. It was a route she knew well. One that always confirmed for her that she was in Paris.

"Do you remember the first time we took this bus?" she asked.

He heard her words but was thinking about the first time Reine-Marie had taken his arm. Like this.

It was their third date, and they were walking along the slippery winter sidewalk in Montréal after dinner.

He'd reached out for her, to keep her steady, just as Reine-Marie had reached for him.

To keep him steady.

She'd put her arm through his. So that their fates would be inter-twined. If one lost their balance, the other would right them. Or they'd fall together.

"You had on that blue cape your mother loaned you," he said, re-membering that chilly night.

"I had on the polka dot dress I'd borrowed from my sister," she said, remembering that warm day.

"It was winter," he said.

"It was the height of summer."

"*Ah, yes,*" he said into the evening air. "*I remember it well.*"

"You nut," she laughed, recognizing the reference.

He smiled. And squeezed her arm. As they passed men and women, young and old, lovers and strangers, strolling like them along rue des Quatre-Fils.

"Ready?" Daniel called upstairs.

"Can't we come with you, Daddy?" Florence asked.

She and her sister were already in the flannel pajamas their grandparents had brought from Québec.

Moose roamed Florence's pajamas, while baby black bears played on Zora's.

The sisters stood side by side in the living room, looking up at their father.

"*Non, mes petits singes,*" Daniel said, kneeling down. "My little monkeys. You need to stay here and play with your cousin."

They looked over at Honoré, asleep on a blanket on the floor.

"He's not much fun," said Zora, uncertainly.

Tante Annie laughed from the depth of the chair she'd sunk into. The babysitters had arrived. They just needed Roslyn.

"Judging by the kicks," Annie said, putting a hand on her stomach, "the next one might never sleep. Want to feel?"

The girls raced each other over, and while they placed their tiny hands on the enormous belly, Jean-Guy and Daniel drifted together.

"I remember that," said Daniel. His deep voice was wistful, soft. "When Roslyn was pregnant. It seemed incredible."

Jean-Guy watched Annie as she smiled and nodded, listening to the girls. Florence, the eldest at six, took after her mother. Slender, athletic, extroverted.

Zora took after her father. Large-boned, slightly awkward, shyer. Where Florence could be impetuous, chasing balls, running into lampposts, skinning her knees leaping off swings, Zora was calmer, gentler. More thoughtful.

28

Where Florence decided she was afraid of birds, shrieking in the park and running away, Zora stood with a handful of bread, feeding them.

Watching them, Jean-Guy was so grateful that their unborn daughter would have them to play with, and Honoré, who was fiercely loyal, as her brother. She'd need it. Him. Them.

And what would Honoré get, in his sister?

A lifetime of love, he hoped. And responsibility, he knew.

He looked at his sleeping son, and felt that pang of guilt, for what he was being given, without his consent.

"I'm here," said Roslyn, hurrying down the stairs from their bedroom. "Sorry I'm late. Here, let me help you."

She put out her hand, and together with Jean-Guy and Daniel, they hauled Annie out of the chair.

"Did you hear a thucking sound?" Jean-Guy asked.

"Thuck off," said Annie.

She put her arm through his, and he held her close as they stepped into the cool September evening.

Armand and Reine-Marie got off the bus at the familiar stop. The Bibliothèque nationale.

Armand glanced around. It would appear, to any fellow passenger also alighting, as though he was just getting his bearings.

In fact, the head of homicide for the Sûreté du Québec was scanning the street. Taking in, instinctively, the brasseries, the shops. The doorways, the alleyways. Their fellow pedestrians. The cars and trucks.

Paris was far from immune to violence. And had a tragic recent history of terrorist attacks.

While comfortable in the city, he was still keenly aware of his surroundings. But then, he did the same thing while walking the dogs through the forest at home.

They strolled down rue de Richelieu and in less than a minute had arrived at the *bar à vins*, with its window display of bottles.

They were greeted with kisses and embraces by the owner's daughter, Margaux.

Now a grown woman and married, Margaux had been there thirty-five years earlier when the Gamaches had run into Juveniles, soaked through in a sudden downpour, and decided to stay for dinner.

Margaux had been just five years old and was working the bar.

Her father had bent down and whispered in her ear, pointing to them. She'd walked over to the newcomers, a white linen towel over her raised forearm, and gravely suggested a nice red wine from Andalusia.

She'd pronounced it carefully. Then looked back at her father, who nodded approval and smiled at the young couple.

Margaux had now taken over the restaurant and her husband, Romain, was the head chef. But Tim remained the owner and was still known as the Big Boss.

This evening the familiar carafe was already on the table waiting for them. They were the first of their party to arrive and were seated at their regular long table by the wooden bar.

Armand and Reine-Marie chatted with the Big Boss, while jazz played softly in the background. Within minutes Daniel and Roslyn arrived, with Annie and Jean-Guy.

There were shouts of delight as Margaux put her hand on Annie's belly and the two women discussed the upcoming birth, while the others exchanged greetings.

Once the hubbub died down, they sat. Daniel poured the wine, and Margaux brought over fresh-squeezed juice for Annie and a Coke for Jean-Guy. Warm baguettes were placed on cutting boards on the table, along with a *terrine de campagne*, whipped butter, and small bowls of olives.

"I thought Stephen was coming," said Annie, looking at the empty chair.

"He is," said her father. "We saw each other this afternoon."

"Let me guess," said Daniel. "At the Musée Rodin?" He turned to Roslyn. "Did you ever hear about when Dad decided to propose to Mom?"

"Never," said Roslyn, with exaggerated interest. Like the rest of them, she'd heard it a hundred times. "What happened?"

Armand narrowed his eyes at his daughter-in-law, in mock disapproval, and she laughed.

"The girls love their pajamas," Roslyn said to Reine-Marie. "I'm afraid they're going to want to wear them everywhere."

"I say let them," said Daniel. "And by the way, Mamma, thank you for not letting Dad pick out the gift."

"He had the paint rollers all wrapped before I stopped him."

Armand shook his head sadly. "I guess they'll have to wait until Christmas."

While the others laughed, Armand watched Daniel.

He was enjoying himself.

Daniel seemed to have made peace with Jean-Guy. Long jealous of the close relationship his father had developed with his second-in-command, now Daniel could establish his own relationship with Jean-Guy.

Still, Armand noticed that Daniel made sure to put Jean-Guy as far from him as possible. Though that might have just been a coincidence.

He himself hoped to find time in the next day or so for a quiet walk or meal with Daniel. Just the two of them. To make sure everything really was okay, after what Stephen had said.

Armand's eyes returned to the empty chair. It was twenty past eight, and Stephen, normally a fiend for punctuality, hadn't arrived.

"Excusez-moi," he said, and made to get up, just as the door to the bistro opened and the elderly man appeared.

"Stephen," exclaimed Annie, and struggled to get up before Jean-Guy hauled her to her feet.

Armand and Reine-Marie stood at their places while the younger ones greeted Stephen, then were corralled back to their seats by Margaux in an effort to unblock the aisle in the tiny restaurant.

Daniel gestured for more wine, while Stephen placed his phone on the table in front of him and nodded to the barman. His usual.

The martini arrived along with a fresh liter of red.

"A toast," said Armand, when they'd all ordered. "To family. New"—he nodded to Annie's belly—"and very, very—"

"Very," they all joined in and turned to Stephen, "old."

Stephen raised his glass and said, "Fuck off."

"My father's a man of few words," said Daniel when the laughter stopped.

"Yeah, you don't know him so well," said Jean-Guy. "Just wait 'til he starts reciting 'The Wreck of the Hesperus.'"

"Just for that," said Armand. He cleared his throat and looked very serious. *"It was the schooner Hesperus—"*

Everyone laughed. With one exception. Out of the corner of his eye Armand caught the scowl on Daniel's face. He clearly did not like being told, even in jest, that Beauvoir knew his father better than he did.

Stephen had also noticed the look on Daniel's face and gave Armand the slightest of nods before glancing at his phone.

Then, turning to Annie and Jean-Guy, he asked, "How're you feeling?"

They talked candidly for a few minutes.

"If you need anything," said Stephen, and left it at that.

"Maybe some ice cream at the Lutetia?" said Annie.

"That I can do," said Stephen. "After Monday. We can all celebrate."

"What's happening on Monday?" asked Jean-Guy.

"Just some meetings. Speaking of which, how's your new job?"

Down the table, Armand was saying to Daniel, "Wonderful news about your promotion. A whole new department, too."

"It is," said Daniel. "Venture capital. Already made one investment."

"What's that?"

"Can't say."

Can't, Armand wondered, *or won't?*

"So, you do a lot of risk assessment?" he asked.

"Exactly."

His father listened closely, asking questions. Gently pulling information out of Daniel until his son relaxed and began speaking freely, even enthusiastically.

Reine-Marie watched as Daniel, after a few minutes, leaned closer to his father.

They were so much alike, in so many ways. They even looked alike.

At six foot two, Daniel was slightly taller than his father. And heftier. Not fat, but there was meat on the bone.

As there was with Armand. But slightly less so.

Daniel had grown a beard, which had come in reddish, with a few strands of gray, which surprised Reine-Marie. Time was marching on.

He had thick brown hair, which he wore closely cropped.

His father's hair was now quite gray, and slightly wavy. And slightly thinning. Clean-shaven, Armand's face had more lines, of course. And that deep scar at the temple.

Like his father, Daniel was kind and almost courtly.

Unlike his father, young Daniel had not been a scholar, but what the boy had was self-discipline. He worked hard, and often excelled past his more naturally talented friends.

He'd been a happy boy.

Until . . .

At the age of eight something changed. A wall went up between him and his father. At first it had been a very subtle step back. Always a polite little boy, there was now a formality. A frigidity. A caution that grew into a coolness.

That grew into a chasm.

Reine-Marie had watched as Armand tried to close the gap, but it only seemed to widen with each embrace.

Armand volunteered to coach his son's hockey team until Daniel had asked him to stop.

He'd then driven the boy to early-morning practices, and sat in the stands with a wretched coffee from the vending machine to warm his hands. Watching.

Until Daniel told him to stop.

Tucking him in at night, he'd always, always told the boy that he loved him.

The words had been met with silence. But still, he'd never stopped, to this day, telling Daniel that he loved him. And he showed, in every way he knew, that he not only loved the boy but also loved being Daniel's father.

Having lost both his parents, Armand wanted his children to have a mother and father who they could trust to keep them safe and always be there.

But it was never enough for Daniel. Something had torn. Some hole had opened inside him that could not be filled.

And yet Armand remained smitten with the boy. Reine-Marie didn't think any father could love his children more.

Then came the teen years, and the real troubles. With the drugs. With the arrests.

As soon as he could, Daniel moved away. Putting a deep blue sea between them.

And then Jean-Guy arrived. Agent Beauvoir. Found in some basement Sûreté servitude. Angry, arrogant. One insult away from being fired from the detachment and booted out of the service.

Chief Inspector Gamache had recognized something in the young man. And had, to everyone's astonishment, not least Agent Beauvoir's, brought him into homicide. The most sought after, the most prestigious department in the Sûreté du Québec.

Armand had become Jean-Guy's mentor. And more.

Jean-Guy had risen to become Armand's second-in-command. And more.

And Daniel had never forgiven either.

Reine-Marie and Armand had talked about that. About possibly putting some distance between himself and Jean-Guy. For Daniel's sake.

But Armand would not do it. Besides, it wouldn't help.

"Have you asked Daniel what's wrong?"

It was the only time she'd ever seen Armand annoyed with her.

"You think I haven't tried that? I've asked. I've begged Daniel to tell me what I've done. He just looks at me like I should know. I can't keep twisting myself around, hoping something will finally satisfy him. Beauvoir's a great investigator and a good man. He shouldn't be punished because of my relationship with my son."

"I know."

What she also knew was that Jean-Guy Beauvoir wasn't some replacement for their son. His relationship to Armand was far different. Far older. It seemed almost ancient, as though the two had known each other for lifetimes.

They belonged together.

"Daniel loves you, Armand." She squeezed his hand. "I know he does. Give him time."

Armand had dropped his head, then raised it. "I'm sorry I was short with you. I just . . ."

"*Oui.*"

As the years went by, and the grandchildren were born, he and Daniel had grown closer. Armand wondered if becoming a father himself had softened Daniel toward his own father. Made him forgive whatever trespass had happened.

There was still, he could sense, a small distance. It was as though there was a thin strand of barbed wire between them, so that he could only get so close before feeling the jabs.

But Armand kept trying, and the distance had diminished. Until, finally, it was imperceptible. No larger than a slight crack in a teacup.

Reine-Marie watched the two in the bistro. Leaning toward each other. And she dared hope.

Down the table, Jean-Guy and Annie were still talking with Stephen.

"What do you know, sir, about Luxembourg?"

"Luxembourg?" asked Stephen, leaning forward and checking his phone.

"You expecting a call?" asked Annie.

"No."

Just then their dinners arrived.

Merlu Breton for Stephen. The tender whitefish was surrounded by baby potatoes, grilled beets, and a delicate sauce.

"That's very light," said Annie as her massive steak frites arrived, with its sauce béarnaise.

"I'm saving myself for the rice pudding," explained Stephen.

"There's a project in Luxembourg," said Jean-Guy as his own steak frites arrived. "A funicular. But I'm having trouble understanding the engineering reports."

Stephen nodded. "So do I. I don't even try anymore. When I invest in an engineering company or project, I just read the emails between the project managers and home office. They're much more illuminating."

He put down his knife and fork and looked at the young man. "Has something in this Luxembourg project caught your interest?"

Jean-Guy frowned as he thought. *"Non."*

"You're sure?"

"Yes."

The steely blue eyes glared at Jean-Guy, and his mind went blank. It was like looking down the barrel of a shotgun.

"Then why are we talking about it?" demanded Stephen. "You must've learned the dark art of banality from your former boss."

Annie laughed, and even Jean-Guy gave a snort of amusement as all three looked down the table.

Armand was focused on Daniel and apparently hadn't heard.

But Daniel had. Not the words, but the laughter. He shot a glance their way. And realized they were looking, and laughing, at him.

"So," said Daniel, breaking off his conversation with his father to speak to Stephen at the other end of the table. "We know Mom and Dad came to see Annie and Jean-Guy. But what brings you to Paris?"

Armand felt the glancing blow. A flesh wound, but a wound nevertheless.

"I came to Paris for meetings," said Stephen. "Arrived yesterday. Timed it to be here when the baby arrives, I hope." He placed his hand over Annie's, then gave Daniel a penetrating look. "Your parents and I also came to see you and Roslyn and the girls."

And Daniel colored. But did not apologize.

"Now," Stephen said, glancing around the table, "have I ever told you about how your father—"

"Planned to propose to Mom?" said Annie. "Never. What happened?"

Armand just shook his head and grimaced.

"A toast," said Stephen, raising his glass. "To *The Gates of Hell.*"

They clinked glasses, and Stephen caught Armand's eye. There was amusement and genuine happiness there, Armand was glad to see. But also a warning.

The old trip wire, the barbed wire, was still in place after all.

"Really," said Reine-Marie once the laughter died down. "The better question is where your father took me for our honeymoon."

"I assumed it was here in Paris," said Annie.

"I think we should order dessert," said Armand, and tried to get Margaux's attention.

"*Non*, not Paris," said Reine-Marie.

"Manoir Bellechasse?" asked Daniel.

"Rice pudding, anyone?" asked Armand, putting on his reading glasses and lowering his head to the menu.

"*Non*. Shall you tell them, or should I?" Reine-Marie asked her husband.

"Why didn't we ever think to ask?" Annie asked her brother.

"Too busy laughing at the proposal," he said. "Attention diverted. Now you have to tell us."

But once again their attention was diverted, this time by dessert.

Daniel and Roslyn shared the huge portion of rice pudding with its drizzle of salted caramel.

Annie ordered her own pudding and fiercely defended it from Jean-Guy, who ended up sharing Stephen's.

Reine-Marie and Armand, too jet-lagged to eat any more, just watched.

When the bill came, Armand reached for it, but Stephen took it instead.

It was one of the rare times Stephen picked up a bill, and Armand looked at him questioningly. But the elderly man just smiled and left, Armand could see, an enormous tip.

The night air was refreshing after the warmth and close atmosphere of the bistro, and revived Armand and Reine-Marie a little. Though both longed for their bed.

By habit and silent agreement, the family headed south, crossing familiar streets, passing familiar shops, on their way to the Palais-Royal.

It was the walk they always took after dinner at Juveniles. It gave them the impression they were working off the meal they'd just had. Though they could walk to Versailles and still not work off the rice pudding.

Annie and Jean-Guy, Daniel and Roslyn were up ahead, pausing to look in shop windows.

Armand and Reine-Marie were about to follow Stephen across rue de Richelieu when Reine-Marie asked, "What time is it?"

Armand checked his watch. "Almost eleven."

They turned toward the Tour Eiffel, and sure enough, as they watched, it lit up in the distance, sparkling.

"Look at that," said Armand, with a sigh, tipping his head back.

Stephen paused on his way across the street and looked up from his phone.

A delivery van, half a block away, had stopped to let him cross.

It started to move. Slowly. Then it picked up speed. Moving quickly now. Armand looked away from the glittering tower just in time to see what was happening. What was about to happen.

He raised his hand and shouted a warning.

But it was too late. There was a thud.

And the vehicle sped away.

Jean-Guy took off after it as Armand ran to Stephen. "Call an ambulance!"

Reine-Marie stepped into the middle of the street, her arms up and waving. To protect Armand and Stephen from the oncoming vehicles.

Armand fell to his knees and, turning to Daniel, he yelled, "Help your mother."

And watched as Daniel backed away.

"Mamma," Annie screamed, and Armand turned just in time to see a car skid to a stop within a foot of Reine-Marie. So close she put her hands on the warm hood.

"Reine-Marie?" Armand shouted.

"I'm fine."

"I'm calling for help," yelled Annie.

Armand turned back to Stephen. His hands hovered over the still body of his godfather. Not daring to turn him over, for fear of doing more damage. If that was even possible.

"No, no, no," he whispered. "Please, God, no."

He could see blood on the pavement, and Stephen's glasses and keys and shoes flung about.

Stephen's legs were at an unnatural angle. His head was obscured by an arm.

Armand felt for a pulse. It was there. Light, wavering.

"Daddy?" Annie asked, approaching her father and the body on the ground as the Tour Eiffel sparkled in the background.

"Get back," her father commanded. "Get off the road."

And she did.

"Armand?"

Reine-Marie knelt beside them as drivers got out of cars and gaped. A few honked. Not realizing what was happening.

"An ambulance," Armand repeated, not taking his eyes off his god-father.

"On its way," said Annie and Roslyn together.

Reine-Marie reached out and picked up Stephen's shattered glasses and keys and put them into her handbag. His shoes she left.

Armand held Stephen's hand and bent close, as close as two people could be, and whispered, "I love you. Hold on. Help is on the way. I love you."

"What can I do?" Daniel asked, joining them.

"Nothing," said his father, not bothering to look at him.

CHAPTER 4

The paramedics arrived within minutes and quickly assessed the situation.

Armand stepped aside but remained close. Watching as they took Stephen's vitals. Carefully turning him over. Fitting an oxygen mask on the bloody face.

Reine-Marie slipped her hand into Armand's, feeling it sticky.

There was no sign of life from the elderly man. He was completely limp.

"He's alive?" she whispered.

Armand nodded, but couldn't yet speak.

He just stared at Stephen as the medics, who were communicating with the emergency doctor back at the hospital, used words both Armand and Jean-Guy had heard too often. About wounds too grave.

"Shock." "Hemorrhaging." "Probable skull fracture."

Had this been a battlefield, Stephen Horowitz wouldn't have passed the triage. He'd have been left on the ground. To die.

It would not have taken long.

The police arrived. Without leaving Stephen's side, Armand quickly introduced himself and said, "This was no accident."

"What do you mean, sir?"

"The vehicle, a delivery van for a boulangerie, hit him deliberately. I saw it."

The officer paused in his note-taking. "That's quite an accusation."

"I saw it, too," said Reine-Marie.

"And you?" The agent turned to Annie, Daniel, Roslyn, and Jean-Guy, who was still catching his breath after sprinting after the truck, then running back.

"It didn't stop," said Annie. "Did you get the plates?"

"I got a photo," Jean-Guy said, and showed it to the cop while the paramedics lifted Stephen carefully onto a gurney.

"That makes it a hit-and-run," said the cop, leaning close to Jean-Guy's phone. "But not attempted murder. This's unusable, sir. I can't make out anything."

Jean-Guy looked at it himself and had to agree. It was just a blur.

"I'm a police officer in Québec," said Armand. "This was a clear attempt on his life."

"Québec," said the cop, and lifted his brows. No need to ask what he was thinking.

"Yes, we're senior homicide investigators with the Sûreté du Québec," said Jean-Guy. "You have a problem with that?"

"Not at all, sir." The cop made a note, then looked at Beauvoir. "Did you actually see the vehicle hit the man?"

Jean-Guy bristled, but shook his head.

"*Bon.* Did any of you?"

Annie hesitated, then shook her head. As did the others.

"I told you. I saw it," said Reine-Maire. "And so did my husband. You have two witnesses."

"Your name?"

She gave it.

"It's Friday night, it's dark," said the cop. "The man's in a black overcoat. The driver might've had too much to drink. Don't you think it's possible—"

"It was deliberate." Armand took out his card, scribbled his Paris mobile number on the back, and handed it to the gendarme. "I'm going with him."

Armand followed Stephen into the back of the ambulance, and after a very brief argument, the paramedics relented, realizing there was no way they'd be able to get the man out.

"I'll let you know which hospital," Armand shouted to Reine-Marie as the door slammed closed.

"Will he be okay?" asked Annie.

Did she mean Stephen or her father?

As the ambulance sped off, Reine-Marie took her daughter's hand while Daniel put his arm around his mother's shoulder.

All emergency waiting rooms looked the same, smelled the same, felt the same.

They'd taken Stephen to the hôpital Hôtel-Dieu, on île de la Cité. Almost in the shadow of Notre-Dame.

Armand stared at the swinging doors, where the paramedics had rushed Stephen. And which now separated Armand from his godfather.

He could have been anywhere. In any hospital in any city. Time, place, did not exist here. Did not matter here.

The others in the room, waiting for news of their loved ones, looked gaunt with anxiety and exhaustion. And boredom.

Armand had washed the blood from his hands and face. But couldn't get it off his clothes. They'd be thrown away, he knew. He never wanted to see them again.

It was ridiculous to blame the shirt and tie, the jacket and slacks, for what had happened. But even the socks would be tossed out.

He'd called Reine-Marie first, to let her know where they were. She'd arrive soon. He suggested the others return home and wait for news.

Then he'd called his friend.

"I'll be right there, Armand."

Reine-Marie arrived within minutes, with Annie and Daniel. Jean-Guy and Roslyn had returned home to the children.

"Any news?" Reine-Marie asked, taking Armand's hand.

"None."

"He must be still alive," said Daniel. He put his hand on his father's arm.

"*Oui.*" Armand gave his son a thin smile of thanks, and Daniel dropped his hand.

"Armand," came a voice from the entrance.

A slender man, in his late fifties, and wearing clothes clearly just thrown on, walked rapidly toward them. His hand out.

Armand took it. "*Merci, mon ami.* Thank you for coming. Reine-Marie, you remember Claude Dussault?"

"Of course."

Dussault kissed her on both cheeks and looked at her gravely, then turned to the others.

"These are our children, Daniel and Annie," Armand said. "Claude is the Prefect of Police here in Paris."

"This is a terrible thing to happen," said Monsieur Dussault. He shook their hands, then turned to Armand, noting the bloodstains and exhaustion. "How is he?"

"No word," said Armand.

"Let me try."

Dussault went over to reception and a few moments later returned to them. "They'll let us in. But only one of you."

"We'll stay here," said Reine-Marie.

"Go home," said Armand.

"We're staying," she said. It was the end of any discussion.

As he went through the swinging doors, Armand felt himself light-headed for a moment. Swept back into memory. As bloodstained sheets were drawn over the faces of officers. Young men and women he'd recruited. Trained. Led.

Whose birthdays and weddings he'd danced at. He was godfather to several of their children.

And now they lay dead on gurneys. Killed in an action he'd led them into.

He'd had doors to knock on then. Eyes to meet and lives to shatter.

He took a ragged breath and kept walking, through those memories and into this new nightmare. His friend and colleague by his side.

"He's in one of the operating theaters," said Claude after speaking with a nurse. "We should make ourselves comfortable."

They sat, side by side, on hard chairs in the corridor.

"Terrible place," whispered Dussault, clearly struggling with his own memories. Of his own young gendarmes. "But they do good work. If someone can be saved . . ."

Armand gave a curt nod.

"On the way over I looked up the preliminary notes of the flic who responded to the call."

The Préfet had used the Parisian slang for "cop." *Les flics.* Learned on the streets before he'd joined the force. Though it was not, strictly speaking, a compliment, most cops, between themselves, had adopted the word. Originally from Yiddish slang, "flic" had become a sort of term of endearment. Or, at least, of camaraderie.

Armand remained silent, his focus on the door leading to the operating rooms.

"He wrote that you said it was deliberate. Do you believe that?"

Now Armand turned to him. His eyes bloodshot with exhaustion. And emotion.

"It was. The vehicle was stopped. Then it sped up. It meant to hit Stephen."

Dussault nodded, looked down at his hands briefly, then back up. "The other witnesses agree that the van left the scene. One of them, your son-in-law, I believe, got a very bad photo of it."

"Reine-Marie also saw it speed up to hit Stephen."

"Did she? After you left, she described what happened. She said you were both looking at the Tour Eiffel that had just lit up."

"That's true. I began to speak to Stephen—"

Armand stopped, and blanched. Suddenly feeling he might be sick.

"What is it?" asked Claude.

"I didn't realize Stephen was in the middle of the street. When I spoke, he stopped and turned. He didn't see the van. Couldn't. He was looking at me."

"This isn't your fault, Armand," said Claude, immediately understanding what he was saying. Feeling.

The swinging doors opened and a nurse came through.

"Monsieur le Préfet?" he asked, looking from one to the other.

The two men stood up.

"*Oui*," said Dussault.

"Mr. Horowitz is alive—"

Armand's face opened with relief, but the nurse hurried on.

"—but he's in critical condition. We honestly don't know if he'll survive the surgery. And even if he does, there's significant trauma to his head."

Armand bit the inside of his lip. Hard enough to taste blood.

Dussault introduced him, as next of kin.

"You might want to go home," the nurse said to Gamache. "If you leave your number, you'll be called."

"I'll stay, if you don't mind."

"We'll stay," said Dussault, and watched the nurse return through the swinging doors before he turned back to Gamache. "Horowitz? The injured man is Stephen Horowitz? The billionaire?"

"Yes, didn't the report say that?"

"It must have, but I guess I was focusing on your statement."

"He's my godfather. *Excusez-moi.* I'm going to tell Reine-Marie and the others to go home."

Claude Dussault watched Armand walk back down the corridor, side-stepping doctors and nurses as they responded to other emergencies.

Once Armand had left, Dussault went over to the nurse in charge and asked for the bag of Stephen's things. Not his clothing, but whatever had been in his pockets.

The Prefect looked through the wallet, checking every slip of paper, then picking up the shattered iPhone and examining it.

Replacing everything, he resealed the bag and gave it back to the nurse.

Reine-Marie, Daniel, and Annie hurried to meet Armand.

The others in the waiting room looked up, alert, afraid, then dropped their eyes when they realized he wasn't a doctor bringing them news.

"He's still in there," said Armand, giving Reine-Marie a hug.

"That's good news, right?" said Annie.

"*Oui.*" Her father's reply was so muted, she immediately understood.

"Dad," said Daniel. "I'm sorry—"

"*Merci.* He's in good hands."

"Yes, but I want to say I'm sorry I didn't react when you asked for help. I think I was in shock."

Now Armand turned to his son and focused on him completely.

If there was one thing the senior police officer understood, it was that everyone had strengths. And weaknesses. The important thing was to recognize them. And not expect something from someone who didn't have it to give.

He knew he should never have turned to Daniel. Not in that moment. Not in a crisis.

Not, perhaps, ever.

"You're here now," he said, looking into that worried face. "That's what matters."

"Do you think the driver meant to hit Stephen?" Annie asked.

"Well, yes."

"No, I mean, do you think he knew it was Stephen?" she clarified. Her lawyer's mind working. "Or do you think it was a random attack?"

Armand had been troubled by that himself. He couldn't see how the driver could have specifically targeted his godfather. And yet, if it was a random terrorist attack, another one using a vehicle as the weapon, why hadn't the driver plowed into them, too? Why take out just the one elderly man?

"I don't know," admitted Armand. He looked over his shoulder at the swinging doors. "I need to get back. I'll let you know. I love you."

"Love you," said Annie, while Daniel nodded.

Reine-Marie hugged him tight and whispered, "*Je t'aime.*"

CHAPTER 5

Once back in their apartment, Reine-Marie sank into a rose-scented bubble bath and closed her eyes. Trying to get the filth of the events off her. She took in deep, soothing breaths and could feel her body relax, though her mind kept working. Conjuring images.

Of Stephen, on the ground. Of Armand's face. Of the van speeding by. And the car—coming straight at her.

She'd stayed rooted in place. Not leaping aside. If she had, the car would have hit Armand. And she'd be damned if she'd let that happen.

And then another image appeared. The expression on the face of the officer. Clearly not believing what she and Armand knew to be true.

This was no accident.

"You okay?" asked Jean-Guy. "You must be exhausted."

He'd carried Honoré home, fast asleep in his arms, the two blocks from Daniel and Roslyn's apartment. After putting his son to bed, he'd waited up for Annie, texting her now and then short messages of support.

Now Annie and Jean-Guy lay in bed as she tried to get comfortable. The lights out. Honoré's baby monitor confirming he was sound asleep.

But sleep wouldn't come for the boy's parents.

Annie was days away from giving birth, and Jean-Guy was worried this shock could be harmful.

"I'm okay. She's kicking. Must know I'm trying to get to sleep."

Jean-Guy smiled and cupped his wife and unborn daughter in his arms. "Who's this friend your father called?"

"Claude Dussault," said Annie.

Jean-Guy sat up in bed. "The Prefect of Police for Paris?"

"Yes. You know him?"

"Only by reputation. A good one."

"Dad met him years ago on an exchange program, when they were just agents."

She almost asked why he'd told that cop at the scene that he was a homicide cop in Québec. When he wasn't.

Or maybe, she thought, he was. Still. Always.

But she didn't ask. As a lawyer, she was trained to never ask a question if she wasn't prepared for the answer.

Instead she said, "That cop didn't believe that the van meant to hit Stephen."

"*Non.*"

"Do you?"

"Yes." It would not occur to Beauvoir to doubt Gamache. "The question is, will this Claude Dussault believe it?"

It was the middle of the night, though they couldn't tell in the windowless, airless corridor.

The activity just down the hall, where emergency cases first arrived, had not let up. Accidents. Coronaries. Strokes. Victims of violence.

There were screams of pain, and shouts for assistance by medical personnel.

Armand was beginning to recognize voices. There was the overwhelmed intern. The harried paramedics. The firm nurse. The cool senior doctor and the janitor with his almost eerie whistle.

The noise and activity had gone from a cacophony, jangling Armand's

nerves and bringing back deeply unpleasant memories, to almost soothing in their familiarity.

Armand found his eyelids heavy and his head falling back against
the wall.

It was two thirty in the morning, and he hadn't slept for two days,
since the overnight Air Canada flight from Montréal.

Claude had found a vending machine and bought them coffee.
Wretched but welcome. But even that weak shot of caffeine couldn't
keep him alert.

Armand's head hit the wall, and he jerked awake. Wiping his face
with his hands, he felt the beginning of stubble, then looked over at
Claude, who was reading.

"You can go, you know. You have to be at work soon."

Dussault looked up. "It's Saturday. The boss gave me the day off."

"You're the boss."

"Convenient, that. I'm staying." He lifted the tablet and said, "The
report from the responding officer mentions alcohol on your breath,
and that your eyes were bloodshot."

"I'd had two glasses of wine with dinner. I wasn't drunk."

"But with jet lag, it's possible it affected you more than you realized."

"It's been a while since I was drunk, but believe me, I know what it
feels like. I was, and am, completely sober. And I know what I saw."

"You think that van meant to hit Stephen Horowitz."

"Not just hit, kill. Not just think, but know."

Dussault took a deep breath and nodded. "Then I believe you. But
it does raise some questions."

"Really?" said Gamache and saw Dussault smile.

"I've assigned this to my second-in-command. She works out of
the Quai des Orfèvres," said Dussault.

"She? I thought your number two was Thierry Girard."

Dussault shook his head. "Like your second-in-command, mine
has also jumped ship. I think they just might be smarter than us,
Armand. They're not getting shot at, and they're managing to make
more in a year than I do in five."

"Ahhh, but we have a dental plan," said Armand.

"Unfortunately, we need it. Still, I have an excellent replacement in Irena Fontaine. I'll arrange a meeting tomorrow morning."

"*Merci.*"

"We'll keep the details, and our suspicions, quiet of course. I had no idea you knew Stephen Horowitz."

"Know him," Armand corrected. He knew he was being pedantic, but he needed to keep Stephen alive, even if it was just grammatically. "He practically raised me, along with my grandmother."

Dussault was familiar with that part of Armand's life, so didn't need to dredge it up again. But he did have more questions.

"How did you meet him?"

"He was a friend of my father's. They met at the end of the war. Stephen was acting as an interpreter for the allies."

"He's German, isn't he?"

There was, quite naturally, an assumption in that question.

"He was born in Germany, but escaped and came to Paris. Worked with the Resistance."

"Escaped, you say. Is he Jewish?"

"Not that I know of. More of a humanist really."

Dussault was quiet, and Armand looked over at him. "What is it?"

"Not that I'm doubting you, or him, but my father used to marvel how many men and women suddenly fought with the Resistance when the war ended."

Armand nodded. "My grandmother used to say the same thing."

"I'd forgotten that she was from Paris."

"The Jewish Quarter. Le Marais, yes. Before . . ." But he left it at that. "Stephen never spoke of the war. She did, but rarely."

"Then how do you know he was in the Resistance?"

"I heard my mother and father talking about him."

"You must've been just a child."

"I was. I didn't completely understand, of course. Later Stephen told me that my father helped him get to Montréal and loaned him the money to start his business. When I was born, they named him as a godparent."

"Awkward, for someone who doesn't believe in God."

"I think maybe he believes, but is just angry. Giving Him the silent treatment."

"Let's hope he doesn't get to meet Him soon. I don't envy *le bon Dieu*."

Armand smiled at that and imagined Stephen, whole and strong, standing at the Gates.

But which Gates?

"Hell is empty," he murmured.

"Pardon?" asked Claude.

"Just something Stephen likes to say. *Hell is empty, and all the devils are here.*"

"Charming. But this's Paris, Armand. The City of Light. No devils here."

Gamache turned an astonished face to his friend. "You're joking, of course." He examined Dussault. "The Terror was partly inspired by the Age of Enlightenment. How many Protestants massacred, how many men and women guillotined, how many Jews hunted and killed? How many innocents murdered by terrorists here in the City of Light would agree with you? There're devils here. You of all people know that."

Dussault had forgotten that his friend was a student of history. And, therefore, of human nature.

"You're right, of course. Monsieur Horowitz has no family of his own?" Claude asked, bringing the topic back to the man fighting for his life just meters away. "Siblings?"

"Not that I know of. Stephen's family lived in Dresden."

No more needed to be said about that.

"A wife? Children?"

Armand shook his head. "Just me."

"I have agents going over the CCTV cameras in the area. Since we know the time of the attack, we'll be able to find the van as it turned onto rue de Rivoli."

"And where Stephen was hit?"

Claude shook his head. "We can't put cameras on every block in

Paris, so no, none on the small side street. But shopkeepers might have their own. They'll be canvassed as soon as stores open. But there's something I can't immediately get my head around."

"Was Stephen the target, or was it random?"

"Yes. If this was an attempt on Monsieur Horowitz specifically, how did the driver know it was him?"

"And if it was random, a terrorist attack like the others using vehicles, why didn't the driver try to hit more people?" said Gamache. "Us. We were as vulnerable as Stephen."

"Yes. We're categorizing this as a hit-and-run, but"—he put up his hand to stop any protest—"treating it as attempted murder."

Claude Dussault looked at his friend. And spoke the words Armand Gamache needed to hear: "I believe you."

Both men looked over as a doctor stepped through the swinging doors.

CHAPTER 6

The moment she heard the creak of the front door, Reine-Marie was instantly awake and out of bed.

"Armand?"

"*Oui,*" he said, whispering, though without knowing why.

Reine-Marie switched on the hall light.

"Stephen?" she asked as she embraced him.

"Still alive."

"Oh, thank God." Though even as she spoke, she wondered if thanks were really owing. "How is he?"

"Critical. He's in recovery. They wouldn't let me see him."

"How are you?"

She looked into his haggard face and saw his eyes well. She grabbed him to her again, and they held on to each other.

Weeping for Stephen.

For themselves.

For a world where this could happen as they strolled happily along a familiar street.

They stepped apart and wiped their faces and blew their noses, then Armand followed her into the kitchen.

All the way home in the taxi, all he'd wanted to do was hug Reine-Marie, have a hot shower, and crawl into bed. But now he just sat at the kitchen table, staring ahead.

Reine-Marie put the battered kettle on the gas ring and brought out the teapot.

The kitchen was old-fashioned. They'd discussed updating it, but somehow it never got done. Probably because neither really wanted to change it. It was the same as when Armand's grandmother Zora was alive and had bustled around it, chatting away in her strange mix of Yiddish and German and French.

She'd learned Yiddish and French growing up in Paris. And German in the camps.

She'd left the apartment to him in her will, along with all she possessed. Which mostly amounted to her love, which was plentiful, and which he carried with him always.

"*Nein. Opshtel*," Armand could almost hear her say. "Stop. Tea always better when *wasser* isn't quite *bouillant*. You should know by now," she'd chastise him.

"Don't *plotz*," he'd invariably reply, which amused her greatly.

His grandmother was long dead, and now he watched Reine-Marie, brushing gray hair from her eyes, move about the kitchen. She brought the teapot over, nicely steeped, with a jug of milk from the cranky old fridge.

"*Merci*," he said, stirring in sugar. "They say he probably has brain damage, but at least there's activity there."

Reine-Marie sipped her tea. She knew Armand was thinking the same thing, but couldn't yet say it.

When they finished their tea, Armand had a hot shower, turning his face into the water. Tasting the salt from his face.

Crawling into bed beside Reine-Marie, he fell immediately into a deep sleep.

Three hours later he woke up, with light streaming through the lace curtains. In the first flush of consciousness he felt completely at peace. Here in this familiar apartment. Surrounded by familiar scents that evoked such a deep contentment.

But a second later he remembered and immediately reached for his phone, checking for messages.

There was none from the hospital.

Reine-Marie was already up. She'd been out to the shops along rue Rambuteau, and brought back fresh croissants from their favorite patisserie, Pain de Sucre.

He followed the scent of strong, rich coffee into the kitchen and saw cheese and raspberries and ripe pears on the table. Along with the croissants. And a *pain aux raisins*, bought with Stephen the day before.

"Up already?" she asked. "How did you sleep?"

"Well. Very well," he said, kissing her. "Not long, but deeply."

"Nothing more from the hospital?"

"*Non.* How are you?"

"I think I'm still in shock. I can barely believe it even happened."

He hugged her, then went off and showered again and shaved. As he dressed, he saw his clothing from the night before, tossed onto the chair. Even from across the room, he could see the blood.

He checked again for messages, scanning for the one he dreaded. But it wasn't there. Surely the hospital would have gotten in touch if . . .

Over breakfast he called Daniel, then Annie. He'd texted them the night before with an update, but wanted to find out how they were.

Jean-Guy got on the phone. "Any word from the cops?"

"*Non.* I'm just about to call."

"Are they treating this as attempted murder?"

"Yes."

Jean-Guy heaved a sigh. "Thank God for that. What can I do?"

"You talked to Stephen last night, more than I did. Did he say anything at all that might be important? Anything he was working on, or worried about?"

"Annie and I have been going over our conversation with him. There was nothing."

In the background Armand heard Annie call, "The phone, tell him about the phone."

"*Oui.* He did keep checking his phone, like he was expecting a call or message."

"Huh," said Armand. Stephen normally despised it when people brought out their phones over a meal, never mind actually used them.

55

"How did he seem to you?" Armand asked.

"The usual. In a good mood."

"What did you talk about?"

"Nothing really. Well—" Jean-Guy gave a small laugh. "I mentioned a project at work, and he seemed interested, but then accused me of wasting his time."

Armand took that in. He'd also been going over their conversation at the Musée Rodin. And while Stephen had seemed his old self, there was that strange moment. When talking about the devils.

"Not here, here," he'd said. Leading Armand to think Stephen knew where they were.

He wished now he'd pressed more, but it had seemed so innocuous.

And then there was Stephen's comment. That he wasn't afraid to die.

Armand hoped that was true, but now he also saw something else in it. Not that his godfather was prescient, but that Stephen actually knew something.

"If this was deliberate," Jean-Guy asked, "who would do it?"

"Stephen made a lot of people angry," said Armand.

"You think this was revenge?"

"Or a preemptive strike. Hitting him before he hit them."

"Mrs. McGillicuddy would know if Stephen was planning something," said Jean-Guy.

Damn, thought Armand. *Mrs. McGillicuddy. I should have called her last night.*

She was Stephen's longtime secretary and assistant.

He looked at his watch. It was six hours earlier in Montréal. Which made it one a.m. Let the elderly woman have a few more hours of peace, he thought, before the anvil dropped. Besides, he'd have more news on Stephen's condition by then.

After saying goodbye to Beauvoir, he called Claude Dussault.

"We have the CCTV images," said the Prefect. "The van was a delivery truck reported stolen earlier in the evening. We have it turning onto rue de Rivoli right after Monsieur Horowitz was hit. From there it crossed Pont de la Concorde, to the Left Bank, and headed southeast. But the van disappeared into back streets. We'll find the vehicle. I have no doubt. How much it'll tell us is another matter. Any more word on Monsieur Horowitz's condition?"

"Not since last night. We're heading over there now."

"Armand . . ." The Prefect hesitated. "After some sleep and time to reflect, do you still think it was a deliberate attempt on Monsieur Horowitz's life?"

"Yes."

It was a clear answer, and the one Dussault had expected. But Gamache's insistence and his involvement were both unsettling and problematic.

"It must be revenge," said Dussault. "How many companies and individuals did he ruin in his career?"

"They ruined themselves. He just caught them. He was one of the first to figure out what Madoff was doing and alert the SEC."

"And Enron, I think."

"Yes. Ken Lay had been a personal friend. But that didn't stop Stephen from testifying against him. Believe me, it gave Stephen no pleasure, but he did it."

"A sort of avenging angel. Is there anyone he was targeting now?"

"Not that I know of. I think he was mostly retired."

Dussault sighed. "Okay. Do you know what brought him to Paris?"

"He said he was here mostly for the birth of Annie's baby, but he mentioned he had some business early in the week. In fact, he was meeting someone for drinks before dinner."

"But you don't know who?"

"No, he didn't say. Do you know if his phone was found?"

"I haven't seen mention of it. It's probably at the hospital with his personal effects."

"I'll look for it when we get there."

"I'll put a guard on Monsieur Horowitz's room," said the Prefect. "When you finish at the hospital, come by the 36. I'll be here all day."

"The 36" was the nickname for 36, quai des Orfèvres. Where the Préfecture de Police traditionally had its headquarters.

Most of the services had been moved to a new building, but some units and some people stayed behind. Claude Dussault, the head of all the forces, maintained an office there. Mostly because he preferred the storied old building on île de la Cité to the modern one.

And also because he could.

"Taxi?" Armand asked as they left their apartment.

"I'd prefer to walk, if it's all right with you."

It was less than ten minutes to the hospital, along streets he'd explored with his grandmother after she bought the apartment with the restitution money.

"Those *askhouls* thought they could get rid of me," she'd said, triumphantly, as she'd slapped down the money for the apartment. "Well, I'm back."

Young Armand did not need a translation.

As they'd walked the *quartier*, Zora told him about her life in the Marais, when she was his age. She'd point out the synagogues, the parks, the old shops that used to be owned by friends of the family.

All said in her cheerful voice, which somehow made it better. And worse.

Now he and Reine-Marie left Le Marais, crossing the Pont d'Arcole and pausing to look at the restoration work being done on Notre-Dame.

How long it takes to build something, he thought, and how quickly it can all be destroyed.

A look. A harsh word. A moment of distraction. A spark.

At the hôpital Hôtel-Dieu they took the elevator to the critical care unit.

Armand identified himself, showing his ID, and said, "We're here to see Stephen Horowitz."

"The doctor has asked if she can speak with you first," said the nurse.

"Of course."

They were guided to a private meeting room. Within minutes a doctor appeared.

"*Monsieur et Madame Gamache?*"

She motioned them to sit.

"You're Monsieur Horowitz's next of kin?"

"I'm his godson. We were with him when it happened."

"You're named as next of kin on his Québec hospital card."

"Which means you can tell us how he is."

"Yes. And you can make medical decisions. There's significant trauma. Honestly, a man his age should not have survived. He must be very strong."

"Strong-willed, for sure," said Reine-Marie, and the doctor smiled.

"He is that," she agreed. "Unfortunately, if will to live was all it took, most of us would never die." She looked at them for a moment. "We have him in a medically induced coma. He's in no pain that we know of. We're monitoring him closely. Since he's survived the night, there is a chance he'll go on."

Armand noticed she didn't say "recover." She confirmed his suspicions a moment later.

"You must prepare yourself for a difficult decision."

She looked into those thoughtful eyes. They were deep brown, and she could tell this was a man who'd had to make many difficult and painful decisions. Who'd known pain himself. That much was etched into his face, and not just by the deep scar at his temple.

She'd seen wounds like that before, when working emergency, and she knew what must have made it. She looked at him with more interest.

Yes, there was pain in that face. But now she saw other lines. This man also knew happiness.

And by the way he and his wife held hands, lightly, they knew love. She was glad. They'd need it.

"Can we see him, please?"

"Yes, but only one of you, and briefly. We have some papers for you to sign, and there are his personal effects. Best to take them with you, for safekeeping."

"I'll get those," said Reine-Marie as they stood up. "While you see Stephen."

"There's a gendarme outside Monsieur Horowitz's door," said the doctor. "I understand there's some concern that this was no accident."

"Yes."

They left Reine-Marie to sort Stephen's things, which arrived in a sealed cardboard box, while Armand was taken down the quiet hall, to a private room.

The gendarme, at a word from the doctor, let him pass.

Opening the box, Reine-Marie shoved aside the bloodstained clothing, cut off by the emergency room medics, then opened the sealed plastic bag. Stephen's iPhone was there. Smashed.

She tried it. It was dead.

There was loose change, and mints, and a handkerchief. His wallet had 305 euros, and credit cards.

She was about to close the bag when she remembered the things she'd picked up from the street the night before. Reaching into her handbag, Reine-Marie placed Stephen's broken glasses and keys into the bag.

Then, pausing, she took a closer look at the keys.

Last night, in the dark and panic, they hadn't struck her as odd. Now, in daylight and relative calm, they did.

In fact, far more than just odd.

CHAPTER 7

⌒

I'm sorry, Madame. I can't let you in."

Reine-Marie stared at the young man guarding Stephen's room.

"Please." She gave him her most matronly smile. "I just need to speak with my husband."

These are not the droids you're looking for, she thought and almost shook her head. Jean-Guy had clearly rubbed off on her.

The young flic examined the woman standing in front of him. Her tone said, *I'm your mother's age and harmless.*

But her eyes were far too intelligent to fool the agent. Besides, his mother had much the same eyes, and she was a judge on the French assize court.

She'd taught him never to underestimate anyone, especially a smart woman.

He smiled back and made a decision, recognizing that sometimes common sense needed to prevail. He'd also learned that from his mother.

For common sense, he opened the door. For his training, he went in with her.

Reine-Marie paused. Unable, for a moment, to go beyond the threshold.

Stephen was breathing with the aid of a machine. There were monitors and drips. His body seemed to be wrapped from head to toe in bandages, including over his eyes.

How could this man still be alive, she thought.

But it also brought flooding back, catching her up and tumbling her around, memories of seeing Armand in much the same condition.

She took a sharp breath in and recovered herself.

Armand sat beside the bed, his reading glasses on. With one hand he held Stephen's hand. In the other he held a copy of that morning's *Le Figaro*.

"Energie Stat is down three points, to 134.9. Produits Cassini is up half a point, to 87.6."

He was reading the report from the Bourse de Paris to Stephen, as though it was a fairy tale for his grandchildren. Giving each an inflection, a drama.

The young gendarme stopped just inside the door, and stared. It was a tableau so intimate he felt as though he'd violated these people by his presence.

"Armand?" Reine-Marie approached the bed.

He looked up, clearly surprised to see her.

"I've found something," she said quietly.

Getting up, Armand kissed Stephen on the forehead and said quietly, "I'll be back soon. Don't go anywhere. I love you."

The box with Stephen's belongings was placed on the table by the window in the hospital room.

Armand went through the contents as Reine-Marie watched. Interested to see if the same thing struck her husband.

Armand went first to Stephen's suit jacket, stiff with blood, and did something unexpected. Turning it inside out, he searched and, with a smile, withdrew a Canadian passport.

"Stephen had his passport stolen many years ago," Armand explained, holding it up. "Since then he's had his tailor put in the hidden pocket. He keeps his important things in there."

Armand brought out one more thing. A slender agenda.

He then went through the things in the box. All predictable.

Except. His brow furrowed.

There, lying amid the other items, was a key. Not an apartment key, but a room key.

"Hotel George V," he read.

"Yes," said Reine-Marie. "That's what I wanted to show you. It was on the pavement. I picked it up last night along with his glasses and put them into my purse. I forgot they were there until just now. Why would he have that? He's staying in his apartment, isn't he?"

"Yes. I walked him there yesterday afternoon. And here's the key to his apartment."

Armand held it up, then went back to the hotel key.

"Do you think someone else is staying at the hotel?" she suggested. "Could it be . . ."

"A lover?" asked Armand.

"Ruth?" said Reine-Marie.

Armand felt a frisson. That might explain the "here, here." The devil was in the George V.

He smiled at the thought. Ruth Zardo, Stephen's friend, was also their close friend and neighbor in their Québec village of Three Pines.

An elderly poet, she was embittered, often drunk. Definitely nuts. And brilliant.

> You were a moth
> brushing against my cheek
> in the dark
> I killed you
> not knowing you were only a moth,
> with no sting.

She and Stephen had proven a good match and fast friends. And while often angry, she was no devil. Perhaps, he'd often thought, just the opposite.

Armand could still see her, waving goodbye with one raised finger.

So who was in room 815 at the George V?

"I guess it's possible the key was already there," said Reine-Marie. "That someone dropped it and I picked it up by mistake."

"Possible." Armand pocketed the key and put the rest back in the box. With the exception of Stephen's agenda, which he also slipped into his pocket. "Let's find out."

The taxi pulled into the entrance to the luxury hotel.

A man in livery opened the door and escorted them in. Armand gave him a twenty-euro note, and the man bowed and backed away.

The marble lobby was chock-full of fresh flowers, in banks and sprays, reaching almost to the twenty-foot ceiling. It was like stepping into a forest of blooms.

"Keep walking," Armand whispered to Reine-Marie, their feet echoing on the marble floor. "Look like we belong."

She smiled at him, then caught the eye of a uniformed bellhop, and, nodding, she swept right by her, with a casual *"Bonjour,"* as though she was a *habituée*.

Armand still carried the cardboard box from the hospital, but walked with such authority no one challenged them.

Mercifully, they had the elevator to themselves and could relax.

But Reine-Marie suddenly turned to Armand. "Have you told Mrs. McGillicuddy?"

"Not yet. I've emailed and asked her to call me when she can."

"She's going to be devastated."

Agnes McGillicuddy had been Stephen's private secretary for fifty-six years. Now in her mid-eighties, she'd refused to be rebranded an assistant, and lorded it over the outer office like a Hound of Hell.

She was married to Mr. McGillicuddy, he of no fixed first name. Sometimes Stephen called him Jeremiah. Sometimes Josephat. Sometimes Brian.

Armand was never sure if he did it because he really didn't know Mr. McGillicuddy's name, or to annoy Mrs. McGillicuddy. Though she refused to rise to it.

They had no children, and despite the fact Stephen was actually older than she, she treated him like a son.

The Gamaches knew her well, though neither had ever actually seen her away from her desk.

When they got to room 815, Reine-Marie knocked once. Then again.

A chambermaid came down the hall, looked at them, then walked right by.

Armand quickly unlocked the door, saying, "Hurry. She's going to call security. We don't have much time."

"*Allô?*" Reine-Marie called once the door closed behind them. Silence.

This was no normal hotel room. It wasn't even a normal suite. It was practically a castle within a castle.

"You take down here," he said. "I'll go upstairs. Hurry. They'll be here soon."

"There's an upstairs?"

But Armand was already halfway up the curving stairway.

While vast, the main floor didn't take long to explore. It was essentially one palatial room, with a sitting area in front of a fireplace and a long, polished dining table under a Murano glass chandelier. A powder room was just off the entrance, and a kitchenette tucked away at the back.

In case the billionaire wanted to make his own dinner, she thought. The only "cooking" she'd seen Stephen do was open a tin of cashews. And even that was a struggle.

Though she did notice a paper bag on the counter. Opening it, she saw one croissant.

Newspapers sat by one of the armchairs, with a book called *The Investment Zoo* on top of them.

There were signs not just of occupation, but of someone having settled in.

Reine-Marie found Armand in a small upstairs study, rifling through the desk.

"Stephen's definitely staying here," he said, looking up briefly. "His things are in the bedroom. But I think someone else is, too. There's

65

another bedroom with an unopened suitcase. Can you see what you can find?"

The second bedroom was larger than most Paris apartments. She went straight to the bag, really more a carry-on than a suitcase, and quickly went through the contents. Toiletry kit. A suit, silk tie, two clean white shirts, underwear, and black socks. Fine handmade leather shoes. Pajamas, and a book.

She searched for something to identify the owner. Clearly a man. Probably older, judging by the style of suit. Not planning to stay long.

Whoever this belonged to hadn't had time yet to unpack.

There was an ensuite with hotel toiletries, but nothing else.

She froze as she heard a chime. The doorbell. They'd run out of time.

Armand appeared at the door to the bedroom. "They're here. Can you stall them?"

"You keep going," she said, heading down the stairs as the chime sounded again. It was cheerful and discreet, but to her it sounded like a shriek.

She was halfway down when the door opened.

"*Bonjour,*" a man's voice called out. "Monsieur Horowitz? It's the duty manager. Is there anyone here? Is everything all right?"

A middle-aged man stepped into the suite and stopped when he saw her.

"Who are you?" he asked.

Two large men in beautifully tailored suits and wearing earpieces stood behind him.

They looked out of place in the almost effete surroundings. Like street fighters at a tea party.

George V was home to many wealthy and powerful people. Clearly there was need of a security presence. And not a very discreet one.

"My name is Reine-Marie Gamache," she said, slowly walking down the last few steps. "I'm a friend of Stephen Horowitz. I'm afraid he's been in an accident."

"I'm sorry to hear that. Is he all right?"

"He's in the hospital."

"There was a man with you. Where is he?" the manager asked, trying to get around her.

Reine-Marie stood her ground, blocking their way. "I've told you who I am. Who are you?"

The man, a little taken aback, said, "I'm the duty manager."

"Yes, but what's your name? I'm going to have to see your ID before I let you in."

He seemed reluctant to give it, then relented. "Auguste Pannier." He showed her his hotel identity card. Which she studied. At some length.

"I don't want to be rude," she eventually said, handing it back. "But what are you doing here?"

Now the manager was really stumped. This woman was clearly a trespasser, yet she acted like she not only belonged but owned the place.

He was, perforce, a judge if not of character, then clothing. He quickly took in her bearing, her good-quality slacks, silk scarf, elegant autumn coat. Her style was classic. Her eyes intelligent.

And yet she was hiding something, he knew. Someone, to be more precise.

He was about to repeat his question when they heard footsteps on the stairs and a man appeared.

Middle-aged. Distinguished. In a good suit, tie. Shoes polished. Well-groomed. He, too, looked like he belonged here.

The only things out of place were the cardboard box he carried and the worn leather satchel over his shoulder.

"*Bonjour,*" said Armand. "We're sorry to have just let ourselves in, but as my wife said, Monsieur Horowitz has been in an accident and we wanted to collect some things for him."

Armand did not offer his hand, preferring to appear cordial but aloof. An attitude he'd observed in his godfather more than once.

But he did offer his name. "My name is Armand Gamache."

"And who are you to Monsieur Horowitz?"

"A close friend."

"I see. Shall we continue this conversation in my office?"

"If you wish," said Armand.

"I hope you understand," said Monsieur Pannier, once in his large mahogany-paneled office behind reception. "But I would like to see what you've taken from the suite."

Armand placed the satchel on the desk and unzipped it.

Inside were pajamas, a dressing gown. Toiletries.

Satisfied, the manager then nodded to the box.

"Unfortunately, I can't show you this," said Armand. "It's from the hospital and contains Monsieur Horowitz's belongings. As you see, it's sealed, and we need to keep it like that so that when he recovers he knows nothing has been tampered with. It's for his protection, and ours."

Armand made it clear the "ours" now included the duty manager.

There was a moment's awkward silence.

In fact, as well as Stephen's things from the hospital, Armand had swept the contents of the desk, including the laptop, into the box. As Reine-Marie stalled them down below, he'd resealed it, then quickly gone into the bedroom and thrown clothes into the satchel.

"I'm afraid I'll have to insist," said Monsieur Pannier.

"And I'm afraid I can't do that."

"Is there a problem?" a new voice came from the door.

Pannier practically shot to his feet. "*Non.* Not at all."

A woman stood partway into his office, and Gamache knew he was now looking at the real boss.

She stepped forward, her hand out. "Jacqueline Béland. I'm the General Manager."

They introduced themselves, and Monsieur Pannier briefly explained the situation.

Madame Béland listened quietly, waiting until he'd finished, then turned to the Gamaches.

"I'm so sorry to hear about Monsieur Horowitz. I expect Monsieur Pannier here has extended the sympathies of the hotel."

The Gamaches looked at him. Then Reine-Marie turned back to the General Manager. "Yes, thank you. He's been most gracious."

They could hear Monsieur Pannier exhale.

There was a slight arch of surprise, and appreciation, to Madame Béland's brow, but that was all. "You're a relation of Monsieur Horowitz's?"

"His godson," said Armand.

Her eyes dropped to the box. "I'm afraid Monsieur Pannier is right. We'll need to see what's inside there, too. I hope you understand."

And, to be fair, Armand did. Thieves took all shapes and sizes. At luxury hotels they were more likely to look like the Gamaches than a street thug.

"It's sealed by the hospital," Armand said. "And I want to keep it that way. But if you'd feel better calling the Préfecture, you might try"—Armand handed her a card—"him."

Madame Béland's eyes widened. "You know Monsieur Dussault?"

"I do. Clearly you do, too."

"He was here just yesterday. A friend of yours?"

"And a colleague, *oui*. I'm the head of homicide."

Gamache decided there was no need to specify his territory.

"Armand," said Reine-Marie. "We should get his things over to him."

"I'm afraid there is," the General Manager said, "a small issue of his bill."

Armand almost smiled. It was a brilliant move on Madame Béland's part. If they were thieves, they would not be at all happy about handing over a credit card.

"Of course." Armand placed a credit card on the duty manager's desk. "I believe he checked in two nights ago."

"*Non, monsieur,*" said the manager, consulting his computer to confirm. "Monsieur Horowitz arrived ten days ago. He was supposed to leave this coming Wednesday."

"Are you sure?" asked Reine-Marie.

"Positive. Should we hold the room for him?"

"If you don't mind," said Armand.

"The suite," said the manager, "is three thousand five hundred euros."

Reine-Marie and Armand exchanged a glance. They could certainly cover that.

"A night."

Reine-Marie's face remained composed, though she could feel her blood, and her children's inheritance, draining away.

Two weeks . . . that would come to . . .

"It comes to forty-nine thousand euros," said Monsieur Pannier. "So far. That is, of course, before tax and any other charges. Monsieur Horowitz often had meals in his room."

Reine-Marie did a rough conversion in her mind. About seventy-five thousand Canadian dollars.

So far.

"Given the circumstances," said Madame Béland, "all we'd need is a ten percent deposit."

"*Avec plaisir,*" said Armand, as though they'd expected it to be more. "I understand someone else is staying there. Can you tell us who that is?"

The manager frowned. "*Non.* Monsieur Horowitz was alone in the suite."

"Are you sure?" asked Reine-Marie.

"Quite sure."

"I'd like you to cancel the old keys," said Armand, handing back the key he had. "And have new ones issued, please."

They did.

As they left, Reine-Marie whispered to Armand, "You're going to have to get a paper route."

"You're going to have to sell a kidney."

She smiled. "Should we at least stay here, if we're paying?"

"Would you like to?"

She thought about it. "*Non.* I prefer our apartment."

"*Moi aussi.*"

"Where to now?" she asked and got the answer as Armand gave the taxi driver the address.

"*Cinq rue Récamier, s'il vous plaît.* It's in the Seventh Arrondissement. Across from the Hôtel Lutetia."

Stephen's apartment.

Armand sat back, the box on his knees, the satchel sitting on the seat between them.

The magnificent Haussmann buildings glided past, but he was lost in thought.

While he definitely liked the finer things, Stephen was notoriously careful with his money. Some might even say stingy.

There was no way he would have paid for a suite at the George V when he had a perfectly good, even luxurious apartment in Paris.

And yet it appeared that's exactly what Stephen had done.

Now why was that?

CHAPTER 8

A rmand put his arm out and stopped Reine-Marie from going any farther.

They'd let themselves into the apartment and were standing in the wide foyer. The archway into the living room was off to their left.

Reine-Marie, slightly behind her husband, couldn't yet see the room, or the problem. But Armand could.

He didn't speak. Didn't have to. She saw his body tense.

He lowered the cardboard box and shoulder bag to the floor. Leaning forward, Reine-Marie saw what he saw.

The living room was a shambles.

"Armand—" she began but stopped when he raised his hand. A clear signal for silence.

He moved slowly into the room, Reine-Marie behind him. They stepped over and around overturned chairs and side tables, lamps and paintings.

She bumped into his back when he suddenly stopped.

Armand remained completely still for a few heartbeats. He was staring behind an overturned sofa. His face grim.

When he crouched down, she saw.

There was a man on the floor. Facedown.

Dead.

She took a step back, blanching.

Armand stood and looked around quickly. What he'd seen, which Reine-Marie had not, was that the man had been shot twice, once in the back. Once in the head.

The man was cold to the touch. It must have happened a number of hours earlier. But . . .

"There's a slight scent in the air. Can you smell it?" he whispered.

She took a deep breath and shook her head. Then she caught it. Hardly there. Elusive. More a suggestion than a scent.

"Try to remember it." His voice was urgent. His eyes sharp. His whole being alert.

Slightly citrusy, she thought. And sort of muddy. Not a perfume, a cologne. Definitely masculine. Not pleasant.

It was disappearing, even as she tried to grasp it.

"Is it his?" she whispered, not looking at the man again.

"I don't think so. And it's not Stephen's."

So it was someone else's, and Reine-Marie immediately followed Armand's thoughts. And understood his extreme alertness.

Colognes, *eaux de toilette*, didn't hang around for long. They might cling to clothes, but did not float in the air. Certainly not for hours. Which meant someone had been there recently. Very recently.

And might still be in the apartment.

Instinctively, Armand moved Reine-Marie behind him and took a step back. Away from the body. Toward the door. His mind working rapidly.

"Armand, if there's someone here, someone who did that . . ." She looked toward the corpse. "Will he . . ."

"Hurt us? *Non*," he whispered. "He'd just want to get away."

He could hear her breathing. Short. Rapid. Her hand on his back was trembling. And with good reason. Despite what he'd said, they were almost certainly still in an apartment with an armed murderer.

And while he didn't say it, Gamache knew that the surest way for the killer to get out was to kill anyone in his way.

Armand said, loudly, "Stay behind me. We're leaving."

As they backed away, he brought out his phone and took several quick photographs.

Once at the door, he gave her his phone, then stooped and picked up the box.

"Take this," he whispered, so softly she could barely hear. "Go to the Hôtel Lutetia. Call Claude. Send him one of the photographs."

"You?"

But he'd already closed the door. She heard the double lock turn as she stood in the hall, holding the box.

Not waiting for the elevator, Reine-Marie took the stairs two at a time.

Armand leaned against the door, using his body to muffle the sound of the key turning in the lock. Then he replaced it in his pocket.

The intruder couldn't leave without the key. There was a possibility he had one, but Gamache had to take that risk.

The other risk he was taking was locking himself in with someone who was almost certainly armed. He'd have disciplined any of his agents who did what he was doing. But whoever murdered this man was probably also responsible for the attempt on Stephen's life. And Armand was not going to just let them go.

But there was another problem. Armand knew the apartment and knew there was another way out. He just hoped the intruder didn't know.

Finding the killer was no longer his goal. Just the opposite, really.

What he needed to do was get to the kitchen, and the back stairwell. If he could lock that door from the outside, the intruder would be trapped.

He could see the kitchen, at the far end of what now seemed a very long and very narrow hallway. With nowhere to hide. Exactly the environment he taught cadets at the academy to never, ever enter.

The scent of cologne was slightly stronger now.

Bringing the keys out, he made a fist around them, the individual keys between his fingers, like brass knuckles. Not much of a defense. More psychological than practical.

He was halfway down the long hall when he heard a bang. He flinched, even as he realized it wasn't a shot.

It was a door slamming.

"Damn."

Racing into the kitchen, he yanked open the fire escape door and heard feet on the concrete stairs. He followed them down, taking the steps two, three at a time.

As he ran, he thought he heard a familiar sound. Muffled. A phone ringing. But not his. His was with Reine-Marie.

The sound of the intruder's feet echoed in the enclosed stairwell. The person he was chasing was not young, Armand unconsciously noted.

But still, whoever this was, they had a head start and were moving quickly. Desperate to get away.

And it looked like they would.

If he could just catch a glimpse . . .

A door banged open, and he saw sunlight a few flights down. Then it disappeared as the door swung shut.

When he got to the bottom, Armand threw himself against it and staggered out onto a busy Paris sidewalk. Surprised pedestrians leaped out of the way as Armand swung around, looking this way, then that.

Nothing. Just men and women walking, some gawking. No one running.

He'd lost him.

Walking rapidly toward the Lutetia, Armand turned the corner and saw Reine-Marie hugging the cardboard box. Staring at the front door to Stephen's building.

Willing Armand to appear.

He called to her, and she turned. Her relief was accompanied by the familiar wail of a police siren quickly approaching.

CHAPTER 9

"What the hell's going on, Armand?"

Claude Dussault and Armand Gamache were standing side by side, looking down at the body while members of the brigade criminelle fanned out in a semicircle, waiting for the Prefect to give them the go-ahead.

Since he didn't know what the hell was going on, Gamache remained silent.

"Do you know him?"

"I don't think so," said Gamache. "But we'll get a better look when he's turned over."

What he could see was that the man was older, perhaps mid-seventies. Caucasian. Slender. In casual but expensive clothes.

Armand lifted his eyes from the body and gazed at the shambles around him. Furniture overturned. Books taken from shelves and splayed on the floor. Drawers pulled out and tossed. Even the art had been taken from the walls, the brown paper at the back of them slashed.

Thankfully none of the art itself appeared to have been destroyed.

Dussault nodded, and the brigade went to work while the two senior officers walked from room to room. Armand hadn't had a chance to look at the rest of Stephen's apartment, but now he did.

"Horowitz's bedroom?" Dussault asked.

"*Oui.*"

The bed had been taken apart, the mattress thrown to the floor. The doors of the huge armoire were open, and clothing lay in heaps.

"Someone's done a number on this place," said the Prefect.

Even Stephen's bathroom had been searched, the medicine cabinet's contents in the sink and on the floor.

They walked down the long corridor, glancing into the other bedroom, the bathroom, the dining room.

"Coming?" Dussault asked.

He'd noticed that Armand had stopped.

"What is it?"

"Nothing, really. *Désolé.*" He looked away, into the second bedroom.

"What?"

Armand turned back to the Prefect, his colleague and friend, and said with a very small, almost sad smile, "Just a memory."

"Did you stay here as a child?"

"Yes."

"Hard to see this," said Dussault. "It must be quite something when not . . ."

"It is."

Stephen Horowitz's Paris apartment spoke of untold wealth and unusual restraint.

The financier preferred the simplicity of the Louis Philippe style, with its warm wood grain and soft, simple lines. Each piece, searched out in auction houses and even flea markets, had a purpose. Each was actually used. The armoires, the bedsteads, the dressers and lamps.

As a result, the place felt more like a home than a museum.

But right now, it could pass as a dump.

"Robbery gone wrong or professional hit?" Dussault asked.

Armand shook his head. "Whoever did this was searching for something. Had Stephen not been attacked last night, I'd have said a robbery gone wrong, but—"

"But it can't be a coincidence," agreed Dussault. "The two must be connected. The simplest explanation is that the killer came here knowing Stephen was at dinner, and the apartment would be empty.

He could search it without fear of interruption. When he arrived and discovered this fellow, he killed him. Then continued the search. Poor guy was in the wrong place at the wrong time."

Gamache raised his hands. He had no idea if that was true. It was just one scenario.

What he did know was that while it was necessary to go through various scenarios, there was folly, there was danger in landing too heavily on one particular theory early in an investigation. Too often the investigators became invested in that theory and began interpreting evidence to fit.

That could lead to a murderer going free, or, worse, it could lead to the conviction of an innocent person.

Don't believe everything you think.

Chief Inspector Gamache wrote that on the board for the incoming cadets at the start of every year at the Sûreté academy, and it stayed there all year.

At first the students in the class he taught laughed. It sounded clever but silly. Little by little most got it. And those who didn't did not progress further.

That phrase was as powerful as any weapon they'd be handed.

No. Right now there were any number of theories, all equally valid. But only one was correct.

"Why was the killer still here this morning?" asked Dussault. "They don't normally hang around."

"Or why did he return? The only explanation I can think of is that he hadn't found what he was looking for."

"Okay, here's a thought," said Dussault. "The original plan was to search the apartment while Monsieur Horowitz was at dinner. When he found what he wanted, the intruder would head over to the restaurant and kill Horowitz, hoping it would look like a hit-and-run. No one would suspect anything other than a terrible accident. Clean. Simple. *Fini.*"

Armand considered that. It could be true. Except . . .

"The place is a mess," said Armand. "If he really wanted Stephen's death to look like an accident, wouldn't he leave the apartment as he'd found it?"

"Yes, that would've been the plan, but it went south as soon as he discovered this man and killed him," said Dussault. "Then there was no need to be careful. In fact, he was in a hurry. He had to find whatever he needed, fast. Then get to the restaurant in time to run down Horowitz."

"By then, why not just shoot Stephen?" asked Armand. "If what you say is true, there was no longer any need to make it look like an accident. We'd find the body in his apartment and realize it was deliberate."

"He needed to buy time," said Dussault. "If Horowitz had been shot, the brigade criminelle would've come here right away."

As they should have anyway, thought Gamache.

The only constant in these theories was that the dead man was killed unexpectedly. One of several big mistakes made that night by the intruder.

Murdering the wrong man, failing to kill the right one, and apparently not even finding what he was looking for. If he had, he wouldn't have still been hanging around when they'd arrived.

"Aaach," said the Prefect. "My head is beginning to hurt."

Gamache didn't believe that. This was the sort of puzzle that people like Dussault, like him, were good at. Trying to unravel what appeared to be a Gordian knot.

But were they working on the same knot?

"It is possible," said Armand, looking at Dussault to see his reaction to what he was about to say, "that it wasn't the killer Reine-Marie and I interrupted, but someone else."

"Who?"

"I don't know."

Claude Dussault sighed. "People coming and going. Mistaken identity. We appear to be looking at two different *mises-en-scène*. I'm seeing an Émile Zola tragedy, while you see a farce straight out of Molière."

It was not unlike what Gamache himself had been thinking a few moments earlier. Though Dussault's description, while said with humor, held an implied criticism. And some mocking.

"Could be," said Armand, with equanimity. "Fortunately, *truth is on the march and nothing will stop it.*"

Dussault laughed and clapped Armand on the arm. Clearly recognizing the Zola quote.

"Touché, mon ami."

Dussault turned and they continued down the hall.

"Is this the way you came, following the intruder?"

"Yes."

"He obviously knew there was a back stairway through the kitchen," said Dussault.

"Exactly. He'd had plenty of time to get to know the apartment. It's unfortunate. I thought I'd trapped him."

"How did you even know there was someone else here?" asked Dussault.

"We heard a sound."

Dussault was shaking his head. "And what would you do, Armand, if one of your agents, unarmed, chased a murderer with a gun down a narrow hallway?"

Armand gave a small laugh. "I'd have them on the carpet for sure."

"You'd probably be scraping them off the carpet. Not very smart of you. He could've shot you, too."

"Interesting that he didn't. Though I am grateful."

"As am I," said Dussault, with a smile. "But I am also a little surprised."

They were standing in the kitchen. Like most older apartments in Paris, it was small. Not much more than a galley, though there was a large window that looked out over the rooftops.

Cereal, sugar, coffee had been shaken out. The cupboards emptied.

It had become obvious, as they'd moved deeper into the apartment, that a methodical search had turned to panic, had turned into a sort of frenzy.

The back door was ajar, untouched from when Armand had followed the intruder through it less than half an hour earlier.

Once it was clear the killer had been swallowed by the Saturday morning crowd, Armand had joined Reine-Marie and waited for Claude Dussault and the rest of the gendarmes.

When they arrived just minutes later, Reine-Marie had taken the box of Stephen's things into bar Joséphine, where she was now waiting.

"I'll show you where he went," said Armand, opening the back door with a gloved hand. "Let's go down."

Just as they stepped into the stairwell, a voice called from the apartment, "*Patron?*"

"Here, Irena," said Dussault, stepping back into the kitchen. "What is it?"

Irena Fontaine stood beside the Prefect. As she'd stood beside and slightly behind him for years. Since she was a junior agent.

When Claude Dussault had been promoted to Prefect after the death of his predecessor, he'd elevated her to head the brigade criminelle.

At thirty-eight, she was the youngest to do so. And only the second woman.

From there, when his longtime second-in-command left the Préfecture, Dussault had promoted her to his number two.

And now, once again, she took her natural place beside him. Tall, blond hair pulled back in a tight ponytail, she emanated competence. The sort of person, Gamache thought, you'd want piloting any plane you were flying in.

"The coroner's here. We're ready to turn him over." She looked from the Prefect to his companion.

"I'm sorry, I haven't introduced you. Commander Irena Fontaine is my second-in-command. Chief Inspector Armand Gamache is the head of homicide with the Sûreté du Québec. He's a friend and trusted colleague."

They shook hands, and Fontaine said, "Québec?"

The slight condescension in the tone had long since stopped bothering Gamache. Her attitude was, after all, not his problem.

"*Oui.*"

"What've you found?" Dussault asked as they walked back down the corridor.

"Shot twice, once in his back, once in the head. Looks like a robbery. The victim returned home, surprised the intruder, and was shot."

"And yet," said Gamache, a step behind, "nothing was taken."

Fontaine stopped and turned. "How do you know that?"

"You can see. The artwork alone is worth a fortune. The intruder took the time to take it off the walls, even tearing the framing paper, but didn't then cut the paintings out."

"He was looking for ready cash, jewelry," said Fontaine. "The victim's wallet is missing."

"A little early to come to that conclusion, surely," said Gamache. "With all this mess, it could be anywhere. It looks more like a search than a robbery, *non*?"

While annoyed at being contradicted by this stranger, Irena Fontaine couldn't quite suppress a smile. The Québécois accent always amused her. It was like talking to a bumpkin.

"*Non,*" she said. "It looks to me like a robbery. Not everyone, monsieur, wants to wander the streets with oil paintings under their arms, trying to fence them."

"There's something I've failed to tell you, Irena," said Dussault. "Monsieur Gamache isn't here in his professional capacity, though that is helpful." He gave her a stern look. Of reproach, Gamache wondered, or warning? "He knows the owner of this apartment. He and his wife found the body."

Fontaine turned more interested eyes on Gamache. "You know the dead man. Why didn't you say so?"

"Because the victim isn't the owner of the apartment. I have no idea who the dead man is, but the owner of the apartment is my godfather. Stephen Horowitz."

"And where is he?"

"In a coma at the Hôtel-Dieu. He was hit by a van last night in an attempt on his life."

Fontaine's eyes widened, and she looked at the Prefect. "That's the case you passed along to me."

"Yes."

"And he owns this apartment?"

"Yes," said Gamache.

"The two attacks have to be connected," she said. "There can't be any doubt now about the hit-and-run last night."

So there had been doubt, thought Gamache. That might explain why the police hadn't come to Stephen's apartment themselves. It was one of the first things you'd expect in an attempted homicide investigation.

"I was with him when he was hit," said Gamache. "It was deliberate."

"And you're here now. You found the body," said Fontaine.

"I did."

He knew full well what she was getting at. It was, in all honesty, not a surprise. He'd probably be wondering the same thing if the same person showed up at the scene of two separate, but linked, attacks.

Irena Fontaine turned and looked down the hall toward the living room, and the body.

"I wonder if he was murdered by mistake."

"We were thinking the same thing," agreed Dussault.

"Someone was obviously trying to kill this Horowitz," Fontaine continued, speaking directly, and only, to the Prefect. "They came here first, found this man, and shot him, thinking he was Horowitz. When he discovered his mistake, the murderer went in search of his real target."

"And how did he know where to find him?" asked Armand.

It was a question that was taking on increasing importance in his mind.

"Maybe someone told him," she said, staring at Gamache. After a moment's pause she said, "What do you think happened here?"

"First, let me tell you what we found earlier today."

"No, I asked you a question. What do you think happened?"

He turned to look at her.

Fontaine expected to see a cold, angry glare. Instead, his gaze was calm, thoughtful. Curious even. She was acutely aware she was being assessed.

She assessed him in return.

Mid-fifties, the Prefect's vintage. Good cut to his clothes. Well-groomed. Distinguished. What struck her were the lines of his face. Not wrinkles. These weren't made by time, but by events.

There was the deep scar at his temple. And then there were his eyes. Bright, intelligent, thoughtful. Shrewd. And something else.

There was, she felt, a sympathy there. No, not that. Could it be kindness?

Surely not.

Still, there was something compelling about this man. An unmistakable warmth, like embers in a grate on a dreary day.

Irena Fontaine fought the urge to be drawn in. Recognizing that embers could erupt into flame at any moment.

"I think, Commander," Gamache said, "I can best answer your question by first telling you what we found among Stephen's things. If you don't mind."

"If you insist."

"*Merci.* After Stephen was hit, my wife picked up his glasses and a key off the street. She put both in her purse and only remembered them this morning."

"So?" said Fontaine. "Natural he'd have a key on him."

"It was to a hotel room. A suite actually, at the George V. We went there and discovered that Stephen had been living at the hotel for the last ten days. He was planning to check out this coming Wednesday."

Claude Dussault turned to him. "You didn't tell me that."

"I haven't had the chance. And it looks like there was someone else staying there," Armand continued, in the face of Dussault's glare. "A man who'd just arrived. He hadn't yet unpacked and wasn't planning to stay long. He only had a carry-on."

Fontaine cocked a thumb toward the living room. "That man?"

"I don't know for sure, but it seems a pretty good bet."

She was shaking her head. "This doesn't make sense. Why would someone with a place like this, and even a second bedroom for a guest, stay at a hotel?"

"To make it even more puzzling," said Gamache, "Stephen's famously cheap. There'd have to be a very, very good reason for him to take a suite at the George V."

"And what's that reason?" she asked.

"I wish I knew."

"Coming?" an agent called to them. "The coroner's waiting."

As they walked back down the hall, Dussault muttered to Gamache, "You should've told me about the key."

"And you should've told me you didn't actually believe that the attack was deliberate."

"Why do you say that?"

"Fontaine herself just admitted there was doubt, and if there wasn't, your people would have come here immediately. They'd have interrupted the intruder. Not Reine-Marie and me."

Gamache stopped. It was his turn to glare at the Prefect.

"Your doubt could have cost her her life."

"And you yours," admitted Dussault. "It was a mistake on Fontaine's part. I'll speak to her."

Armand almost pointed out that the error didn't rest solely with Fontaine, but kept his mouth tightly shut.

CHAPTER 10

~

The coroner knelt beside the body.

"You're here, good," she said, her voice heavy with impatience and annoyance. "We can finally start."

Reaching out gloved hands, she expertly turned the stiff body.

It was their first good look at the dead man.

Even in death, he had an air of success about him. Healthy. Wealthy. But was he wise? One thing was certain: Gamache had never seen him before.

The coroner described her observations.

"Male, Caucasian. Approximately seventy-five years of age. Shot in back and head. No apparent wounds to the front of the body. There's rigor. Death was more than twelve hours ago, less than twenty-four. Nothing in his hands. Nails look clean. There doesn't appear to have been a struggle. Slight bruising to the face, probably caused in the fall." She looked up at the Prefect. "I'd say he was dead before he hit the ground."

"Excuse me," they heard. "*Excusez-moi.*" Everyone turned to see a younger man in jacket, jeans, and scarf tied around his neck trying to get through the wall of cops.

"Who are you?" demanded one of the gendarmes.

Instead of answering, he turned to Gamache. "Reine-Marie called me. I came right over."

"This's Jean-Guy Beauvoir, my son-in-law," explained Gamache.

"Well, he shouldn't be here," said Fontaine. "Please wait outside. This's a crime scene."

"Yes, I know," said Jean-Guy. He had sympathy for this officer, who was obviously the agent in charge. But instead of leaving, he took a step forward and stood beside Gamache.

"Jean-Guy was my second-in-command," Gamache explained to Dussault and Fontaine. "He ran homicide for more than a year before moving to Paris. He also knows Stephen. Do you mind?"

"If he stays?" Fontaine looked at Beauvoir as though he was something she'd scraped off the bottom of her shoe.

Then she appealed to the Prefect, who shrugged.

"Fine," she said. "As long as I don't have to deal with him."

"Is there a wallet?" Dussault asked. "Any ID at all?"

"None," she said, kneeling beside the coroner now. "All his pockets are turned out."

"May I?" asked Gamache.

"Oh, what the fuck," muttered Fontaine. Then gestured toward the body, inviting Gamache forward and watching as he pulled aside the dead man's jacket and felt inside. He lifted a flap to reveal a hidden zipper and pocket.

But he didn't undo it, preferring to let Fontaine do that.

A moment later she pulled out a thin wallet.

"How did you know?" she asked.

"It's something seasoned travelers often do. Have hidden pockets in their clothes."

He chose not to explain that Stephen also had one. Nor did he tell them that he and Reine-Marie had found Stephen's agenda and passport there.

Fontaine handed the wallet to the Prefect, who walked away from the activity around the body. Gamache and Beauvoir joined him by the window.

"His name's Alexander Francis Plessner," said Dussault. "Mean anything to you?"

Armand thought. "*Non.* Stephen never mentioned him. You?"

Jean-Guy shook his head.

"Driver's license is from Ontario," said Dussault.

Irena Fontaine joined them and gave Dussault a passport. "We found it under that dresser. But no phone yet, and no keys."

"If they found his passport," said Gamache, "they must've realized they hadn't killed Stephen Horowitz."

"They killed the wrong man," said Dussault.

"Or not," said Gamache, and the Prefect nodded. Or not.

"Canadian," said Jean-Guy, looking at the passport. "Issued a year ago."

Claude Dussault flipped through it and sighed. "With kiosks at most customs now, passports aren't stamped anymore. We'll have to be in touch with Interpol."

"I'll scan the bar code over later today," said Irena Fontaine.

"Best to do it as soon as possible," said Gamache. "In my dealings with Interpol, it can take a little while for them to get the information. Even days."

"This's the brigade criminelle, monsieur," she said. "In Paris. Not the Sûreté du Québec. Interpol responds quickly to us. They know if we ask, it must be serious."

Beauvoir opened his mouth, but at a small glance from Gamache remained quiet.

This Fontaine obviously didn't know that Gamache had been approached in just the last six months to move to Lyon and take over Interpol. He'd refused, preferring to hunt murderers in Québec.

If Gamache wasn't going to tell her, he sure wouldn't. Though he was longing to.

"Thank you for explaining that, Commander," said Gamache. "Does the passport have any stamps at all?"

"Only one," said Dussault. "A trip to Peru a year ago."

"Peru?" asked Beauvoir.

"Big tourist spot," said Dussault. "Machu Picchu. The Nazca Lines."

"The what?" asked Fontaine, and Beauvoir was glad she was the one who showed ignorance. Normally that was his job.

He'd actually thought the Prefect had said "Nascar," and was about to ask about that.

"Look them up," said Dussault. "One of the great mysteries of the world."

"Two hundred and fifty dollars Canadian," Fontaine reported as she went through the wallet. "Seventy euros. Two Visa cards and"—she held up a white business card—"this."

She handed it to Dussault.

He read the name on the card. "Stephen Horowitz. That confirms it. The dead man knew Horowitz. But how? Friend? Business associate? Must be more than an acquaintance to be in his apartment."

"May I?" asked Armand, and held out his hand for the card. "Monsieur Plessner was much more than an acquaintance, to have this."

He handed it back to Fontaine.

"Why?" she asked. "It's just a simple business card."

"But without an address?" said Beauvoir. "Not even a phone number or email? What business card has just a name?"

"Not just that," Dussault pointed out. "Someone's written *JSPS* after his name. What does that mean, Armand? 'Justice of the Peace'? Is it an honorific?"

Gamache was smiling. "Not exactly."

Bringing out his own wallet, he removed a dog-eared, slightly scruffy business card. The paper was thin and worn, but the printing was exactly the same.

Stephen Horowitz. And after the name exactly the same four letters. Written longhand.

JSPS.

"It's something my grandmother Zora always called him," Armand explained.

"But what does it mean?" asked Dussault.

"'JSPS' stands for 'Just Some Poor Schmuck.'"

Dussault laughed. "Really? But 'schmuck,' that's an insult, isn't it? Why did your grandmother call him that? Was it a private joke, a term of endearment?"

"Just the opposite," said Armand. "She loathed him. Did from the moment they met in the late 1940s. He was an easy man to dislike."

Jean-Guy smiled. It was true. Stephen Horowitz could be a real piece of *merde*. And it wasn't an act. It was genuinely who he was. But Beauvoir knew that was just one side of a complex man.

"How did she know him?" asked Fontaine. "Come to think of it, how did you?"

"My father hired him to do odd jobs. Stephen had nothing when he came to Québec after the war, but my father quickly saw his potential. They were roughly the same age, and only fate decided that one would lose his home and family, and the other would have both. My father had huge admiration for Stephen, but Zora hated him from the get-go. She called him—"

"Just some poor schmuck?" said Dussault.

"*C'est ça*. And that was when she was being polite." Armand smiled, remembering her muttering "*Alte kaker*" whenever Stephen showed up.

"Why did she hate him so much?" asked Fontaine. "What did he do to her?"

"Nothing, except to be born German. I think it was asking a bit too much of her, at that time, to like or trust anyone who was German."

"But you told me he fought for the Resistance," said Dussault.

"I don't think my grandmother ever believed it."

Armand glanced out the window, at the Hôtel Lutetia. That was another reason Zora distrusted Stephen.

Because he chose to live right next door to the Lutetia.

It had taken Armand many years to understand her hatred of the beautiful hotel.

He knew he'd have to explain the complex relationships in his family, eventually. Now seemed as good a time as any.

"My father met Zora in Poland, in the final days of the war. She and her family had been deported from Paris and sent to Auschwitz. There were more than a thousand people in that transport. Three survived the war. Zora was one of them."

He looked at Claude Dussault, who dropped his eyes.

Paris might have a lot of light, but there were also strong shadows.

"She never called it the Holocaust. It was, for her, 'the Great Murders.'"

He'd been raised to consider Zora his grandmother, which he did to this day. She'd impressed on him that murderers had to be stopped. No matter the cost. That was, Armand knew, the reason he'd joined the Sûreté.

To stop them. No matter the cost.

"My father was with the Canadian Red Cross and was helping with the 'displaced persons,' as they were called. Those liberated from the death camps but with nowhere to go. No home left. He sponsored Zora to come to Montréal. She lived with us and raised me after they were killed."

"They?" asked Fontaine. "Killed?"

"My parents. Car accident. I was nine years old. Stephen was my godfather and helped raise me. He brought me to Paris once a year. I practically grew up in this apartment."

He looked around, trying to recapture that sense of security.

But it eluded him amid the wreckage. And the murder.

"So, wait a minute," said Commander Fontaine, nodding toward the card. "Go back. If it was an insult, why would Horowitz write *JSPS* on his business card?"

"It was an inside joke. He actually liked Zora, and I think as he got more successful, it was a way for him to keep his considerable ego in check. It was also a code."

"For what?" asked Fontaine.

"For his senior management, his bankers, his security. Most importantly, it was code to his secretary, Mrs. McGillicuddy. Whoever had that card was to be given all access. All help. No matter what was asked."

"But what would stop anyone from writing *JSPS* on a card and getting that access?" asked Fontaine.

"Stephen made it known that anyone who tried would be dealt with severely. It wouldn't be worth it."

Fontaine looked over at the body of Alexander Plessner.

"Not that severely," said Gamache.

"Do you know how many of these he gave out?" Fontaine asked.

"I actually thought I had the only one," said Gamache, returning his thin card to his wallet. For safekeeping.

Stephen had given it to him after the funeral of his parents. He'd taken Armand aside and, under the watchful, wrathful eye of Zora, had brought out a business card and written, *JSPS*.

"Do you know what that stands for?"

Armand had shaken his head. He didn't know, and he didn't care. Nothing mattered anymore.

Stephen told him, and for the first time since the knock on the door, Armand smiled. He could hear Zora saying it, in her thick accent.

"You keep this card with you always, Armand. And anytime you need help, you come to me. If someone won't let you in, you show them that. They'll give you everything you want."

"Ice cream?"

"Yes, any flavor. Money. A safe place to stay. And they'll find me, no matter where I am, and I'll come to you. You understand?"

It was a good question. Stephen's German accent was still thick at the time. And while Armand couldn't understand each and every word, he understood the meaning.

He put the card in his pocket. Then went outside with his best friend, Michel.

Every now and then, as the day moved to evening, moved to night, he'd put his hand in his pocket. Touch the card. And look at the house.

Zora would be watching over him. And now he knew Stephen would be, too.

He was not alone.

Half a century later, it was Armand's turn. To watch over Stephen. To protect him.

To find out what had happened. What was happening.

But what was happening?

He looked over at the dead man.

Was Alexander Plessner the intended target, or was he, as they suspected, killed by mistake? Mistaken for Stephen.

Just some poor schmuck.

"Armand," Dussault said, taking Gamache aside while Beauvoir examined the body. "I don't mind you being involved with the investigation. In fact, I welcome it. You know Monsieur Horowitz better than anyone. But this fellow? He'll only get in the way. He's already annoying Fontaine."

"Beauvoir is an experienced homicide cop," Gamache explained. Again. "And ended his career as head of homicide—"

"In Québec."

"*Oui.* But murder is murder, and people are people. Even in Québec. No one is better at tracking down killers than Jean-Guy Beauvoir."

"You forget," said the Prefect, looking from Gamache to the men and women collecting evidence. "This is the brigade criminelle. In Paris. We choose the very best France has to offer. And these are the best. Not just in Paris. Not just in France. But in the world."

They stared at each other.

"You're right, of course," Armand conceded. "But Jean-Guy stands with the best of them."

"Does he really? I looked you up this morning, to get caught up on your career. A lot has happened, my friend."

"True."

"In my reading, I saw his record, too. He's an alcoholic and drug addict—"

"In recovery," snapped Armand. "He's been clean for years. Don't tell me you don't have fine officers who've battled addiction. The incidence in our line of work is—"

"Yes. Yes," admitted Dussault. "Too much damage done."

"And often to the best," said Gamache. "Those who care. Those who stand in the front line. Jean-Guy Beauvoir cares. There's no better officer anywhere. And that includes here." He paused for a moment. Challenging Dussault to challenge that. "I know no one braver."

"Or smarter?" suggested Dussault. "I read that he jumped ship to go into private industry. He probably gets paid ten times what we make. And doesn't get shot at. As you know, my own second-in-command also left. We're the foolish ones, Armand."

"Thank God we're so good-looking," said Armand, smiling.

Dussault clapped him on the arm. "Have you ever been tempted, *mon vieux*? To take a job with a private security firm, for instance? They'd pay a fortune for someone like you."

"No. You?"

Dussault laughed. "Don't tell anyone, but there's only one thing I do well, and this's it."

He looked at his team, with fondness.

"That's not true," said Armand. "I seem to remember you took a sabbatical a couple of years ago to play saxophone in that polka band."

Claude lowered his voice. "Shhhh. Everyone thinks I was studying international money laundering."

"I think they might be onto you. Your mistake was telling them you'd joined the Interpol Anti-Terrorist Glee Club."

"Yeah, they did find that hard to believe. Comforting, really, that I'm not surrounded by idiots. I seem to be the only one."

Armand laughed.

The truth, and Armand was one of the few who knew it, was that Claude had suffered PTSD after a spectacularly brutal year of terrorist attacks. Culminating in the hit-and-run death of his mentor, the former Prefect.

Music, particularly his beloved saxophone, had helped heal the man.

"All right," said Dussault. "Beauvoir stays, but in the background. And I deal with you, not him."

"Agreed," said Gamache.

"Will you excuse me? I see the Procureur wandering around."

Jean-Guy was walking through the rest of the apartment, examining each room.

Irena Fontaine had gone back to supervising the team from the brigade criminelle.

Claude Dussault was standing by the window, conferring with the Procureur de la République, who was needed to officially launch any murder investigation.

The conference did not take long. Two bullets in the back was a pretty convincing argument.

No stranger to homicide investigations, Armand stood in the middle of the familiar room. Lost.

This space, this place, had always been safe for him. Almost sacred. But no longer.

His eyes moved to the picture hooks on the walls and the paintings strewn on the floor.

The Gauguins and Monets, the Rothkos and the huge Cy Twombly ripped down from over the fireplace. The sublime Kenojuak Ashevak lying faceup.

And among them, easily overlooked, a little frame, like a single mullion in an old window. The watercolor was unspectacular in every way, except for the comfort it had offered a grieving child. The tiny window into the possible.

Smoke still rose from the cottages. Perpetual. Predictable. A river still wound through the village in the valley. There were thick forests filled, young Armand had been sure, with marvelous creatures. And in the very center of the painting of the village, there was a cluster of trees.

Armand looked across the crime scene, at the small frame on the floor, and had a nearly overwhelming desire to turn around and go home. Back to Québec.

To sit in the bistro with Reine-Marie. Henri, Gracie, and Fred curled together in front of the log fire.

Gabri would bring them café au lait, or something stronger. Olivier would grill maple-smoked salmon for their meal, while Clara and Myrna joined them to talk about books and art, food and what the Asshole Saint's horse had done now.

Mad Ruth and her possessed duck Rosa would toss out insults, and sublime poetry.

> I just sit where I'm put, composed
> of stone and wishful thinking:
> That the deity that kills for pleasure will also heal,

He could, even now, from what felt like an impossible distance, see through the mullioned windows of the bistro to the thick forests, and the leaves that would already be changing.

As everything eventually did.

Except in the picture tossed so casually on the floor.

> That in the midst of your nightmare,
> the final one, a kind lion will pick your soul up gently
> by the nape of the neck,

Home. Home. He wanted to go home. And sit by the fire. And listen to their friends talking and laughing. To hold Reine-Marie's hand and watch their grandchildren play.

> And caress you into darkness and paradise.

But not quite yet.

Gamache went over to the tiny painting and replaced it safely on the screw in the wall. Where it belonged.

But before he did, he noticed, written on the back, *For Armand.*

CHAPTER 11

———

Reine-Marie Gamache sat in the Hôtel Lutetia's bar Joséphine, her hand resting on the box beside her.

She stared past the elegant patrons, through the huge windows of the Lutetia, at the chic men and women of Paris's Sixth Arrondissement.

They strolled by on rue de Sèvres. Many holding shopping bags from the nearby Le Bon Marché.

Reine-Marie was aware of the activity around her in the magnificent Belle Époque brasserie, but all she saw was the body on the floor and blood on a carpet where her children had played.

And she tried to recapture that scent. Would she ever be able to identify it again?

She could still, to this day, identify her mother's scent. Not perfume, but ammonia cleanser. Clinging to her, ingrained in her very pores, from her job cleaning houses.

And Reine-Marie knew she'd go to her grave with Armand's scent of sandalwood. At least, she hoped she would. That she'd go first. In his arms.

It was selfish of her. To make him go through that. To leave him behind. But she wasn't sure if she could go on without him. If he . . .

She refocused her mind. Back to the events. The facts. The body.

As a trained librarian and archivist, she was used to not just sorting and cataloguing information but also making connections. What had made her so good at her job, and led to her rise within Québec's

Bibliothèque et Archives nationales, was that her mind worked on many levels.

Where others might see facts, Madame Gamache could see the relationship between them. She could connect two, three, many apparently disparate events.

Between the aboriginal name for "the Stargazer," an account of a dinner party in 1820 with the geologist Bigsby, and a pauper's grave in Montréal.

She'd put all that together and come up with David Thompson. An explorer and mapmaker who turned out to be possibly the greatest cartographer who ever lived. An extraordinary human who'd disappeared into history.

Until the librarian and archivist Madame Gamache had found him.

And now she was presented with a whole different set of facts, of events. Not safely residing in history, these had a pulse. And blood all over them.

She pulled the box closer and narrowed her eyes. Trying to see . . .

"Hello?"

Reine-Marie was jolted back to the Joséphine and looked up into her husband's smiling face.

"*Désolé*," he said, bending to kiss her. "I didn't mean to startle you. You were a million miles away."

"Actually, not that far." She kissed him back and heard him whisper, "Don't react."

She kept the smile on her face and tried not to betray any confusion.

He stepped aside and revealed Claude Dussault.

"Claude," she said.

But she was confused. What had Armand meant? Was she not supposed to recognize this man she knew well?

Had seen the night before in the hospital?

But as the Prefect bent to kiss her on both cheeks, with an exaggerated *politesse* that had become a joke between them, she understood.

She tried not to react, but she feared she might have, momentarily, given it away. In the slight widening of her eyes. In surprise.

She was pleased to see Jean-Guy and focused her surprise on him.

Everyone got settled in the banquette and ordered drinks as Armand brought Reine-Marie up to speed.

She listened, asked a few questions that had no answers, then fell silent.

But her mind was racing. So quickly she actually felt it was spinning. Kicking up dust. Obscuring what should have been clear.

Jean-Guy pointed to her brioche. "Are you . . . ?"

She pushed it toward her son-in-law, who was always, it seemed, ravenous.

"One big question is whether Monsieur Plessner was mistaken for Monsieur Horowitz, or whether the attack on him was deliberate," said Claude Dussault. "What've you got there?"

He gestured toward the box, where Reine-Marie's hand still rested, protectively.

"Oh, yes," said Armand. "We wanted to show you." He looked around and caught the maître d's eye.

"Jacques."

"*Oui*, Monsieur Armand?"

The two men went way back. Jacques had been a busboy when Stephen first brought Armand, at the age of nine, to the Lutetia. They were a decade apart in age, and while they'd known each other for almost half a century, there remained a formality between the two. A good maître d'hôtel was never overly familiar with guests. And Jacques was among the best.

"Is there somewhere we can go to talk privately?"

"Of course. I will find you a room."

A few minutes later they found themselves in the presidential suite.

"I was expecting some basement storage closet," said Dussault, looking around with amusement. "You clearly have some pull here, Armand."

"As do you at the George V."

Dussault laughed. "I wish. I haven't been there in years."

"My mistake. I thought you said you had."

"No. You're thinking of the flophouse around the corner from the Quai des Orfèvres."

"Right. The Gigi V," said Armand.

As Dussault laughed, Armand caught Reine-Marie's eyes, with another warning. But he could see it was no longer necessary.

Claude Dussault sat on the deep sofa and, putting the box on his knees, he opened it with all the anticipation of a child on Christmas morning.

"Let's see what we have here. This's a hospital container, *non?* Monsieur Horowitz's belongings. Sealed. You haven't opened it? But I thought—"

"We opened it," said Armand. "And resealed it."

He explained for Dussault and Jean-Guy what had happened at the George V.

"*Bon,*" said Dussault. "Good thinking. So everything's in here? Laptop, phone, clothing?"

"Everything that Stephen had on him last night, and that I could find in his study."

Dussault paused, his hand hanging into the box and a perplexed expression on his slender face. "It's so strange, that he'd be staying at the hotel. You have no idea why?"

"None."

Dussault brought out the laptop. "I don't suppose you know his password for this?"

"No. Nor the phone. Though it's smashed."

"The SIM card?" Dussault asked.

"Broken."

He sighed. "That's a shame."

"*Oui.*"

"What's this?" Dussault asked.

"Looks like an Allen wrench," said Reine-Marie.

She'd assembled enough big-box furniture for Daniel and Annie when they'd gone away to university to know an Allen wrench.

"That was on the desk beside the laptop," said Armand. "I just swept everything into the box."

"Including these," said Dussault, holding a few screws in his palm.

"All we need is a roll of duct tape and we'll know more than we want to about the George V."

"This's interesting." Jean-Guy picked up a couple of Canadian nickels. "They're stuck together."

"Ha," said Reine-Marie, reaching for them. "That's fun. One of them must be magnetized. I used to show Daniel and Annie that trick when they were kids."

"What trick?"

"Older coins have a high nickel content, which means they can be turned into magnets."

As she spoke, Jean-Guy tried to pull them apart. "They're not magnetized, they're glued. Now why would Stephen have two old nickels glued together?"

"He probably found them on the street and picked them up," said Armand.

"As a good-luck charm?" asked Dussault.

"You would've hoped," said Armand.

Dussault tossed the soldered coins in the air, caught them, then put them in his pocket. "For luck."

"Actually, Claude, if they are Stephen's good-luck charm, I'd like to take them to the hospital. Put them by his bed."

Most people, Armand knew, had some degree of superstition, and imbued objects and rituals with power. From crucifixes to the Star of David, from a rabbit's foot to a lucky pair of socks.

This could be Stephen's. Nickels stuck together. Money he could not spend.

"Of course," said Dussault, and without hesitation he gave them to Armand. "Selfish of me, to want all the luck."

He went back to the box and examined the torn and bloody clothing. Armand noticed that he looked for, and found, the hidden pocket. Which held Stephen's passport. But not his agenda. That was sitting in Armand's pocket. And would stay there.

Finally, from the bottom of the box, Claude Dussault brought out a publication.

"An annual report. You said he was here for meetings. Could this be one?"

Dussault placed the document on the sofa.

Armand watched as Jean-Guy picked it up. It was for GHS Engineering. Beauvoir's company.

His face, at first, showed some confusion. That never lasted long with Beauvoir.

"Stephen?" he said quietly. "You?"

Armand was prepared for this, but no less dreading it. He'd known since the attempt on Stephen's life, since they'd found the annual report on Stephen's desk, since bringing it with them, since calling Beauvoir into the investigation, that this moment would come.

"What does this mean?" Jean-Guy asked, holding up the document.

There was no mistaking the barely contained anger in his voice.

"It means that Stephen helped find you your job, at my request."

And there it was.

"You told Stephen to use his influence to get me my job at GHS?"

Armand stood up. "Let's talk in the bedroom."

Not waiting for Jean-Guy to agree, Armand walked across the huge living room, down the corridor, and into the farthest bedroom.

A moment later Beauvoir appeared, his lips thin. His eyes hard.

"Close the door, please," said Armand.

Beauvoir gave it a sharp shove. Creating a bang that got the message across.

"I'm sorry," said Armand.

Beauvoir opened his hands, indicating *Is that it?* while remaining mute. Partly because he didn't know what to say. Partly out of fear of what he would say.

This was a betrayal, on so many levels. To not just do this thing, but to keep it from him.

They'd been through Hell together. Crossed the River Styx together. Paid the boatman in blood and agony and sorrow. Together.

They'd come back to the land of the living together. Scarred. Marked.

They were as connected as two humans could be.

And Armand had played God with Jean-Guy's and Annie's lives? He'd conspired to get Jean-Guy his job at GHS Engineering, without asking first? Without consulting him?

Armand sat on the side of one bed, while Jean-Guy sat on the other. Facing each other.

"I was afraid if I told you I had anything to do with the job offer, that you'd think I wanted you to leave the Sûreté. That it was some sort of veiled message that you weren't up to the job of Chief Inspector."

"Was it?"

"Are you really asking that?" said Gamache. "You were a gifted Chief Inspector. A natural leader. At the time I believed I'd be fired, maybe even put on trial. My one consolation was that the homicide department was in good hands. Your hands. But the brutality of the situation weighed heavily on both of us. I could retire. I'd had a full life. A good life. Reine-Marie and I would live quietly in the country.

"You're just beginning. You and your family. I wanted to give you a choice. That's all. But I was wrong not to discuss it with you before approaching Stephen. I am sorry."

"Is Stephen on the board of GHS?"

"Maybe. I don't know. When I asked him to find you a job offer in private industry, I assumed it would be in Québec. Not Paris. And not specifically GHS."

Jean-Guy nodded, rocking back and forth slightly on the bed.

"The offer was legitimate," said Armand, reading his thoughts. "GHS would never have hired you for that position if they hadn't known you were perfect for it."

"Did Stephen approach Carole Gossette, my boss?"

"I honestly have no idea." Armand hesitated before going on. "You leaving the Sûreté was painful for me. You and your family leaving Québec broke my heart."

Jean-Guy nodded. He knew the truth of that.

"Still," Armand went on, "it was a terrible mistake, not asking if you wanted the option to leave the service."

His use of that word reminded Jean-Guy that Gamache almost never called the Sûreté a force. He called it a service.

Jean-Guy took a deep breath, then nodded.

Armand reached into his pocket and brought out the nickels. He looked at them, then handed them to Jean-Guy.

"Compensation?" asked Jean-Guy.

Armand gave a short laugh. "*Non.* If this really is Stephen's good-luck charm, I know he'd want you to have it."

Jean-Guy closed his fist around the fused coins. "We might need it." He looked his father-in-law in the eyes. "*Merci.*"

He made to get up, but Armand motioned him back down.

"There is something else."

"*Oui?*"

"When Reine-Marie and I found the body, we noticed a scent in the air. A man's cologne. That's how we knew someone was still in Stephen's apartment."

"It wasn't the dead man's or Stephen's?"

"No. This was fresh."

"What did it smell like?" asked Jean-Guy.

When Gamache paused, Beauvoir assumed it was to think about how best to describe a scent. But he was wrong.

Gamache's answer not only surprised Beauvoir, it changed everything.

"It smelled like Claude Dussault."

CHAPTER 12

"What was that about?" asked Dussault as the two men returned to the living room.

"I'm not sure if you know that I work at GHS Engineering," said Jean-Guy, pointing to the annual report. "I hadn't realized until I saw that that Stephen must've had a hand in my hiring. I thought I got it on my own merits."

"And you did," said Armand. "But I needed to explain how it happened, and apologize for my part in it."

"Which was?" asked Dussault.

Armand explained.

"Well, Horowitz must be on the board of GHS," said Dussault, holding up the annual report. "That's how he got Beauvoir the job, and why he has this."

He put it back in the box and replaced the lid.

"I'll check with Mrs. McGillicuddy, his secretary," said Gamache.

"I've heard from Fontaine," said Dussault. "They're removing the body. I need to be at the autopsy. Would you like to be there, too?"

He looked at Gamache, then, slightly reluctantly, widened the invitation to include Beauvoir.

"Please," said Gamache while Beauvoir nodded.

After they set up a time to meet the Prefect at the Quai des Orfèvres later that afternoon, Dussault said, "Commander Fontaine wants to interview you and the family. You're witnesses to the attack on Horowitz."

It was agreed that Fontaine would interview them at Daniel and Roslyn's apartment in the Third Arrondissement, mid-afternoon.

Dussault left the Hôtel Lutetia with the box, while Reine-Marie, Jean-Guy, and Armand returned to bar Joséphine.

They needed to talk.

A waiter asked what they'd like to order.

Reine-Marie asked for tea then quickly scanned the menu, taking the first thing she saw. Thankfully it was lobster mayonnaise.

Armand ordered an herb omelette. He wasn't hungry and knew he'd just push things around on the plate. Beauvoir had a burger.

Finally, the waiter left, and Reine-Marie turned to Armand.

"Claude? That cologne we smelled in Stephen's apartment. It's the same one Claude's wearing."

"*Oui*. I told Jean-Guy while we were in the bedroom."

"You don't think . . . ? He's a friend. He's the head of the Préfecture de Police, for God's sake."

Armand shook his head. "I don't know."

"A lot of people might wear that cologne," suggested Jean-Guy, who'd made sure he got a good whiff of the Prefect before he left.

Reine-Marie hesitated, but knew this wasn't the time to shy away from the truth. "I've never smelled it before. Have you?"

Jean-Guy had to admit he hadn't. "But it might be more popular here. Like *tête de veau*."

He'd never quite recovered from the first time he and Annie, with Honoré, had wandered the Marché des Enfants Rouges, near their new home.

Turning from a bank of éclairs, he came face-to-face with a row of skinned calves' heads. Glaring at him.

He'd scooped Honoré up and made sure the little boy didn't see.

"What kind of people eat that?" he'd hissed at Annie as he hurried away.

"What kind of people eat poutine?" she'd countered.

"That's different. It doesn't have eyes. You're okay with eating the head, and brain, of a calf?"

"*Non*. It's disgusting. But the French like it."

Reine-Marie and Armand understood the slightly tortured point Jean-Guy was making.

"I wonder what the cologne is," Reine-Marie said, and thanked the waiter, who'd just brought her a pot of tea, already steeped.

She poured a cup and looked out the window, across the park, to the huge department store on rue de Sèvres.

Picking up her cup, she noticed a line down the side and a drip.

"It's leaking," she said, putting it back down.

"A lane to the land of the dead," said Jean-Guy, to the astonishment of the Gamaches.

"What did you just say?" Reine-Marie asked.

"Sorry. Part of a poem, I think. I heard it recently. Can't remember where. Oh, right. We were flying to the Maldives—"

Since Annie wasn't there to moan, Reine-Marie did.

"—and Carole Gossette said it." He closed his eyes, remembering. *"And the crack in the tea-cup opens / A lane to the land of the dead."*

"Why would she say that?" asked Reine-Marie.

"I'm beginning to wonder," said Jean-Guy.

Turning to Armand, Reine-Marie said, "You do suspect Claude, don't you. If you didn't, you'd give him everything."

"Pardon?" said Jean-Guy.

Armand reached into his jacket and brought out Stephen's slender agenda. "I haven't had a chance to go through it yet."

"While you do, I'm going shopping." Reine-Marie got up.

"Now?" asked Jean-Guy.

"Now."

"But your lunch?" said her son-in-law.

"Save it for me, please," she said. "I don't think I'll be long."

She was wrong.

Reine-Marie paused in the sun-filled atrium of Le Bon Marché department store. It hadn't changed. The bright and airy space was an unlikely and perfect confluence of commerce and beauty. And now, with the passage of time, history.

Le Bon Marché was the oldest, the first, store of its kind in Paris. Practically in the world. Opened in 1852, it predated Selfridges in London by more than half a century.

In fact, the Hôtel Lutetia was built by the owner of Le Bon Marché, primarily to give his customers someplace to stay while spending money in his remarkable store.

He was a visionary. What he saw was wealth. What he could not have envisioned were the other uses his magnificent hotel would be put to.

As children, Daniel and Annie had loved nothing better than to ride up and down the famous white-tiled escalators, looking out over the wares, the people, gawking at the huge installations that were as much art as marketing. They'd visit the toy department, the bonbons department, before returning to the Lutetia for a hot chocolate.

This near-perfect commercial creation was filled with happy memories.

But not today.

She was there for a reason, a dark purpose.

Reine-Marie Gamache made her way to the parfumerie. And from there, to the colognes.

Gamache and Beauvoir had their heads together, looking at Stephen's cramped writing.

They'd first checked his entries for the day before. There were several.

Stephen had written *Armand, Rodin,* and the time.

Below that he'd written *AFP.*

"Alexander Francis Plessner?" asked Beauvoir.

"Must be. That's when he arrived in Paris."

Below that Stephen had written *dinner, family, Juveniles,* and the time.

"You said he was meeting someone for drinks before coming to dinner," said Jean-Guy. "Do you think he meant Plessner?"

Gamache was nodding, staring at the page.

"Jacques?"

"*Oui*, Monsieur Armand?"

"Was Monsieur Horowitz here yesterday?"

"*Bien sûr.* He came in for ice cream."

"Who was he with?"

"No one, monsieur. He was alone. I personally waited on him."

"You're sure."

"Certain. Will he be joining you?"

Armand stared at him and realized the maître d' had no idea what had happened. Why would he?

Gamache got up and stood facing Jacques. "I'm afraid there's been an accident."

Jacques's face slackened. "*Non,*" he whispered. "Is it serious?"

His blue eyes, sharp as ever, trained to pick up the most nuanced of movements, the smallest change of facial expression in his patrons, now betrayed his own feelings.

Jacques had known Monsieur Horowitz from the first day he started at the Lutetia. The visiting Canadian's water glass was practically the very first one he'd filled.

In his nervous state, Jacques had tipped the silver beaker too steeply and ice cubes plopped out, spilling water onto the linen.

Jacques, all of fifteen, stared in horror, then lifted his eyes to the man sitting there.

The patron's face was placid, not revealing that anything was wrong. But he gave a small smile and nod of encouragement.

It was okay.

While everything else about his first few days was a blur, the Canadian businessman had made an impression. And not just for that act of kindness.

His accent, for one. It was a mixture of German, English, and French. And was, for the new busboy, a little hard to follow.

Where other patrons were clearly wealthier, more powerful, this one had an assurance. As though he belonged.

And then there'd been the tip. Slipped into his pocket.

Three hundred francs. As much as he'd make in a week.

At the time, though Jacques didn't know it, Stephen wasn't yet rich. But he recognized, and rewarded, a hard worker. A worker who cared.

Besides, Stephen Horowitz knew the courage it took to bus tables for difficult, even scary, patrons. Courage must always be rewarded.

The other thing Jacques remembered was looking down the long corridor as Monsieur Horowitz paused at the mosaic in the tile floor by the entrance to the Hôtel Lutetia. It was the symbol of the hotel, and also the ancient symbol of Paris.

The city had originally been called Lutetia. And her emblem was a ship in peril on a stormy sea.

That symbol was imbedded in the hotel floor.

Monsieur Horowitz had turned to young Jacques and said, *"Fluctuat nec mergitur."*

Every schoolchild in Paris learned those words. It was the motto of the ancient settlement of Lutetia. And of Paris.

"Reminds me of *The Tempest*," Monsieur Horowitz had said, nodding to the mosaic.

Jacques had looked around at the hushed corridor. A place less like a storm would be hard to find.

"We are such stuff as dreams are made on," quoted Monsieur Horowitz. He'd turned his clear, clear crystal-blue eyes on the puzzled busboy. "And sometimes nightmares, eh, young man?" He gazed around before returning to Jacques. "Who knows where we're going to find the devil?"

"Oui, monsieur." Though Jacques had no idea, at the time, what the man could possibly be talking about.

That had been almost fifty years earlier.

Now young Armand, for Jacques couldn't help thinking of this man that way, stood before him. With news.

Jacques was no fool. Monsieur Horowitz was elderly. Getting frailer. He expected, one day, to receive bad news. But he had not expected it to be this bad.

"He's in the Hôtel-Dieu hospital. A hit-and-run." *No need to say more*, thought Gamache.

"*Merde,*" whispered Jacques. "*Désolé,*" he quickly added, shocked at himself for swearing in front of a patron. He'd have fired a waiter on the spot for doing the same thing.

"You're right," said Armand. "It is *merde.* We're trying to work out where he was yesterday, and who he met with."

"I see."

If Jacques really did see, Armand couldn't tell. The maître d's professional mask was back.

"He came here at three thirty and ordered his usual peppermint ice cream."

Armand almost smiled. "With hot fudge?"

"Of course."

Three thirty, thought Armand. The time he'd walked Stephen back there. That fit.

He'd sat here, alone, eating his ice cream. And?

Was he expecting someone? Monsieur Plessner maybe? But was he already lying dead across the street?

Why would Stephen be waiting here and not in his own apartment?

He heard Jean-Guy on his phone to Isabelle Lacoste, back at the Sûreté headquarters in Montréal. He was asking her to find out all she could about Alexander Francis Plessner.

"*Oui,* Canadian citizen, probably living in Toronto."

"Did Monsieur Horowitz meet anyone here in the last ten days?" Gamache asked.

"Ten days? I assumed he'd just arrived."

Armand brought up a photo on his phone. "Does this man look familiar?"

It was a close-up of Plessner's face. He appeared asleep. Except for the pallor.

"Is he dead? He looks dead."

"Please, just tell me if he's been here recently, or ever. Do you recognize him?"

"No."

Armand nodded. "*Bon. Merci,* Jacques. Oh, what time did Stephen leave yesterday?"

"I'd say just after four."

"He met us at eight," said Jean-Guy. "Four hours unaccounted for."

"For now," said Armand.

"May I visit him?" Jacques asked.

"I'm afraid not. But I'll let him know you were asking after him."

"Yes, please. And can you tell him, *Fluctuat nec mergitur*?"

"What does it mean?" Jean-Guy asked.

"'Beaten by the waves,'" said the maître d'. "'But never sinks.'"

Armand and Jacques stared at each other, then nodded. And went about their jobs. Jacques to command the army of staff in the bar and restaurant, and young Armand to find a murderer.

CHAPTER 13

⁓

"May I help you, madame?" a young man asked.

"I'm trying to find a cologne. I smelled it recently but don't know the name," Reine-Marie said. "I'm sorry. That's not much help."

"Not to worry," he said. "I love this sort of thing. Now, are you sure it was a man's cologne and not a woman's *eau de parfum*?"

"Absolutely."

"*Bon,*" he said. "That helps. We can ignore all those." He waved toward the archipelago of women's scents. And then asked the question she'd been dreading. "Can you describe it?"

Short of saying it smelled like a senior police officer, she racked her brain. What were the words she'd used when first trying to imprint it on her brain in those horrific few seconds in front of the corpse?

"Was it earthy?" the salesperson asked, trying to help. "Did it smell like moss or bark? Lots of men's fragrances do. They think it's masculine."

He made a face, and Reine-Marie smiled. She liked this man.

"No. It was lighter than that."

"Fruity?"

"*Non.*"

"Citrusy?"

"Yes."

"Good."

"Maybe a little woody," she added, and grimaced to show her uncertainty.

"Okay," he said.

"With a kind of chemical-y smell?"

"Are you asking me?"

"Telling?" she said.

"It seems we're looking for a lemon tree made out of plastic. It's a good thing you're not trying to sell fragrances, madame."

Armand pushed his omelette away after one bite. It was moist, with aged Comté cheese and tarragon. Just as he remembered it. Just as he liked it.

But not today.

Adjusting his reading glasses, he leaned over the agenda once more.

Jean-Guy had wolfed down the juicy burger, with the young, runny Gorgonzola, Mont d'Or, and sautéed mushrooms, and was now also reading while absently dipping the herbed frites into mayonnaise.

"Stephen arrived on the eleventh of September," said Jean-Guy. "Air Canada flight from Montréal. That was ten days ago, just like the manager at the George V told you. So, what's he been doing?"

The rest of the agenda, from the eleventh to the day before he was hit, was empty. Until the entry about meeting Armand in the garden of the Musée Rodin. Then AFP, which they now knew stood for Alexander Francis Plessner.

Below that, Stephen had written in the dinner with the family. His family, Armand noticed. His family.

Armand brought out his own notebook.

"This's ridiculous," said Jean-Guy as he leaned back against the sofa. "Stephen came to Paris for a reason. Why didn't he write anything down? The rest of the agenda is packed with meetings and notes."

It was true. They'd been through it once, scanning, and would need to go over it a few more times, carefully. The ten days previous were empty.

But the days going forward were not.

On Monday Stephen was planning to attend an eight a.m. board meeting of GHS Engineering.

"He has a reservation on the Air Canada flight back to Montréal on Wednesday," said Armand. "But there's a note beside it." He leaned closer to read the cramped writing, then smiled. Stephen had written, *only if baby has arrived.*

Armand sat back and took a deep breath.

Going more slowly through the agenda, they found notes on meetings with an AP, presumably Alexander Plessner, in the past year. And lunches with friends, including Daniel.

But nothing about what he was up to, if anything. And certainly no suggestion of concern on his part.

But then, Stephen was a careful man. He wouldn't write anything like that in his agenda.

"Do you think the attacks have something to do with the board meeting?" Beauvoir asked.

"The timing is suggestive. We need to get our hands on that annual report, preferably Stephen's copy. He might've made notes in the margin."

"Dussault has the box. We can ask him." When there was no answer, Beauvoir looked at his father-in-law. "Do you really suspect the Prefect just because of his cologne?"

Gamache opened his mouth, then shut it. Not sure what to say.

"It's slightly more than that," said Gamache. "He said he hadn't been to the George V in years, but the manager said she'd seen him yesterday."

"Yesterday?" Beauvoir's brows shot up. "She could be wrong."

Gamache made a noncommittal guttural sound.

Still, it seemed absurd. Was he going to suspect a friend, a colleague, of murder based on such flimsy evidence? A whiff? And a possible sighting in a crowded hotel?

Was loyalty so fragile?

What he did know about Claude Dussault, and had seen time and again over the years, was that he had both courage and integrity.

But people changed. Sometimes for the better. Often for the worse.

And there was something else.

"The intruder Reine-Marie and I surprised this morning. If he was responsible for the murder, and the attack on Stephen, then he should have killed us. I told Reine-Marie that he wouldn't. It would cause too much of a mess, but that was a lie. The truth is, once he'd made one body, he wouldn't hesitate to make two more. And he certainly should have killed me when I was chasing him. It would've been easy enough."

"Yes," said Beauvoir.

His father-in-law had hit on the one great argument against trusting Claude Dussault.

A stranger would not have hesitated to murder the Gamaches. But a friend . . . ?

"And when I was chasing him down the stairs, I heard a phone ring. It was muffled, but I'm pretty sure it came from the intruder."

"Yes?" said Beauvoir, not sure how this linked up with the Prefect.

"Reine-Marie would've been calling Claude at about that time."

There it was.

"Maybe we don't tell the Prefect everything," said Jean-Guy. "But we do need to get our hands on that annual report."

"How did Stephen seem to you last night?"

"He was in good spirits. As good as it ever got with Stephen."

"But not especially giddy," said Gamache. "Not like a man about to expose some big swindle?"

"Not giddy, no. You're thinking he found something out about GHS? That's why he wanted to go to the board meeting?"

If Stephen was about to topple a tower of malfeasance he'd probably be quite bubbly. It was just about his favorite thing to do.

As it was, he was clearly pleased to see everyone and to be there, but there was no sense of triumph. Nor did he seem guarded or nervous.

"But he did check his phone a few times," said Beauvoir. "That was strange."

"Yes, you mentioned that before. I wonder if he was looking for a message from Monsieur Plessner. There was no phone found on the body or in the apartment?"

"*Non*, but they might find one eventually."

"I doubt it," said Armand, and so did Jean-Guy. The killer would have taken it.

And there was something else.

"Stephen helped me get the job at GHS," said Jean-Guy. "Could there have been a reason? But if he had suspicions about the company, he'd have told me, right? Or at least hinted?"

Gamache shook his head. His godfather was a complicated man. He kept his own counsel, and always had. His early experiences in the war had taught him that the fewer people who knew what was going on, the safer everyone was.

It was a quality he and his godson shared. A quality others did not always appreciate.

It seemed obvious that someone knew what Stephen Horowitz was about to do. And needed to stop him.

It was their turn now to connect the dots. But first they had to collect the dots.

"If he put you in GHS because he had suspicions, he might've wanted you to figure it out on your own," said Gamache. "And not prejudice your thoughts."

"Yeah, well, he obviously overestimated my 'thoughts.' I have none. At least, no suspicions. Though—"

"*Oui?*"

"Well, it's just that my number two—"

"Madame Arbour."

"*Oui*. She was pushing some file on me yesterday afternoon. A project we have in Luxembourg."

"Luxembourg?"

"Yes. Small by comparison to others. When I changed the subject to Patagonia, she seemed miffed. I put it down to a very tiring power struggle we still seem to be having. I thought she might be testing, to see if I was up on even the smaller projects. What is it?"

"I'm remembering my conversation with Stephen in the Rodin. A mistake he made."

"He made a mistake?" Jean-Guy had never heard of the financier making, or certainly admitting to, an error.

"More like a memory lapse. He said that he'd convinced me to propose to Reine-Marie in the jardin du Luxembourg. But that was wrong. He'd actually suggested a small garden in the Marais, just off rue des Rosiers."

"And that's where you did propose?"

"Yes. I put the mistake down to his age and lingering jet lag. But clearly he wasn't suffering from jet lag since he'd arrived days earlier."

"So, what was it? If it wasn't a mistake, you think he might've said it on purpose?"

"I'm not sure I'd go that far. He might've had Luxembourg on his mind. What's the project there?"

"A funicular."

"An outdoor elevator?"

"Yes, up the side of a cliff. But this's a newer, safer design. We're incorporating it into elevators all over the world, not just funiculars. Jesus, could Stephen be worried about the design? Could something be wrong?"

"Stephen isn't an engineer. He can read a financial statement in moments, but I doubt he could make heads or tails of an engineering report."

They were now wandering in the dark, and in danger of believing they weren't totally lost. It was at about this point, as Gamache warned his people, that many investigations went over a cliff.

"You say that when you changed the subject, Madame Arbour got upset?"

"A bit, yes," said Beauvoir.

"Did you tell Stephen this?"

Beauvoir thought. "No. You think there's something in it?"

"I think it would be helpful to get a copy of the engineering report on that funicular."

"But Stephen didn't have the report with him. If he was going to expose something, don't you think he'd take it to the GHS meeting?"

"Maybe he hid it. Maybe that's what the intruder was trying to find. Not just the report, but the proof something was wrong."

"True. I'll see what I can do. Might slip into work later today. But it would mean missing the autopsy."

"A shame."

"*Oui.*"

"But even if I find it, I'm not sure the engineering report will be helpful," said Jean-Guy. "I still can't understand them."

"Then we'll find someone who can."

Beauvoir sat up straighter. His brows drawing together in concentration.

"I told Stephen last night that I was struggling to understand the engineering. He said he did, too."

"Which means he tried," said Gamache. "Maybe even the funicular report."

"Yes. He also said that he found it helpful to read the emails between the engineers and home base."

"Home base being Paris. Your head office. Can you get those?" Gamache was leaning forward now.

"I can try." Jean-Guy's eyes were narrowed, his quick mind going through the options. And the conclusions. "But if there is something wrong with the design of the funicular, and Séverine Arbour saw it, wouldn't she tell me? Why bring the Luxembourg report to my attention but then not say anything?"

"Maybe she was going to, but you changed the subject. Maybe that's why she was annoyed."

"God, that might be true," said Beauvoir. "But still, if it was a serious flaw, you'd think she'd set aside her feelings and insist on telling me."

Gamache sat back and took his glasses off as he, too, tried to see the answer. "Madame Arbour's an engineer, right?"

"Yes. Carole Gossette, the head of operations, says she's a very good one."

"Interesting, then, that she should be put in a department meant to police the others."

"That's what I thought," said Beauvoir.

"So, she's either there to help find problems," said Gamache. "Or to cover them up."

"Jesus. She brought me the Luxembourg report not to tell me about the flaw," said Beauvoir, his eyes widening. "She wanted to test me, to make sure I hadn't seen it."

"I think it's possible. With the board meeting so close, and your connection to Stephen known, they might've wanted to see how much you knew."

"To add my name to the hit list?" Jean-Guy asked. "Fuck me. How many people were they willing to kill?"

"How many people have already died?" asked Gamache. "A flaw in an engineering design, in an elevator for example, could kill hundreds before it's stopped."

"How sick do you need to be to cover up something that could kill hundreds, maybe thousands?"

Gamache looked at him.

It happened more often than he cared to admit. But couldn't deny.

Airlines. Car manufacturers. Pharmaceuticals. Chemical companies. The entire tobacco industry.

Companies knew. Governments knew. Even so-called watchdogs knew. And remained silent. And got rich.

While hundreds, thousands, millions died. Were killed.

The Great Murders.

It had been, and still was, Gamache's job to find those responsible, and stop them. Jean-Guy, as Gamache's second-in-command, had followed him into that cesspool.

And while Jean-Guy Beauvoir had left, he hadn't actually escaped. The sludge had followed him. Found him. In Paris. He was in it again, this time up to his neck, it seemed.

Beauvoir considered. Was Séverine Arbour that ambitious? That sick?

The former homicide investigator knew that the desire for power and money could infect. Could fester. Could hollow out a person.

How many bright young executives, fresh off an MBA, or a P.Eng., dreamed of mass murder? None. No, that sort of sickness took time and a certain environment.

Was GHS just such an environment?

Is that why Stephen had placed him there? He knew Jean-Guy Beauvoir could not read an engineering schematic, but he could read people.

Was GHS corrupt?

He'd have to admit, he didn't think so. But he also knew his energies had been put into getting up to speed with the job. And in thinking about the imminent arrival of their daughter.

And, yes, maybe he'd been dazzled by the private jets, the luxury hotels, the exotic locations. Blinded to what was really going on.

"You say the new design is going into elevators around the world," Gamache broke into his thoughts. "Office buildings, apartments?"

"Everything, yes."

"When?"

"Next week." Beauvoir blanched. "Oh, God, it is possible, isn't it? It could be GHS's finances, but it could also be the design. Oh, *merde*."

They looked at each other.

Elevators. They were where both men's fears intersected.

Heights for Gamache. Tight spaces for Beauvoir.

The thought of being stuck in a malfunctioning elevator, many stories up, made them both light-headed. The thought of it, of hundreds, thousands, plummeting, made them sick.

Gamache took a long, slow, deep breath. "We need those plans."

"I'll get them. You think maybe what Stephen found wasn't a financial swindle, but some engineering flaw?"

"Maybe. But if he did, I doubt he'd bring it up at the board."

"Why not?"

"If he somehow came across a serious flaw in a design, he'd go straight to the head of the company. He'd want to tell someone who could stop the projects and have the flaw fixed. Who's the head of GHS?"

"Eugénie Roquebrune. Should I try to get a meeting?"

"*Non*, not yet. We need more information. If she's behind the cover-up, she'll deny it, and without hard evidence we're just exposing ourselves."

"Maybe that's exactly what Stephen did," said Jean-Guy. "And maybe that's what triggered the attacks."

"Do you know if GHS is owned by anyone else? Whether it's a subsidiary of another corporation?"

"Not that I know of. GHS is massive. That would make the parent company the equivalent of"—he hesitated—"something really big."

"You were going to say the Death Star, weren't you."

"Well, yes. If you can quote poetry, I can reference *Star Wars*. But it's not a bad analogy."

No, thought Gamache. It wasn't.

He stared out of the Joséphine, onto the crowded sidewalk, and warned himself that they were manufacturing motives. Almost certainly with serious flaws.

"We've been through Stephen's agenda," said Jean-Guy, flipping the pages. "There's no meeting with Roquebrune noted. Nothing at all about GHS until the board meeting."

"True. But the one undeniable fact is that someone tried to kill Stephen, and someone succeeded in killing Alexander Plessner. Three days before the board meeting. The timing must be more than a coincidence."

Whoever had killed Plessner had ripped Stephen's apartment apart, searching for something. Whoever ordered the hits had the advantage of knowing what that was.

They did not. But Gamache knew he had perhaps an even greater advantage. He knew Stephen.

It was now a race.

"We need to figure out what Stephen's been doing for ten days," he said.

One person who might be able to help was Agnes McGillicuddy. Armand checked his phone, but there was still no message from her.

The other thing Armand really wanted to know, with increasing importance, was what Stephen had done for those four missing hours, between leaving the Lutetia and meeting them for dinner.

A rogue thought appeared. Was it possible he went up to his apartment? Was it possible Stephen killed Plessner? Is that what the AFP notation was about?

But no.

But . . .

Who knew what Stephen Horowitz was really capable of? What he'd done in his youth, with the Resistance. When there was so much at stake.

What he'd do in his extreme old age? When there was very little left to lose.

But what could possibly drive Stephen to murder?

He looked over at Beauvoir, to see if he was thinking along the same lines. Connecting phantom dots to form a monster.

Jean-Guy was watching him closely, but didn't say anything.

Gamache shifted under the gaze. Then, putting his reading glasses back on, he flipped to the back of the agenda, where people often made random notes. They'd already looked, and there was nothing there.

He tipped the page up to the sunlight, to see if there was the imprint of something written there and torn out.

Nothing.

But . . .

Something had slipped out from under the back flap of the booklet. The corner of a tiny scrap of paper. Shoved there. Hidden there?

He pulled it out.

"What's that?" asked Jean-Guy as he leaned closer.

There were numbers and letters on the paper. Not *JSPS* this time.

In his cramped, clear hand, Stephen Horowitz had written *AFP.*

"Alexander Francis Plessner," said Jean-Guy. "And the numbers must be the dates they met."

Just then Jean-Guy's phone rang. It was Lacoste, from the Sûreté in Montréal.

He answered it, listened, thanked her, and after hanging up he turned to Gamache.

"Alexander Francis Plessner is, was, an engineer."

"Is this it?"

The sales clerk had pulled out a Tom Ford bottle and spritzed it on Reine-Marie.

No.

Then Versace's Eros.

Definitely not.

Then Yves Saint Laurent—

"No, those are all pretty common," she said. "It's something I've never smelled before."

"Are you sure it was a cologne?" he asked. "Not something you stepped in? Some do smell like that."

"Quite sure."

They went through more. The young man spraying, or dabbing, various scents onto, or around, her.

Reine-Marie felt more and more queasy, but kept going. Finally, they came to the end. Without success. Unless the goal had been to make both of them nauseous. In which case it had been a triumph.

"*Désolé*," she said. "But there is one more thing you can help me with."

Fifteen minutes later, at the door to Le Bon Marché, she pressed a fifty-euro note into his hand.

He did not decline it. He had, he felt, earned every stinking centime.

Reine-Marie returned to bar Joséphine.

Armand and Jean-Guy's plates had been taken away, but as soon as she sat down, Jacques put her lobster mayonnaise in front of her.

Normally without expression, and certainly without judgment, the maître d's face now contorted into a scowl.

"Madame," he said, and backed away.

"I'm sorry, Jacques. I'm no longer hungry. Can you package this up for me to take away?"

"Of course," he said.

Taking a deep breath through his mouth, he leaned forward and whisked the plate off the table.

"Good God, Reine-Marie, what've you been doing?" Armand asked, his eyes almost watering.

She explained.

"It was a good try," he said as he shoved a few inches away from her and gestured to Jacques to bring their bill. Quickly.

From a distance, Jacques waved the suggestion, or something, away. Their food and drink were on the house.

As Reine-Marie and Beauvoir stepped into the fresh air and sunshine on boulevard Raspail, they noticed that Armand was still inside.

He'd paused at the entrance and was, once again, staring down at the mosaic in the floor.

Jostled and shoved by impatient guests, Armand stood his ground and contemplated the ancient symbol of Paris before it was Paris.

Jacques had quoted the Latin motto. *Fluctuat nec mergitur.*

Beaten by the waves, but never sinks.

For the first time, despite seeing it for decades, Armand realized the mosaic looked like a scene from *The Tempest*. Shakespeare's play opened with a terrible storm, and a ship in peril.

As a young man leaped from a sinking ship to almost certain death, he screamed, "Hell is empty, and all the devils are here."

Armand raised his head and looked around.

Here, here? In the Hôtel Lutetia?

CHAPTER 14

———

Beauvoir sat on the Paris métro as it rumbled out of the center of the city to the area known as La Défense, where he worked.

The district sounded more romantic than it actually was.

When Jean-Guy heard that's where he'd be working, he'd been excited. The very name, La Défense, conjured childhood images of chivalry. Of bold and brave deeds. Of towers erected to defend the City of Light.

There were indeed towers in La Défense. Incredible numbers of them. But they wouldn't repel a rock, never mind an army. They were made of glass.

There was barely a tree, barely any grass to be seen. Just concrete. And glass. With helicopters droning overhead, ferrying presidents and CEOs to important meetings.

Beauvoir wondered if their feet ever actually touched the ground.

It was a place of industry, of finance, of unimaginable wealth.

Of inconceivable power.

And that, he suspected as the train approached his stop, was what they were defending.

As he got off, he looked around.

This man, born and raised in inner-city Montréal, was beginning to yearn for a tree. Or two. Or maybe even three.

* * *

Reine-Marie parted with Armand at the Quai des Orfèvres, but not before giving him the paper bag with her purchase from Le Bon Marché.

While she went home to take a long, long, hot, hot shower, he approached the old building overlooking the Seine.

The 36, as it was known, had once been the bustling headquarters of the Paris police. How many cops, how many criminals, had walked through that archway?

Most of the operations had been moved to more modern facilities, leaving just the BRI. The Brigade de recherche et d'intervention. The serious crimes squad.

It was also where the Prefect chose to have his main office.

As Gamache approached the door, his phone vibrated.

Before he even had a chance to bring it to his ear, he heard a gravelly voice say, "Is it Mr. Horowitz? Has something happened?"

It was Agnes McGillicuddy.

"He's alive, but he was hit by a van last night."

"Is he all right?"

He could hear the fear, and delusion, in that question.

How could a ninety-year-old man be all right after that?

"He's in a coma," Armand went on. His voice gentle. Though he knew nothing could soften the blow he was about to deliver to an eighty-year-old woman who also loved Stephen. "He might not recover."

As he spoke, Armand walked away from the 36, down the stone ramp to the walkway along the Seine.

"How could you let this happen?" Mrs. McGillicuddy demanded.

Armand opened and closed his mouth. Surprised by the accusation and trying to work out an answer. Should he have, could he have, prevented it?

"I'm sorry," was all he could think of to say. "I didn't see it coming. Mrs. McGillicuddy, do you know why Stephen was in Paris?"

"To see you, of course. And because of the baby. He wants to be there to support you all."

"He isn't here just for that. Stephen's also in Paris for a board meeting."

"No, he isn't."

"We found the annual report on his desk. For the engineering company GHS. It's in his agenda."

"Not in the one I have."

"His personal agenda."

"Mr. Horowitz isn't on any boards anymore. He gave them all up."

"Why?"

"Most corporations have bylaws saying board members must step down at a certain age. Mr. Horowitz passed all those ages. And then some."

Bikers pedaled by. Kids on scooters passed. Pedestrians walking dogs glanced at the man staring into the river.

"Why would he have the annual report then?"

"He liked reading annual reports, like others like reading celebrity magazines."

"Was he ever on the board of GHS Engineering?"

"No."

"Does he own shares in the company?"

"I'd have to check." He heard clicking as she looked it up on her laptop. "No. It's privately owned. Not publicly traded on the stock exchange."

"Did he ever talk about Luxembourg?"

"Luxembourg? The country? Or is it a city-state? Why would he talk about that?"

Armand sighed. "I don't know."

There was a pause before she spoke again, softly, almost gently. "You think this was no accident, don't you, Armand?"

He hesitated. Considering.

Stephen Horowitz had trusted Agnes McGillicuddy with his business and personal life for decades. If anyone knew his secrets, it would be her.

If Stephen trusted her, so could he.

"I'm certain of it. Stephen knew something. We need to find out what it was. He never gave you anything, any documents, for safe-keeping?"

"No."

No, thought Armand. Even as he asked the question, he had known that Stephen would never drag her into this. Just as he hadn't mentioned it to him, or Jean-Guy, or anyone else.

Except Monsieur Plessner, and he was dead. Confirming Stephen's worst fears, and his need for extreme caution.

"And you have no reason to suspect he'd found something out, something extremely damaging, about a corporation?"

"No, and he'd normally crow to me if he had. He loved having a secret, and loved nothing better than knowing the shit was about to hit the fan." She hesitated before going on. "If he didn't tell me, that means it must be really bad. And they tried to kill him to stop him?"

"I think so. You have his business agenda?"

"I do. What do you want to know?"

"What he was doing between September eleventh and the twenty-first."

"I don't see anything here. But he must've been spending time with you."

"Reine-Marie and I only arrived in Paris yesterday."

There was a pause and then she said, "Oh."

"So you have no idea what he was doing in those ten days?"

"No." Now she was clearly confused. Something new for Mrs. McGillicuddy. "I didn't book anything for him. No dinner reservations. No theater or opera tickets. And I don't have the meeting next week. He might've made that plan since arriving in Paris."

"Did you make a reservation for him at the George V?"

"No. I just told you. No dinner reservations."

"Not at the restaurant. For a suite."

"A suite? At the George V? Have you lost your mind?"

Well, that answered that, thought Gamache. He began to pace back and forth along the riverfront as they talked.

The great medieval buildings of île de la Cité rose behind him, while across the Seine he saw the Rive Gauche. The historic home of artists and writers.

Over the centuries, people looking out of those windows had seen far more shocking things than a man walking back and forth along the riverfront.

They'd have witnessed the Terror, for instance.

This was more like watching the Agitation.

Though if they could see his thoughts, his feelings, they'd have drawn the curtains and locked their doors.

"Do you know a man named Alexander Francis Plessner?"

"Alex Plessner? Yes."

Armand stopped pacing. Finally, a sentence that didn't start with "no."

"Mr. Horowitz has lunch with him at the club whenever Mr. Plessner's in Montréal. He lives in Toronto, I think."

"They were friends?"

"Were? Mr. Horowitz's still alive." The reprimand was immediate and whip sharp. "Don't bury him yet."

The past tense was because of the death of Plessner, but Armand wasn't ready to give up that piece of information.

Instead, he apologized and asked, "They know each other well?"

"They're more like acquaintances than friends. Not especially close."

"Can you find out if Alex Plessner ever sat on the GHS board?"

"I think so."

"Is there anything else you can tell me about Mr. Plessner? Anything Stephen might've said?"

There was a pause as she thought. "I believe Mr. Plessner has a great deal of money. Mr. Horowitz said he made most of it all at once, through some speculation. I think it might've been venture capital."

"Like seed money for Apple or Microsoft?"

"Something like that. Mr. Horowitz always kids Mr. Plessner about falling into a bucket of luck."

That bucket, it seemed, had run dry yesterday, thought Gamache.

"Mrs. McGillicuddy, there's something else I need to tell you. Alex Plessner was found murdered this morning, in Stephen's apartment."

There was a soft moan at the other end. The sound of a person who'd seen a lot in her long life. And had now seen too much.

Armand gave her time to absorb that news.

"What's happening?" she whispered down the line from Montréal.

"I'm trying to find out. The apartment was ransacked. They were looking for something."

"What?"

"I don't know. We think it might be evidence of some sort that Stephen and Plessner found. Alex Plessner had Stephen's business card on him—"

"Well, that's no sur—" She'd interrupted him. And now Mrs. McGillicuddy interrupted herself. "Are you saying . . . That's not possible."

"What isn't?"

"You were going to tell me that Mr. Horowitz gave him a JSPS card."

"Yes."

"I don't believe it. You know what that card does? Anyone with it can get into Mr. Horowitz's bank accounts, his safety-deposit boxes. His homes. As far as I know, Mr. Horowitz only gave that card to three people. You, me, and your grandmother."

"Zora?"

"Yes."

"Zora?" Armand repeated. "Are you sure?"

"I was there when he gave it to her. He made sure I saw."

"At my parents' funeral?"

"No. When you were going away to Cambridge. He thought she might need a friend one day. He was offering to be that friend."

"She hated him."

"Yes. But that didn't mean he hated her."

Armand thought for a moment. Could the card they found on Alex Plessner have been Zora's? But no. She'd been dead for more than twenty years. And Mr. Plessner's card was newer. Thick, sturdy. Zora's would have been the much older, flimsier version.

He wondered what had become of Zora's. It hadn't been among her belongings when she died. Perhaps his grandmother hadn't understood the magnitude, and significance, of what Stephen was offering, and had thrown it away.

"Would you necessarily know if Mr. Plessner used his card?"

Mrs. McGillicuddy thought. "If he used it to get into one of Mr. Horowitz's accounts, or homes, or business, yes. But you know that card can be used for so much more. In the international business world, it's pretty much a *laissez-passer*."

That was a good way of putting it, Armand thought. The Just Some Poor Schmuck card, as silly as it might sound, was anything but. It was akin to a travel document issued by rulers and despots of old, guaranteeing safe passage.

Within the international business community, Stephen Horowitz's JSPS card had become legendary. Mythical.

"You don't know, then, if Mr. Plessner ever actually used it?"

"No."

"You still have yours?"

"Of course."

"I have a colleague, Isabelle Lacoste. She's the acting head of homicide for the Sûreté. She's going to need to get into Stephen's home and work. Into his safety-deposit boxes at the bank, to make sure they haven't been searched in the last day or so, and to search them herself."

"Tell her to call me. I'll make sure she gets in."

"If she needs the JSPS card, can you give her yours?"

"No."

"No?"

"Mr. Horowitz trusted me with it. I'll help her with whatever she wants, but I need to be there when she uses it."

"Agreed. There is something else I need you to do," said Armand.

"Please. Anything."

"I found a scrap of paper in Stephen's agenda," said Armand. "With dates that seem to be in reference to Monsieur Plessner. I'm wondering if they're meetings the two of them had, either in person or on the phone. If I email them to you, can you cross-check with Stephen's old agendas? See what he was doing on those days? Some go back a number of years."

"I can do that."

Armand paused before speaking again. "Can you think of anyone who might want Stephen dead?"

"I can think of any number of people."

Armand gave a small laugh. "True. *Merci*, Mrs. McGillicuddy."

"You'll let me know—"

"I will."

"I didn't mean to blame you, Armand. It's just that . . ."

"*Oui*. It is . . . that."

CHAPTER 15

R eine-Marie looked at her watch as she left their apartment. It was two o'clock. She had one hour to do what she needed, and then get to Daniel and Roslyn's in time for the meeting with Commander Fontaine.

She walked rapidly down rue des Archives, stopping to drop her clothes at the dry cleaner before continuing on.

How the neighborhood had changed since Zora bought the apartment in the 1970s.

As much as Reine-Marie loved history, she had no desire to live in it. A city, a *quartier*, a street, a person needed to evolve. Though the fact she was walking in Zora's footsteps always comforted her. She was retracing a route the elderly woman had taken almost every day of her life in Paris. Both before and after the war, Zora would have come along this same sidewalk, with her familiar string bag, to get to the kosher deli, the butcher, the boulangerie, the seamstress, and, finally, the Bazar de l'Hôtel de Ville, or BHV. The huge department store on rue de Rivoli had been there, in one form or another, since the mid-1850s.

Reine-Marie walked up the steps and into the store.

When she came out again, she had in her purse a small blue-and-gold box. Containing a cologne.

* * *

Jean-Guy sat at his desk and was about to log in to his computer when he paused. Considering the options and the consequences. But not for long. It was already just after two, and he needed to meet Annie and the others in less than an hour.

Making up his mind, Beauvoir walked next door into Séverine Arbour's office. He looked around. As far as he knew, there were no cameras here. Though he couldn't be sure.

It was a risk he had to take.

Sitting down, he first rifled her desk, or tried to. The drawers were locked, and all he succeeded in doing was rattling them.

Then he turned to her computer. It, too, was locked, but as head of the department he knew her code.

Her computer sprang to life. There was a document already up. The Patagonia project. He'd managed to rattle her after all.

Minimizing it, he began typing, and up came the file on Luxembourg.

Beauvoir knew that their cybersecurity unit could find out who had accessed which files, and on which terminal.

If anyone wanted to know who was snooping around the Luxembourg dossier, on a Saturday, all they'd see was Séverine Arbour. Not him.

He couldn't get into her emails, he'd need her password for that, but he could get into the main files and bring up internal reports.

Which is what he did.

He was just about to send it to himself when he stopped. That would be a fatal error. Instead, he hit print.

Out in the main office, over by the wall, a large industrial printer sprang to life.

Now he needed to find the emails between the engineer on-site and the executive overseeing the project. Scanning the file, he found the name of the engineer.

And the name of the executive.

Carole Gossette.

He sat back, staring at the name. Madame Gossette. Head of operations. His boss. His mentor.

Now why would such a senior executive be overseeing such an

apparently minor project? Because, he thought, it wasn't such a minor project after all.

There was a soft ding.

"*Merde,*" he whispered, his heart leaping in his chest. He recognized that sound.

The elevator door at the end of the hallway opened. Without glancing up, Beauvoir tried to stop the printer, but it wouldn't be put on pause. Hitting the button several times, Beauvoir eventually gave up and put the screen to sleep.

Across the large open room, the Luxembourg file was still printing out. And the guard was getting closer.

There was no way to get to the printer before the guard arrived. Instead, Jean-Guy quickly left Arbour's office and ducked into his own, leaving the door open.

In the background, he could hear the large machine making what now sounded like a racket.

And then it stopped, and there was silence just as the guard entered the offices.

"Monsieur Beauvoir," he said. "I'd heard you were in."

The man was in his late twenties. Tall and sturdy. Fit.

He stopped just outside Beauvoir's office. Then he turned toward the printer before returning his gaze to Beauvoir.

"Working?"

In his early days at the company, Jean-Guy had come in on weekends, when it was quiet and he could bumble around without anyone seeing. Never had a guard shown any interest.

So why was this guard here. Now. Very interested.

The look, while disconcerting, wasn't threatening. He seemed to be puzzled, trying to work something out.

"*Oui.* Can I help you?" Beauvoir asked, looking up from his laptop, as though interrupted.

"No, sir. I'm just checking."

"Checking what?"

"To make sure everything's as it should be."

"Well, it's not. I should be outside, playing with my son. Instead I'm here." He smiled and got up.

"Why are you here, sir?"

Beauvoir had never had a guard ask him that. It wasn't any of his business. And yet the guard seemed to think it was. And maybe, thought Beauvoir with some unease, it was.

"I have a baby coming any day now. Little girl." He picked up his mug, and the guard stepped aside to let him pass. "When she's born, I'll be on leave. I just need to get some of the crap out of the way before the blessed event."

He'd remembered that the coffee maker was on the wall farthest from the copier. He walked over there now.

"Coffee?"

"No, sir."

The guard did as Beauvoir had hoped. He followed him to the espresso machine.

"You have children?" Beauvoir peered at the guard's nametag. "Monsieur Loiselle?"

"No."

Not a big talker. Now Loiselle began to turn around.

"I was a cop once, you know," said Beauvoir, desperate to stop the man from turning completely. And possibly seeing the papers the printer had coughed up. "In Québec, as you can probably hear." Jean-Guy had intentionally broadened his accent, giving his words a twang. He'd been in Paris long enough to know that they viewed the Québécois as slightly thick country cousins.

While this was insulting and ignorant, he now found it useful.

"Got tired of being shot at," Jean-Guy continued. "And with a family coming . . ." He left it at that.

The guard's stare was now intense. Scrutinizing him. Practically, Jean-Guy felt, dissecting him.

Beauvoir could see past Loiselle, into Arbour's office. Something was happening. The computer had come back to life, and images were flashing across the screen.

Even from a distance, he could see what it was. Emails. Schematics. Being erased.

Fuck. Fuckity fuck, thought Beauvoir. *Shit.*

But his face remained placid, and his eyes returned to the guard.

"You don't happen to know how this works?" he said, pointing to the espresso machine. "Trust them to have something you need an engineering degree to work. All I've managed to figure out in five months is how to grind the beans."

"Sorry. Can't help," Loiselle said.

With one final look around, he turned away.

Jean-Guy pretended to play with the machine while watching the guard walk back to the elevator.

Come on, come on. Hurry up.

When the elevator doors opened and finally closed, Beauvoir sprinted across the room, bringing out his phone as he ran. He knew he couldn't stop the files from being erased, so he did the next best thing.

He recorded the messages as they flashed up and disappeared.

CHAPTER 16

———

"M*erci,*" said Gamache when Claude Dussault's assistant put the espresso in front of him.

"*Je vous en prie,*" said the young man, and withdrew from the office.

Armand had been in the famed 36 many times, and in this very office quite often. With its grimy old windows, long since painted shut. No doubt with lead-based paints. The coal-burning fireplace thankfully no longer worked. And there was probably asbestos in the ceiling.

It smelled musky, as though there might be dead things mummified in the walls.

The building was damp and chilly in winter, and stifling in summer. And yet it contained so much history, it thrilled Gamache every time he entered.

He could understand the need to modernize, and that meant moving to a new location, but he'd been glad to hear the Prefect had maintained an office here.

Claude's desk had framed pictures of his wife and children. And dog. The walls were covered with photos of colleagues, though not one, he noticed, of Dussault's predecessor, Clément Prévost.

Dussault accepted his espresso with thanks, then dismissed his assistant with a nod. Leaning forward, he asked, "How're you doing, Armand?"

"I'm holding it together."

"Are you?"

Dussault could see the strain around his friend's eyes and the slight pallor that came from little sleep and a lot of worry.

Does he know Horowitz is going to die?

Does he know why?

What exactly does Gamache know?

Armand took a long sip of his espresso. It was rich and strong and exactly what he needed.

He regarded the man in front of him and wondered, *What exactly does Claude Dussault know?*

"I just spoke to Stephen's assistant," he said, leaning back and crossing his legs. "Agnes McGillicuddy. I'll give you her coordinates. She's probably someone you'd like to connect with. But it was . . ." Armand paused to gather his thoughts. "Difficult. Emotional. She's in her eighties and has been with Stephen almost since the beginning."

"Did you tell her everything?"

"I told her I thought it was deliberate, yes. And about Monsieur Plessner."

"We haven't released the news about Monsieur Plessner, but Stephen Horowitz is making headlines."

"You put it out as an accident. A hit-and-run. Best thing to do," said Armand.

"Still, the press will be onto her. She'll need to be careful about what she says."

"She'll say nothing."

Dussault looked skeptical.

"I can guarantee it," said Gamache. "Stephen chose her for that reason, and kept her for that reason."

"Even under torture, Mrs. McGillicuddy wouldn't reveal anything," Stephen used to say. And Armand knew he wasn't joking.

Stephen Horowitz knew who would crack, and who would not. It was how he measured people. Most, of course, came up short. But not Agnes McGillicuddy.

Fortunately, the press in Canada, though capable of tormenting, hadn't yet stooped to actual torture.

Gamache, while often in their crosshairs, had a great deal of respect for journalists.

He now filled the Prefect in on everything Mrs. McGillicuddy had said.

"So she claims not to know why Monsieur Horowitz was in Paris," said Dussault.

"If she says it, it's true."

"She did admit Monsieur Horowitz knew Alexander Plessner," said Dussault. "That's something."

Gamache uncrossed his legs and placed the demitasse on the table. "Monsieur Plessner was an engineer."

"*C'est vrai?*" said Dussault.

He sounded as though this was news, and yet he didn't look surprised. Not by the information, at least. Perhaps slightly by the fact Gamache knew.

"*Oui.* My second-in-command, Isabelle Lacoste, passed along the information a few minutes ago. Trained as a mechanical engineer. Worked in the field for several years before making a fortune in venture capital."

Dussault was taking notes. "*Merci.*"

It seemed incredible, and unlikely, to Gamache that Dussault's own people hadn't found this out themselves.

"I'd like to go through the box of Stephen's things again," he said. "I didn't get a good look the first time."

"I don't have it. Handed it over to Commander Fontaine. I'll ask her to give you what you want. But that reminds me. Monsieur Horowitz's laptop is in there. We need the password and any codes he might've used. Do you know them?"

"No, but I can ask Mrs. McGillicuddy."

"That's okay, I'll ask."

"I doubt she'd give them to you."

Dussault's eyes widened. "She'll have to. She wants to help the investigation, doesn't she?"

"Of course, but she doesn't know you. She knows me. Let me ask."

Dussault hesitated, then nodded. "Of course. And I have some news for you. We found the van."

Armand leaned forward.

"It was wiped clean. Our forensics team's going over it for DNA. But . . ." Dussault put up his hands to express faint hope.

"Clean clean?" Gamache asked.

Dussault nodded. Both men knew it was extraordinarily difficult to take away all physical evidence. It meant using special cleansers designed to destroy DNA. Not everyone knew about them. Fewer had access.

And the person had to be meticulous to get every molecule. A pro.

Either that, or the forensics had to be incredibly sloppy. Could that be it? And not just incredibly but intentionally sloppy?

"The coroner called me about an hour ago. She's preparing Monsieur Plessner's body for the autopsy—"

"By the way, I won't be able to make it. I need to get back for the interview with Commander Fontaine."

"Right. That's at three?"

"*Oui.*"

They looked at the clock on the old mantel. It was quarter past two.

"You were telling me about the coroner," said Gamache.

"Two bullets were used. That much was obvious."

"Back and head, yes," said Gamache.

"Not just back, it severed his spine."

Gamache held his colleague's gray eyes. Both knew what that could mean. "Commando? The GIGN?"

Dussault nodded. "Possible."

They knew that was how commando units were trained to kill. Use as few bullets as possible and make sure each one counted. Spine to guarantee incapacitation. Head to guarantee death. Then move on. And do it again.

Even as he stared at Claude Dussault, Gamache remembered his colleague's CV. Dussault liked to say he'd washed out of the elite corps, the GIGN, but Armand knew that wasn't true.

He'd completed his training and was about to be assigned when he'd suddenly transferred to the Préfecture in Paris.

Or appeared to.

But the reality was, Claude Dussault had stayed with the GIGN, only leaving several years later to move up the ranks of the Préfecture.

Did Dussault realize that Armand knew the truth?

Was he looking at the man who'd killed Alexander Francis Plessner and been involved in the attempt on Stephen's life? He had the skills, but did he have the motive?

"It could be a former member of the GIGN," conceded Dussault. "Or the Sayeret Matkal, or the SAS. The SEALs. Even"—he smiled at Gamache—"Joint Task Force Two. There're any number of highly trained former special forces floating around this city, hiring themselves out as security and intelligence contractors."

"Mercenaries."

"Why not use their skills?"

"Depends on which skills, doesn't it?" said Gamache. "Have you had a chance to look at the security cameras around Stephen's apartment?"

"We're going through the footage. Unfortunately, most of the cameras are facing the Lutetia and Le Bon Marché."

"So the cameras don't show people entering or leaving Stephen's apartment building?"

"No."

"A shame."

"*Oui.*"

Dussault knew Gamache well enough to know the man was almost always calm and courteous. Gracious, in an almost old-world manner. It was what made him an effective leader. Armand Gamache never flew off the handle. Never lost control. Unless he wanted to.

But Dussault also knew that the angrier Gamache became, the more contained, the more polite he became. Putting iron straps around any violent emotion.

As he regarded his colleague and friend, Claude Dussault realized with surprise that Armand's *politesse* was being directed at him.

He was, at the moment, the target of Gamache's brutal courtesy.

Claude Dussault leaned back in his chair.

"You were telling me about the van," said Gamache. "Where was it found?"

"It was abandoned just outside the bois de Boulogne."

Armand brought up, in his mind, the map of Paris. And the location of the huge park, the Woods of Boulogne.

"The bois is close to the headquarters of GHS," he said.

"Yes, and Mr. Horowitz had the GHS annual report in his possession," said Dussault. "Probably just a coincidence."

"More than that. He was planning on going to the GHS board meeting on Monday morning."

Dussault stared at him. "How do you know that?"

"It's in his agenda."

"What agenda?" The stare had become a glare.

It was the moment of truth. The moment for truth.

"The one Mrs. McGillicuddy has," Armand lied. "She told me his plans."

"Was he a member of the board?" the Prefect asked.

"No."

"Then why would he go? And would they even let him in? Why're you shaking your head?"

"If GHS Engineering is somehow involved, why would the attacker abandon the van pretty much on the corporation's doorstep?"

"He might not have known who his employer was. The bois de Boulogne, as you know, has become a dumping ground for all sorts of things."

"True. Which is why you have cameras all over it. Do they show anything?"

But Armand already knew the answer. If they did, Dussault would have said something.

"We have cameras, but as soon as we put them up, they're smashed."

"So, once again, no footage?"

"No." Dussault was quiet for a moment before asking his next

144

question. "Your former number two, Beauvoir, works for GHS, isn't that right?"

"It is." Gamache's tone was relaxed. Reasonable. But his guard was up.

"In fact, Horowitz helped get him the job," said Dussault. "That was the drama this morning in the Lutetia."

"Right."

Gamache made up his mind.

His suspicions of the head of the entire Préfecture were so paper-thin as to be almost irrational.

He had to share some information.

"Does Luxembourg mean anything to you?"

"Luxembourg? The country or the garden?"

"Country." Armand was watching him closely.

Dussault considered, then shook his head. "Why?"

"Beauvoir had an odd experience at work with his own number two."

Gamache described what had happened.

"So you do suspect GHS," said Dussault. "And that's why you asked about the box. You want their annual report. Monsieur Horowitz is a financier, not an engineer. If he was studying their annual report, he must've been looking for financial wrongdoing, and obviously found something if he was planning to go to their board meeting. Corruption, fraud. Maybe money laundering. Luxembourg has traditionally been a harbor for that. Is that what you think?"

"I honestly don't know what's going on, but yes, I do think Stephen found something out about GHS, and was planning to confront them at the board meeting."

"Which is what the killer was looking for in his apartment. The evidence. If it's that important, we have to find it first. Do you have any idea what it might be?"

"I wish," said Gamache. "We don't even know if it was GHS he was after or some other company."

"I've found out a little about GHS Engineering since this morning. But it's surprisingly very difficult, even for us. It's a multinational. Mostly engineering, but with interests in oil and gas, some manufacturing.

It's a private company, with emphasis on 'private,' and has friends powerful enough to keep their interests secret. If it was GHS Horowitz was tilting at, they'd make a formidable adversary."

Stephen was famous for bringing a cannon to a fistfight. Was it really possible, Armand wondered, that he'd underestimate his opponent?

But he was in a coma and Alexander Plessner was in the morgue, so clearly he had. But Armand was also curious about Claude's turn of phrase. Describing Stephen as "tilting at" GHS. That conjured images of Don Quixote, who tilted at windmills, mistaking them for adversaries.

Was Claude suggesting, however subtly, that Stephen was also mistaken?

"Is that why Stephen got your Beauvoir a job at GHS?"

"It's possible. If that is the reason, he didn't share it with Beauvoir."

"So Beauvoir knows nothing?"

"Nothing except what I've told you."

"The Luxembourg thing."

"Yes."

"Seems pretty thin. Could a business rival be setting GHS up? Knowing we'd investigate? But would they really go this far to discredit, maybe ruin, another company?" Dussault stopped and grimaced. "Sorry. That was stupid."

Yes, it was.

Corporations that put profit before safety would not stop at killing two old men to protect themselves. That would be considered a slow day.

Dussault made a note. "I'll pass along our thoughts to Commander Fontaine."

"Poor her," said Armand.

Dussault chuckled, then glanced at the clock. "You need to be off soon."

It was now half past two.

"I do."

As he walked Gamache to the door, Claude Dussault said, "You were a member of Joint Task Force Two, Armand. *Non?*"

Armand cocked his head and looked at his friend. How did Dussault know about his relationship with the elite Canadian force? But then, how did he know about Dussault's background as a commando?

Because that's what they did. If knowledge was power, both wanted to be the most powerful in any room. Neither carried a gun. What they carried was a brain, and in that brain was information.

"*Non.* I've trained recruits," said Armand, his voice steady. "But that's all."

"In counterterrorism and hostage situations," said Dussault.

"Correct."

"And how to kill effectively."

"Mostly how not to have to kill."

"Far more interesting," conceded the Prefect. "And challenging."

With some surprise, Gamache realized that while he harbored suspicions of Claude Dussault, it was actually a fairly crowded harbor.

It seemed Dussault might have some suspicions, too.

And Gamache could see why. He'd been essentially on the scene of both attacks. While not there for the murder of Alexander Plessner, he had discovered the body. And come away unharmed from a confrontation with an intruder no one else saw.

It would have been amusing, these two men in late middle age suspecting each other of commando-style murders. If one of them wasn't, possibly, right.

At the door Dussault spoke quietly and gravely. Holding Armand's eyes.

"I'm happy for your insights into Monsieur Horowitz, but please, Armand, after your talk with Commander Fontaine, it's time for you to leave this investigation to us. Step away. You're too close."

"Close to what?"

The truth?

"Leave it."

"Would you, Claude? If you were in Montréal and a man who was pretty much your father was attacked. Would you just step back?"

"If you were in charge of the investigation? Yes."

Armand left, knowing he'd just heard at least one lie. And told at least one himself.

He called Mrs. McGillicuddy and asked her to agree that the board meeting was noted in Stephen's agenda.

"Just, perhaps, don't say which agenda."

After leaving the BHV, Reine-Marie Gamache hurried back home. Showering and changing again, she placed a call before she thought better of it.

"Dr. Dussault? Monique?"

"*Oui?*"

"It's Reine-Marie Gamache."

"Oh, I was just about to call to invite you and your husband for dinner." Monique Dussault's voice was deep and warm. "Claude told me what happened last night. I'm so sorry."

While Reine-Marie had only met her a few times, she'd immediately liked the woman. Dr. Dussault was a pediatrician who had a practice in Montparnasse, not far from the catacombs.

"Seems like some sort of karma," she'd told Reine-Marie. "I live with a secretive man, and now I live over those secret tunnels. The only difference between them is that the catacombs have hidden depths."

She'd laughed and looked across the table at her husband with undisguised affection.

"Why don't you come to us," said Reine-Marie. "Something simple. To be honest, once home I'm not sure I'll want to go out again. I know the men will want to talk, and honestly, I'd like the company."

"But you must be exhausted."

Reine-Marie was, and could barely believe she was inviting company for dinner. But it was the only way . . .

"I find cooking relaxing. Please come. It'll be just us. *En famille.*"

"Let me at least bring a dessert."

And so it was decided. No going back now, thought Reine-Marie, and wondered how Armand would feel about this.

She looked at the box on their dresser. Then, opening the bottom drawer, she hid it under a layer of sweaters. Not from Armand, but from their dinner guests.

It was twenty to three when Jean-Guy signed out.

This was a different guard than the one who'd visited him. But no less fit. No less focused. Why hadn't he noticed that before? No flab on these men and women. Their eyes were sharp, intelligent. Watchful. Suspicious.

Once out the door, he kept walking, his pace measured.

He was longing to look at what he'd printed out and recorded on his phone.

Up ahead was the entrance to the métro. He took the escalator down, used his Navigo Liberté card to get into the station, and waited for his train.

Once on, he pulled out his phone to check he'd actually recorded.

Before clicking it on, he glanced to the left and saw bored passengers reading *Le Monde* or looking at their phones.

Then the other direction.

And there he was. The guard Loiselle. The one who'd come up to the office.

The man was staring at him. Not even trying to hide his presence, or his scrutiny.

It was twenty to three when Reine-Marie once again emerged from the dry cleaners.

The first time that day she'd dropped off a reeking set of clothes, they'd smiled and been polite. Pretending not to notice the shrieking smells.

This time there was no pretense.

"Do you work in a perfume factory, Madame Gamache?" the young woman asked as she used two fingers to pick up the clothes, holding them at arm's length.

"No. I was just testing some."

"With a fire hose?"

Reine-Marie laughed, and got out of there as quickly as possible.

Stepping onto rue des Archives, she first turned toward Roslyn and Daniel's place. Then, changing her mind, she walked in the opposite direction.

It was twenty to three when Armand entered the hôpital Hôtel-Dieu.

The nurse had a brief word with him. Nothing had changed. Which, she said, was actually good news. At least Monsieur Horowitz hadn't gotten worse.

After exchanging a few words with the guard outside Stephen's room, Armand went in. He kissed Stephen on the forehead. Then, walking to the end of the bed, he opened the paper bag Reine-Marie had given him.

Uncovering Stephen's feet, he squirted moisturizer on his hands, and gently massaged Stephen's feet while telling him about the day. The family. Mrs. McGillicuddy.

"And Jacques at the Lutetia says, '*Fluctuat nec mergitur.*' I think that means 'pay your hotel bill, you schmuck.'"

Armand waited, as though expecting a reaction.

Then he covered the feet up again, put on his reading glasses, and, sitting beside the bed, read out loud stories about the bumper grape crop in Bordeaux, and the nuclear power plants coming online around the world to cut down on fossil fuels.

Then he found a wire service story from Agence France-Presse about a tortoise in Marseilles that could predict horse races. He read it out loud, just to annoy Stephen.

But he only got a few lines in before stopping. Taking off his glasses, he reached out and held his godfather's cold hand, warming it in both of his.

Then Armand closed his eyes and whispered, "Hail Mary, full of Grace. Hail Mary, full of Grace."

Over and over. He knew the rest of the prayer, but just kept repeating that first line.

"Hail Mary, full of Grace."

And then, dropping his head to Stephen's hand, he whispered, over and over, "Help me. God, help me."

Reine-Marie quietly entered the hospital room and stood in the shadows, watching.

Armand's head was resting on Stephen's hand. His voice muffled by the bedding.

But she knew what he was doing.

Hush, hush, she thought. *Whisper who dares. Armand Gamache is saying his prayers.*

CHAPTER 17

⁓

It was just after three o'clock when Irena Fontaine and her second-in-command entered Daniel and Roslyn's apartment.

They were met at the door by a man in his early thirties. Bearded, tall, substantial. That much was obvious. But Fontaine was skilled at seeing what others might miss.

His eyes, while serious, were thoughtful, warm even. Here was a man it would be easy to like, she thought. And trust.

Which meant she immediately distrusted this Daniel Gamache, despite the fact he was Chief Inspector Gamache's son.

But then, Commander Fontaine was far from sure she trusted the father.

When she entered the living room, she saw the rest of the family, on their feet and turned to her. The large room felt even bigger thanks to the three floor-to-ceiling windows that looked out over the metal roofs, the garrets, the chimney pots.

It was a timeless Paris view.

Before starting the interview, her number two took down the particulars of everyone in the room.

Reine-Marie Gamache was a senior librarian and archivist. Retired.

Annie was an *avocate*. A trial lawyer who'd trained in Québec but qualified for the French bar and was on maternity leave.

Roslyn worked in marketing for a design label, and Daniel was a banker.

He looks, thought Fontaine, *a lot like his father. If you removed the beard, the resemblance would be remarkable.* And she wondered if that was why the son had grown the beard. So that he needn't see his father in the mirror, examining him at the beginning and end of every day.

When they were asked for their addresses, Daniel shifted in his seat, and he and Roslyn exchanged glances.

"There's something we need to tell you," he said, then turned to the rest of them. "This won't be our home much longer. We're moving."

"Moving?" asked Reine-Marie. "Home?"

There was no mistaking the hope in her voice and the gleam in her eyes.

"This is home, Mama," he said. "No, we're putting in an offer on a place in the Sixth Arrondissement."

"Three bedrooms," said Roslyn. "The girls will each have their own. And it's close to their school in Saint-Germain-des-Prés."

"But they go to school around the corner here," said Annie.

"Not next semester," said Roslyn. "They've been accepted into the Lycée Stanislas."

Everyone's eyes opened wider, including the investigators'.

The little boys and girls, in their dark blue and crisp white uniforms, were as much a part of Paris lore as Madeline and her adventures. The boys and girls could be seen solemnly holding hands as they crossed the boulevards of the Sixth Arrondissement, and played in the jardin du Luxembourg.

It was, without a doubt, the very best private school in Paris. Probably France. And one of the most expensive.

"How . . . ?" Reine-Marie began, then stopped herself.

"Did we get them in?" asked Daniel, beaming.

"Yes."

Though it was clear she'd actually meant to ask another question.

How were they going to pay for it? And a new apartment?

But some things were best not asked. Not in front of a homicide investigator.

"Congratulations," said Armand. "It's a great school. The girls will love it."

But Annie was glaring at her brother. Not sharing her parents' enthusiasm, however forced it might have been.

"Terrific, my ass," said Annie, unable to hold it in. "We decided to live two streets over to be close to you, and now you leave?"

"We're not going far," said Daniel.

"Do you rent here?" asked Fontaine.

"Yes. Shouldn't be a problem subletting," said Daniel. He turned to his sister. "Maybe you could take it?"

"Maybe you could—" began Annie.

"Maybe we can talk about this later," their mother interrupted.

But if she was hoping to change the subject, it was too late.

"You're going from renting to buying?" said Commander Fontaine. "A larger apartment in a better neighborhood."

"Yes," said Daniel.

"And sending both of your daughters to the Lycée?"

If Daniel didn't hear the subtle implication, his father did. He remained quiet, though watchful.

Daniel took Roslyn's hand and smiled, his face open and without guile. "*Oui.* Sorry, Mom, I know you hoped we'd eventually move back to Montréal, but Paris is our home now."

Armand put his own hand lightly over Reine-Marie's.

It was true. They'd always hoped, expected even, that Daniel, Roslyn, and the children would one day return to Québec. But now it seemed that wouldn't happen. Paris had taken their son and their grandchildren. And now Annie and her growing family had been beguiled.

It wasn't the city's fault. It couldn't help being luminous.

But just at this moment, Reine-Marie hated the city. And Armand wasn't so enamored either.

"Well, that sucks," said Annie as Jean-Guy took her hand and squeezed.

Commander Fontaine watched. But try as she might, she couldn't see this as a family riddled with hatred and resentments. If anything, their reaction to Daniel's announcement was driven by affection.

They wanted to be closer, not farther apart.

After listening to their recollections of the events of the night before, Commander Fontaine once again turned to Daniel.

In the few minutes she'd been there, she'd come to realize that while he looked like his father, he was not actually like him.

They both, *père et fils*, seemed kind. Not at all threatening. But where in Gamache the elder it took the form of confidence and authority, in the younger it came across as charm. Which, while pleasant, could be superficial. Often was. A sort of genial wrapping paper hiding, what? Neediness? Insecurity?

"Monsieur Horowitz had been in Paris for ten days before being hit. Did you get together with him in that time?"

"No," said Daniel, surprised. "Not until last night. I thought he'd just arrived."

"Had any of you heard from him?" asked Fontaine.

They shook their heads.

Jean-Guy Beauvoir had gotten up and wandered over to a window.

"Am I boring you, Monsieur Beauvoir?" Fontaine asked.

"*Non, désolé.* I just wanted to make sure I could see the children and their sitter in the park."

He returned to his seat beside Annie, and reaching into his pocket, he began playing with the nickels that were stuck together. He'd meant to show them to Honoré but had forgotten he had them.

"Monsieur Horowitz had planned to go to a board meeting this coming week," said Fontaine. "We're wondering if there could be a connection between that and the attacks."

"Which board meeting?" asked Daniel.

"GHS Engineering." She turned to Beauvoir. "Monsieur Horowitz got you your job at GHS, I believe."

"That's true," said Beauvoir.

"He did?" said Daniel. He seemed surprised, and surprisingly pleased.

"Did you ask him to?" Fontaine asked Beauvoir.

"It was a favor for me," said Gamache. "I asked him to find a position in private industry for Jean-Guy."

"In private industry, or in GHS?" asked Fontaine.

"No, not specifically that company."

"So as far as you know, Monsieur Horowitz didn't plant you there"—she turned back to Beauvoir—"to get information for him? Insider information even."

"To spy?" asked Jean-Guy. "No. He never asked. And I'd never pass along insider information. And if I thought something was wrong, I'd have gone to my immediate superior."

"And who's that?"

"Carole Gossette."

"But you saw nothing suspicious?"

"No."

"Not even the Luxembourg project?"

"How do you know about that?" Beauvoir asked.

"Monsieur Gamache here told the Prefect about your questions."

Beauvoir shot Gamache a quick look before turning back to Fontaine. "That was odd," he admitted. "But from what I could see, there's nothing wrong there."

"Would you necessarily know?" Fontaine asked.

It was a good question. "No."

"And you have no idea why Monsieur Horowitz was planning to go to the board meeting on Monday?"

"Can I interrupt?" said Daniel. "Do we know if Stephen is on the board?"

"He is not," said Fontaine.

"Then he might've had it in his agenda, but he'd never get in. It's a private company. Only board members are allowed in board meetings. Confidential things are discussed. No outsider would be allowed anywhere near it."

"Monsieur Horowitz would know that?"

"Yes, absolutely."

"Was he an investor in the company?" Annie asked.

"No," said Armand. "I asked Mrs. McGillicuddy. Stephen didn't hold any shares in GHS. In fact, as Daniel says, they're a private company, and not listed on the stock exchanges."

"Then what's his interest?" asked Daniel.

Gamache looked at Fontaine to answer. It seemed Claude Dussault had, quite rightly, briefed her on their discussion, and their suspicions. He was very interested to see how much Commander Fontaine would say.

But even as he looked to her, she was studying him.

The man confused her.

She didn't like that.

She didn't like Gamache's ease and natural authority. She didn't like his accent. She sure didn't like that he seemed oblivious to the fact that he was not their equal, socially, culturally, intellectually, professionally. Couldn't be. Not coming from Canada. Not coming from Québec.

She didn't like his relationship, his close friendship, with the Prefect.

She didn't like that when something bad had happened in the past twenty-four hours, Armand Gamache wasn't far behind.

And she sure didn't like that she actually liked the man. That her instinct was to trust him. The Prefect had warned her about that.

"We have no idea why he wanted to go to the board meeting," admitted Fontaine. "But you know Monsieur Horowitz. Was it more likely he planned to go to congratulate them on their success? Or to expose some wrongdoing? What's more in character?"

It was clear by their expressions that they knew the answer to that.

"That's what we thought. But he can't go now. One question we ask in a homicide is, who benefits? Isn't that right?"

She'd turned to Gamache, who nodded.

"Who benefits if Monsieur Horowitz is killed?" she went on. "It seems clear that GHS Engineering does."

"But what could he have on them?" Annie asked.

"We don't know, and right now the specifics don't matter. What matters is motive. And it seems GHS had a big one. Silence a whistle-blower."

"You're guessing," said Beauvoir. "Look, you could be right, GHS might be behind it. But there're all sorts of people who might want Stephen Horowitz dead. He's made a lot of enemies."

"That's true," admitted Fontaine. "But there's only one company he was planning to visit just before the attempt on his life. You know, of course, that a dead man was found in Monsieur Horowitz's home this morning. His name is Alexander Francis Plessner."

She was speaking directly, and exclusively, to Annie and Daniel. Watching them closely.

"Does the name mean anything to you?"

The siblings looked at each other, then back to the investigator, shaking their heads.

"No," said Annie. "Should it?"

Armand's brows lowered as he watched the investigator examine his children.

Fontaine turned her focus on Annie. "Are you sure?"

Annie's face opened in surprise. "Alexander Plessner? I've never heard of him."

Fontaine continued to stare at her.

"What's this about?" Gamache asked of Fontaine. "Do you know something?"

She turned to him.

This was clearly the Chief Inspector's Achilles' heel. His family. She knew it. And he knew it.

"I know that your daughter's firm handles his business in Paris. Did he help you get your position there?"

"I've never heard of the man," Annie repeated. "Not personally, not professionally. But I can help you get whatever information it's legal to give out."

Good for you, Armand thought.

"That won't be necessary. *Merci*." Fontaine turned to Daniel. "And you, sir? Do you know him?"

Daniel frowned in concentration, then shook his head. "Sorry. No. Was he a friend of Stephen's?"

"Alexander Plessner was an investor. Venture capital mostly."

It took a force of will for Armand not to look in Daniel's direction.

"Ahh, then he might've had investments with some GHS subsidiary," said Daniel. "Maybe he invested in one of their riskier ventures."

And now his father did look over at Daniel.

He'd just had time, before the investigators had arrived, to warn them not to volunteer information, no matter how banal it might seem. Answer the Commander's questions honestly, but not more than was asked.

Everything can be misinterpreted.

"This's very helpful," said Fontaine. "Do you happen to know what those subsidiaries are?"

"Well, it's not listed on the Bourse," said Daniel, ignoring the sound of his father clearing his throat, "so it's hard to get accurate information. The great advantage of being a private company is just that. Privacy."

"Perhaps you mean secrecy," said Fontaine, smiling at him in a conspiratorial way.

Daniel smiled back. Clearly enjoying showing off his expertise.

It was, Gamache knew, a technique in investigations. Appeal to the ego of a suspect. And watch them spill.

"That's probably more accurate," conceded Daniel. He opened his mouth to go on, but his father interrupted.

"Regulators would know what the company's into, wouldn't they, Commander?" he asked, making it clear who should answer the question.

"You'd be surprised," said Fontaine.

"By what?" asked Reine-Marie.

"By how little they actually regulate," said Daniel, leaping in again. "By how little they really know about corporations."

"Tell me more," said Fontaine, leaning toward him.

"Well, the French government checks compliance," Daniel said. "But if a large corporation like GHS is slow to respond, the bureaucrats just move on to another company. Something smaller. Something simpler. So they can at least show progress."

"So you're saying, sir, that these corporations, in your experience, aren't deliberately hiding anything?"

"From competitors, yes. But from the regulators, no. In my experience they try to be as transparent as possible. The problem is that there are too many companies, and too few watchdogs."

Fontaine looked over at Gamache, who was listening, stone-faced. Showing absolutely no reaction to what his son just said.

But what must he be thinking?

Probably exactly what she was thinking. Daniel Gamache's answer was naïve at best. Deliberately misleading at worst.

And while his father might want to think the best, Commander Irena Fontaine absolutely thought the worst.

"Let's move on—" began Fontaine.

"Wait a minute," said Gamache. "I have a small question for Daniel."

He was breaking, shattering, his own advice to his family, but he had no choice.

"*Oui?*"

"Here in France there are a number of agencies that oversee corporate governance, right?"

"Yes. There's the AMF, for instance."

"But that's mostly financial institutions, like banks," said his father. "It wouldn't oversee a private multinational company like GHS."

"That's true. But there are government bodies that enforce French commercial codes."

Daniel was beginning to color. Not comfortable, it seemed, being essentially cross-examined by his father

But Commander Fontaine knew exactly what Gamache was doing.

This wasn't a cross-examination. This was a rescue mission.

He'd seen the danger his son was in. He was giving Daniel another chance to explain. To not appear to be covering up for unethical companies.

To admit there was often complicity and collusion, bribery and intimidation. That sometimes watchdogs looked the other way while corporations got away with murder.

"You've been here for a while, Daniel. What do you think?" asked his father. "Could a private corporation intentionally hide its activities from regulators?"

He's leading him right to it, thought Fontaine. And she found, despite herself, that she was rooting for Daniel to come through.

"Yes."

Daniel was glaring at his father. Not understanding that the man had just saved him.

But Gamache wasn't finished yet.

"How?" he asked.

"With billions of euros at stake, there can be bribery, blackmail," said Daniel, his tone brusque. "Payoffs. Politicians can be in the pocket of private industry. Or it can be something as simple as a bureaucrat turning a blind eye to some problem, in hopes of being rewarded by the corporation."

"A flaw in the system," said his father, nodding. "Paying the enforcers so much less than the criminals make. Opens people up to temptation."

"But most are honest," said Daniel. "In my experience anyway. Unlike you, I don't always want to see the worst in people."

The shot was unmistakable. And had hit its mark.

Armand, despite years of practice, had never developed a defense against his son's barbs.

And Irena Fontaine made a mental note. This might be a tight family circle, but she'd just found the weak link. The crack through which spite passed.

She wondered what the father could have done to the son to create such animosity.

"*Bon*, let's shift back to Monsieur Horowitz. Madame McGillicuddy gave me a lot of information about his, what? Empire?"

The family, as one, smiled.

Stephen would have liked that. It made him an emperor.

"But," continued Fontaine, "she refused to give me the codes to his computer and phone. The Prefect says you'll get them for us. Have you done that, sir?"

"Not yet. I haven't had the chance to call her back."

161

"I see."

Clearly, she was thinking, if she had found the time to speak to Mrs. McGillicuddy, he could, too. And Fontaine was right.

What she hadn't known was that he'd spent that time with Stephen. But now, Armand realized he needed to focus on the investigation.

He couldn't help his godfather. Stephen was in other hands. Good hands. But he could help find out who'd done this to him, and to Alexander Plessner.

"She did give me the name and number of Monsieur Horowitz's personal lawyer in Montréal," said Fontaine. "I'll be calling soon, but you can save me some time."

"How?" asked Roslyn, leaning forward.

"Who benefits?" said Fontaine, looking around the room.

"Didn't we just talk about that?" said Roslyn. "That company benefits, if he had something on it."

"She means the will, don't you?" said Annie. "If Stephen dies, who gets his money."

"Yes. He's a billionaire with investments, property, impressive collections of art, rare first editions. And no one to leave it all to. Except you. Oh, come on, you can't tell me you haven't thought about that. You're his family. Who else is he going to leave his fortune to? Chief Inspector?"

"Stephen never spoke about it," said Armand. "And I never asked."

"Neither did I," said Daniel. "If I thought about it—"

Be quiet, be quiet, his father thought. *For God's sake, be quiet.* But it was too late.

"—it was that he'd use his wealth to set up a foundation," said Daniel. "He wouldn't leave it to us. We don't need it."

"It sounds as though you have thought about it," said Fontaine.

And there it was, thought Gamache with dismay.

"And you don't need the money?" she continued. "Not even to buy an apartment that must cost several million euros? And put your children into private school?"

"I've had a promotion at work," said Daniel, red spreading up his neck and across his cheeks.

"You can't possibly think—" began Reine-Marie, then stopped, unable to say the words out loud.

But Beauvoir could. "You think one of us tried to kill Stephen? For money?"

"You don't need to look so shocked," said Fontaine. "You'd ask the same question if this was your case. Wouldn't be the first time greed was a motive for murder. And as magnificent as you might think you all are, you're still human."

But it was Gamache's reaction that interested her the most.

Instead of exploding, as she'd expected when she'd deliberately and clearly accused his family, attacked his family, he'd grown even calmer.

Claude Dussault, had he been there, would have recognized the warning signs.

But Irena Fontaine did not.

"It's a legitimate question," he said. "But let me make this clear. No one in this family would ever hurt someone, not for personal gain."

The tone might be polite, but the force of his personality was almost overwhelming. The outrage so much more powerful for being contained. It was, Fontaine thought, like watching a centurion control a team of snorting and stamping warhorses. Prepared for battle, but holding back. Choosing, with infinite patience, his own time to take to the field.

"Not personal gain, you say. But there are other reasons they might kill?" Fontaine continued to provoke.

It seemed everyone else had faded into the furniture. And they were alone. Locked in a duel. This senior cop from Québec, with the strange accent. And her. The second-in-command of the cops in all fucking Paris.

She would outrank him, had they been in the same force. She tried to find comfort, and confidence, in that. Even as she felt herself wavering. Wondering if it had been such a good idea to cross that line.

But she had to know. Had to push him. The Prefect had instructed her to do all she could to find out what this man knew. And the best way was to hit him where it hurt.

"No," said Gamache. "Nothing could make anyone here try to kill Stephen. At least"—his stare was unrelenting—"not any member of this family."

Had he really just insinuated that she could be involved? she wondered. And that, by extension, the Préfecture could be involved?

Maybe even the Prefect himself?

He'd hit back, and hard.

She could now see why Monsieur Dussault had warned her about this man.

"Do you know the contents of his will?" she asked, trying to modulate her tone to match his.

"I'm one of the executors. Mrs. McGillicuddy and his personal lawyer are the others. But I haven't seen the will."

"He never mentioned any bequests to you or your family?"

"No."

"Though it wouldn't be unreasonable"—with great effort, she held his stare—"to expect something. Maybe even something substantial."

"It's certainly possible that Stephen's left his billions to us. And it would be only human to imagine what that would be like." He smiled. "Wouldn't you?"

"Would you?"

"Me?" His smile faded until he looked almost wistful, and shook his head. "No. I never wanted anything from Stephen except his company."

A snort of derision escaped her. But he continued to look at her, unapologetic. Almost, she saw now, in a kindly way.

Inviting her, it seemed, to understand. What it meant to love so completely that all you wanted from that person was companionship.

She remembered what he'd said while in Horowitz's apartment.

Dead parents. Godfather. Nine-year-old boy.

And for a moment she understood what the crotchety financier must've meant to the boy. To the man.

She found that she believed him. But that didn't mean his lawyer daughter and his banker son with the expensive new apartment hadn't dreamed of riches beyond belief. And maybe even done more than dream.

Now Gamache leaned forward. "No one in this family had anything to do with the attacks. Think about it. Even if, even if"—he stressed the "if"—"we had a motive to kill Stephen, why murder Monsieur Plessner?"

"Mistaken identity," she said, not yet willing to give up her theory. "None of you knew Monsieur Horowitz was staying at the George V and not at his apartment."

"For God's sake—" Reine-Marie began, then stopped when she heard her husband laugh.

"I'm sorry," he said, sitting back in the sofa. "But are you really suggesting that one of us went to the apartment, mistook Monsieur Plessner for a man we'd known all our lives, then shot him in the spine and head?"

He'd been specific for a reason. Hadn't said "back." Had said "spine." And he could see that his logic had landed. Except.

Now Commander Fontaine turned slightly. Until she was looking at Jean-Guy Beauvoir.

"Oh, come on," said Beauvoir, clearly following her thinking. "Me? You think I did it? This's bullshit."

"It was, as you pointed out, a commando-style hit," she said, turning back to Gamache. "I understand, sir, you were a member of the Canadian special ops unit, Joint Task Force Two."

"Do I look like a commando?" Gamache said, opening his arms.

Fontaine had to admit he looked more like her history prof at the Sorbonne. If you didn't look into his eyes.

Elite forces were led by people like this. Who thought as well as acted. Who thought before they acted. And who could be ruthless if need be.

"Now?" she said. "Maybe not. But a hundred years ago . . ."

Gamache laughed and shook his head.

"You deny it?" she said. "But then, aren't commandos sworn to secrecy, even after they've left? To say, if pressed, that they washed out, or were simply an instructor?"

"Really? If I admit it, then I'm a member. If I deny it, I'm still a member? You'd have done well in the Inquisition, Commander." His smile had disappeared. "Now, this's a little awkward, but I was actually an instructor for JTF2. Not a member."

"Really? That's your official statement?"

"That's the truth."

"I see. That means you probably also train your own people in commando tactics. Why wouldn't you? As the Sûreté, your people are often first in."

"Then you must know, Commander," said Gamache, "that anyone schooled in those tactics is also trained to make sure the person they're killing is the actual target. Not an innocent bystander."

"Mistakes happen."

"Yes, when a situation gets out of control. But this would not. It was contained. One unarmed elderly man in a private apartment. There would be no mistake. Whoever killed Alexander Plessner almost certainly meant to kill Alexander Plessner."

That sat in the room. A bald statement so certain of itself that Commander Fontaine could not think of an argument.

"What have you found out about him, the dead man?" Beauvoir asked, hoping to draw some of her fire.

Fontaine disengaged from Gamache and turned to Beauvoir.

"We've tracked down one of Monsieur Plessner's colleagues in Toronto. She was, of course, shocked. The news of his murder isn't public yet, and I have local investigators searching his office and home. As we know, Monsieur Plessner was trained as a mechanical engineer and seems to have used his training to invest in venture capital, mainly in small, apparently insignificant inventions or innovations that others dismissed, but ended up making him a fortune."

"There can't be many that come to anything," said Roslyn.

"No, but if even one hits," said Daniel, "a fortune is made."

Reine-Marie heard Armand sigh, a long exhale of exasperation with a son who just could not shut up.

"That's right, I'd forgotten, you're in venture capital, too," said Fontaine, who clearly had not forgotten.

If there was a trap to step into, Daniel would find it. If there was no trap, Daniel would create one. Then step into it.

"And yet, you don't know Monsieur Plessner?" asked Fontaine, pleasantly.

"Never heard of him. If he's based in Toronto, I wouldn't. There're a lot of people who think they can find the next Apple or Facebook. And some do. That's where lives are changed."

And sometimes, thought Gamache, staring at his son, lives lost.

CHAPTER 18

◠

When the interview ended, the others went across the street to join the children and their sitter in the park. But Gamache and Beauvoir stayed behind.

Jean-Guy was dying to tell Gamache what had happened at work, and to check out what he'd recorded on his phone. But Fontaine and her number two also lingered in the apartment.

"Did you bring the box, Commander?" Gamache asked, looking around the foyer.

"The box, sir?"

"Monsieur Dussault said he'd ask you to bring Stephen's things so we could go through them again."

"Were you looking for anything in particular?"

"Well, yes. I wanted to look at the annual report from GHS."

"The Prefect did ask, but I'd already left. Perhaps tomorrow."

"*Merci,*" said Gamache, doubting he'd see that box the next day, or ever. He went to open the door for them, but Fontaine didn't move.

"I'd like to speak with you. Privately, sir." She glanced at Beauvoir.

"Yes? You can speak in front of Jean-Guy. What is it?"

He could see it was something. Something even more sensitive, it seemed, than accusing his children of murder.

They were standing in the front hall, and she pointed to the dining room. When they sat down, she said, "Are you aware of Monsieur Horowitz's background?"

Armand opened his mouth to answer, then changed his mind. Finally saying, "I think so, but what do you know?"

"He's German by birth."

"Yes."

"And fought with the French Resistance during the war," said Fontaine. "His family was arrested for protecting Jews, and shot. Monsieur Horowitz managed to escape."

"*Oui.* His family stalled the Gestapo long enough to allow him to lead the Jewish family out a hidden door in the back garden."

This was news to Jean-Guy, who listened in astonishment. He knew about the Resistance, but not this.

"That's the story, yes," said Fontaine.

Gamache shifted in his seat but remained silent. He was beginning to get an inkling of what was coming.

"As you can imagine, sir, we have access to files that aren't public. That were suppressed after the war, for all sorts of reasons."

"Go on."

Armand had tensed his muscles, like a boxer preparing for a body blow.

"The reports we have in the archives tell a different story," said Fontaine. "His family was indeed killed in the war. His mother and siblings in Dresden. His father and uncle survived the war but were shot by the Russians."

"Why?"

"They were senior Gestapo officers responsible, according to the Russians, for sending thousands to the camps."

Armand sat perfectly still. Struck dumb. Almost blind and deaf. His senses shutting down. Not breathing. Not blinking. This was far worse than anything he could have expected or imagined. Or steeled himself against.

It was so great a lie, it staggered him.

And then an image exploded in his mind. Of his grandmother. Zora. Looking at Stephen, as though the devil himself had entered the house.

Did she know something? Sense something?

But no. That wasn't possible. This wasn't possible.

With a jolt, like a man coming up for air, he was back in the peaceful dining room of his son's apartment in Paris. Diffused light came in through the sheer curtains, giving it an ethereal quality.

"That's not true," he finally managed to say.

"I can show you the documents."

He nodded. Knowing he had to see them, but not wanting to. He wanted to crawl back to an hour ago, when things were just terrible, not monstrous.

"Even if it is true, about his father and uncle, that doesn't mean Stephen was part of it. He still escaped to France. Still fought in the Resistance."

"Did he?" asked Fontaine. "Are you so sure? If he lied about his family, maybe he lied about that, too."

"What he told us is the truth." Gamache's grip was slipping. The horses straining. "The man is ninety-three, fighting for his life in a hospital bed after being attacked, and now you . . . you . . . attack him again? With wild accusations that are impossible to prove, or disprove? Jesus Christ."

The stamping horses had broken loose.

Beside him, Jean-Guy jerked. He'd rarely heard Armand Gamache shout, and never, ever heard him swear. Not with those words anyway. Never.

And now the Chief was literally trembling with rage.

Across the table, Irena Fontaine smiled. She'd hit a nerve, just as Dussault had predicted. And not just hit but shattered a nerve.

Gamache had managed to remain calm, contained, when she'd accused his children of murder. But this accusation against Horowitz had made him lose it. Why?

Because, she thought, he's afraid it might actually be true.

"What I know," she said, "is that the Allies had their doubts. The leaders of the Resistance had their doubts."

"But not enough to prosecute."

"That's hardly a measure of innocence, as we all know."

She opened the slender folder and produced a grainy black-and-white photograph.

It showed German officers laughing and raising glasses. Among them a thin-lipped, humorless man who looked like a failed accountant. Heinrich Himmler. Head of the Gestapo and father of the Holocaust.

Food and drink were in front of them. A celebration in progress.

And behind Himmler, a slender hand resting comfortably on the Nazi leader's shoulder, was a young man with a familiar grin, looking straight into the camera.

Armand felt light-headed and thought he might be sick. It was the same hand he'd gripped as a child. He'd gripped that morning in the hospital.

Stephen. Impossibly young. Happy. Joining in the fun. Joining in the joke.

Armand recognized the fresco behind them.

The photo was taken in the Hôtel Lutetia after it had been commandeered as the headquarters of the Abwehr, the Nazi counterespionage unit, in occupied Paris.

Gamache had sat at that same table with Stephen. Eating ice cream as a child, sipping scotch as an adult. Perhaps the very same drink, from the same glasses, in the very same chair, as that creature.

"After the war, when questioned, Horowitz claimed to have taken a job at the Lutetia to spy on the Germans and pass the information on to his comrades in the Resistance," said Fontaine.

"That makes sense," said Armand, struggling to regain his equilibrium.

In the photo Stephen was in uniform, but not that of the Abwehr, or any German unit. It was the crisp uniform of a Lutetia waiter.

"It's what every collaborator claimed, monsieur, as you must know."

"And it's what members of the Resistance actually did. How else would they get information except to cozy up to the Nazis? And Stephen, being German, would be in a perfect position to get information. He was telling the truth. The man I know wouldn't do what you're suggesting."

"Help the Nazis? He was one."

"He was German. There's a huge difference."

"I agree. I meant that he was raised in a house that supported the Nazi party. His family were members. Senior officers. They rounded up men, women, children and sent them to camps. Death camps this man"—she thrust a finger onto Himmler's face—"created."

"And that's why Stephen escaped to France and fought the Nazis," said Armand, raising his voice again, before pulling it back so far he was almost whispering. "Because he couldn't support that."

Even to his own ears, he'd begun to sound like an upset child insisting on something that might not be true.

"You could be right," she admitted. "Monsieur Horowitz was investigated. The Allies decided, with his perfect German and French and his smattering of English, he could be of more use to them free than as a prisoner. And they had far worse criminals to go after. After your father helped Horowitz get to Canada, the dossier was closed and buried."

She paused, almost hating to take this next step. Almost.

"Your father was a conscientious objector, is that right? He refused to fight?"

"*Pardon?* My father? What's he got to do with it?"

"Just answer the question, please."

Gamache glared at her, and composed himself before answering.

"He didn't believe in killing people in a war so far from home. But he volunteered as a Red Cross medic."

Would she know what that meant? Unarmed, their job was to drag wounded soldiers, often under intense fire, back to safety.

The casualty rate among medics was the highest of any unit except paratroops. The commandos.

"My father came to regret his opposition to the war. He was deeply scarred by what he saw in the camps. He spent much of his time after the war trying to make amends."

"By bringing the woman Zora to Québec and into your family."

"*Oui.* And by helping Stephen, among other things. He wouldn't have done that if there was any suspicion that Stephen was a collaborator. I heard him and my mother talk about it. I remember clearly."

"You were a child, sir. Eight, nine years old? Children can mishear, misunderstand."

"What? That my godfather was a Nazi collaborator who my father essentially helped escape justice? You think I'd misunderstand that? You think he'd do that?"

"I didn't know your father." She held his intense stare. "And neither did you."

Below the table, below everyone else's line of sight, Jean-Guy saw Gamache's hands clutching each other so tight his knuckles were white.

But Gamache held his outrage. Held his tongue. Held his horses. Just.

"Why bring this up now? What can this possibly have to do with the attack on Stephen and the murder of Alexander Plessner?"

"It speaks to Horowitz's character. You might not want to see it, and I don't blame you, sir, but that's who your godfather is. All his life Stephen Horowitz has betrayed friends in exchange for freedom. He betrays colleagues in exchange for wealth. It's how he stayed alive. It's how he got to Canada. It's how he made his billions."

"He made his fortune by being smart and working hard," said Armand. "By being more ethical, having more integrity and courage, than anyone else out there."

"That's what he wants you to believe, but the truth is Stephen Horowitz is out only for himself. Why do you think he's left a trail of enemies? He sat on boards collecting confidential information, then used it against the very people he sat beside. He went to their weddings and baptisms and bar mitzvahs, then turned on them. Betrayed their trust, just as he betrayed his comrades in the Resistance. He's a traitor. It's in his nature."

"It is not." Gamache leaned toward her.

"The only thing that changed after the war was his location," Fontaine said, leaning toward him. "Horowitz was, and is still, interested in only one thing. Himself. A snake sheds its skin, but nothing else changes. It's still exactly the same creature."

"Stephen Horowitz fought against the Nazis in his youth. And in his career he's fought against corruption, against wrongdoing. He never betrayed anyone. They betrayed themselves, by cheating and stealing from investors, many of them small. Many in danger of losing life savings. He was, is, ruthless. Yes. But he's on the side of the angels."

Beauvoir couldn't believe Gamache had just brought angels into the argument, but the Chief Inspector did not look at all embarrassed. And for her part, Commander Fontaine didn't laugh.

In fact, what she said next surprised him.

"Angels? Are you so sure? Is it possible that *Hell is empty, and all the devils*"—she brought her index finger down again on the grainy photograph, this time on top of Stephen's face—"*are here?*"

Gamache leaned back, slowly, almost casually, and continued to regard her. When he spoke, his voice was calm, reasonable. Thoughtful.

"Dussault told you about Stephen's favorite saying?"

"He did."

"Did he also tell you that he called Stephen an avenging angel?"

"*Non.*"

"But I think now he was wrong, and you're right," said Gamache, to everyone's surprise. "Stephen's actions during the war were a prelude to what he did all his life. He tracked down the devils among us. He's not an avenging angel. He's an exorcist. I'm going to join the others in the park, unless there's another member of my family you'd like to attack."

He got up.

"No, I think that does it," said Fontaine.

They all rose. Gamache gave a curt nod and left.

Beauvoir waited until the door closed, then turned to Fontaine. "Give me the dossier. I'll pass it along to him."

"I don't have it on me. I only brought the photograph. But we can get it to you."

"Do. And by the way, just so you know, you're wrong. About Stephen, for sure. But you've made another mistake."

They'd walked to the door, and now he paused. "Monsieur Gamache might look old to you. Did you call him a hundred? Over a hundred?"

"It was a joke."

Beauvoir nodded. And smiled. Then leaned closer to her. "Just a word of warning. You don't want to fuck with him."

"Oh, really? And what's he going to do?"

"Not him. Me."

CHAPTER 19

⌒

Armand stood in the bright sunshine of the small park. He knew
he should read his emails, make some phone calls.

But he needed this more. This moment watching his grandchildren
play. Watching his own children be parents. Turning his back on life
as it was, he watched life as it should be.

Walking over to Daniel, who was pushing Zora on a swing, he said,
"Can we grab a beer later? Just us."

"Why?"

"Because I like your company. Because it would be nice to catch
up. Hear more about your new job, your new home."

"Continue the interrogation?"

Armand managed not to be drawn in. "I just want to catch up. We
don't get to do that often."

Ever.

"I'm a little busy right now," said Daniel. "Maybe tomorrow."

"Daniel—"

"See you later, Dad."

He gave Zora another push, turning his back on his father.

Across the park, Reine-Marie was watching, and caught Armand's
eye.

"You okay?" Reine-Marie asked when he joined her. "That looked
tense."

"He's angry about the interview. About my questioning him."

"He'll settle down. Realize you did it to help him."

"I don't think he will. I tried to talk to him, but . . ." He raised his hands.

She saw in that gesture all the pain and futility of the last twenty-five years. The frustration and sadness of trying to connect with a child who'd one day vanished. His sweet boy. Gone. Replaced by a grim, angry child.

And they didn't know why.

She looked at her husband and thought, not for the first time, that here was a man who spent his life working out what had happened to others, but who couldn't figure out what had happened to his own child.

"I've invited the Dussaults for dinner tonight," she said.

"I'm sorry? You what?"

"Claude and Monique are coming for dinner."

He stared at her. Of course, she couldn't have known the awkwardness of the conversation at the 36 just an hour or so earlier. But she did know that the cologne they'd smelled in Stephen's apartment, while standing over the body, was the same as Claude Dussault wore. That there was a suspicion that the Prefect was somehow involved.

"Why?"

"I think I've found the cologne," she said. "The one we smelled. But I want to be sure. I thought if we had them over . . ."

"We could just ask him? *Claude, were you in the apartment with us? Did you kill Alexander Plessner? Cheese?*"

She laughed. "No. Of course not. But it might come up."

"Cologne?"

"He doesn't know we smelled it in the apartment, does he?"

"No."

"Then there's no harm in asking."

"There's a great deal of harm," said Armand, turning to her. "Reine-Marie, please. Promise me you won't ask him. Please. These are dangerous times. He might be a friend, but if he isn't, if he feels threatened, cornered—"

"So you do suspect him."

177

"I'm afraid at this stage I suspect everyone. Except our own family. Please, promise me you won't ask him about his cologne."

"I promise. Did I make a mistake in inviting them over? I can cancel."

Armand thought about that. "No, it might actually be a good thing."

He looked around for Jean-Guy. He was anxious to hear what Beauvoir had learned at GHS earlier in the afternoon.

Armand spotted him and watched as Jean-Guy gave Honoré the nickels that were stuck together. While the boy tried to pull them apart, Jean-Guy turned full circle. Scanning the area.

Gamache recognized that look. It was not casual.

Honoré, in frustration, tossed the nickels into the grass.

When Jean-Guy turned back to his son, the nickels were gone. He immediately knelt and opened Honoré's mouth, frantically sweeping his fingers in as the boy began to cry.

Armand ran over, calling, "It's okay. He threw them away."

"Oh, thank God. If anything happens to Honoré . . ." He looked over at Annie. "I don't want to be blamed."

Armand laughed. Out of the corner of his eye, he saw Daniel pick up the nickels, making sure no other child swallowed them. Putting them in his pocket, Daniel walked away from his father and Jean-Guy.

"Are you all right?" asked Jean-Guy. "After what Fontaine said . . ."

"It was a shock. I know it's not true, about Stephen, but just hearing the accusation was sickening."

"I've asked for the file."

Gamache turned to him now. "Does it strike you as strange that she should have it? They only began the investigation this morning, but they already have some old dossier on Stephen that had been buried in the archives for seventy-five years."

Jean-Guy nodded and watched as Honoré ran over to play with the other children. Then he looked at Annie, so pregnant she was about to explode. She was sitting on a bench, chatting with another mother.

"You all right?" asked Armand.

"I'm sorry. I'm a little distracted."

Armand followed his glance. "Tell me."

Jean-Guy lowered his voice, becoming almost furtive. As though what he was about to say was shameful.

"I'm so worried. Have we done the right thing? What's going to happen? Jesus, I'm standing right next to Honoré and I can't stop him from swallowing coins. How'm I ever going to keep our daughter safe? All her life. It'll never stop. And, and, God help me, I think of how happy we are, just the three of us. Have we made a mistake? I'm so afraid."

Armand paused, then asked gently, "What're you afraid of?"

"I'm afraid we won't be able to do it. That we, I, won't love her enough. I'm worried for Honoré. And yes, I'm worried for me. What it'll mean to me. I wake up in the middle of the night and think, what've we done? And I just want to run away. Oh, God, am I really so selfish?"

Across the park Daniel, now talking with other parents, saw his father and Jean-Guy in a clearly intimate conversation. Turning his back, he focused on the strangers in front of him.

"No, of course you're not. Listen." Armand held Jean-Guy's arm. "Are you listening? Look at me."

Jean-Guy raised his eyes.

"It would be insane not to be afraid. To worry. The very thing you just admitted is what will make you a great father to your daughter. We're all afraid. Of something bad happening to our children. Of not being there when they need us. Of not being enough. We all want to pull the sheets up over our heads some days and hide. But not all of us admit it. Your daughter is one lucky girl. I don't know what it's going to be like, but I suspect you'll find that she is much more like other babies than she is different. And I do know you will love her, Jean-Guy."

Beauvoir looked into his father-in-law's eyes and hoped that was true.

Just then little Zora started crying. They watched as Daniel took her in his arms and held her, rubbing her back. Letting her wail. And whispering, "It's all right. It's all right."

Reine-Marie and Armand joined them.

"Did she fall?" asked Reine-Marie.

Daniel put her down and asked, "Are you hurt?"

Sputtering, trying to catch her breath, Zora shook her head.

"Why are you crying?"

"Nothing."

"It's okay, you can tell me."

"Nothing."

Armand gave a handkerchief to his son, who used it to wipe Zora's face and have her blow her nose.

Florence, her older sister, had come over and was hovering in the background.

"It's the other kids," Florence said.

"Is not," muttered Zora.

"What about them?" asked Daniel.

"They make fun of her."

"Do not."

"Why?"

"Because of her name."

Now her little sister was quiet, though her face had again crumpled, and she was on the verge of tears.

"They say it's weird. That she's weird."

"I hate it," said Zora. "I hate my name, and I hate them."

"Has anyone told you about your name?" her grandfather asked. "Where it comes from?"

"Grand-mère," she muttered. "Or something."

Armand knelt down now. "Your great-grandmother, yes." He looked at the other kids, staring, then at Daniel. "Can we all go for a walk?"

Daniel nodded and put out his hand for his daughter to hold, while Reine-Marie took Florence's.

As they strolled through the park, Armand told Zora all about Zora. Leaving out the worst bits, the nightmare parts, time enough for that later. He told her how brave her namesake was. And how loved. How funny and kind. And strong.

"Zora is a beautiful name," said Reine-Marie. "It means 'dawn.' Every name means something special."

"What does my name mean?" asked Florence.

"It means 'to flower,'" said Daniel. "'To blossom.' And to blossom, you know what you need?"

"Candy?"

Her father laughed. "*Non.* Flowers need the sun." He looked over at Zora. Florence followed his gaze and nodded. But said nothing.

"And maybe," Daniel said to both his girls, "some ice cream. But first"—he leaned toward them—"a horse kiss."

At that, they shrieked and ran away, laughing.

Armand watched his son be a father, and smiled. Yes, it was far more important he be a great father than a good son. Hanging back, he joined Jean-Guy. "We need to talk."

Reine-Marie went across to the Marché des Enfants Rouges to get food for that evening, while Daniel and Roslyn took the girls home for ice cream.

Annie walked with Honoré back to their apartment, for a nap.

"Coming?" she asked Jean-Guy.

"Do you mind if I speak to your father?"

"Not at all. Don't forget the key."

"The key," Jean-Guy said as he and Armand flagged down a taxi, "is a box of mille-feuilles. I'm not allowed in without them."

Armand smiled. With Reine-Marie, it had been spicy sausage pizza.

"*Hôtel Lutetia, s'il vous plaît,*" he told the driver and closed the glass partition between them.

It was the first chance they'd had to be alone since Jean-Guy's visit to his office at GHS Engineering.

"What did you find out?"

"Well?" said Claude Dussault. "What did you find out?"

"Nothing concrete, sir," said Fontaine over the phone.

Dussault could hear it in her voice. The hesitation. "But?"

"But I think Monsieur Gamache has suspicions. He was courteous, but I don't think he was completely open."

"I see. How did he react to the file on Stephen Horowitz?"

"Angrily. It shifted the focus, as you predicted."

"Good. Maybe he'll focus on that and not so much on the investigation."

"He did ask to see the box. I told him I didn't have it. Why can't you just tell him to back off, *patron*?"

"I tried. Didn't work. Besides, best if we can keep an eye on him. I'm going to their place for dinner. I might find out more."

After he hung up, Dussault sat back and considered. He'd initially been annoyed at Monique for accepting the invitation to the Gamaches' for dinner that night. It would, at the very least, be awkward.

Now he thought it might be a good idea.

CHAPTER 20

⌒

Gamache sat in the back seat of the taxi and looked down at the printout Beauvoir had given to him.

The Luxembourg funicular project. There was a schematic and all sorts of technical language Gamache could not begin to understand.

Taking off his reading glasses, he looked at Jean-Guy. "Do you have any idea who was erasing all those emails and progress reports?"

"No, but obviously it was someone familiar with the system."

"It at least confirms that GHS has something to hide. I wish we knew what was in those messages."

Beauvoir smiled and hit play on his iPhone.

Both squinted in concentration as the video he'd taken at GHS came on.

"The emails?" Armand asked.

"And reports, *oui*. I recorded them as they were being erased."

"Clever."

But the taxi ride was too bumpy, the video already too shaky, the messages flashing by too quickly, for them to make anything out.

"Damn," said Beauvoir, clicking it off. "Have to wait until we arrive."

"Those messages, they were to and from Carole Gossette?" said Gamache. "Your boss? A senior executive? Is that—"

"Unusual? Very. She oversees some projects, but only the really big ones."

"And she's the one who quoted Auden, right? About the crack in the teacup leading to death. About something small, some everyday issue, that can be devastating. It was an odd thing to say. What were you talking about at the time?"

Jean-Guy threw his mind back. "About my job. Whether I was there to police."

Gamache looked out the window as Paris slipped by. Thinking. "We don't know what those messages are about. She might've placed herself on the project because she had suspicions."

"That's true," said Beauvoir, brightening.

Gamache turned to him. "You like her."

"I do. I can't see her being involved in anything criminal."

"Let's hope you're right." But he wondered how much they ever really knew anyone. Even someone they'd known all their lives. "They must've panicked when they realized you'd opened the files."

"Except that I used Arbour's computer."

"So they'd think it was her?" said Gamache, nodding. "That was smart. But . . . still . . ." His mind was working quickly, trying to put it together. "If someone was monitoring that project and noticed that Séverine Arbour had accessed it, and that set off alarms, that would mean—"

Beauvoir's eyes opened wider. "That she's not in on it. If she was, they wouldn't be concerned, and they sure wouldn't erase those files. By using her terminal, have I just put Arbour in danger?"

"It's possible. Do you know where she lives?"

"*Non*. But I have her number." He lifted his iPhone, but Gamache touched his arm.

"Just a moment. She might still be in on it. It's possible what set off alarms wasn't the computer but the security cameras. They might've seen you at her desk."

Gamache thought, then remembered something curious. "You went to the window of Daniel's apartment during the interview with Fontaine. You told her you were checking on the kids, but you can't see the park from there. What were you really looking for?"

"I'm not sure it's anything, but a guard came up while I was at GHS. They'd never done that before. He asked all sorts of questions."

"Did he go over to Madame Arbour's desk?"

"*Non*. But I saw him again on my ride back. In the métro. He got onto the same car as me."

Gamache had grown very still. Very focused. His eyes on Jean-Guy were sharp. Quickly absorbing the information.

And Jean-Guy wondered if, maybe, Irena Fontaine had been right. And Chief Inspector Gamache had done more than just instruct recruits to Canada's elite tactical team, Joint Task Force Two.

Though it did occur to Beauvoir to wonder what had happened to Task Force One.

"You were looking out the window for him," said Gamache.

"Yes. But no sign of him. He was probably just going home. He didn't get off at my stop. I think I was just spooked." Jean-Guy tapped his phone then showed it to Gamache. "I took a picture of him. His name's Xavier Loiselle."

Gamache studied the photo, in case he saw the man again, then looked at Jean-Guy. "You have good instincts. What do they tell you?"

Jean-Guy shifted. He really hated it when Gamache talked about instincts, or accused him of being intuitive. It was, he was pretty sure, an insult.

But he was equally sure his father-in-law saw it as a compliment.

"I think the guard Loiselle was following me. But I don't know why he would've stopped."

"Maybe his orders were to scare you. What do you think is going on at GHS?"

Beauvoir exhaled and shook his head. "I wish I knew. I wish I could understand that report." He pointed to the printout in Gamache's hands. "The engineering could be flawed and they're covering up. Could be money laundering. Drugs? Arms dealing? The company has the scope for it. Projects all over the world. Shipments of equipment going back and forth to places known to traffic in drugs and weapons and people. But the Luxembourg project?" Beauvoir shook his head. "A funicular in a grand duchy? It seems unlikely. Too small. Too time-limited. They'd choose something that would go on for years, not months."

Gamache was quiet, nodding slightly, as though listening to music. Or some internal voice.

"What is it?" asked Beauvoir.

"There's either something very wrong about the Luxembourg project, or there isn't."

That was a little cryptic even for Gamache.

Beauvoir was about to ask for clarification when he suddenly understood. "You think they were erasing all those messages so that we wouldn't see that there's nothing wrong with it. So we'll continue to focus on the Luxembourg project, and not where the issue really is."

"I think it's possible."

"Shit," said Beauvoir, leaning back in the taxi seat and staring ahead. His mind working rapidly. "The problem will be understanding the report and emails well enough to spot a flaw."

"We need a financial analyst and an engineer," said Gamache, staring at Beauvoir.

"*Oui.*" And his eyes widened. "Jesus. Like Stephen and Plessner."

Gamache's phone vibrated. It was Mrs. McGillicuddy.

Jean-Guy could hear her voice, high-pitched with anxiety.

She was at Stephen's office with Isabelle Lacoste—

Just then his own phone vibrated. It was Lacoste.

Both Stephen's office and home had been broken into, the security systems circumvented.

"They've thrown things everywhere," said Mrs. McGillicuddy.

"Agents at his home report it's been searched, too," said Lacoste, her voice calm, stating facts. "I can't tell what they were looking for, but seems like papers."

"Did they find them?" Jean-Guy asked.

"I'm not sure. The place is a mess."

"Ask her about his safety-deposit boxes," said Armand, covering the mouthpiece of his phone. In the background, Jean-Guy could hear Mrs. McGillicuddy still talking. Upset. Shocked.

"I heard," said Lacoste. "We're going there next. Mrs. McGillicuddy has the card that'll get us in."

"The JSPS card, *oui*," said Beauvoir. "Let us know."

He hung up. Armand was talking with Mrs. McGillicuddy, who'd calmed down a little. As he listened, Gamache pulled out his notebook and made notes.

Thanking her, he hung up.

"The code to Stephen's laptop. Claude wanted it."

"Are you going to give it to him?"

"I'll have to, yes. Let's just hope Stephen didn't have anything important on his laptop."

"Yes, because people don't," said Beauvoir, all but rolling his eyes.

The taxi had arrived at the Lutetia.

Getting out, Gamache took a step toward the liveried woman holding the heavy door open for them.

Then stopped.

Though he'd known the history of the hotel, including during the war, what Gamache had heard most about was that this was where the survivors of some of the concentration camps had been brought immediately after liberation.

He'd seen photographs of emaciated men, their striped clothing still hanging in tatters from their bones. They sat glaze-eyed in the opulent surroundings.

This was an act of brutality. Though unintentional. What had the liberators been thinking, to bring the survivors there?

What had those ghostly men and women been thinking as they looked around?

There was no celebration, no triumph, in those blank faces. Those photographs spoke only of savagery. Of an unspeakable cruelty, made even more hideous, if that was possible, by the luxury around them.

Yes, he'd known about what seemed a misguided attempt at kindness.

But now another image superimposed itself. Of Stephen. His hand on the shoulder of the monster who had done that.

"*Patron?*" Beauvoir broke into his thoughts.

Gamache turned away. "I'm going across to Stephen's apartment. I have some questions for the concierge."

187

Beauvoir watched as his father-in-law jogged across rue de Sèvres, between oncoming vehicles.

He'd seen Gamache go into homes, warehouses, forests where they knew heavily armed gunmen waited.

Armand Gamache had never hesitated. Had only ever moved forward, the first in. His agents following him.

And now Beauvoir followed Gamache as he ran away.

"You know she was messing with you," said Beauvoir once he'd caught up with Gamache.

"Fontaine? I don't think she was," said Gamache, walking rapidly along the sidewalk. "I think she believes what she said about Stephen."

"Do you? Believe it, I mean."

To Jean-Guy's surprise, Armand hesitated, then shook his head. "No. Not in the least."

At the huge red-lacquered doors into Stephen's building, Gamache pressed a button. A minute later the door was opened by a thin older man, who peered out, then smiled.

"It's the boy," he called behind him. Then opening the door fully, he let Armand and Jean-Guy in.

Claude Dussault sat in his office, going through the box. Again.

Was it just the annual report Armand wanted to see, or was there something else?

There were the predictable items. Stephen Horowitz's wallet, with euros and some Canadian money. Various credit cards and ID.

Dussault took out Stephen's passport and examined it. There were no stamps, but then there wouldn't be if he'd traveled elsewhere in Europe.

Like Luxembourg, for instance.

There were pens and paper clips in the box. Two screws and an Allen wrench. Scotch tape and a pristine notepad with the George V logo. All of which Armand had swept into the container while Reine-Marie stalled the manager.

Then there were the interesting items.

The slender laptop. The crushed phone.

The Préfecture's technical department had examined the phone, taking out the chip and declaring that it was destroyed. And Stephen Horowitz had not used any cloud-based system to store information. Either because he was too technically challenged, or because he didn't trust it. Or, most likely, thought Dussault, Horowitz trusted technology. It was people he distrusted.

"The boy'?" whispered Jean-Guy, as they took seats at the kitchen table.

Madame Faubourg had just brought a *pain au citron* out of the oven, filling the kitchen with a citrusy baking scent. Now she put a kettle on the gas stove, while Monsieur Faubourg opened a cupboard and brought out three bottles of warm beer.

"He doesn't want tea, Madame," said Monsieur. "He's a grown man. He wants beer."

"Actually—" Gamache began but was drowned out.

"Beer and *pain au citron*?" said Madame. "Whoever heard of that? And after what happened? He needs tea." She turned to Armand. "Unless you'd prefer *chocolat chaud*?"

"Actually—" Armand tried again.

"We'll put it all out," Monsieur announced, grabbing some glasses, "and let the boy decide. Brewed it myself."

He tipped the bottle toward his guests.

"*Non, merci,*" said Armand, managing to hold Monsieur's hand to stop him from popping the top off the beer. "I think tea, actually."

On seeing his disappointment, Armand went on, "For my son-in-law. But I'd love a beer."

When they'd all settled around the Formica table, Madame Faubourg asked, "How is he?"

"Well, you know Stephen," said Armand. "Indestructible."

"So he'll be all right?" asked Madame.

"I hope so." That at least was true.

"What happened, Armand?" asked Monsieur Faubourg. "First he's hit by a car, and now a man's killed in his apartment. We don't understand."

189

"It can't be a coincidence, can it?" asked Madame Faubourg.

"*Non*," said Jean-Guy. "We think what happened to Monsieur Horowitz wasn't an accident."

"*Voilà*," said Madame, while Monsieur crossed himself. "That's what I said."

"But why would someone do this?"

"That's what we want to know," said Jean-Guy. "When did you last see him?"

"Monsieur Horowitz?" Madame looked at Monsieur. "Was it June? July?"

"Not since then?" asked Jean-Guy. "Not in the last couple of days?"

"Days? No," said Monsieur. "We only knew he was in Paris when we heard about the accident, this morning. We thought he must've just arrived. We haven't seen him here."

Madame's hand was shaking as she reached for the teapot.

"Here," said Jean-Guy, gently taking the heavy pot from her. "Let me be mother."

"*Pardon?*" asked Monsieur.

"*Désolé*," said Beauvoir, reddening. "Just something a friend back home says when pouring tea."

Damn Gabri, he thought, remembering the large man in the intentionally frilly apron, pouring the Red Rose from the Brown Betty teapot.

Oh, dear God, thought Beauvoir. *Why do I know these things?*

Madame closed her hands into fists to stop the trembling. "We've known Monsieur Horowitz for so long. We knew one day . . . but not like this."

Armand had no idea what their first names were. They only ever called each other Madame and Monsieur. Childless, they'd adopted the residents of the building as their family. As their children, their aunts and uncles, brothers and sisters.

Stephen was somewhere between an uncle and an older brother.

When in Paris, his godfather almost always had Sunday lunch with Madame and Monsieur. And as a child, young Armand had joined them around this kitchen table for roast chicken, or fish pie. The food provided by Stephen, the cooking by the apron-clad Madame. The men would drink beer in the courtyard while Armand helped in the kitchen.

This kitchen, this home, had not changed. Though he had. From child to adult. Father and grandfather now. From boy with flour on his hands to man with blood on them.

Still, he'd always be "the boy" to them. And they'd always be Madame and Monsieur to him.

Monsieur watched as Armand took a long sip of beer, coming away with a slight foam mustache, which he wiped away.

"*Délicieux.*"

And it was. Monsieur had obviously had long practice making beer.

Madame Faubourg, back in control of her movements, cut thick slabs of *pain au citron* and put out a ceramic tub of whipped butter.

"You want to ask us about what happened," she said, shifting the point of the knife from one to the other. "Well, we didn't see anything, and thank God for that."

"Wish we had."

"Don't say that, Monsieur. They'd have killed us, too." She put down the knife and touched his hand, in an act as sacred as the sign of the cross.

"Monsieur Horowitz has the whole top floor, as you know. And you can't see his windows from here," said Monsieur. "He looks out over the street, not into the courtyard."

"The police are still up there going over things," said Madame. "We expect they'll want to talk to us eventually."

"They haven't yet?" asked Beauvoir, glancing at Gamache.

"No."

"And you saw no stranger cross the courtyard yesterday?" asked Armand. "No one rang you?"

"Do murderers normally ring the concierge for admittance?" asked Madame, and Jean-Guy smiled.

"*Non,*" admitted Armand.

The apartment building was fairly typical of the *quartier*. The large wooden door from the sidewalk opened onto a private courtyard. The residents walked across it to access another door that led to the elevator, though most took the stairs if they could.

The elevator was the cage type, tiny, old, rickety.

"And this morning?" asked Gamache. "Did you see anyone arrive?"

"I saw you and Madame Gamache," said Monsieur. "That was mid-morning. I came out to say *bonjour*, but you'd already gone into the building. You found the body?"

"*Oui*."

"*Pauvre* Madame Gamache," said Madame. "You must give her some cake."

Gamache considered declining, but realized it would just hurt her feelings. He accepted the slab of warm *pain au citron* wrapped in wax paper and put it in his pocket.

"You saw no one else?" asked Beauvoir.

"No strangers," said Monsieur. "The children of the family on the third floor came in from Provence for the weekend, but we know them well. And the woman on the second floor had a delivery from Le Bon Marché. We know the deliveryman. See him often. He came and left right away."

"And you didn't see Monsieur Plessner arrive?" asked Jean-Guy.

They looked blank.

"The man who was killed," Jean-Guy explained.

"No," said Madame. "But Fridays are always busy. I'm doing the cleaning, and Monsieur here is dealing with the garbage and recycling."

"There was a leak in the radiator of the apartment on the first floor," he said. "I was fixing that. It's always something in these old buildings."

But what had happened the day before, thought Armand as they left, was something else entirely.

Once in the courtyard, Gamache touched Beauvoir's arm in a silent request to pause.

A single tree, thick-trunked, tall and gnarled, dominated the space.

Lace curtains fluttered at windows where boxes were planted with bright red geranium and soft blue pansies.

Even Beauvoir, not given to appreciating aesthetics, could appreciate this.

It was one of the many peculiarities of Paris. Hidden behind many of the simple wooden doors were these courtyards and secret gardens.

It was a city of façades. Of beauty, both obvious and obscure. Of heroism, both obvious and obscure. Of dreadful deeds, both obvious and obscure.

"Is it possible," Armand began, his voice low so that none of the other residents, whose windows opened onto the courtyard, could hear, "Alexander Plessner let his killer into the apartment?"

"But why would he do that?"

"Two reasons," said Gamache. "Either Plessner had been bought off, and the killer was actually an accomplice—"

"Then why kill him?" asked Beauvoir. "Especially before he'd found the documents? The place was turned upside down. They were pretty desperate to find something. And apparently never did."

"Or," continued Gamache, "Plessner was working with Stephen to uncover something. He'd hidden the evidence in his apartment and sent Plessner there to recover it. And to meet someone else there. Someone they trusted."

"But who would they trust that much?"

"Who were you told to always trust, as a child?"

"Not the man with the candy, that's for sure." Beauvoir thought, then turned to his father-in-law. "A cop."

"*Oui.* Stephen wouldn't trust just any cop, but a senior one . . ."

"The most senior one," said Beauvoir. He glanced around and lowered his voice still further. "The Prefect of Police?"

"Stephen wouldn't go to the apartment himself for fear it was being watched and he'd be recognized. So he sent Plessner, who no one would know, and arranged for a senior cop, Claude Dussault or someone else, to meet him there."

"Let in through the fire escape so no one could see."

"Could be."

"But again, why kill Monsieur Plessner before the evidence was found? The place was turned upside down. Plessner obviously hadn't handed it over."

"Maybe he suspected something," said Gamache. "Maybe Plessner refused to do it, and was shot trying to get away."

Some of the pieces fit.

Some did not.

"So, to recap," said Beauvoir. "There might or might not be something wrong with the Luxembourg project, GHS might or might not be involved, Alexander Plessner might or might not have been working with Stephen to expose some wrongdoing. And the Prefect of Police might or might not be involved."

"Exactly," said Gamache.

"You know," said Beauvoir. "Can't say I really miss homicide investigations."

Gamache gave a small grunt of amusement.

They'd arrived at the elevator, Beauvoir blanched. "You first."

"I'll take the stairs, *merci*," said Gamache.

"Me, too."

Beauvoir took them two at a time, arriving at the top wheezing.

Gamache walked up slowly. Arriving at the top with another question.

Could Stephen have discovered Alexander Plessner, his friend and colleague, ransacking his apartment, and killed him? Is that what he was doing in the hours before dinner?

CHAPTER 21

⁓

O h, God," said Annie, lowering herself into the armchair in her living room. "That feels better."

She and Honoré had had their naps, then invited Daniel and Roslyn and the girls around for tea.

"Okay," she said, looking at her brother. "What's going on?"

"What do you mean?"

"Your answers to the investigator. Not very satisfactory."

"She practically accused me, us, of killing Stephen for his money. That didn't upset you?"

"She had to ask," said Annie. "They're legitimate questions. We know the truth."

"Tell that to Dad. He piled on fast enough."

"He was trying to save you, you asshole. Sorry, it's the baby talking." She placed her hand on her belly.

"Are you carrying the anti-Christ?" Daniel asked, and Annie laughed.

"Dad just wanted to give you another chance to say what everyone in that room, especially the cops, knew to be true. That corporations get away with murder."

"Still, he could've let it go, but instead he deliberately made me look bad."

"Really? You can't believe that, you fuckhead."

"The baby again?" asked Roslyn.

"No, that was all me," said Annie. "You made yourself look bad, and while we're on the subject, the baby wants to know how the hell you can afford that new apartment?"

"You want to know?" said Daniel, getting red in the face. His daughters looked over, and he took a deep breath to calm himself.

Lowering his voice, and making his tone friendly, he said, "It's none of your business, but I'll tell you anyway." As he spoke, he ticked the points off on his fingers. "We saved up. I got a raise. Ros has a great job, and I get a favorable mortgage rate from my own bank. Satisfied?"

"I'm happy for you. For both of you. I really am. But you have to see that it looks suspicious. Why didn't you tell the cops all this? It looks like you knew you were going to come into money when Stephen died. Dad was trying to help you."

Daniel shook his head.

Honoré walked over to Daniel, offering his uncle the toy duck his godmother, Ruth, had given him when they'd left Québec.

When squeezed, it said "duck." They thought. They hoped.

"*Merci*," said Daniel, taking it. He squeezed it twice and Honoré laughed.

"I need to call work," Daniel said, getting up.

She watched him leave the room, the phone to his ear.

Then Annie pulled out her own phone and made a call.

"I'm afraid you can't come in, sir," said the gendarme guarding the door to Stephen's apartment.

"Is it possible to speak to the agent in charge?" asked Gamache.

"He's busy."

Beauvoir was about to say something, but Gamache stopped him. Bringing out his wallet, he handed the agent his card.

"Do you mind giving him this, please?"

The cop glanced at it. Unimpressed. A lowly chief inspector, from Québec.

"*Un moment*," he said and swung the door shut in their faces.

"Well," said Beauvoir, "this's humbling. For you."

Gamache smiled. "Humility leads to Enlightenment, Grasshopper."

"Well, you are brilliant, *patron*."

The door was opened a moment later and a plain-clothed officer in his mid-forties stood there.

"*Désolé*," he said, putting out his hand. "Inspector Juneau, Stefan Juneau."

"Armand Gamache. This's my former second-in-command, Jean-Guy Beauvoir. He now works in Paris."

"For us?"

"No, for a private company."

"A security firm? SecurForte?"

"No, GHS Engineering."

"*Ah, oui?*" said Juneau, walking into the apartment as they followed. "Out at La Défense?"

"Yes."

Juneau stopped in the hall. "Commander Fontaine filled me in on what happened last night and this morning." He dropped his voice. "Please forgive Agent Calmut. He's young and, frankly, just a little stupid. I'm having him flogged as we speak. How can I help?"

Gamache could actually see the young officer going through the pile of books flung onto the floor.

"We'd like to take a look around the apartment, if you don't mind. I know it well. It might be some help to you."

"Absolutely. Are you looking for something in particular?"

"Not really. I was here earlier, but I thought it might be helpful to come back. Get a better look. Have you spoken to the neighbors yet?"

"Yes. No one heard or saw anything. The concierges are next on my list."

Gamache and Beauvoir were given gloves and the freedom to roam the apartment.

"It looks worse now than this morning," said Beauvoir as they picked their way through the mess in the living room.

Beauvoir watched as his father-in-law took several photos of the room, then moved aside a chair to get at a large oil painting. Leaning it against the wall, he stared at it. Then he turned it around and looked at the brown paper, slashed to expose the canvas behind.

Another painting was examined, the front and back photographed by Gamache.

"We did wonder if the intruder found something hidden behind the paintings," said Juneau, joining them.

"I don't think so," said Gamache as he put a Rothko back on the wall.

"Why not?" asked Juneau.

"Because the intruder kept searching after he'd slashed them," said Beauvoir.

He pointed to the remaining art on the floor. Some almost hidden beneath splayed books and pillows.

"Good point," said Juneau. Though he didn't sound so happy that the Québec guy had seen it and he hadn't.

Gamache spent the next few minutes digging out the paintings, photographing them, and replacing them on the wall.

Juneau walked over to Beauvoir. "Is he okay?"

Gamache was just standing there, staring at the paintings.

"Ça va, patron?" asked Beauvoir.

"Yes, yes," said Gamache. "Everything's fine."

Though he sounded distracted. Not exactly upset, but definitely preoccupied as he returned to the art.

Then he looked at his watch and turned abruptly. "I'm afraid I haven't been any help. I can't see that anything's missing." He stripped off the gloves and held out his hand to Juneau. "We need to be going. Thank you for your understanding."

"Thank you, Chief Inspector."

"If the backs of the paintings were slashed, that means the intruder thought something was hidden there," said Beauvoir as they left. "Papers. Documents."

"I agree," said Gamache. "The paintings are important."

Annie Gamache was staring out their apartment window at the Tour Eiffel in the distance.

Daniel, Roslyn, and the girls had left, and Honoré was sitting at his little table having applesauce.

Her hands rested naturally, protectively, on her belly. On her baby. Their daughter.

She dropped her eyes to the fromagerie across the street. At least soon she'd be able to eat all the cheese. And she planned to.

Then she stood up straighter.

There he was. She'd spotted him earlier and now there he was again. The man. Looking up. At the window. At her. There was no mistaking it this time.

She grabbed her phone, but by the time she brought up the camera he was gone.

Just then her phone rang. It was the office returning her call.

Annie listened, interrupting only once to ask, "Are you sure?"

Hanging up, she sank into a chair.

From across the room came the sound of Honoré's squeeze toy. Saying what they all feared and suspected.

"I agree," she said to him. "This's all ducked up."

CHAPTER 22

⁓

Jean-Guy stared at the printout.

"Holy Mother of God," he said, and looked up into the steady eyes of the General Manager of the George V. "You charge that much for a pot of coffee?"

"Service is included," said Jacqueline Béland.

She'd joined them in Stephen's suite, at Gamache's request, and brought the statement of room charges with her. Also at his request.

"How many people were serving this coffee?" Beauvoir asked, his voice almost squeaky with shock. "How big is the pot? Have you seen the total, *patron*? Thank God Stephen's good for it."

"Yes," said Gamache, not bothering to tell Jean-Guy that he and Reine-Marie were covering the bill. Though he had discouraged Beauvoir from ordering up a club sandwich.

"Look," said Gamache, running his finger down the first sheet, then turning it over. There were three sheets of room charges. "Stephen ate all his meals in his room. Alone. For ten days. But look at this."

He pointed to the day before. In the afternoon. There was a room charge for two beers. Stephen's usual and an Abbaye de Leffe beer.

"He had company," said Jean-Guy, examining the bill. "The beers were ordered up after he left the Lutetia at four, and before he met us at Juveniles."

"*Oui.* This's where he was for at least part of the time." Gamache turned to Madame Béland. "He made a note of Plessner's arrival, before dinner."

He brought out Stephen's agenda to double-check, and there it was. *AFP.* Alexander Francis Plessner.

"You have security cameras?" Jean-Guy asked the General Manager.

"Many, yes. Everywhere except the actual guest rooms."

"We'll need to see the footage."

"I'll have my assistant bring up my laptop and we can view it here," she said, understanding their need for privacy. And speed.

She placed the call.

"Do you know an Alexander Plessner?" Beauvoir asked.

"No. The Inspector in charge showed me a picture of him." She paused. "Is he . . . ?"

"So he wasn't staying here?" asked Gamache.

"No. I looked him up. No one named Alexander Plessner has stayed here. He might've visited, of course."

Neither Beauvoir nor Gamache mentioned that Plessner was in fact a guest. And staying in this very suite.

"How about Eugénie Roquebrune?" Beauvoir asked.

"The head of GHS Engineering? I've heard of her, but we've never met. Not that I haven't tried."

"Why would you?" asked Gamache.

"Because I'd like her business. Their account would be worth hundreds of thousands of euros a year."

"But you don't have it?" asked Beauvoir. "Their account, I mean."

"*Non.*"

Just then there was a quiet knock on the door and a young man with a laptop appeared. Sitting at the long dining table, Madame Béland opened it up and logged in.

"What day and time are you interested in?" she asked.

"Yesterday," said Beauvoir, sitting on her other side and looking at the screen. "From four o'clock on."

"We have a lot of cameras," she explained as she tapped keys. "Even knowing what date and time you need to see, it'll take hours to go through them all."

"Just the main entrance," said Gamache.

Within a minute the image and time stamp popped up.

They watched for a few minutes at double speed. People whizzing in and out, their now frantic movements made comical. Then Beauvoir said, "Stop. Back up slightly. There." The image froze. "Stephen."

The time was 4:53.

Armand leaned closer.

Stephen looked haggard. More tired, Armand thought, than when they'd parted.

The video started again. Stephen walked across the Art Deco lobby and disappeared.

He was alone.

"Can we see where he went?" Gamache asked.

Madame Béland hit more keys. They were able to track Stephen's progress through the lobby, down the hall to the right. Through the large open room where elegantly dressed men and women were having afternoon tea or drinks. Stephen looked around before heading down the hall to the bank of elevators.

Madame Béland brought up the camera outside his suite. The elevator doors opened, and Stephen stepped out and disappeared into his suite.

"Can you go back? To the elevator?" asked Gamache.

Madame Béland did.

"Stop, please," said Gamache.

There, frozen on the screen, was Stephen. Alone in the elevator. Armand realized he'd never actually seen his godfather when he thought no one was looking.

And what he saw was a very elderly man. Grim. Vulnerable. Determined. Afraid.

A Burgher of Calais in the George V elevator.

"Is that such a good idea, sir," asked Irena Fontaine. "To take everything?"

Claude Dussault smiled at her as he replaced items in the box.

"We've been through it, more than once, and didn't find anything. It's possible Monsieur Gamache will. And I suspect he'd notice if anything's missing. Even this."

He held up a screw, then dropped it into the box.

"We need to go back to the front door," said Beauvoir. "See who else arrived. Who Stephen was expecting. He ordered that second beer for someone."

The video played. They saw guests and visitors and staff entering and exiting. And then they saw him.

At 5:26 Alexander Plessner walked confidently through the lobby of the grand hotel, a satchel over his shoulder.

"He must've come straight from the airport," said Beauvoir.

A hotel official stopped Plessner, and they watched as the older man chattered, gesturing toward the hotel bar. The official nodded and watched him walk away.

"Your security?" asked Gamache.

"Yes. Private firm. Very good. Trained to be courteous, and to take down an assassin."

Beauvoir raised his brows. "Has that happened often?"

"Once. And two kidnapping attempts. We also get a lot of protesters. Our clientele are rich and powerful. We take security seriously."

"As I saw," said Gamache. "Your people came up quickly, to see who we were."

"Yes, well, not fast enough. We're looking into that. Had you been intent on harm, you might have gotten away with it."

But looking at the man, she understood how he and his wife got past security in the lobby. He managed to look both authoritative and trustworthy. Here was a man who naturally belonged.

It would take an extraordinary person to challenge him. And, once challenged, to stop him.

Now, the other fellow? She looked at Beauvoir. Handsome, she thought. But there was something almost wild about him. As though he was just pretending to be civilized.

Yes, he'd be stopped. Though if he wanted to get by, or through, their security, she had no doubt he would do so. But it wouldn't be subtle and it wouldn't be pretty.

On the screen, they watched Plessner take the same route as Stephen. A minute later he entered the suite.

Madame Béland put it into double speed. The beers arrived. The time stamp said 7:14 when the door opened again and Plessner stepped out. At the door Stephen said something.

They zoomed in.

"Looks like," said Beauvoir, leaning close, "'Good luck.' But I can't make out the rest."

"Monsieur Horowitz is saying, 'Text me when you have it.'" They looked at Madame Béland, who explained. "You get good at lip-reading in my job."

"Stephen checked his phone a few times over dinner," said Jean-Guy. "That explains why."

He also, Armand knew, had his phone in his hand when he was hit.

It became even more frustrating that the chip was smashed and they couldn't retrieve his messages. Had Plessner managed to get something off before he was killed?

On the screen, they followed Monsieur Plessner out of the hotel. And to his death.

Gamache's brow furrowed. He always found it moving to see someone in the final images. Oblivious to what was awaiting them.

They continued to watch the door, but no one followed him.

On the exterior camera the doorman waved over a taxi and Plessner got in.

At 7:53 Stephen himself left. He'd changed into a slightly more formal suit. Before getting into a taxi, he checked his phone.

"Is there a way to know if the video has been tampered with?" Gamache asked.

The GM looked at him, astonished, but didn't argue the point. "Well, yes. There's a time stamp generator. If it was edited, there'd be a slight fluctuation when it was reset. The time would appear to be correct, but the video would speed up slightly to catch up with the piece that was removed."

"Can you check, please?"

"It'll take a few minutes."

While Madame Béland did that, Jean-Guy brought out his phone and Armand nodded.

Leaving her in the living room, they went upstairs to the study.

Armand closed the door. Jean-Guy tapped his phone, and the video of the disappearing messages began to play.

Reine-Marie picked up the phone on the first ring.

"Annie?"

"No, it's not time, Maman." For the past week every time she had called, her mother asked, *Is it time?* "But can you come over?"

"Is everything all right? Are you all right?"

"Yes, but I just need to show you something."

"I'll be right there."

Reine-Marie threw on a coat and left behind all the things that still needed doing for their dinner that night with the Dussaults.

The emails between Beauvoir's boss, Carole Gossette, and the Luxembourg project engineer were ambiguous.

"See here," said Beauvoir. "She writes, *We need to be careful. We don't want anything to go wrong.* That could mean anything. Could mean there's a cover-up."

"Or it could mean the opposite," said Gamache. "That she's making sure all the plans, all the safety measures, are in place." He shook his head. "Go back to the previous email, please."

They leaned in. But it was blurred on Beauvoir's camera.

"Looks like they're talking about something unique." Gamache pointed to a word. "Is that word 'not'? Is she saying it's not unique?"

"I can't tell. But again, he could be referring to the weather for all we know. Or some government official who was actually helpful."

Gamache took a long, deep breath. Then, exhaling, he took off his glasses and stepped away. "We need to send these to Lacoste back at the Sûreté. They can get a clearer picture."

Just then Madame Béland called up the stairs. "Got something."

Reine-Marie read the email from Annie's office, about their dealings with Alexander Francis Plessner.

Then she raised her eyes to her daughter.

"What should we do?" Annie asked. "Should we talk to him?"

Reine-Marie shook her head.

"We can't go to the police," said Annie, her voice rising.

"No, of course not." At least that much was clear. "But we do need to tell your father."

"And Jean-Guy."

"Yes. Do you two have plans tonight?"

"No."

"We have guests. I've asked the Prefect of Police and his wife for dinner. We'll call you when they've left."

Gamache and Beauvoir stared at the screen.

"There," said Madame Béland.

They had to watch it three times before seeing what she saw. The slightest fluctuation.

"If I slow down the time stamp, you can see it jumps one one-hundredth of a second. That's where they made the splice."

"On all the cameras?" asked Beauvoir. He was almost cross-eyed by now and had to open his eyes wide, then screw them shut just to see her properly.

"No. The ones in the elevators and outside Monsieur Horowitz's suite haven't been tampered with. Only the ones in the lobby, then into the Galerie lounge."

"So what happened in the Galerie?" asked Jean-Guy. "Something did. Yesterday at . . . ?"

"At about five o'clock," said Madame Béland. "That's when the edits were made."

"Who could do this?" asked Gamache. "Who has the access and the ability?"

"Well . . ." She took off her own glasses. Now she looked both bleary and weary. "Obviously, I could. But didn't. The videos are in a virtual library. Our security oversees all that. But unfortunately, where humans are involved nothing is completely safe and secure."

"You have your own private security," said Beauvoir. "Could they do it?"

"Well, yes. They're trained in many things, including cybersecurity. It's not just about muscle anymore."

"Who trains them?" asked Beauvoir.

"Mossad. Spetsnaz," she said with a smile. "They train the best, and once finished there, we hire them."

"GIGN?" asked Gamache.

"Preferably, yes," said Madame Béland. "We ask for them specifically because they already speak French and know Paris well."

"Is there any way to know how much was taken out and restore it?" Jean-Guy asked.

"You know," she said, "I'm not sure. This's never happened to me before. I'll try to find out."

"*Bon,*" said Gamache. "Can you back up what's left so we don't lose more?"

"Already have, Chief Inspector. I'll send you a link."

"*Merci.* And please don't tell anyone about this."

"The investigators from the Préfecture might ask to see the security video. I'm actually a little surprised they haven't."

So were Beauvoir and Gamache.

"Can you show them without volunteering this information?" Beauvoir asked.

She thought, then nodded. "But if they ask outright, I'll have to tell them."

"Understood, but keep it to yourself if you can," said Gamache. "The firm who does your security, who is that?"

"SecurForte."

"That sounds familiar," said Gamache.

"Stephen's apartment," murmured Jean-Guy. "The flic."

Gamache nodded. Yes, the investigator in charge had asked Jean-Guy if he'd joined SecurForte. It was obviously well-known to the Paris police.

After she left, Gamache looked at the time. Almost six. Far later than he'd thought.

"We need to go," he said.

"I forgot to ask her one question," said Beauvoir.

"We can stop in on the way out," said Armand.

"Not important. I was just surprised that the George V uses Ikea furniture."

"Why do you say that?"

He looked at his father-in-law with amusement. "Have you never put together an Ikea bookcase or desk?"

"Actually, yes. For both Daniel and Annie when they went away to university. Clever design but almost drove us mad."

"Then you must've recognized the screw and Allen wrench. They're Ikea."

"Huh, you're right. Though others use Allen wrenches."

They were at the door, but Armand stopped, turned, and walked up the stairs to the office area. Beauvoir followed.

"It's certainly not Ikea," said Armand, and even Jean-Guy could see that.

It was a fine original Louis XV desk.

Armand pulled out the drawer and looked under it. But there was nothing there.

"Have you ever actually found anything taped under a drawer?" Jean-Guy asked.

"*Non.* But wouldn't it be nice?"

"A note, maybe, saying, *The murderer is . . .*"

Gamache laughed. "Seems we'll have to do this the hard way."

"You mean I do all the work while you sit on a bench sipping Pernod?"

"Good God, young man. What've you been reading? Pernod? Never had one in my life. Now, a nice lager . . ." He looked at Beauvoir. "Shouldn't you be doing something useful?"

"Come along, old man. I have to get you home to your wife."

"And I to yours."

Beauvoir wasn't fooled by this. In the taxi back, he could see Armand staring out as the wide boulevards slid past. A slight furrow between his brows.

Thinking. Always thinking. Though it wasn't the thoughts that had created the lines in his face, Jean-Guy knew. It was the feelings.

Then Armand roused himself and sent off a few emails, including, Jean-Guy noticed, one back home to their neighbor in Three Pines, Clara Morrow. Checking on the dogs and whatever little Gracie was, thought Beauvoir, as he went back to his phone and got caught up on his own messages.

Armand got out at the hospital, while Beauvoir continued on home.

After sitting with Stephen for a few moments, reading the news and telling him about the day, Armand put on his coat, wrapped the scarf around his neck, and walked out into the fresh air and gaiety of Paris on a Saturday evening. He passed young couples, arms linked, on their way to a brasserie. Or to a tiny walk-up apartment. A hot plate, a small table by the window. A bed. And Paris.

All they could possibly need.

Ah, yes, he thought. *I remember it well.*

Armand paused in front of Notre-Dame, and tried to see beyond the scaffolding to the remarkable face of the cathedral. He could see the huge rose window that had, incredibly, survived the fire. It looked, behind the works, like a giant third eye. Gazing perpetually out at the City of Light and its citizens, while also gazing inward, at their motivations, their characters, their hearts and souls.

He wondered if that was why the great cathedral had burst into flames.

Then he placed the call he was loath to make.

"Mrs. McGillicuddy? No, he's still with us. Holding on. Yes. But I need to know something. The terms of Stephen's will." He listened while she protested, then said quietly, "I agree. It's an awful thing to ask, but I need to know. Yes. I'll wait."

The early evening was growing chilly as the sun set. The spires and monuments and museums were outlined against the soft shifting pinks of the sky.

"*Oui*, I'm still here."

He listened. Then, thanking her, he dropped his head and sighed. Before lifting his gaze to the rose window.

Once home, Jean-Guy could see right away that Annie was stressed.

"What is it? The baby?" His voice rose on the last two words.

"No. I think someone's watching the apartment, Jean-Guy."

He took three quick strides over to the window. There was no one there. But it was getting dark, and the shadows between the buildings hid all sorts of things. And people.

"A cop has been assigned to protect you. It's probably them. But I'm going to make sure."

From the window, Annie saw her husband run across the narrow street, darting in and out of alleys and looking into doorways.

Then he looked up at her and shook his head.

"Nothing," he confirmed when he got back. "Not even the god-damned flic."

"Why would one be protecting us?"

"Just to be extra safe. You're kinda important, you know."

She smiled. "I'm sorry. I must've been imagining things."

"Well, you're not the only one," he said, holding her close.

Her next words came to him muffled by his jacket.

"There's something else. Something I didn't imagine."

CHAPTER 23

—

"A hostess gift?" Reine-Marie asked, eyeing the familiar hospital box Claude Dussault held. "Too kind."

"Yes, Madame, but I need it back," said Dussault.

"That's the gift part," said Monique Dussault, who was standing just behind her husband.

Armand took the box from Claude as Reine-Marie laughed.

She kissed Monique, who was carefully holding a much smaller box. This one had the familiar logo of Pâtisserie Pierre Hermé.

"Is it . . . ?" she began.

"An Ispahan? *Oui.*"

Both women sighed.

"You'd have thought George Clooney was in the box," said Claude.

"Better," said Monique. "Oh, something smells delicious."

The Gamaches' small apartment, with its wooden beams, fresh white walls, and large windows, was already welcoming, but the scent of garlic and basil made it even more so.

"Just a simple pasta dinner," said Reine-Marie. "As I said, *en famille.*"

"I also brought these, Madame." The Prefect of Police pulled two wine bottles wrapped in brown paper out of his deep pockets.

"Ahhh," said Reine-Marie. In a regal voice she pronounced, "You may stay."

Claude laughed, then turned to his wife. "Just wait until she realizes the pastry box is empty. *Sauve qui peut.*"

Now it was Reine-Marie's turn to smile. They didn't see the Dussaults socially all that often, and now she wondered why not. She liked them. A lot. And so did Armand.

But when she leaned in to kiss Claude on both cheeks, it all came flooding back. And she remembered why they were actually there. Not as friends, but—

His scent washed over her and brought with it, on the tide, Alexander Plessner's body.

The uninvited guest lay sprawled in front of her, as real at that moment as any of the living ones.

She struggled to keep her smile as she and Armand walked their guests into the living room.

They sat in front of the gentle fire in the grate, lit more for comfort than heat, and over drinks and dinner they talked about children and grandchildren. About books and plays. About newly discovered restaurants.

About anything other than Stephen and Monsieur Plessner, who sat at the table with them. Staring at her. Waiting for her to ask the question.

But it wasn't time yet.

Now the conversation turned to retirement plans.

Reine-Marie, having stepped down as head of the Bibliothèque et Archives nationales du Québec, told them of her new passion.

"I'm a freelance researcher."

"What does that mean?" asked Monique as she dabbed a piece of baguette into the last of her pasta sauce.

"People hire me to track down information on items, documents, photographs."

"Like genealogy?" asked Claude.

"*Non*, others can do that," she said. "Suppose a relative dies, and in sorting through their things you find something strange, unexpected. I can find out more about it."

"And you, Monique?" asked Armand. "Any plans?"

If they'd noticed he'd changed the subject, they didn't show it.

Monique, it turned out, was considering cutting back her hours in the clinic.

"We've just bought a place in Saint-Paul-de-Vence," she said. "Our daughter is close by, and there's an airport in Nice for Claude."

"You'd commute?" asked Armand, pouring more wine, then bringing out the cheeses he'd picked up on rue Geoffroy l'Angevin on his way home.

"*Non, non.* At least, not to my current job," said Claude, spreading creamy Pont l'Évêque onto a water biscuit. "This's after I retire. Like Reine-Marie, I might pick up the odd private commission. Always a market for certain skills, right, Armand?"

"Are you talking about the saxophone?"

Monique laughed. As did Reine-Marie, but Armand kept his eyes on Claude. He knew exactly what skills he was talking about.

When the cheese course was finished, Reine-Marie suggested they take a break. The others rose as she got up.

"We can have coffee and dessert in the living room." She spoke as though it was a whole separate room, where, in fact, the round dining table shared space with the comfortable sofa and armchairs in front of the muttering fire.

They helped clear the table. Then Reine-Marie ushered the men out. "Go. Have your cigars and plan the storming of the Bastille."

"We will do as we're told," said Claude, "though it's possible, Madame, you have spent a little too much time in archives. Now, Armand," they heard him say as the men took their drinks and left the kitchen. "Which side of the barricades would you be on, if we were at the storming of the Bastille?"

"Need you ask?" said Armand.

While Claude's tone was light, his eyes were sharp, searching. It seemed more than just a silly question.

And Armand had the uncomfortable impression the two old friends would, in fact, find themselves on opposite sides. Not a problem when it was simply a political disagreement. It became a big problem when it meant trying to kill each other.

Once back in the living room, he refreshed Claude's glass, but left his as it was. He'd had enough and needed to remain as clearheaded as his weary brain would allow.

When he'd gotten home with the provisions, he'd gone to take off his coat, only to remember at the last minute that he had something in his pocket.

"This's for you," he said, handing Reine-Marie the wax paper filled with *pain au citron* crumbs. "From Madame Faubourg."

She took it with a smile.

He longed to talk with her. To just be with her, quietly. To sink into an armchair, with a cup of tea, and go over the events of their day since he'd last seen her. To hear about her day and tell her about his.

About the edited security video.

The mounting evidence that Stephen had discovered something about GHS and its funicular project in Luxembourg.

And then there were the records and photograph Commander Fontaine had produced, throwing suspicion on Stephen during the war.

But he only had time for a quick shower and change of clothes before the Dussaults arrived.

If anyone could get at the truth of those documents from the archives, it was Reine-Marie. Which was why he'd cut off discussion of her particular skill set. Better if the Prefect didn't realize just how good Reine-Marie really was.

He hoped that Claude, his old friend, wasn't involved. But if ever there was a time for caution, it was now.

For her part, Reine-Marie was equally anxious to tell Armand what she'd heard from Annie. And about the box hidden in their dresser drawer.

But first, she had to know if she was right.

Annie had gone to bed, and Honoré was tucked in and fast asleep.

Jean-Guy lingered in the doorway, looking at the boy sleeping so soundly.

Then his eyes drifted to the crib. With the mobile over it that he'd installed. Winged unicorns and stars and rainbows would dance over his daughter's head, while it played Brahms's Lullaby.

There was the comfortable chair in the corner, for Annie to nurse.

And where Jean-Guy imagined holding their daughter and singing the songs his own mother had sung to him.

Les berceuses québécoises.

"It snows on the wood and on the river," Jean-Guy sang softly to the empty crib. *"A little one, just like you, we will deliver. It is a mystery."*

He left the bedroom door open a crack and returned to the living room. Imagining the soft snow that would soon be falling on the forests and the near-frozen rivers. Back home.

It is a mystery, he hummed.

What Annie had told him was deeply disturbing, though he tried not to overinterpret.

Instead, after checking out the window yet again and muttering, "Fucking flics," he sat at his computer. There was a message from Isabelle Lacoste, back in Montréal.

They were cleaning up the blurry video, in hopes of making more sense of the emails he'd recorded.

She'd also sent the plans for the Luxembourg funicular to their contact at the École polytechnique, to see if anything was off.

Beauvoir couldn't bring himself to believe that Carole Gossette was involved. Nor did he really believe that GHS was the culprit. It still looked to him like they were being set up.

But he was also beginning to realize that he might not know as much about GHS as he'd thought.

He started a search. Finally, after digging and digging and finding nothing beyond what he already knew about his company, he changed course and tried something else.

And there, in an article by Agence France-Presse, he found it.

Printed in an obscure American paramilitary magazine several years earlier was a small piece not on GHS Engineering, but on its president, Eugénie Roquebrune.

Accompanying the item was a studio photo of an elegant middle-aged woman. The telling detail about the woman wasn't her intelligent eyes or her warm smile. It was her hair. It was gray, almost white.

Beauvoir was beginning to understand that this was the ultimate power move by a female executive in Paris.

It signaled she did not need to impress anyone. Eugénie Roque-brune could be, would be, herself.

The article said that she ran a corporation with engineering projects around the world. But the point of the article was that, because of global unrest, they'd just bought a boutique security and intelligence firm. Which was recruiting.

SecurForte.

His eyes widened. Wasn't that the one George V used? And the one that cop mentioned?

Jean-Guy stared at the insignia on the screen. He recognized the design. He'd seen it on the uniform of the guard Loiselle.

The emblem was unmistakable because it was unusual. It was delicate, even pretty, and looked like a snowflake.

It wasn't the sort of macho, aggressive insignia you'd expect with a private security contractor. Screaming eagles. Pouncing panthers. A death's-head skull.

This was the logo equivalent of the CEO's hair. The message being, SecurForte was too powerful to need to impress.

Besides, Jean-Guy Beauvoir, who'd grown up in Québec winters, knew that a snowflake might look harmless, but it was a harbinger, a warning, of worse to come. The snowflake-like emblem of Secur-Forte was in fact quietly terrifying. Mostly because it wasn't trying to terrify.

Was GHS using its security company to gain access to competitors' files and projects?

What corporations, what hotels, restaurants, clubs, might it work for? What information could it collect, both professional and personal?

Is that what Stephen and Plessner had discovered? A vast network of industrial espionage? Even blackmail?

Jean-Guy leaned forward and began digging again. Digging deeper.

Armand picked up the screw, examined it, then replaced it in the box.

"Those were in the desk, I imagine," said Claude, watching his host.

"On the desk, yes. Thank you for bringing the box. Have you found anything?"

"No, though the password for this"—Claude held up Stephen's laptop—"would help."

"And I happen to have it." Armand retrieved his notebook, and, writing the word down, he ripped the page off and gave it to Claude, who read it with surprise but without comment.

Lutetia.

"*Merci.*" Claude Dussault put the paper in his pocket.

"Aren't you going to try it?" asked Armand.

"*Non.* It'll take hours to go through the laptop and analyze what's on it. I'll hand this over to Fontaine."

Armand went back to the box and brought out the GHS annual report. The first page had a greeting accompanied by a photo of the president, Eugénie Roquebrune, as she nursed peregrine falcon chicks. And another of her releasing baby sea turtles into the ocean.

Madame Roquebrune, even in these rustic surroundings, managed to look elegant, with her perfect, and lightly applied, makeup, and her beautifully done gray hair. Not unlike, he thought, Reine-Marie.

Though these photos were filled with artifice. Reine-Marie had none of that.

Then he turned to the list of board members and raised his brows. "Impressive."

"Incredibly so, *oui*," agreed Claude. "Do you mind?"

He indicated his jacket, and Armand said no. It was indeed quite warm in the apartment.

Armand scanned the rest of the report while Claude got up and took off his jacket, then wandered the room, examining the paintings on the wall and the books on the shelves. He drifted, apparently aimlessly, over to the tall windows and, pulling aside the lace curtains, looked down onto the street below.

The annual report was upbeat in its broad statements about the financial success of the past year. It described the engineering giant's ongoing commitment to the environment. To improving lives in developing nations. To equality. Sustainability. And to profit.

But there was precious little hard information. And no list of its actual projects or holdings.

When he'd finished, Armand took off his reading glasses and rubbed his eyes.

"Not much here. I wonder why Stephen was interested in it. I've read a few annual reports in my time, and most are far more informative."

As Claude returned to his seat, Armand noticed a small stain on his shirt, on the inside of his left elbow.

A bloodstain. Plessner's blood?

"It's probably just the corporate culture," said Claude. "Secretive."

"But that begs the question—"

"What're they hiding?" asked Dussault.

"Yes."

"You must be excited about the baby," said Monique.

"We are." Reine-Marie plugged in the old percolator.

She was suddenly exhausted, and just wanted them to go home so that she and Armand could talk, then go to bed. Bed. Bed.

But there was too much still to do before that could happen.

The aroma of coffee filled the tiny kitchen, and she watched as Monique sliced the bright pink Ispahan cake. The sharp knife cut through the layers of macaron and rose and raspberry cream.

Alexander Plessner stood at the doorway, watching her. Reine-Marie nodded acknowledgment and, taking a deep breath, she turned to Monique.

"Our anniversary is coming up, and I'm looking for a gift for Armand. Please, please don't tell him, or Claude, that I asked, but I noticed Claude's cologne and really like it."

"You do? I think it smells like bark. And mud. I like Armand's. A lot. What is it?"

"Sandalwood."

"You're not thinking of having him switch, are you?"

"Well, it's just that sometimes it's nice to have a choice. What is Claude's cologne?"

"Something his second-in-command gave him a few years ago after they'd been to a conference in Cologne together. His number two bought a bottle for each of them when they toured the factory where it's made. Have you ever been to Cologne? Beautiful city. Or at least once was. All but destroyed in the war."

This conversation was hardly linear, and Reine-Marie wondered if she could continue to steer it back to a stinky cologne when there were other more interesting topics on the table.

One more try.

"He and his second-in-command wear the same scent?"

She knew the Prefect's second-in-command was a woman, Irena Fontaine, the investigator who met them at Daniel's apartment.

She was a protégé of the Prefect. They were obviously close, professionally, but this sharing of scents seemed a little beyond that.

"Oh, yes. Claude doesn't wear it all the time, thankfully. Only when they're going to meet."

Reine-Marie stared at Monique. Didn't she see how convenient this was? If Claude came home after this "meeting" smelling like his younger, female second-in-command, there would be no suspicion.

But this wasn't her business. And maybe there was nothing there.

After all, Armand's new number two was also a young woman. Isabelle Lacoste. She'd become a close family friend. A cherished and valued colleague. He'd brought her into homicide and mentored her. Isabelle had repaid Armand by saving his life, at a terrible personal cost to herself.

They were like father and daughter. There was never any suspicion of more between them.

But then, Reine-Marie didn't know Monique's husband as well as she knew her own.

"Do you know the name of the cologne?" Reine-Marie asked again, casually.

"No, but I can tell you the bottle looks more like booze than scent. It's quite ornate. Attractive, actually. The only thing I do like about it.

Oh, wait. It's not a name, it's a number. Made me laugh. I thought it said *112* at first. Seemed appropriate."

Yes, thought Reine-Marie as she put the coffeepot on the tray. 112 was the French emergency number. Alarms should be going off for Monique Dussault.

"Maybe we can find it," said Reine-Marie, reaching for her iPhone on the counter.

She put in *cologne from Cologne* and up popped the image of a blue-and-gold box.

"Yes, that's it," said Monique. "It's called 4711. I knew it was a number. Says here it's the first cologne ever made. Ha, probably why Claude wears it. He loves history. As does Armand. Something they have in common."

"*Oui,*" said Reine-Marie.

As she closed the phone, she thought it might be the only thing the two men had in common.

The cologne was exactly the same as the one hidden in their bedroom. She'd confirmed the scent. But in doing that, she'd uncovered another, more important question.

Was it Claude Dussault they'd surprised in Stephen's apartment or Irena Fontaine?

Jean-Guy got up from his laptop and went to the open window. He scanned the dark street below and breathed in the fresh night air. Trying to clear his mind. To get the clutter out and to see more clearly the connections that were appearing.

SecurForte was the link.

The security firm owned by GHS Engineering. It looked after security at the George V and almost certainly the Lutetia.

And where else?

He looked at his watch. Almost ten. He'd call the Gamaches at ten thirty. By then their guests might be gone.

Returning to his laptop he clicked on the link the GM of the George V had sent, to access the tapes from the hotel cameras. They'd been edited, almost certainly by SecurForte. To hide something or someone.

But it had to have been done quickly, and something might have been missed.

And sure enough, after twenty-five minutes of going back and forth, he found something. Someone.

Not Stephen. Not Alexander Francis Plessner.

What he found was a grainy image of a gray-haired, elegant woman.

She was just emerging from behind a huge floral arrangement in the lobby. It was a split second of tape they'd failed to erase.

There was no mistaking Eugénie Roquebrune, the president of GHS, entering the George V yesterday afternoon. She was there one moment, then the next there was no trace of her on the video. She'd disappeared.

But why was she there, and why had she been erased? Could she have been the one Stephen was meeting before dinner Friday night?

He got up and walked around the living room, unable to settle. What could this mean?

Had Stephen sat across from her, looked her in the eyes, and told the president of GHS Engineering that he'd found out about their industrial espionage?

Was that what he was going to announce at the board meeting on Monday?

Is that why they tried to have him killed? That might explain the lack of finesse in both attacks. They were ordered at the last minute.

But something wasn't quite right.

For a man who'd survived the war as a member of the Resistance. Who'd been cunning then and throughout his long life. Why would he make such a foolish strategic error now? Effectively signing his own death warrant.

Presumably he was in the George V to hide. Why invite over the very person he was hiding from?

After another circuit of the small living room, Jean-Guy sat back down and went through the video again. The lobby. The hallway to the elevator. The elevators, including the service elevators.

Nothing. Eugénie Roquebrune had disappeared.

He broadened the search.

And that's where he found her. In the reflection of a waiter's large silver tray. Polished and gleaming. It showed, for 2.7 seconds, three guests at a private corner table in the Galerie lounge.

The head of GHS Engineering sat with two male companions. Stephen Horowitz and Alexander Plessner?

Back and forth Jean-Guy went, over and over the footage. Until he was certain that he recognized one of the men at the table.

Just hours before the attacks, Claude Dussault, the Prefect of Police, was having tea with Eugénie Roquebrune.

Beauvoir got to his feet. It was almost ten thirty. He could call, but . . .

Dussault was at the Gamaches'. He didn't want to say anything that might be overheard.

A man naturally given to action, Jean-Guy had come late to the value of pausing.

"It is solved by walking," Gamache had often said.

In the middle of a stressful case, the Chief would leave his office, and instead of doing something, he'd go for a walk. Often just up and down the corridors of Sûreté headquarters, hands clasped behind his back, occasionally muttering, while Beauvoir, figuratively, danced Tigger-like around him.

Gamache had patiently explained, over and over, over the years, that he was doing something.

He was thinking.

It had taken Beauvoir years to see the power of pausing. And of patience. Of taking a breath to consider all options, all angles, and not simply acting on the most obvious.

After looking in on Annie and Honoré, he put on a light jacket and went out for a walk.

CHAPTER 24

When the men returned to the living room with dessert and coffee, Reine-Marie nodded toward the box. "Find anything interesting?"

"Look at this," said Armand. "And tell us what you think."

He handed them the GHS annual report, open to the page listing the board of directors. "My God. The former President of France?" said Monique. "An ex–American Secretary of State?"

"Look, a Nobel laureate," said Reine-Marie. "I read her book. *Formidable.*"

They scanned the list of diplomats, world leaders, philosophers, and artists.

"Anything strike you?" asked Armand.

"Besides the caliber of members?" said Monique. "GHS must be incredibly powerful to attract such people."

"Yes," said Armand. He was watching Reine-Marie as she stared at the list. Then, after taking a large forkful of creamy cake, she turned to the President's Report. There was a photo of the CEO, Eugénie Roquebrune. And below it a précis of their corporate philosophy.

"Seems interesting to me," she said slowly, "who's not on the board."

"What do you mean?" Monique reexamined the names.

"This's an engineering firm, right?" said Reine-Marie. "So why aren't there any engineers? There're no scientists of any kind. Nobel laureates, but not in economics or physics. They're in literature. And why aren't there any accountants? Anyone who could read a financial statement and see if there's anything wrong? They're all politicians and diplomats. Minor royalty and celebrities. There's this one fellow, head of a media empire, but that doesn't mean he can read a spreadsheet even if he wanted to."

And that, thought Armand, was the crux. How much did these people actually want to know?

"Not exactly the checks and balances you'd hope for in a board of directors," said Monique.

The photo of Madame Roquebrune smiled out at them. She seemed pleasant enough, but did not give the impression of immense power or even authority.

But then, that might've been the idea. Gamache suspected nothing, no word, no image, not even the font, was chosen without intense scrutiny.

Reine-Marie also studied the photograph. She saw a woman in her early fifties. Elegant, warm. Kindly even. Not at all intimidating or formidable. In fact, as she looked closer, Reine-Marie saw there was a very small eyelash on Madame Roquebrune's cheek.

It was almost unnoticeable, except as a tiny human flaw.

It was actually quite endearing. She wanted to brush it away.

And that, Reine-Marie knew, was the trap. Even as she felt herself drawn into it.

Could this, she found herself wondering, really be one of the most powerful people in France? In Europe?

But then, her own husband was often mistaken for a college professor. Not a man who hunted killers.

The GHS president was not kindly and benign, and its board was not oversight. It was a façade, a stamp of legitimacy. The men and women on the board gave the corporation access, and cover, should anything go wrong.

"Claude, do you know this Eugénie Roquebrune?" Armand asked.

"No," he said. "Though that's some impressive board. I wonder if Monsieur Horowitz really did have anything on GHS. Hard to believe people like that could be taken in."

"People believe what they want to believe," said Reine-Marie. "It's just human nature."

"Reminds me of the story of the oilman who went to Heaven," said Claude. "He shows up at the Pearly Gates and Saint Peter says, 'I have some good news and some bad news. The good news is, you've got into Heaven.'

"'Fantastic,' says the oilman. 'But what's the bad news?'

"'I'm afraid the part of Heaven reserved for oilmen is full.'

"'Well, I know how to solve that,' says the oilman. 'Take me to them.'

"When Saint Peter does, the oilman calls for their attention and announces, 'Exciting news. They've struck oil in Hell.'

"And with that, the place empties out.

"Saint Peter turns to the oilman and says, 'That was amazing. You can go in now.'

"'Are you kidding?' says the oilman. 'I'm going to Hell. I hear they've struck oil there.'"

The other three laughed.

"It's true what you say, Reine-Marie," said Claude. "People believe what they want to believe. Beginning with their own lies."

"Hell is the truth seen too late," said Reine-Marie as she poured out more coffee. "Thomas Hobbes."

For a moment, Armand could feel Stephen's steely grip on his wrist, and see his laser-blue eyes, staring at him as they sat in the garden of the Musée Rodin. In front of *The Gates of Hell.*

I've always told the truth, Armand.

Jean-Guy glanced around to see if he could spot anyone watching.

But he was alone in the park.

He walked along the path, unconsciously clasping his hands behind his back. As he strolled, Jean-Guy Beauvoir went over what he'd found. And what it could mean.

And, equally disturbing, what Annie had told him. And what that could mean.

Jean-Guy stopped. Supposedly to stare into the duck pond. But actually, he'd picked up the fact he wasn't alone. Someone was quietly watching from the shadows.

A thief? Was he about to be robbed?

It is a mystery, he hummed as he slowly circled the pond. *It is a big mystery.*

Then, turning quickly, his hand shot out, but the man had lightning reflexes and jumped out of his grasp, then turned and took off.

Jean-Guy ran after him, and while the man was younger and had the advantage of age, Jean-Guy had the advantage of rage.

The man ran out into the traffic along rue de Bretagne. Horns sounded and curses followed them down rue du Temple, the distance between the men growing. The man turned down an alley, knocking over bins to slow his pursuer.

While all his survival instincts, all his training, told Jean-Guy it was a mistake to follow a suspect into a dark alley, his instincts as a husband and father were stronger.

The man disappeared around a corner.

Skidding around the corner, Beauvoir saw a brick wall at least ten feet high blocking their way. It was a dead end.

The man didn't slow down. Didn't hesitate. He ran full tilt at it, leaping and grabbing the top. Pulling himself up, he went over the other side.

At the very top, he twisted and looked back.

Directly at Beauvoir.

Then he dropped from sight.

Beauvoir got to the wall and jumped. Clutching for the top. His fingers scraping the bricks. Clawing at them for purchase. But he skidded down. Once, twice, three times he tried. Then stopped. Bending over, holding his knees. Gasping for breath.

"Fuck, fuck, fuck," he muttered, pounding the wall with each word.

Then he turned and jogged back to the apartment, picking up speed, breaking into a run as his mind raced ahead of him.

Had he actually been lured away? Was he meant to chase one man while another broke in?

He was running across streets as cars slammed on brakes.

At his building he took the stairs two at a time, yanking himself up with the handrail.

The door to their apartment was closed. And still locked. But . . .

Hands trembling, he unlocked it and ran to Honoré's room, then checked on Annie.

Both were asleep. Both snoring lightly.

Returning to the front door, he double locked it. Then, leaning against it, he slid down, landing on the floor, his knees to his chin and his head in his hands.

What could have happened to his family?

He got up and walked unsteadily into the living room. The chase had not been totally futile. He'd found out one thing.

The man had turned at the top of the wall on purpose. So that Jean-Guy could get a good look at him.

It was the guard Loiselle.

Jean-Guy's bloody hand reached for the phone. The Chief was right. Some things were solved by walking. And some by running.

Armand put down the phone and turned to Claude.

"Did you assign an agent to guard Annie?"

"I asked Irena to do it. Why?"

"Because," snapped Armand, "there's no one there, except, as it turns out, a security guard working for GHS. They're watching the apartment."

"Armand?" said Reine-Marie, standing up.

"They're all right. No thanks to you," he said to Dussault. "Jean-Guy chased him away."

Claude Dussault picked up his phone and made a call. A moment later he hung up. "An agent has been assigned, but his shift won't start until midnight. I'm sorry. I didn't make it clear to Fontaine that this was a priority. A flic is on his way now."

Armand continued to stare at the Prefect, who colored under the unrelenting glare.

"*Désolé*," Dussault repeated.

Gamache was far from convinced this man was *désolé*. He was also concerned that any gendarme Dussault sent would be there not to guard, but to watch. And maybe do more, if it came to that.

The Dussaults were on their feet, understanding that the evening was over. But as Claude bent to pick up the box, Armand stopped him.

"I'd like to keep this for a day."

The two men locked eyes. Over the box. Over the barricade. And the Prefect, knowing he was in a difficult position after his failure earlier, conceded. But he wasn't surrendering completely.

"I'll just take this then." He picked up the laptop.

Had they actually been at the barricades, Armand had the impression Dussault would have pulled the trigger.

And he'd have shot back.

CHAPTER 25

⌒

"What was that about?" Monique asked as they got in their car.

"The Horowitz case," said Claude, tossing the laptop into the back seat.

"I know that, but there was tension. More than tension. Is something wrong?"

"*Non.*" But her husband was distracted. Enough to actually get lost for a moment in the narrow streets of the Marais. "I'll drop you at home. I need to speak with Irena."

"At this hour? It's almost eleven. Claude, what's going on?"

"Nothing. I need to get her the laptop, now that we have the password. I'll be home before midnight."

He dropped her at the door to their building and made sure she got in safely, then drove off.

Monique walked up the stairs slowly. Thinking. Her husband's scent, even more rank than she remembered it, clung to her clothing.

Beauvoir opened the door.

Once in, Reine-Marie hugged Jean-Guy.

"You all right?" Armand asked, noticing the scrapes on Jean-Guy's hand.

"A bit shaken, to be honest. It really is different when it's your own family." His eyes were wide. "Thank you for coming."

"Annie?" asked Armand.

"Asleep. So's Honoré."

Despite the reassurance, Reine-Marie and Armand walked to the bedrooms, peered in, then returned to the living room.

"We brought this." Reine-Marie held up the pastry box. "I'll make some tea."

They followed her into the small kitchen and put out the tea things.

"What happened," Armand asked.

Jean-Guy described it, then said, "I'll tell you, Armand, that guy barely touched the wall as he went over. That's no ordinary guard. And I'm pretty sure he wanted me to recognize him."

"Bit of psychological warfare," said Armand.

"But the good news is, his orders were to follow me, not to do any harm to Annie or Honoré. There's something else. He works for SecurForte."

"The same company that has the contract with the George V," said Gamache. "Who almost certainly doctored the tapes."

"It gets worse. SecurForte is owned by GHS."

Armand paused for a beat, taking that in. "How do you know?"

"I found an old article in some American mercenary magazine. Let me show you."

They returned to the living room and took seats side by side on the sofa, in front of the laptop.

Armand read, then looked up. "What are you thinking?"

"That GHS is using SecurForte to spy on other corporations."

"And Stephen found out. It's possible."

Annie walked, waddled, into the room in her bathrobe.

"What time is it? Is it morning? What's going on?" She looked at the clock on the mantel. "It's eleven thirty. Why're you here? Has something happened?" Her eyes landed on the cake. "Is that an Ispahan?"

"She seems to be giving birth to questions," said Jean-Guy.

"Careful." Annie placed a hand over her stomach. "You don't want the baby to join the conversation, do you?"

Once they were all sitting down, Jean-Guy told her about the GHS guard.

Annie turned white. "You chased him? Are you crazy? Are you all right?" She took his hand. "You're hurt."

"No, no. I'm fine. They're just trying to scare us."

"Are you sure?" She looked at her father, who'd been silent. "Daddy?"

She only used that word when something awful had happened, or was happening.

Just then there was a knock on the door.

Jean-Guy went to it and returned a minute later. "It's the cop, come to guard us."

"I've been thinking," Armand said, "that maybe you need to move into Stephen's suite at the George V."

"But will it be any safer?" asked Reine-Marie. "SecurForte's there, too."

"Mom's right," said Annie. "They'll be all over the George V. Why would we be safer there?"

"Because you wouldn't be alone," said her father. "There'll be other guests, staff. Support."

"You mean witnesses? I see your point." Annie turned to Jean-Guy. "A few days in a luxury hotel? If we must . . ."

"Just don't order the caviar, dear," said Reine-Marie. "Or toast. Or anything."

"I need to show you something on the security cameras," said Jean-Guy. "Something they didn't erase."

They huddled around his laptop while he showed them the clip, gone in the blink of an eye, of a woman arriving at the George V.

"This was yesterday, late afternoon," he said.

"It's the head of GHS," said Reine-Marie. "I recognize her from the annual report."

Eugénie Roquebrune was indeed recognizable. The only woman in the lobby, perhaps in the entire hotel, maybe in all of Paris, with gray hair.

"Now," said Beauvoir, bringing up the next clip. "This's half an hour later. Look at the reflection in the tray the waiter's holding."

They watched as the uniformed waiter put a teapot and a three-tiered tower of little sandwiches and petit fours on a table. While he spoke to the guests, he lowered the large silver tray to his side. So that it reflected the guests at another table.

They watched it twice through before Armand hit pause.

"It's Claude Dussault," he said, and sighed, staring at the screen. "Meeting with the head of GHS. That's it then."

His fear confirmed.

Despite the tension that evening, and Armand's growing discomfort with his old friend and colleague, he'd still held out hope that he'd gotten it wrong.

But he could no longer hide from the truth.

Having afternoon tea with the head of an engineering giant was hardly a crime. But he was the Prefect of Police for Paris. And GHS appeared up to its neck in this business.

The business of murder. Attempted murder. And whatever it was Stephen had discovered.

Besides, when asked directly if he knew the CEO, Claude Dussault had denied it.

He'd looked Gamache in the eye and lied.

"Who's the other man?" asked Annie.

They could see the back of his head and a bit of his face as he turned to listen to Madame Roquebrune.

Dark hair, close-cropped. Clean-shaven.

"Madame Roquebrune's security?" asked Reine-Marie.

"I don't think so. A security guard wouldn't sit down for tea with a client," said Armand. "He's part of whatever meeting's happening."

"But what is happening?" asked Reine-Marie. "I can't imagine the CEO herself is telling the Prefect of Police, in a public place, to go kill a man."

"They obviously didn't know that Stephen was actually staying right there," said Jean-Guy. "Was just a few flights above them."

Armand leaned closer to the image. And remembered the grainy photo of Himmler in bar Joséphine.

Terrible things were discussed by confident people in public places.

And there was a reason this recording had been erased. When the killings and search were bungled, they had to kick over all trace.

Innocent people holding innocent meetings didn't erase the evidence. As SecurForte had done. And deny that it ever happened. As Claude had done.

"What would they have to offer, to get him to do it?" asked Reine-Marie.

"He talked tonight about retirement," said Armand. "They must've offered him more money than he could ever make as a cop. A lifetime of peace and security for himself and his family."

Armand rubbed his forehead, his fingers naturally finding the long, deep scar at his temple.

What would it take?

"Ummm," said Reine-Marie. "There's something you should know. I asked Monique—" She turned to Annie and Jean-Guy and explained, "Dr. Dussault. Claude's wife. I asked her tonight about his cologne. I'm sorry, Armand, but it seemed the only way."

"That's all right," he said. "I'm sure you were careful."

"I think I was. I found out that it's called 4711. I have a bottle of it at home that I bought this afternoon at the BHV."

"You found it?" said Armand.

"*Oui.* I wanted to be able to confirm it really is the same scent we smelled, and that Claude really does use it. I didn't show Monique the bottle, I just said I was looking for a gift for you, Armand," she said, turning to face him directly. "It is Claude's cologne. Monique confirmed it."

He gave a very small nod.

"She told me his second-in-command bought some for him and for herself," Reine-Marie continued, "when they were on a trip together in Cologne. They toured the place where it's made. Monique says Claude only puts it on when they're going to meet."

There was silence as they took that in.

"That means," Reine-Marie said, deciding they were taking too long to get there, "that it could've been Irena Fontaine we interrupted in Stephen's apartment."

"It could also mean they're closer than we realized. We need to find out more about her," said Jean-Guy.

"And SecurForte," said Reine-Marie.

She took over the laptop and put the name in. Up came a website.

It was spartan, to say the least. All they could see was the home page. They needed a security code to access more.

The home page photo showed a handsome, well-groomed, muscular man in a suit standing alert beside a Maybach, while a woman, smiling but also alert, held the door open for a little girl and her mother.

In the bottom right corner was their logo.

"That's the same emblem I saw on the guard's uniform," said Jean-Guy. "The same one in that article."

"It looks like a snowflake," said Annie. "Why would they have a snowflake as a corporate logo?"

"Look closer," said Reine-Marie, doing just that. "Those are spears, tridents, in a circle."

The spears were radiating out from a central point, as though protecting it.

"That's no snowflake," said Reine-Marie. "That's a promise, and a warning. Clever." She smiled. "Making it look like one thing while actually being something else. Hiding its real nature. An insignia like that is more than just a corporate logo. It's a symbol. It means something. Most paramilitary emblems do."

After a few dead ends, she sat back and turned the screen to the others. "*Voilà*. The Helm of Awe."

"You're kidding, right?" said Annie, leaning in. "Sounds like a comic book."

"The Helm of Awe," Reine-Marie read, "is an ancient Norse symbol of protection and overwhelming might."

"What's the Sûreté du Québec logo again?" Jean-Guy asked as they stared at the Helm of Awe. "A kitten?"

"Playing with a ball of yarn, *oui*," said Armand.

Annie laughed. They all knew the Sûreté logo was a fleur-de-lys. A flower. Appropriate, but hardly awe-inspiring.

Fortunately, they didn't need a symbol to be inspired.

"Does it say who runs SecurForte?" asked Armand.

"No," said Reine-Marie. "But I'm sure I can find out."

"Actually, there's something else we need you to look into," said Armand.

He told her and Annie about the documents Irena Fontaine had produced, questioning which side Stephen was on in the war.

"But that's ridiculous," said Annie. "There's no way he was a Nazi."

"Those documents were supposedly suppressed by the Allies, you say?" said Reine-Marie. "Hidden in the Archives nationales. I have experience with those archives. They're immense. If those documents were buried seventy-five years ago, they wouldn't be easy to find. And yet she had them within hours of the investigation beginning. That doesn't make sense."

"Go on," said Armand.

Reine-Marie thought. "They must've already had them, ready to use if necessary."

"By 'they,' you mean Fontaine's boss. The Préfet de Police," said Beauvoir.

They were back to Claude Dussault. All leads led them there.

"Looks like it, yes," said Armand.

"But why?" asked Annie.

"Suppose Stephen found out that GHS was, for example, stealing corporate secrets," said her father. "They'd have to stop him before he exposed them. How would they do that?"

"They could kill him," said Annie.

"Yes, that would do it. But it's pretty drastic, and risky. I think they'd try something else first."

"Blackmail," said Jean-Guy. "They went looking for some dirt to hold over him. Maybe something criminal."

"They found those documents from the war," said Reine-Marie. "And threatened to use them. If he exposed them, they'd tar him as a collaborator."

Jean-Guy nodded. He'd been in France long enough to know that the Second World War was never that far away. Especially the tender issue of who worked for the Resistance, and who claimed to but actually worked for the Nazis.

He'd learned early on that he should never suggest "collaborating" with a colleague. It was an incendiary word.

"Well, if that was the strategy, they don't know him," said Reine-Marie. "That would just make him more determined than ever."

"So they moved to plan B." Armand turned to Reine-Marie. "Is there a record of who asks for which files at the archives?"

"There is, and I can look it up." She paused. "But I have to be there. There's something else, Armand. Something Annie found out."

"I asked a colleague at my law firm to look into the work we did for Alexander Plessner," said Annie. "He got back to me late this afternoon. Monsieur Plessner had an agreement drawn up, to form a limited partnership here in France. This was earlier this year."

When Annie hesitated, Armand said, "Go on."

"The agreement was with a newly created department within the Banque Privée des Affaires. The venture capital division."

"Daniel?" Armand said and saw Annie nod. "But maybe he didn't actually know Plessner."

"He did. His name's on the incorporation certificate."

Daniel had lied.

CHAPTER 26

Armand stood up. "I'm going over there."

"You can't," said Reine-Marie. "It's almost midnight."

"Then he's sure to be in." He was walking to the door.

"Armand, stop." It was a command. From Reine-Marie.

And he did. But he remained with his back to her. Not, for the moment, wanting her to see the rage, the outrage he felt toward their son. The hurt.

"He lied."

"Yes," said Reine-Marie. "But storming over there isn't going to help. You know that."

Now he did turn and held her eyes. "He lied. Not just to the police, but to us."

To me.

"He was probably in shock when Commander Fontaine said it was Alexander Plessner who'd been killed," said Reine-Marie. "You know Daniel. He feels things deeply and takes his time to think things over. But he gets there."

"What would you have me do?"

"Come home," said Reine-Marie. "Sleep on it. You can speak with him in the morning. If you go over now, who knows what'll happen. What'll be said that can't be unsaid. Please."

She held out her hand. Armand looked at it. Then, nodding, he took it.

"You're right. It'll keep 'til morning." He turned to Annie. "Will you be going to the hotel?"

"First thing in the morning, yes," said Annie. "Once Honoré's awake. Dad?"

"Yes?"

"Daniel's a good man. He's not involved in this. You know that, right?"

"I do."

But he didn't dare look Jean-Guy in the eye. He knew what he'd find there.

If anyone else in a homicide investigation had blatantly lied about knowing the victim, they'd move way up the suspect list.

And Daniel's actions were suspect, at the very least.

Once home, they decided to leave the dishes for the morning and dropped into bed, exhausted.

Armand expected to toss and turn, but instead he fell into an immediate and deep sleep and awoke to the sound of rain pelting against the bedroom window.

It was dawn on a drizzly Sunday morning. As he closed the window, Armand looked out and into the living room of the apartment across the narrow street.

It belonged to a young couple with a child. He didn't know their names, though they sometimes waved to each other. But it was too early for anyone to be up.

Except, maybe. He scanned the street below but saw no one watching their apartment. But then, anyone SecurForte-trained would make sure not to be seen.

Though, oddly, Jean-Guy's man had not only been spotted, several times, but made sure he was recognized. No doubt a scare tactic.

It seemed, this Sunday morning, that no one was trying to scare him.

He looked at the bedside clock. Six fifteen.

As he showered, he thought about Daniel. As he dressed, he thought about Daniel. Then, leaving Reine-Marie fast asleep in the bedroom, he did the dishes as quietly as he could.

And thought about Daniel. About what to do. What to say.

Putting the coffee on to perk, he went for a walk.

Glancing casually about him, he could see no sign of surveillance. It was, he thought as he put up the umbrella, a bit of an insult.

Gamache strolled through the familiar streets of the Marais, the rain, heavy at times, hitting the umbrella. It was, in its familiarity, a restful sound. *Pat. Pat. Pat.*

He walked past rue du Temple, pausing, as he always did, to study it. His grandmother had explained that it was named not for a Jewish temple, as he might have imagined, but for the Templars. This was where the Knights Templar had their headquarters, eight hundred years ago.

"This is where," she'd told the boy, "they hid the treasure looted from the Holy Land in the Crusades. And when there was the putsch, when the Templars were rounded up and tortured, not one of them revealed where it was hidden."

"The treasure?" young Armand had asked.

"Never found. Apparently still here, on rue du Temple, somewhere."

Though by then Armand had understood that the treasure that was really lost were the lives.

Armand had gone to bed the night before hoping, praying, that he'd wake up to find a message from his son. Asking him to come around. Saying there was something he needed to tell his father.

But there was nothing.

Well, not nothing. There was an email from Isabelle Lacoste saying the engineer she'd consulted couldn't find anything wrong with the Luxembourg plans.

And there was one from Mrs. McGillicuddy that he hadn't read yet. Her messages tended to be long and rambling. And he couldn't quite take that, first thing.

Gamache realized he'd have to tell Reine-Marie about the contents of Stephen's will. But he wouldn't, he thought, tell Daniel and Annie. Not yet.

Armand found himself on the Pont d'Arcole. The bridge that led across the Seine to the hôpital Hôtel-Dieu. Its name, Arcole, was a bit of a mystery, as with so much in Paris.

Some said it was named after a great victory by Napoleon over the Austrians, at the Battle of the Bridge of Arcole. Some said it was named for a young man killed in the French Revolution. He'd planted the tricolor and shouted, with his dying breath, "Remember, I am called Arcole."

Daniel in particular had preferred that version, speaking as it did of valor and sacrifice.

The sort of heroics that would appeal to the young. And untested.

But it was, Armand thought as he continued his walk, an old and dangerous lie. There was nothing right or good in dying for your country. A necessity, sometimes, yes. But always a tragedy. Not an aspiration.

His anger toward his son had dissipated in the night, and now he thought of Daniel and how frightened he must have been, to lie like that.

Was he waiting in his apartment for the knock on the door? Knowing that, eventually, someone would discover the lie. Someone would come?

Armand walked over to the hôpital Hôtel-Dieu and spent half an hour with Stephen, rubbing the cream on his hands and feet. Then reading him the world news.

The ventilator continued to pump, and the beeping of the machines was steady, almost rhythmic.

But the man was still and silent.

After a hushed conversation with the nurse and the doctor on duty, Armand kissed Stephen on the forehead, told him he was kind and strong. Brave and loved.

"And I know that you always told the truth," he whispered.

Then he left.

Though the nurse and doctor stopped short of saying it, he could see in their eyes that soon, very soon, they'd be asking him to make a decision. But he couldn't think about that. Not yet.

The boulangerie on his way home was open, and he picked up half a dozen fresh croissants. By the time he got back, Reine-Marie was up.

"Five?" she said, after looking into the bag.

"One must've fallen out."

"Of course it did, Chief Inspector. Did you sleep?" she asked, brushing crumbs off his coat.

"Very well."

"How are you feeling about Daniel?"

"Calmer. You were right to have me wait. I'll go around after breakfast."

He took a long sip of rich, strong coffee while Reine-Marie spread strawberry jam on her croissant.

"I spoke with Mrs. McGillicuddy yesterday, about Stephen's will," he said. "He made a new one a year ago. After some sizable bequests, to his foundation and one to Mrs. McGillicuddy"—Armand hesitated for a moment, before going on—"he left the rest to us."

Reine-Marie lowered her croissant to her plate, staring at him. To say it was a shock would have been disingenuous. But still, if she'd thought about it at all, she'd have said Stephen would leave Annie and Daniel small bequests. And them nothing at all.

And certainly not the whole thing.

"His estate would be split equally among Annie, Daniel, and you and me."

Before she could ask, or fight the temptation to ask, he volunteered the information.

"According to Mrs. McGillicuddy, after taxes and fees, it will come to several hundred million each."

Reine-Marie's mouth opened slightly, and her lips went pale. Armand wondered if she was about to pass out.

"Armand," she whispered. "We can't—"

He nodded. That had been exactly his feeling, too. But there was a solution to that.

"If you want, when the time comes, we can start a foundation. Annie and Daniel can decide if they want to contribute."

"Yes, yes," said Reine-Marie. "Oh, I know. A home for wayward cats. And financiers."

Armand laughed. It felt good. Then he called Daniel, who answered on the fourth ring. Yes, they were home and he could go over.

Armand could hear the chill in Daniel's voice. *He knows*, thought Armand. *Or suspects.*

"Do you want me to come with you?" asked Reine-Marie.

"No, better if I do this myself."

"Are you sure?" She searched his eyes. "You're prepared for whatever Daniel will say? You won't . . ."

"Make it worse? I'll try not to."

It was a pretty low bar, but still, Armand wasn't completely confident he could get over it.

"What'll you do?"

"It's Sunday. The Archives nationales will be closed. Which is a perfect time to go. I've already contacted the head archivist. She'll meet me there at ten. Are you going to tell Daniel about the will?"

"No. Nor Annie. Not while Stephen's alive."

She tied a scarf at his neck, and kissed him, and sent him back into the rainy day. And didn't say what he already knew.

It would not be long.

CHAPTER 27

⁓

Armand spent some time on the floor playing with his grand-daughters, who were still in their Canadian pajamas and were insisting on being called Bloom and Dawn.

"What does Mommy's name mean?" Bloom asked as she climbed on her grandfather's back.

"'Roslyn' means 'rose,'" he said.

"And Daddy?" asked Zora.

"Your daddy's name is Daniel," said their grandfather. "It means 'The Lord is my judge.'"

That silenced them. Florence was back on the ground, and Zora was now pouring tea for her grandfather.

"What about your name?" asked Florence.

"Do you know my name?" he asked, accepting the imaginary cup poured from the imaginary teapot.

"Papa."

"Exactly," he said, and, putting out his little finger in a gesture that always made them laugh, he sipped his tea.

"His name's Armand," said Roslyn.

"Armand," said Zora, looking at him in that disconcerting way she sometimes had. So pensive.

"It means . . . ," said Roslyn, tapping her phone to find out.

Getting to his feet and brushing off his knees, Armand turned to Daniel. "Maybe we can get some fresh air?"

"In the rain? No, here is fine."

"Please. A little walk, maybe find a café. Just us?"

Daniel looked at Roslyn, who nodded.

"Fine. Where do you want to go?" he asked as they headed for the door.

"You decide. Anywhere. Except the top of the Eiffel Tower."

That made Daniel laugh, and he relaxed. A little. This was something they shared. A fear, a terror, of heights.

Armand had first discovered his when he was a boy and Stephen had taken him up to the second level of the tower. Excited, Armand had raced out of the elevator, right to the edge, and, curling his fingers around the wire fence, he looked out across Paris.

And almost passed out.

His fingers tightened until they were white, and he stiffened. Petrified. Stephen came up behind him and was pointing out landmarks. It took Stephen a minute or so to realize what was happening.

"Armand?" But there was no answer. The boy stared straight ahead, barely breathing, almost comatose.

Stephen knelt and, prying his fingers loose, he turned his godson so that he faced away from the edge. And hugged Armand to his chest, holding him tight. Whispering, "I've got you. You're safe. You're safe."

Daniel discovered his own fear of heights while hurtling on a toboggan down the huge ice slide during *carnaval* in Quebec City, with his mother and sister. While Dad waited down below.

Where Reine-Marie was laughing and Annie was shrieking with delight, Daniel's wail was completely different. A gut-wrenching sound Armand immediately recognized.

When they reached the bottom, Armand swept the terrified boy off the still-moving toboggan and held him in his arms.

Whispering, "You're safe. You're safe." And feeling the heaving sobs against his own chest. As though they were one. While Annie and Reine-Marie looked on. Baffled.

"Feet on the ground it is," said Daniel as they put on their coats and grabbed umbrellas.

Once outside, Daniel looked this way and that before deciding.

"You know where I'd like to go? Rue des Rosiers. Haven't been there in years."

"Perfect. I haven't been for a while either. Did I tell you—"

"That you proposed to Mom there? A few times, yes. You climbed the wall into some private garden and popped the question. Didn't Stephen suggest that place after you said you wanted to propose in front of *The Gates of Hell*?"

"Yes. Though I'm not sure he suggested trespassing."

"Bet he did."

It felt relaxed, for the first time in a long time. Like the Daniel he always knew was there but hidden behind a wall Armand couldn't scale, though God knew he'd tried.

This was the Daniel everyone else met. Cheerful, warm, unguarded. Happy.

Armand wasn't fooled. He was still on the outside, but it was nice, wonderful really, to occasionally be given a glimpse into Daniel's garden. Before being banished again.

They walked and chatted about the children. About Paris. About home. Armand brought him up to speed on their friends and neighbors in Three Pines.

They were silent for a few minutes. The rain had slackened to drizzle and now seemed to have stopped. They lowered their umbrellas just as they reached rue des Rosiers.

It was the heart of the historic Jewish Quarter of Paris. There was a synagogue, a Hebrew bookstore, delis, and falafel joints. And among the bustle were plaques commemorating the Shoah.

"Hey, Dad, look. It's still here. We have to get one."

He'd spotted the bright blue front of La Droguerie. Going to the window, Daniel was thrilled to see that Omar was still making his famous crêpes.

He knew exactly what he wanted, and a few minutes later father and son resumed their walk. Daniel with a Nutella-and-banana crêpe, and Armand with a *beurre sucré*.

"I don't know why I haven't brought Roslyn and the girls here," said Daniel as he took a huge bite of crêpe. "I guess I forgot."

This was the closest father and son had been to normalcy in years, but Armand knew that was about to change.

But . . . did he really have to shatter this calm?

Maybe they could just keep walking and chatting. And leave it at that. Did it really matter what Daniel did, or did not, know about Alexander Plessner?

But yes. It mattered. And Armand knew if he didn't do this, Fontaine would. And it would be worse, much worse, for Daniel.

Bells began to ring, calling the faithful to worship. They sounded from every church on every street, filling the air with music both joyful and haunting. Ordinary and magical.

"There's something I need to ask," Armand began. Keeping his voice steady, neutral. "You knew Alexander Plessner, didn't you."

Daniel kept walking as though he hadn't heard.

"I'm on your side, Daniel. But you have to tell me."

Now Daniel stopped and turned. "So that's why you're here. Not because you want to spend time with your son, but to question a suspect."

"Daniel—"

"No, no. Have it your way. But why even ask? Sounds like you already know."

"What I don't know is why you didn't say anything. You can tell me. I'm your father."

"You're a cop. That's why you're asking, isn't it? Don't try to say you're asking only because you're my father."

"Only your father?" said Armand, struggling now to keep his own voice calm. "That's the only thing that matters."

"That's bullshit. It's never mattered. Not enough. You're a cop first and a father way far down the list."

The streets were crowded now with people brushing by and bumping by, and others staring. At the two versions of the same man, thirty years apart, arguing.

Armand looked around. Putting his half-eaten crêpe in a bin, he said, "Come in here."

They were at the entrance to a garden. The very one he and Reine-

Marie had trespassed in when he proposed. It was now open to the public, with one proviso. On the gate hung a sign.

En cas de tempête, ce jardin sera fermé.

In the event of a storm, this garden will be closed.

Well, thought Armand, *hold on to your hats.*

Grudgingly, Daniel followed his father, recognizing that there was no avoiding it now. The tidal wave that had been moving toward father and son for decades was upon them.

As he stepped forward, Daniel wondered if his father had any idea what was about to happen.

Reine-Marie looked at the stacks of dossiers on the long table in the reading room of the Paris archives.

The head of the Archives nationales, Allida Lenoir, put the last stack down, then sat across from her.

They were alone in the great room. The sun was barely making its way through the huge high windows. The lamps on their table were the only source of light.

In her early sixties, Madame Lenoir was a legend in the world of archives. She was tiny, and solidly built.

Her wife was the head of the Bibliothèque nationale. When the two started their relationship thirty years earlier, it was deemed inappropriate. Not because, they were assured, both had uteruses, but because it was a conflict.

Though the women knew what was really being said.

This was a dangerous alliance of two powerful women. Who now held the keys to too many documents. Too much information. They wielded too much control. Which was code for power.

Refusing to end their relationship, they stared down the establishment and won.

"Okay, spill. Why do you want these, and what's the rush?"

Reine-Marie took off her reading glasses and placed them on a manila folder bursting with thick paper. On it, in a careful hand, was written *September 1944.*

She told Madame Lenoir. Everything.

Archivists knew how to not just keep secrets, but keep them safe.

And none better than Madame Lenoir, who listened, nodded. Then, digging into the pile, she found a dossier and shoved it toward Reine-Maire.

"You'll want to see this."

On it, some long-dead hand had doodled a ship, but instead of masts it had the Cross of Lorraine.

Below it was written *Lutetia*.

Armand turned and held his hands, palm out, in front of him. Asking for, and offering, calm.

"Why didn't you tell Commander Fontaine that you knew Alexander Plessner?"

His voice was gentle. Almost soothing. Trying to hold on to, and invite, civility. He was clinging to the wreckage of his relationship with his son. No longer sure if it could be saved.

But there were, now, more important things.

"Because I was shocked that he'd been killed," said Daniel. "Because I needed time to think."

Armand was grateful Jean-Guy wasn't there. He could imagine what he'd say to that. And what he himself would have said, had this been any suspect in any murder investigation.

"What did you need to think about?" Armand's voice remained reasonable. Reassuring.

"Forgive me, I'm confused. Is this my father asking, or the Chief Inspector? That is your rank now, isn't it? It's hard to keep track."

The collapse had begun. Here, in this garden that had always held a special place in his heart. Another sanctuary sullied.

"No matter what my job is, I've always been, and always will be, your father."

"First? Are you my father before anything else?"

"Yes."

The answer was swift, absolute. "Were you my father in the meeting yesterday when you humiliated me?"

"I was trying to help, to protect you."

"I'm a grown man. I don't need your help."

"We always need help."

"Maybe, but not yours. If I'm in trouble, it's because of you."

They were alone in the garden, enclosed by old mansions on all sides, and one of the ancient towers of the wall of Philip Augustus, built during the Crusades.

Once formidable, it was now crumbling.

Armand took a deep breath. He could see that Daniel was lashing out. And he could see the pain behind the words, even if he had no idea where it came from.

"Why didn't you say something about Monsieur Plessner after you'd had time to think?"

"Because his death has nothing to do with me or his work with us."

"How do you know that?"

"Because I know the work. He and I'd only met a few times. We'd barely started."

"What were you working on?"

"Venture capital."

"*Oui.* But was there a particular project?"

"That's confidential."

Fighting words once again, but Armand chose not to pick up the gauntlet. He hadn't lived to be an old warrior by responding every time someone wanted to fight. Even his son. Especially his son.

"I can find out," said Armand.

Daniel smiled. Satisfied. "Yes. The father might trust me, but the cop will find out."

"You seem to think the two are separate. They aren't. Any more than they are with you. You're a banker. I expect that extends to looking after your family's finances. You and Roslyn make sure they're safe. I'm doing the same thing. Yes, I'm a cop. And I'm just trying to make sure you're safe."

"I'm not a child. Stop treating me like one. I can look after myself. And I can provide for my family. So stop trying to protect me, and stop giving me money."

"What do you mean?"

"Like you don't know. You're always slipping me envelopes with money."

"I honestly don't know what you mean. I haven't done that since you were at college."

"Really? That day on Mount Royal, a few years ago? I was already a banker, already in Paris. Making good money. Way more than you ever made. And what do you do? You shoved an envelope into my hand, like I'm some broke teen working at McDonald's. Do you have any idea how insulting that was?"

"Did you open it?"

"No. I threw it away."

Armand fell silent and glanced at the wet grass at his feet.

"I don't want, or need, your money," Daniel was saying. "I can look after my own family. And I don't need you to keep me safe. Never did. And this—" Daniel raised the half-eaten crêpe. "What's this? More patronizing? Treating me like a child?"

"What're you talking about?" Far from being angry, Armand was completely confused. "Coming here was your idea, not mine."

But Daniel was beyond rational thought.

"I'm not the only one who lied yesterday." Daniel's voice was raised. Almost shouting. "You did, too."

"Me?"

"Don't. Just don't. I know the truth. Mom knows the truth. And I at least didn't betray you to the cops. Didn't humiliate you. Neither did she."

"What do you mean?"

"You said you weren't in the special forces. Because to admit it would be to admit you could've killed Monsieur Plessner. But you were, weren't you."

"*Non.* Never. Why do you say I was?"

"Oh, for fuck's sake," Daniel shouted, and threw his crêpe at his father. It hit his jacket and fell to the grass, but Armand didn't move. "I heard. That's how I know."

"Heard?"

"You and Mom talking, downstairs. It was Christmas Eve. I was excited about Père Noël, so I crept onto the landing. And I heard."

"What?"

"You told Mom about taking a job with the special forces. You told her about the hostage takings, the terrorists, the raids on organized crime. All the terrible things. You said it was dangerous, that the death rate was high. But it was something you had to do."

Armand's eyes widened, and his mouth opened slightly. He remembered that conversation. Years ago. But that wasn't how it went.

"I never accepted the job. The job I agreed to do was to train recruits. That's all. To try to get them as prepared as possible for whatever they'd face. You have to believe me."

"Right, like you believe me? I know you're lying. I know what I heard. I saw Mom crying. You made her cry. And every day after that, when you went to work, I knew you weren't coming home. I hated you for that."

"Oh, my God, Daniel, is that why you shut me out? Because you thought I was going to be killed?"

"Because you cared more for others than you did for us. For me. And yes, because you were going to die. And I couldn't . . . How could I love you . . . how could I care . . . when . . ." The words came out haltingly, as a wail. The same sound he'd made as a boy, hurtling down from too great a height. "How could I . . . ?"

"All these years?" Armand whispered, unable to find his voice. His eyes burning. "All this time?"

Who hurt you once, so far beyond repair / that you would greet each overture with curling lip?

The lines from Ruth Zardo's poem exploded in his head. In his chest.

Me, he realized with horror. *I did.*

"I used to have nightmares," said Daniel.

"I remember."

And he did.

Daniel crying out in his sleep. Armand and Reine-Marie had gone to him, gently waking the boy with hushed assurances. Then the look of horror on Daniel's face when he saw his father.

He'd push Armand aside, and reach out thin arms for his mother.

Two, three times a week this happened. He never told them what the nightmares were about. Until now.

"It was always the same one. There was a knock on the door. I'd run to answer it, and there you were." Daniel was heaving now, sobbing. Barely able to get the words out. "But. You. Were. Dead."

Armand was pale, his breathing shallow and rapid. He reached out, but Daniel stepped back. Away.

"Every time I look at you, that's what I see. A dead man. My friends knew their parents would live forever. But I knew that fathers and mothers leave home and never come back. Your parents did. And now you would, too."

"Ohhh, no," said Armand.

He'd deliberately not talked about the death of his parents in front of Daniel and Annie, for fear of scaring, scarring, his own children. Not until they were old enough to understand.

So how?

And then it came to him.

That rainy Saturday here in Paris, years, decades ago. They were visiting Stephen's apartment and the kids were playing hide-and-seek. They'd found a false door in the armoire in Stephen's bedroom and crawled in.

And heard. Their father and Stephen talking. About his parents, and about that day. About the knock on the door. About the very worst thing that can happen to a child. Annie must've been too young to understand. But Daniel did.

Parents died.

Nightmares came true.

"You couldn't be a teacher, a plumber? Even a normal cop? You had to do the most dangerous thing. I know you never loved us. If you did, you'd have picked us."

"But I did. Oh, my God. Oh, God, I'm so sorry. I didn't know—"

He moved toward his son. Daniel stepped back and raised the only thing he had. His umbrella. "Don't come closer. Don't you dare try—"

"I love you. With all my heart, I love you. I'm so sorry."

He stepped forward, and Daniel swung, at the last moment leaning away so that the handle of the umbrella swept by his father's face, close enough for Armand to feel the air ripple.

Armand hadn't flinched. Hadn't closed his eyes. Keeping them on his son the whole time. Though it was hard to see clearly.

Daniel looked like he was underwater.

Throwing the umbrella on the ground, Daniel strode away. Leaving Armand staring after him.

When Daniel was out of sight, Armand raised trembling hands to his face and wept. For all the pain he'd caused. For all those hours, days, years they'd lost.

For the happy, safe, contented little boy who'd died on the stairs that Christmas Eve, waiting for Père Noël.

CHAPTER 28

A h, look. There's a second floor!"

Annie was standing in the living room of Stephen's suite at the George V, wide-eyed. Marveling.

While the bellhop took their luggage upstairs to the bedroom, she turned serious eyes on Jean-Guy. "We must never leave."

Jean-Guy parted the curtains and was looking outside as Annie gave the young man a tip and closed the door.

"Anyone?" she asked.

"No."

"Now," said Annie, picking up the room service menu. "What'll we have, little man?"

"I hope you're asking Honoré," said Jean-Guy, and heard her laugh.

For all her apparent lightheartedness, he knew Annie was putting on a front. For Honoré. For him. In reality she was alert. Vigilant. And worried.

"I need to leave for a few hours," he told Annie. "Are you and Honoré all right? The flic will stay outside the door."

"I wonder what the other guests must think."

"They'll think that someone very precious is staying here," said Jean-Guy, kissing her.

As he stepped out of the hotel, he looked to his right. Then to his left, as though trying to get his bearings.

He turned right and strolled, apparently aimlessly, along avenue George V. Pausing now and then to glance in the shop windows, he continued his walk, turning into a smaller street.

And there he stopped.

He'd lied to Annie. Loiselle had been outside, watching.

Reine-Marie slowly closed the dossier and looked across the table at the Chief Archivist.

"This file is inconclusive. It quotes anonymous sources as saying Stephen Horowitz was possibly a collaborator. That he claimed to have been working with the Resistance, but might have been turning them over to the Gestapo for interrogation in the Lutetia."

"No, not the Gestapo. Common mistake. Many of the documents even from the time say Gestapo, but it was actually a division called the Abwehr that occupied the Lutetia," said Madame Lenoir.

"Who were they?"

"Intelligence. As bad as the Gestapo. Their job was to wipe out the Resistance. They'd arrest suspected members, take them to a room in the Lutetia, and torture them until they gave up others. Then kill them and move on. Many, most, died without a word."

Reine-Marie had to pause and gather herself. "You know a lot about it."

"My grandmother was one of those killed. And the Lutetia, to its credit, has been very open about that time in its history. Many employees fled when the Nazis took over—"

"So they'd have to hire new people."

"*Oui*. Maybe that's where your Monsieur Horowitz comes in. The fact he was German would work in his favor for the Abwehr, but would've raised suspicions among other employees, and understandably so. Some were definitely working with the Resistance, but others were collaborators. And some were just trying to keep their heads down and survive. It was a confusing time."

"To say the least. It would be easy to tar someone's reputation, to make a false accusation."

Madame Lenoir grunted agreement. "Many of the executions after the liberation were reprisals, but not for working with the Nazis. Neighbors took it as an excuse to do away with someone they just didn't like, or who they felt had cheated them. Or whose property they wanted. Private vendettas. Hundreds were shot or hanged without any trial at all. Though serious effort has been made to go back and sort the real from the manufactured. But it's hard. Documents were destroyed. The archives themselves were in a shocking state after the war. They'd been ransacked by the Nazis, who burned anything that contradicted their worldview. We lost countless irreplaceable manuscripts. For instance, their insistence on an Aryan race. We had document after document proving there's no such thing. It was a construct, a myth, created hundreds of years ago and resurrected by the Nazis."

"They destroyed anything proving it?"

"They tried. Fortunately the people they sent to do it weren't exactly geniuses. Some evidence survived. Though, let's be clear, the Germans weren't the only ones to ransack and rewrite. It served the Allies well to bury, even destroy, much of the evidence. They needed former Nazis in their own programs. How do you think the Americans got to the moon?"

Reine-Marie shook her head. As a librarian and archivist herself, she knew that history wasn't just written by the victors. First it had to be erased and rewritten. Replacing troublesome truth with self-serving myth.

"If Stephen was working for the Resistance," she said, "wouldn't he pretend to be a friend of the Abwehr officers? Wouldn't that be the best way to get the information he needed?"

"Yes. And that became the problem. Identifying those pretending and those who really were helping the Nazis."

Reine-Marie sorted through the small pile of photos in front of her until she came to the one of Himmler. Repulsive. Toad-like at the table. And behind him? An impossibly young and impish Stephen in a waiter's uniform. Beaming.

Putting her hand to her face, she stared at it. Thinking.

She knew Stephen wasn't a collaborator. The question was, how to prove it. They couldn't let the smear mar a courageous man's legacy. And they sure couldn't let a lie undermine whatever truth Stephen and Alexander Plessner had discovered.

But there was another question that came to mind as she stared at the photos.

"The police investigating the murder of Monsieur Plessner had copies of some of these documents within hours of his death. Is that possible?"

"*Non.*" The answer was unequivocal.

"Why not? It didn't take you long to find them."

"I'm the Chief Archivist. I was practically born in a file drawer. I know this place, these files, better than I know my own family."

"But Allida, you can't know all the documents in the archives. Even just the ones on the war. There must be hundreds of thousands."

"Which is why I know there's no way anyone could've put their hands on that"—she pointed at the file in front of Reine-Marie, with the doodle of the ship in peril—"so quickly. It would take weeks, months, to dig through all the documents. I think they found what they needed, then left them here, to be used when needed."

"Which means—"

"Someone must've been planning this for a while."

Not just someone, thought Reine-Marie. The file was in the possession of the police.

She felt physically sick. Her head was spinning with the effort of trying to grab hold of something too immense to grasp.

"When was this file last requested?" she asked.

Madame Lenoir got back on the electronic catalog. It didn't take long before she looked up, meeting Reine-Marie's eyes.

"Five weeks ago."

"Does it say by whom?"

Madame Lenoir was no longer able to make eye contact.

"Daniel Gamache."

* * *

Armand stood outside Daniel's apartment and stared at the door.

Then he knocked.

It was opened by Roslyn, who stepped outside into the corridor and closed the door behind her.

"I'm sorry, Armand. He doesn't want to speak with you. What happened? I've never seen him so upset."

"He'll have to be the one to tell you. But please, Ros, I need to speak with him. It's urgent."

Roslyn looked at her father-in-law. Normally so well-groomed, he was disheveled, his eyes red and his hair messy. Dark strands, mixed with gray, were plastered across his forehead, and his coat was smeared with something brown.

It looked like *merde*, but smelled, thankfully, of chocolate.

"Stay here. I'll see what I can do."

A few minutes later the door opened again and Daniel stepped out. Armand took a deep breath.

"I can understand that you won't believe me, but I want you to know that I love you. With all my heart. Always have. Always will. I didn't join Task Force Two because I wanted to be there for my family. For you. I didn't want you to go through what I did. But I did agree to train them, and I am so, so sorry that wasn't clear. This's my fault and I'm sorry for all the pain I've caused you."

"I don't care anymore. You're twenty-five years too late."

Armand nodded. *"Oui."*

The truth, too late.

He took another deep breath, exhaled. And took the plunge.

"If you don't believe I'm saying this as your father, then please believe that I'm saying this as a homicide investigator. I know how these things work. How an investigator's mind works. You need to go to the police and tell them everything you know about Alexander Plessner. They'll find out anyway."

"From you?"

"No. Not from me. I won't tell Commander Fontaine anything. I know you had nothing to do with Plessner's murder, and I know for sure you'd never ever do anything to hurt Stephen. But there's a sophisti-

cated, powerful organization behind this, and what they need is someone to take the blame. Someone to set up. And I'm very afraid it's you."

"Thanks for your advice, Chief Inspector. I'll consider it."

Armand nodded and held out his son's umbrella, which he'd picked
off the grass in the garden. Daniel looked at him then closed the door
in his face.

Resting the umbrella against the wall, Armand left.

Jean-Guy waited in the shadows.

Pedestrians glanced at him, then moved along. Not wanting to
draw the attention of this tightly coiled man.

And then, there he was.

Loiselle paused for just an instant at the opening to the narrow
side street, but it was all Beauvoir needed.

He grabbed him, swinging the much larger man around. With his
knee he dropped Loiselle to the pavement and knelt on his back as he
patted him down, coming away with a Sig pistol.

People shouted, some screamed, all leaped away. But before anyone could raise their phone and take photographs, Beauvoir hauled
Loiselle to his feet and shoved him into a boutique.

"I'm a cop. I need your back room."

The wide-eyed manager pointed. Then, rushing ahead, he unlocked a door.

"Lock it after us," commanded Beauvoir.

"Should I call the police?"

"No. I've already done that," he lied.

When the door slammed shut, he pushed Loiselle against the wall
and put the gun to his throat.

But something was wrong. The man wasn't struggling. Wasn't
fighting back. This was far too easy.

Then Loiselle did something unexpected. He put up his hands.

They stared at each other. Beauvoir's adrenaline was so strong, his
anger so great, it was all he could do not to pistol-whip the man anyway, surrender or no.

Then Loiselle did something even more unexpected.

"You said you were a cop, in Québec," he said. "You were Inspector Beauvoir, with the Sûreté du Québec. That was you, in the factory. I've been wanting to talk."

Armand's phone rang. It was Reine-Marie.

"Can you meet me at the archives?" she said.

"I'll be there in five minutes."

Armand walked quickly, and tried to get his thoughts straight. He'd told Daniel that he wouldn't say anything to Commander Fontaine, and he wouldn't. But still, he had to find out what Daniel and Plessner were working on. And whether it had anything to do with Plessner's murder.

He checked his emails as he walked. Finally clicking on the one from Mrs. McGillicuddy that had come in during the night. Far from being long and convoluted it contained only two words.

Call me.

He looked at his watch and did the calculations. It was six hours earlier in Montréal. That made it five thirty in the morning. She'd be asleep.

He'd wait and call after he'd met with Reine-Marie.

"I recognized you from the video, the one in the factory," Loiselle said, an urgency to his voice. "I saw what you did. You and the other agents. I saw what your boss did. I saw what happened."

Loiselle was whispering, as though what had happened that terrible day a few years earlier was a secret. Instead of leaked and splashed across the internet. Seen by millions.

The Sûreté raid, to free a hostage. To stop heavily armed gunmen. It had been a desperate fight to prevent something even more horrific from happening. But it had been a bloodbath. They'd prevailed. Barely. And at a terrible price.

"That was Gamache I saw you with yesterday, right? The older man? I recognized him, too. That's why I wanted to speak to you."

260

"Why?"

"In the factory, none of your agents broke and ran. You were disciplined, trained, dedicated. A tight team. But still, no one faces that kind of hell and keeps moving forward unless they know there's a good reason. A higher purpose."

Beauvoir's grip on the man's jacket remained tight, but the pistol dropped a little. Allowing Loiselle to meet his eyes.

"I used to believe that, too," Loiselle said. "That what I did was important. That it mattered. But I don't anymore. That's why the video is watched over and over by ex–special forces. It reminds us of what we once were. What we once had."

"And what's that?"

"Self-respect."

Beauvoir pushed himself away from Loiselle, the better to judge the man.

"I don't want to do this shit anymore," said Loiselle. "When I left the GIGN, I was burned out. I just didn't care. I'd hire myself out to whoever would pay. But seeing you at the office the other day, it was like a slap in the face. I woke up."

"Bullshit."

"I let you catch me. I could've gotten away. Easily. I could've killed you. Easily. But I wanted to warn you."

"About what?"

"They killed that Plessner man and tried to kill Horowitz. It was a shit show. And now they're scared. They see you as a threat. They told me to scare you off."

"And if that doesn't work?"

"They'll come after you. And maybe even your family. You moved them to the George V. That was unexpected. I think my bosses will take time to consider what that means and what to do next. They're ruthless, but they're not stupid. Killing you and your family in the George V would create far more problems than it would solve, but they'll still do it, if cornered. You've bought a little time. But not much."

"Who are they? Who's giving the orders?"

"My orders come from the top of SecurForte, but I don't know who's giving them to the company."

"Are the cops involved?"

Loiselle looked at him, shocked. "Everyone's involved. You really have no idea how powerful SecurForte is, do you? The information it holds over politicians, cops, judges, the media. I could blow up the Tour Eiffel in full view, and if it was on the orders of SecurForte, I'd walk. Man, you better get up to speed fast, before you get run over."

"How do I know this isn't part of their plan? How do I know this isn't a trap?"

"I guess you don't. But what choice do you have?"

"You must know what this's about," insisted Beauvoir.

"All I know is that whatever they were looking for, whatever they killed that old man for, they didn't find it. And they're scared shitless that you will. But they have options. Kill you before you can find it, or stand back and let you find it. Then kill you. Either way . . ."

"Were those your orders? To follow me, try to scare me off, but if that didn't work, and I found the evidence, you were to kill me and take it?"

Loiselle smiled. "You're catching on."

"You're following me," said Beauvoir. "Is someone following Gamache?"

"I think so. But I don't know who, and I don't know what their orders are."

"You mean to just follow, or to do harm?"

"Yes."

"Fuck," said Beauvoir. He stared at Loiselle. He couldn't hold the gun on the man and text Gamache at the same time.

Loiselle understood what he was thinking, and said, "I won't move."

Getting as far from Loiselle as he could in the tight office, Jean-Guy put the gun down and took out his phone. Keeping his eyes on Loiselle, he sent off the quick text, then picked the gun back up.

"What's in Luxembourg? What's so important about that project?"

"I have no idea, but I can try to find out."

"Is Séverine Arbour involved?"

"Madame Arbour? In your department at GHS? Not that I know."

"Is Carole Gossette?"

"I think so. I heard them talking about her. But I don't know for sure."

Jean-Guy stared at the man across from him. He had a decision to make that would affect the rest of his life, and the lives of those he loved.

Taking a deep breath, he gave the gun back to Loiselle.

CHAPTER 29

~

Gamache read the text from Jean-Guy. Then, replacing his phone in his pocket, he scanned the road.

Pedestrians walked by, some on their way from a service at the nearby Notre-Dame-des-Blancs-Manteaux. None looked in his direction.

"Monsieur Gamache?"

He turned just as the front gate to the archives building was unlocked. "Madame Lenoir. *Merci.*"

She shepherded him past security and down what looked like a dark alley, to the less-than-grand entrance to the archives.

The Musée des archives nationales, next door, was spectacular. In an old château, it was approached through a quadrangle of manicured lawn and garden.

But the archives themselves looked like they were housed in a bunker. In Moscow. In the fifties.

Reine-Marie greeted him.

"What is it?" he asked, seeing her face.

"Come with me."

He followed her to a terminal in the reading room.

This building in the Paris archives held almost one hundred kilometers of documents, dating from 600 A.D. to 1958. But it all came down to one tiny entry.

One name.

Whatever Armand had expected to see, it wasn't that.

"Oh, Daniel," he whispered.

Jean-Guy looked out the window and tried to imagine he was not in a jam-packed elevator. Pushed up against the glass.

He shut his eyes and imagined himself sitting with Annie and Honoré in the bistro in Three Pines. Listening to friends and neighbors talking and laughing. The scent of wood smoke and coffee and sweet pine in the air.

He inhaled. But instead of pine, or coffee, or even the oddly comforting scent of mud, he smelled Sauvage by Dior. And felt elbows digging into him.

There was no escaping the fact he was in a crowded elevator, with Paris at his feet. Literally.

The elevator climbed higher and higher, and the space grew tighter and tighter. The scent grew more and more suffocating.

And then the elevator stopped, and he was expelled onto the very highest platform of the Tour Eiffel.

The wind was bracing. Going to the edge, he breathed in the fresh air.

"Why're we here?" Séverine Arbour demanded.

Beauvoir was looking around, and then, spotting what he was looking for, he waved the man over.

"Xavier Loiselle, this is Séverine Arbour."

"We've met," said Loiselle, putting out his large hand.

Madame Arbour stared at it, then at Beauvoir.

"He's a security guard at GHS. I've seen him when I've signed in. What's this about? When you came to my house, you said something about the Luxembourg project. I thought we were going into the office, not coming here."

She looked around.

Séverine Arbour was not afraid of heights, which was just as well. She was standing as high as a person could get in France without wings.

Le Comptoir was hopping when Reine-Marie and Armand pushed their way inside.

When they caught the owner's eye, a spot was made for them at a small table at the back.

Armand and Reine-Marie knew this bistro in the Odéon well. Knew the *patron*. Knew the patrons. And would spot any strangers trying to overhear their conversation.

After they ordered two salade Niçoise, Armand told her about Jean-Guy's brief text.

UR followed.

It was not a huge surprise. He'd assumed. What perplexed him was how skilled his shadow was, and how ham-handed Jean-Guy's had proved.

Even if he couldn't spot the tail, Gamache knew they were almost certainly being watched and overheard. Listening devices were so sophisticated it was almost impossible to get far enough away to prevent someone from monitoring their conversation. But they could obscure it by being surrounded by other, louder conversations.

Once they reached Le Comptoir and could finally talk, all Reine-Marie needed to say was one word.

"Daniel."

"They planted his name," said Armand.

Reine-Marie looked relieved, though Armand knew this was actually reason to be even more worried.

"They wanted us to think he was involved," she said.

"*Non.* I think they knew we wouldn't believe it. But they want us to see the threat. As a warning."

Like a head on a stake during the Terror, he thought.

"To show us what they can do, to Daniel, to any of us, if they want," said Reine-Marie.

"Yes."

"Armand, that request at the archives was made five weeks ago. They've been planning this for that long?"

266

"At least."

"They're ready for us," she said. "They know exactly what we'll do."

"Not completely," said Armand. "They couldn't have foreseen that we'd be right there when Stephen was hit. Or for us to be the ones to find Alexander Plessner's body. This was all supposed to happen when we were at home in Québec. By the time we arrived, Stephen's death would be ruled a hit-and-run, Plessner's body would be removed. And whatever they were looking for would be found. We've messed up their careful plans. They're scrambling."

"But Daniel's name in the archive requests?"

"They had to put someone's name," said Armand. "Whoever found those documents couldn't use their own."

"But how did they even know about Daniel?" She looked at him, and blanched. "Because they knew about you. Claude Dussault knows you. Knows Daniel. He did it."

"I think so."

"But how did he know we'd go looking?"

"He couldn't have," said Armand. "Not then. He was preparing for all the scenarios. What would happen if I came over, if I had my doubts about Stephen's accident. If I started looking deeper."

"You'd find Daniel. Oh, God." But then her face cleared. "Could this be a good thing? If they found the old file and threatened Stephen with it, expecting he'd back down, then they clearly don't know Stephen. And if they used Daniel's name to threaten us, they clearly don't know us. They think they do, but they don't. They might be powerful, but they're also arrogant. Surely that's an advantage."

Now Armand also smiled. "You're right. They don't know us."

The waiter brought their salads. After she left, Reine-Marie said, "You spoke to Daniel this morning about Monsieur Plessner. How did it go?"

"He admitted he knew Plessner."

"And?"

"And that's all. It didn't go well." He was quiet for a moment. "But I did find out what's come between us all these years."

Reine-Marie put down her fork and listened as he told her.

After he'd finished, she sat back and stared at him. "He heard? That Christmas Eve?"

"But he didn't understand."

"He was a child. He thought I was crying because I was upset. Any child would. But they were tears of relief that you didn't take the job. Once you explained, did he feel better?"

"*Non.* I don't think he believed me."

"He's invested too much in this," she said. "If he admits he's wrong, it means admitting he's wasted all those years shutting you out. Give him time. At least he's told you. At least we know."

"*Oui.*"

But Armand also knew the trauma of losing parents.

And now he knew that every day, since the age of eight, his own boy had waited for the inevitable knock on the door.

What did that do to a sensitive child? To live with such anticipated grief?

Daniel's only hope, the only way to survive, was to get it over with. To emotionally "kill" his father and get on with life. Get on with loving those who would not leave him.

It was a brave, a brilliant solution. With one flaw.

Once dead, how could he possibly bring his father back to life?

"I advised Daniel to go to Commander Fontaine and tell her everything he knows about Alexander Plessner. And whatever they were working on."

"But Fontaine's involved," said Reine-Marie. "She must be. She had the archival documents. She must've been the one who put Daniel's name on the search. She might've even been the one who killed Monsieur Plessner. You have to stop him. He can't go to her."

"I don't think he will, but I hope he does. It'll show Fontaine that we don't suspect her. It'll stay their hand against Daniel. They'll know he has no idea what's really going on. If he did, he wouldn't confide in her. Still, I think they'd be safer moving to the George V, too."

"Maybe we should go home, Armand. Back to Three Pines."

The thought of the little village made her heart ache.

"We can't," he said softly. "You know the airline won't let Annie on the plane. Not days before delivery. Besides, they'd find us wherever we go. No, whatever happens, it happens here."

Here, here, he thought. *Where the devils are.*

She nodded and closed her eyes briefly. Taking a last look at the peaceful village before putting it out of her mind.

"Armand," she said, playing with a piece of baguette. She scrunched the fresh bread in her fist, feeling the shards of crust biting into her palm. "There's no way Daniel . . ."

"No. He's not involved."

"*Bon,*" she said. "What do you think they'll do next?"

Armand had been considering that. What would he do? What would Claude Dussault do?

He thought about Stephen. About the files buried in the archives. He thought about the Lutetia.

"I think they'll try to place someone close to us. Get someone into our inner circle."

"But how could they do that?"

"We're alone," said Xavier Loiselle, as he, Jean-Guy Beauvoir, and Séverine Arbour made their way around the circular platform.

"What do you mean, we're alone?" demanded Arbour, looking at the crowd. Thinner than usual for a Sunday, but then the low cloud and occasional drizzle had turned many off.

"What he means is, no one followed us," said Beauvoir.

"Why would they? What's this about?"

"I think you know. And now I want you to tell me."

She lifted her chin and stared him in the eyes. "Are you threatening me?"

"Not at all. In fact, I've decided to trust you. I think you've found something out, something about the Luxembourg project, and I want to know what it is."

"What makes you think something's going on, never mind that I know anything?"

"Your behavior Friday. You came into my office, uninvited, and started asking questions about the funicular project. Why?"

"Why did you change the subject?"

"Did I?"

"You know you did. From Luxembourg to the Patagonia project," she said. "What do you know about that?"

"Patagonia?" Was she changing the subject now? "Nothing. It's a water treatment plant."

Now she was openly staring at him. "It's a mine."

"It was a mine. It was found to be the source of the pollution, so GHS bought it and closed it down. That would solve the contamination problem for the communities downriver."

"So why's a plant still necessary?"

"To be safe."

"Really? How long have you been in private industry? Since when do they do things to be extra safe?"

"What're you saying, Séverine? You need to be absolutely clear. Tell me."

"Have you looked at the equipment going to Chile, and what's being shipped back?"

"No. Why would I? And even if I did, I wouldn't know what's needed."

"Well, I do. There's mining equipment mixed in with gear for the treatment plant."

Beauvoir noticed Loiselle turn very slightly toward the elevator. And the stairs.

Had he seen something? Sensed something?

Beauvoir had brought them to the top of the Eiffel Tower so they wouldn't be overheard. They were now far too high up, and there were far too many people, for anyone to eavesdrop. Even drones would have a hard time getting up this high, certainly without being spotted.

And if anyone was following them, they'd be mighty conspicuous on the small platform.

They were safe. Unless, Beauvoir thought as he watched Loiselle, they'd brought the threat with them.

270

"They reopened the mine five years ago," said Madame Arbour.

"Why?"

"Have you ever heard of rare earth minerals?"

"No."

"Well, that's what they found when they tested to see what pollution they'd have to treat. In the tailings GHS found evidence of a rare earth mineral."

"And that's an important find?"

"Well, yes. Why do you think they're called rare earth minerals? Because they're rare." Beauvoir knew that tone. The "numbnuts," while not said, was implied. "But, more than that, they're versatile. Different ones are used for different things."

"Like?"

"Like batteries and cell phones, magnets. Some next-generation telecommunications, I think."

"What kind did they find in the Patagonia mine?"

"I don't know. I've tried to get the water samples, but I can't find them."

"But if there was something that valuable in the mine," said Beauvoir, "why was it abandoned?"

"The original owners were mining silver. When it tapped out, they walked away, not realizing what else was in there."

"So then GHS buys the mine to close it, but discovers these rare earth minerals. Why hide it?"

"You really are thick, aren't you."

"Just tell me."

"It's obviously not that they've found a rare earth mineral," she said. "It's what they're doing with it."

Beauvoir felt himself get very still. Very alert. "What could they be doing with it? Can it be used in weaponry? Munitions?"

"Not that I know of. Unless they've come up with a new use, it's all fairly benign."

"You mentioned next-generation telecommunications."

"True, but again, not illegal."

"But it could be worth billions?" asked Beauvoir.

"If it works, yes, and if that's the type they found."

"People have killed for a lot less."

"Killed?" asked Arbour, and Beauvoir realized she didn't know the whole story.

He told her about Alexander Plessner. About Stephen. About the upcoming board meeting.

By the time he stopped, Séverine Arbour was pale. "And you've now dragged me into it."

"No, you were already in. If I found out about your snooping, they will, too. But if the issue is the mine in Patagonia, why are you so interested in Luxembourg?"

"How do you know I am?"

"I searched your files."

"You what?"

"Look, let's just assume you're mad at me, I apologize, and you accept, okay? Let's just skip to the important part. Luxembourg."

Arbour glared at him and gave a curt nod. "Fine. Carole Gossette's in charge of the Patagonia project. I've been digging and saw references to her and the Luxembourg funicular. But I can't figure out the connection."

"So Madame Gossette is involved?"

"Up to her neck, from what I can see. So much for your mentor."

And my ability to spot wrongdoing, he thought. Still, if Madame Gossette was trying to hide what she and GHS were doing, why go all the way to Montréal to hire a senior cop, the former head of homicide for the Sûreté? Why not just go with someone dense and easily manipulated?

Though, come to think of it . . .

He put that uncomfortable thought out of his head.

Séverine Arbour was looking at Loiselle. "He works for GHS. Won't he report back?"

"No. He's with us."

She nodded, but was deeply unhappy. Things were getting way out of control. Confusing. This was not at all what she'd signed up for.

* * *

"Mrs. McGillicuddy emailed me last night," said Armand. "She should be awake now. Do you mind?"

"*Non.*"

He placed the call, pressing his phone to his ear in an effort to hear above the din of the restaurant. He said a few words, then listened.

Reine-Marie saw, for a split second, a look of astonishment on his face.

He hung up and stared into space. Then he made another call. This time to one of their neighbors in Three Pines.

"*Oui*, Clara? No, Stephen's still in critical condition. Yes. I will, *merci*. But I have a question. Who do you know at the Louvre?"

Now it was Reine-Marie's turn to look astonished.

"Séverine," said Beauvoir. "What do you know about our company?"

"What do you mean? It's a huge engineering firm. What else is there to know?"

He took another tack. "How could the Luxembourg funicular figure in?"

"Maybe payoffs, funds for the mine siphoned through the Freeport in the duchy. Or bribes for Chilean officials."

Yes, thought Jean-Guy. That made sense. The financial angle. That's how Stephen would have first suspected something was wrong.

Beauvoir put his hands behind his back and walked in silence, gazing out over Paris. The great monuments were spread out at his feet. The boy from East End Montréal, who played ball hockey among garbage cans in the alleyways, could see the curve of the earth.

And all he wanted to do was go home.

273

CHAPTER 30

—

The taxi on the way to the Louvre stopped briefly at their apartment so Armand could pick up the GHS annual report.

While he was upstairs, Reine-Marie called Daniel and convinced him to move with Roslyn and the girls to the George V. To join Annie and her family in Stephen's suite.

"Shouldn't we take another room?" he asked. "It'll be a little tight."

"You'll be fine."

She hadn't told him about his name in the archive system. Not yet. Not while there was still a chance he'd go to Commander Fontaine and tell her all he knew.

Best he didn't know that.

When Armand returned to the taxi, she told him of her success with Daniel.

"That's good." He sighed with relief, knowing if he'd asked, Daniel would never have agreed.

He gave the driver the directions.

"We don't want to go to the main entrance. I'll guide you."

Ignoring the snorting and muttering from the front seat, Armand pointed out the way to the Porte des Lions.

"You won't get in," warned the driver when he dropped them off.

Armand and Reine-Marie stood between the two huge sculptures of lions, and looked up at the tall wooden doors.

"Do you think there's a doorbell?" Reine-Marie asked.

Just as they began to think the surly driver might have been right, the doors slowly, slowly opened.

"We're here to see Monsieur de la Coutu," said Armand, and showed the guard his ID.

Within minutes the curator arrived, hand extended. "Madame, Monsieur Gamache. Clara Morrow phoned and asked me to help. What can I do for you?"

To be honest, Reine-Marie had the same question.

All she knew was that Bernard de la Coutu was a curator in the Louvre's Department of Paintings.

"I'd like you to come with us," said Armand. "I promise, it won't take long."

The curator raised his brows and studied the couple, then nodded. "Absolutely. I'm a huge fan of Clara's paintings, especially her portraits. She's become a good friend. I'll do whatever you need."

Daniel's mouth dropped open. He understood why his mother wasn't worried about them being crammed into the suite. The space, even by Stephen's standards, was insane.

But even more striking than the suite was the officer at the door. He looked grim and held a machine gun.

He remembered the look on his father's face, in the garden that morning.

In his outrage, he'd interpreted it as his father being afraid that Daniel knew the truth about his being a member of Task Force Two. And would tell the cops.

Now he understood that his father wasn't afraid of him. He was afraid for him.

Leaving his family behind to explore the hotel, Daniel got into a taxi.

"Thirty-six, quai des Orfèvres, *s'il vous plaît.*"

"Are you sure this is smart?" asked Xavier Loiselle.

La Défense loomed up ahead, like its own great kingdom.

"It's so stupid, it's probably brilliant," said Séverine Arbour. "Or it's so brilliant, it's stupid."

"That gets my vote," said Loiselle.

They'd taken the métro to the familiar stop. Once they exited the station, Loiselle dropped back and pretended to be tailing them.

Beauvoir and Arbour signed in and showed their IDs. There was a tense moment when the guard double-checked.

Had SecurForte twigged to what was really happening? Maybe Loiselle had turned them in after all, or—

Just as Beauvoir's mind sped through the possibilities, none of them good, they were waved through.

Beauvoir and Arbour got off the elevator at their floor, then took the stairs two flights up to Carole Gossette's office.

"We probably don't have much time," said Beauvoir.

He tried Gossette's office door, but it was locked. Then he nodded toward the assistant's desk.

He and Arbour started pulling out drawers. Looking for a document. A file. A note. Anything that might tell them what was in the water sample from the mine.

He sat at her desktop and tried various codes to get in.

"So, here you are."

Beauvoir looked up. Standing at the door was Xavier Loiselle, and beside him was a man in his mid-forties.

He was fit. His arms hung loosely out from his sides, like an old-time gunslinger. It was the stance of someone prepared, preparing, to act. It wasn't hard to sense aggression in this man.

Beauvoir recognized him. Even though he'd only seen his profile, and that only briefly. But he'd stared at the image long enough to recognize the third person at the table.

The one sitting with Claude Dussault and the head of GHS, drinking tea from fine bone china in the George V.

Beauvoir could feel Séverine Arbour tense. Could hear her ragged breathing.

"Do I know you?" asked Beauvoir.

"I'm the head of security here," said the man. "Thierry Girard."

"Jean-Guy Beauvoir, and this is my number two, Séverine Arbour. Can I help you?"

"What're you doing here?"

"I beg your pardon?"

"This isn't your office."

"No. It belongs to Madame Gossette."

"Then why are you here?"

Beauvoir's brows lowered in annoyance. Getting up, he walked around the desk. "I don't think that's any of your business."

"We don't like people trying to get into offices that are not theirs."

"And I don't like being questioned by a security guard," said Beauvoir. "I'm senior management here. We haven't met, but that doesn't mean you don't know who I am."

"Oh, I know, sir. What I don't know is why you're here."

"I'm looking for Madame Gossette. Since you're so efficient, please check and see if she's in the building."

Xavier Loiselle's eyes had opened wider. Clearly surprised anyone would speak to Thierry Girard like that.

Beauvoir now knew that Loiselle hadn't sounded the alarm. In fact, he suspected Loiselle had accompanied his boss in order to protect them.

Girard was glaring at Beauvoir.

"Go on," said Jean-Guy calmly. "We'll wait."

They stared at each other until Girard took out his phone, made a call, then put it away.

"Unfortunately, Madame Gossette isn't in today. Why don't we show you out."

As all four stood in the elevator, Beauvoir decided to really push.

He turned to Loiselle.

"I spotted you last night, you know. And you've been following me all day. Why is that?"

"You must be mistaken, sir," said Loiselle.

"Yes. I agree. A mistake has been made."

* * *

Commander Fontaine's office was dreary, like the rest of the famed 36.

Daniel could see why they'd want to leave the rambling old building. It was probably rat-infested. What he couldn't figure out was why the Prefect had chosen to keep an office here.

He looked at the mishmash of items on display. There were photos of suspects mixed in with what seemed to be family pictures. Holiday shots and crime scenes.

As though this woman's life and work were so tightly intertwined, she could no longer distinguish between flesh and blood, and her own flesh and blood.

"Did you like it?" Daniel asked, trying to break the ice. "My oldest daughter's dying to go. She's been to Brussels to see the Pissing Boy, but—"

"What are you talking about?" Fontaine interrupted his babbling, glancing up from her notes.

He gestured toward a poster of Copenhagen Harbor. Florence had become obsessed with the story that Copenhagen Harbor had once been the home of all mermaids.

"I don't even know where that is. Never been out of France. Why would I?"

"Right. Why would you?"

She closed the file and focused on him. "Why did you lie to us about knowing Alexander Francis Plessner?"

"I should have told you," Daniel admitted. "I'm sorry. I think as an investment banker, especially with venture capital, it's ingrained to be careful. We let something slip, any tiny detail, and suddenly a potential investment is blown."

"So you lie? To the police? In a murder investigation?"

"It was a mistake," he said, sitting forward. "I was shocked when you said the dead man was Alexander Plessner. But I barely knew him, and I knew that what we were working on couldn't have anything to do with his death."

"What were you working on?"

"Some small company had come up with a new design for a screwdriver."

Now it was her turn to raise her brows. "Screwdriver? The tool?"

"Yes. I wanted to look for something bigger to invest in, but Monsieur Plessner thought the bank should start small."

"The screwdriver."

"*Oui*. You see why I knew it couldn't have anything to do with me. Unless he was killed with a screwdriver."

He smiled. She did not.

"And did you?"

"Kill him?"

"Invest."

"Yes. Monsieur Plessner is, was, an engineer, so he had some idea what was interesting about the design."

"You didn't?"

"Not a clue. But I'd looked at their financials and it seemed a low-risk investment. If it failed, we hadn't plunged a lot of money in. And if it succeeded, well . . ."

"Well, what? You'd make a fortune?"

Daniel gave a single snort of amusement. "Not with that company."

"Then why invest?"

"It was a dry run. What Stephen would call a starter pancake. The one that you drop on the floor but learn from."

Irena Fontaine didn't take her eyes off him. "Do you not find it strange that you're the only one in this whole case who has a relationship with both victims?"

Daniel felt his face tingle as the blood rushed first to it, then away. Like a wave with an undertow. Dragging the last of his bravado out to sea.

"And then," she added, leaning forward, "you deliberately misled us. Why're you here now? What changed your mind?"

"Nothing. My father told me to come."

"Is that right? I had the impression that if your father told you to do something, you'd do the opposite."

"You're very perceptive."

"No need to patronize me, Monsieur Gamache. Why are you really here?"

Now he was confused. He'd actually already told her the truth.

"My father told me you might suspect me if you found out I'd lied, so I wanted to come in and tell you the truth. I knew Monsieur Plessner, but not well. Hardly a relationship."

"Did Plessner ever mention Stephen Horowitz?"

"Yes, they were friends. It's how Monsieur Plessner came to me."

"Through Monsieur Horowitz? Was he directing the investments? Was he part of the venture capital project?"

"I don't think so. Stephen never asked about what we were investing in, and I never volunteered any information."

Commander Fontaine stared at him, but, while blushing even more furiously, Daniel didn't drop his eyes.

This was, after all, the truth.

"Did you know that Stephen Horowitz has quite a large account at your bank?"

"No, but I'm not surprised. He'd want money in France. He spends quite a bit of time here."

"But Horowitz never approached you about investing in venture capital?"

"No. Never."

"When was the last time you saw Monsieur Plessner?"

"Six weeks ago."

"And you haven't spoken since?"

"We spoke yes, on the phone. He called a few times. We discussed other possibilities."

"Like what?"

"Well, honestly, we didn't get far. The screwdriver people had told him about a company that makes screws, and another that makes washers. You know, the metal ring thing you put before a screw."

"And?"

"And nothing. These things take months of investigating, sometimes years. Monsieur Plessner was doing some digging around, but he didn't seem all that enthusiastic. Look, I can guarantee you that whatever the motive was for killing him, it had nothing to do with what we were working on. No one's going to get rich, or poor, in those investments."

Fontaine rose. "Thank you for coming in."

Daniel also got up, surprised the interview was over so quickly and so abruptly. "Thank you for listening."

She walked him to the door. "Will you tell your father you've been to see me?"

"Probably, eventually. I might let him squirm for a while. He sure made me squirm yesterday."

"The difference is, he didn't mean to. He was trying to help."

The small rebuke wasn't lost on Daniel, though he was surprised that she'd defend his father like that. He'd had the impression she didn't much like him.

Daniel decided to walk back to the George V. He felt better for telling her the truth. And when all this was over, he and Roslyn should take the girls to Copenhagen, to see the home of the mermaids.

His girls would not be like that cop and never see the wonders of the world.

CHAPTER 31

⸺

A rmand paused at the door to Stephen's apartment, to warn Professor de la Coutu what he was about to see.

The academic had closely examined countless horrific scenes of beheadings, of rapes, of maulings and stonings and crucifixions. Dreadful torments.

All while standing on the other side of the picture.

He was, for the first time in his life, about to step into the frame.

The professor listened and nodded.

Monsieur and Madame Faubourg, the concierges, had told them that the flics had left.

Just before he unlocked the door, Armand's phone buzzed. He snatched it up and looked at the text. Reine-Marie understood his speed.

It might be the hospital. It might be about Stephen.

But it was from Mrs. McGillicuddy and read, *We're here. Will let you know.*

He replaced the phone and opened the door.

The apartment was a shambles. No surprise there, though as he looked around, Armand had the impression it was even worse than when he was last there.

The investigators, of course, would do a thorough search. But a well-trained unit, while not tidying up, did not generally make a crime scene worse.

The curator walked in, curious, as though looking at a new exhibition. Until he saw the stain on the floor. And the outline of the body. Like skin around a hollow man.

De la Coutu stared. Overcome with the realization that somewhere between standing and hitting the ground, a person had become a corpse.

And someone else had done it.

He began to sway, and felt a hand on his arm, leading him away.

"Come over here. Sit down."

A chair was righted, and when he sat, the same large hand was placed on his back and firmly, carefully, bent him over until his head was between his knees.

"Breathe."

And he did.

When he raised his head, he was a different man. No longer would he look at a scene of violent death as though it was simply a series of brushstrokes.

"Better?" asked Armand.

He nodded and stood, a little shakily. And looked around. He knew he was there to evaluate the paintings.

Professor de la Coutu took a deep breath, almost a gasp.

"Is that a Rothko?" He went right up to it, his nose almost touching the oil paint. "The one that sold at auction twenty years ago? We had no idea who bought it. Look at all this."

The curator turned full circle, in wonderment.

"They'd been taken off the walls and their backing ripped," said Reine-Marie.

"They slashed the paintings?"

He ran over to another one. His arms out in front of him, like a parent rushing to save a falling infant.

He picked up the Vermeer and turned it around.

The brown framer's paper had indeed been slashed, but not the painting itself.

Holding it at arm's length, he studied the work, his eyes luminous.

It was a classic Vermeer domestic scene of a kitchen table with fruit and meat, and a calloused hand just reaching into the frame.

"You can tell not just by the subject matter, but by Vermeer's use of light," said de la Coutu, almost in a whisper. "By the pigments. Oh, my God, what a find."

"How much would that be worth?" Armand asked.

"Armand!" said Reine-Marie, shocked.

"Priceless," said the curator under his breath, shaking his head in wonderment.

He rubbed his hand over the engraved dark wood frame, caressing it.

Then he replaced it on the wall and took more paintings off their hooks, turning them around, too.

None of the actual art had been damaged.

Finally, after walking from room to room, examining the works of Old Masters, Impressionists, Modern Masters, he turned to the Gamaches.

His excitement, at first bordering on hysteria, had died down.

"This apartment belongs to Stephen Horowitz, am I right?"

"How do you know?" Reine-Marie asked. They hadn't told him.

"The collection. He's a huge financial contributor to the Louvre, and every now and then we'd hear rumors of another of his acquisitions, mostly through auctions. He was never named, but the world of high-end collectors and collections is small, tight-knit. I heard the news, but I thought it was a car accident. Not . . ." He looked at the outline on the floor.

"That wasn't Stephen," said Gamache. "We need you to be discreet about what you're seeing."

"Do you know what I'm seeing?" The curator turned from reexamining the Vermeer to examining Gamache.

"I believe I do, but tell us."

Professor de la Coutu rested his critical gaze on them. "I take it you asked me here for an evaluation. In the event of his death."

Armand remained silent.

"I'm afraid these are all copies. Excellent ones, certainly. Able to fool most people, though I'm surprised they fooled Monsieur Horowitz. Worth thousands each, even as copies, but not tens of millions. Not priceless as I first thought."

"All of them?" Reine-Marie looked at Armand and saw that he looked grim, though not surprised. "You knew?"

"I suspected. I knew that most originals from the Renaissance, as many of these would be, don't have framing paper at the back. And the frames themselves, while clearly good, aren't old. Even if Stephen had them reframed, he'd make sure they were from the same era."

"That's what made me suspicious, too," said the curator. "The fake Vermeer has a staple in its frame. Monsieur Horowitz would never stand for that, for an original."

Armand walked over to the smallest painting and, taking it off the wall, handed it to the curator. "Is this original?"

"It's nice," said de la Coutu, bending close to it. "Watercolor. Landscape. Probably from the early to mid-twentieth century. Signed *VM Whitehead*." The professor turned it around. "Funny that it has a nylon thread at the back and plastic eye hooks." He handed it back to Gamache. "Probably original, but worthless."

"Not completely," said Armand as he replaced it on the screw.

"What a shame," said the curator. "Someone must've come in while Monsieur Horowitz was away from Paris, and methodically replaced originals with copies. Probably done over time. I've never seen anything like it. What a loss. Did the dead man surprise the forger, do you think?"

"And was killed," said Armand. "Could be. Any idea how much this would all be worth, if they were originals?"

The curator frowned, thinking. "Vermeer did very few paintings. This one? In London or Hong Kong, probably close to a hundred million." He turned full circle. "All told, there might be half a billion dollars' worth just here, never mind what he must have in his other homes and offices." Now he turned shocked eyes on Armand. "You don't think—"

"That they're all fake?" Armand nodded. "I've asked his assistant to have them evaluated. She's at his home now with the curator from the Musée des Beaux-Arts de Montréal. When they're finished there, they'll look at the art in his office."

"Mon Dieu," whispered the curator. Feeling light-headed again, he sat down and gazed around the room.

Then his expression turned quizzical.

"Have you noticed that all the works are either pastoral or domestic? Peaceful. No torture, no death. Not even any hunting scenes. Huh. It can't be a coincidence. I wonder why."

Armand was so used to the paintings that he hadn't actually noticed this. Neither had Reine-Marie.

But now that the curator had pointed it out, they saw it. Stephen, the exorcist, had covered his walls floor to ceiling with scenes of peace.

"I'm sorry to have given you this bad news," said de la Coutu. "Will you alert the authorities, or should I?"

"I will. Could you keep this to yourself for now?"

"Of course. Clara told me you're a senior officer with the Sûreté du Québec. I hope you find out who did this. And, more to the point, who did that."

He looked at the drawing on the floor.

They put Professor de la Coutu into a taxi and watched as it headed back to the Louvre.

"Poor Stephen," said Reine-Marie as Armand took her hand. "He's going to be devastated."

"I doubt it," he said, quietly.

She looked at him. Armand was coming to terms, she thought, with the reality that Stephen would almost certainly never return home, and never find out that his collection, the work of a lifetime, had been stolen.

They waited for a gap in the traffic on rue des Sèvres, then darted across the street.

Jacques led them to a secluded table in bar Joséphine. But Armand pointed to a table right beside a rowdy group of visitors speaking Spanish. "Over there, perhaps?"

The maître d' raised a brow but showed them to the table.

Reine-Marie found herself glancing around the bar, trying to make out where those photographs she'd seen in the archives, from the war, had been taken. She felt a knot in her stomach and understood why Zora had loathed the place.

Was she one of the ones who'd been brought here straight out of the concentration camp? Had she searched for her family through these corridors? In the grand ballroom, in bars and restaurants, in guest rooms? In vain.

Once Jacques had taken their orders, Armand leaned close to Reine-Marie. But just as he opened his mouth to speak, another text came in.

His phone was on the table, and she could see it, too. It was from Mrs. McGillicuddy. *At office now. We were right.*

Armand typed. *Same here.*

"His whole collection is fake?" asked Reine-Marie, eyes wide. "Even the ones in Montréal? All of it stolen? What happened to it?"

"I don't think those paintings were stolen," he said, leaning close to her and keeping his voice low. "I think Stephen sold them."

It took Reine-Marie a moment to take that in. "Why do you say that?"

"Because Stephen knew art. He'd know immediately if there was even one fake, never mind all of them."

"Why would he sell them?"

"To quietly raise capital. And a lot of it. He couldn't cash in hundreds of millions of dollars' worth of stocks or holdings without anyone noticing, but he could discreetly sell his collection. Then he had to have each painting replaced so no one would know."

Reine-Marie's mind raced. "Why would he need that money? Was he in financial trouble?"

"No, not at all."

"Was he being blackmailed? That dossier? Was he paying to have it suppressed?"

Armand shook his head. "That file was found weeks ago. To quietly sell his collection must've taken years. Whatever he was doing, it was a long time in the planning."

"You had Professor de la Coutu come, but it was just to confirm what you already suspected."

"Yes. And I think I know where most of the money went. When I spoke with Mrs. McGillicuddy this morning, she told me she'd found papers in one of Stephen's safety-deposit boxes. He'd been siphoning money to Alexander Plessner. And a lot of it."

"What for?"

"Investments. Those papers were buy orders. Confirmations. It looks like he'd instructed Plessner to slowly accumulate holdings in several companies. But not all at once. The buys were spread over years, in relatively small amounts at a time so that no alarms would be sounded. When Mrs. McGillicuddy added it up, it came to slightly more than a billion dollars."

"And no one knew it was Stephen?"

Armand shook his head. "This looks like a hostile takeover, done a millimeter at a time. Have you ever seen the game Jenga?"

"Sure. Our nephews have one. You remember last Christmas, they were playing it? It looks like a solid tower but is actually made up of lots of small pieces, like little logs. You pull out one at a time, trying not to have the whole thing collapse."

"Right. Stephen and Plessner were playing financial Jenga. Pulling out tiny pieces of companies one at a time. He was a wily one."

Reine-Marie wondered if Armand realized he'd just, for the first time, referred to Stephen in the past tense.

"Which companies?" she asked.

"Mrs. McGillicuddy's studying the buy orders, but it's complex and many are numbered companies."

"He wanted to control them?"

"Or just one. It's possible the rest are camouflage, misdirection."

"Is one of them GHS?"

"*Non.*"

"No," she said. "That would be worth far more than even Stephen could raise. And the directors would definitely notice a hostile take-over, no matter how subtle. But he could be buying up one or more of the subsidiaries."

Armand pointed at her. *Got it.*

That was his thinking, too.

"But why?" And since there was no answer, she asked another question. "Is that why you stopped at home to get the annual report? To see if any of the companies are listed?"

"Yes. But the report doesn't name any of its holdings."

"If there are any," said Reine-Marie.

"Well, we know of at least one. SecurForte. And I suspect there are many more."

But there was another piece of information he had found out from Mrs. McGillicuddy. He waited for the shouts from the table next to them to reach a crescendo before leaning close to Reine-Marie.

She leaned in.

"Six weeks ago Stephen wired huge amounts into his bank account here in Paris. The funds were frozen, of course, following the anti-money-laundering laws. But they'd be available to him as of tomorrow morning."

She knew her husband and could see there was more to come. "Go on."

Armand paused, wishing he didn't have to actually say it. He studied her eyes. So familiar, he knew every fleck. Had looked into them at all the high, and low, moments of their lives together. As he stared into them now.

"The money's in the Banque Privée des Affaires."

Reine-Marie became absolutely, completely still. They were alone now. Far away from the shouts of laughter, the clink of cutlery, the scraping of chairs on marble floors. The murmurs of discreet waiters. Far away from the familiar.

It was just the two of them, in the wilderness.

"Daniel's bank?" she whispered.

"*Oui.*"

"So Daniel knew, knows, what they were doing?"

"I don't think so. I doubt Stephen would've told him. There was no reason for Daniel to know. And the less he knew, the better."

"Why would Stephen involve Daniel at all? If he thought it was dangerous, why in the world would he drag Daniel into it?"

"He wouldn't. I think at the time, six weeks or so ago, the only danger Stephen probably saw was that his carefully laid plan would collapse. That he'd fail. But he'd never have thought any of this would happen."

"Five weeks ago Daniel's name was put on the archive request for Stephen's war file. That's no coincidence. Something happened. Someone noticed."

Armand exhaled. "I think you're right. Stephen miscalculated. As soon as they threatened him with that file, he knew he had to be more careful. Which was why when he came to Paris he stayed at the George V. Laid low."

"But still they got him. Monsieur Plessner's dead and Stephen's in a coma. Oh, God, Armand, is Daniel in danger?"

"No. If they were going to hurt him, it would've been that same night they attacked Plessner and Stephen." He took her hand. It was freezing cold. "They're setting him up, but they need him alive for that. They won't hurt him."

"Are you sure?"

"Yes. He's safe. Especially if he can be convinced to go to Commander Fontaine and tell her about Alexander Plessner and the venture capital. That will prove to them he has no idea what's really happening."

Reine-Marie snatched up her phone. "I'm going to call and make him do it."

But he stopped her. "Let's get in a taxi. Call from there."

Reine-Marie strode down the long corridor, almost breaking into a run.

"*Hôpital Hôtel-Dieu, s'il vous plaît,*" said Armand.

Reine-Marie had the phone to her ear and was listening to the ringing. Ringing.

Paris slid by, unseen.

She looked at Armand, who was watching her. "No answer."

"Try again."

She did. Still no answer. The hospital was up ahead. She called Roslyn, who confirmed that Daniel had left a couple of hours earlier, but she hadn't heard from him. And no, she didn't know where he'd gone.

"Armand?" said Reine-Marie.

"We'll find him."

His mind was racing. Where could Daniel be? He'd been so sure, genuinely certain, that SecurForte, or whoever was behind all this, needed Daniel alive.

Didn't they?

Dear God, didn't they?

The taxi pulled up to the entrance to the hospital. Armand was on the phone. He no longer cared if he was giving himself away.

"Claude? Armand. Can you tell me if there're any reports of violent crimes in the last couple of hours?" He was pale as he asked, holding on to Reine-Marie's eyes. "Accidents? Where?" He held up his hand to reassure Reine-Marie. "*Merci*. No, just checking. *Merci*."

He hung up. "A woman fell off her bicycle and was hit by a car, but will recover. Nothing else."

"But that doesn't mean—"

"I know."

"We have to find him. There must be a way."

"There is." Armand stared at his phone. About to do something he loathed. Something he knew Daniel would find hard to forgive.

But there was so much unforgiven already—what was one more violation?

He pressed the app. And waited, staring at the screen, as it changed to GPS. To a map of Paris. To the île de la Cité.

"But it's not working," said Reine-Marie. "It's showing our location."

"*Oui*." Armand stared up. At the façade of the old hospital. "Daniel's here."

The cop at Stephen's door let them in. Daniel was sitting beside Stephen's bed. With one hand, he held Stephen's hand. In the other, he held his phone.

And Armand saw the outrage in his son's eyes.

CHAPTER 32

"We need to talk," Armand said to Daniel as soon as they'd returned to Stephen's suite at the George V.

Jean-Guy was there and introduced his colleague Séverine Arbour.

They greeted her, but before Beauvoir could explain, Armand said, "*Excusez-moi,*" and turned to Daniel. "Come with me, please."

Armand walked up the stairs, but Daniel stayed behind until his mother said, "Go. Please."

His father had asked him, in the taxi over, if he'd gone to see Commander Fontaine, but Daniel had refused to answer. As he'd done since he was a child, when angry, Daniel clamped shut. Refusing to talk. To make eye contact. To acknowledge anything and anyone.

Now he slowly followed his father up the stairs while the others exchanged glances.

Honoré was having a nap in the second bedroom, and Roslyn had taken the girls into the courtyard garden of the hotel for afternoon tea.

Those in the living room tried not to listen, but still, they heard enough.

"What?" demanded Daniel when they got into Stephen's bedroom and his father had closed the door.

"What?" said Armand, turning to face him. "One man is dead, another probably dying. We're in the middle of God knows what scale of crime, and you're sulking?"

"Sulking? You spied on me. You tracked my movements. My own father suspects me of having something to do with all this shit. I'm not sulking, I'm in a rage, you . . . asshole."

"You never speak to me like that, do you understand?" His father stared at him until Daniel dropped his eyes. But did not apologize.

"I'm deeply, deeply sorry for what happened twenty-five years ago," Armand went on, barely containing his own anger. "I wish with all my heart it hadn't. I wish I'd realized what had gone wrong. I wish we hadn't lost all that time together, but it's happened. I've apologized and I'll spend the rest of my life saying I'm sorry, if you want, but you need to set it aside for now."

"No, you don't get off that easily. Do you have any idea what it feels like, to have your own father not just suspect you of a crime, but spy on you?"

"I used a tracking app to find out where you were, yes. Because we were afraid. Your mother and I called over and over. When you didn't answer, we got worried. You know why?"

Daniel scowled, and remained silent.

"Because we love you. I used that tracker not because I suspect you, but because I love you. Because the thought of anything happening to you had me terrified. I'd do anything, anything, to find you. To protect you. Anything. And if it means you're safe, but you hate me for the rest of your life, that's a price I'm willing to pay. I hope to God you'd do the same for me."

He dropped his voice almost to a whisper. "If you don't know by now, Daniel, how much I love you, then I'm afraid you never will."

Downstairs in the living room, Jean-Guy took Annie's hand as they stared at the stairway. No longer pretending not to listen. They'd tried small talk, but all conversation about the weather was blown away by the words tumbling down.

"You want me to say that I know? That I love you, too?" said Daniel. "You're going to wait a long time, old man."

Armand's mouth opened slightly as he absorbed the blow. A sharp inhale and his hands closing tight were the only indications of the magnitude of pain.

"That doesn't change my feelings for you," he managed to say. Quietly. "Never will. I will love you until the day I die. And beyond."

He held out his hand. It trembled, very slightly, as he offered it to his son.

Not to shake. But to take.

As he'd reached out to his little boy when crossing the street. Or in a crowd.

Or hiking along a trail when there was a rustle in the woods.

To let Daniel know he was not alone. His father would protect him, no matter what.

He would not lose him.

"I'm not a child," snapped Daniel. "I don't need you. Never have, never will."

He turned his back on his father and left.

Annie, Reine-Marie, Jean-Guy, and Séverine got to their feet when Daniel appeared.

"Everything's fine," he said.

Though Reine-Marie wasn't fooled. She knew what "fine" meant.

Armand came down a few minutes later. He'd needed the time to splash water on his face. And gather himself. He stopped in to see Honoré, and kiss the sleeping boy lightly on the forehead.

As he went down the stairs, Armand heard Daniel say to his mother, "I'm sorry I didn't answer your call. I was with Stephen and didn't want to be disturbed." He turned to Séverine Arbour. "Who are you?"

"I work with Jean-Guy."

She explained about Beauvoir coming to her home and asking for help.

Armand came down and greeted her, thanking her for joining them.

"Let's sit at the dining table," he suggested.

As they walked over, Reine-Marie took his arm and whispered, "Is she really here to help? You said they might try to place someone among us. Her?"

"Possible," he whispered. "But Jean-Guy went to her, not the other way around."

"What're you two whispering about?" Annie asked.

"Food," said Reine-Marie. "What to order."

"Oh, good, I'm starving."

The order was placed for sandwiches, patisseries, and drinks.

"There goes my other kidney," muttered Reine-Marie.

Armand also called down for an easel, paper, and magic markers.

"In case you're still wondering," said Daniel, speaking to his mother and ignoring his father, "I did go to see Commander Fontaine. I told her that I knew Alexander Plessner. That he was a sort of mentor to me in the venture capital division."

"And what was her reaction?" Armand asked.

What had happened upstairs needed to be set aside. There were far more immediate, if not more important, issues to deal with.

Daniel turned to him, and for a moment Armand thought he'd refuse to answer.

"She didn't seem surprised." His tone was brusque, but at least he replied.

"She probably knew already," said Armand. "Did she ask any questions?"

"She wanted to know what we invested in."

"And?" said Jean-Guy.

"We've only done one buy so far. A small company that needed capital to expand. Won't come to much. It's a trial run to work out any kinks in the division."

"What's the name of the company?" asked Jean-Guy, bringing out his pen and notebook.

"Screw-U."

"*Pardon?*" Jean-Guy looked up at Daniel.

"That's the name of the company." When Daniel smiled, his entire face changed, as most people's did. "It was started by a couple of recent grads from the polytechnique. Mechanical engineers. They thought it was funny. We think it's infantile. We're in the process of changing the name. To Screw-Up."

"That's better?" asked Annie.

"Well, less aggressive, more playful."

"Right," muttered his sister. "That's not infantile at all."

"What does it make?" asked Reine-Marie.

"Screwdrivers."

"As in the tool?" Jean-Guy asked.

"Yes."

"Why that company?" asked Armand.

"Monsieur Plessner saw potential. It was his idea, not mine."

Daniel's answers to his father remained curt, though they were getting slightly longer.

"And nothing since?"

"No."

"Plessner didn't suggest anything else?" his father prodded.

"Well, we were looking at two other small companies. One that makes washers, those metal rings you put around a screw. And one that makes screws."

"Huh," said Jean-Guy. "That's interesting."

"Is it?" asked Annie. "Really?"

"Actually, yes. There were screws in Stephen's box. We thought they were from the desk upstairs, but maybe they were part of this venture capital research."

Armand turned to Séverine Arbour. "Does any of this sound familiar?"

She thought, then shook her head. "I've never heard of the company, and never seen particular mention of screwdrivers in any of the documents. They do mention screws, but we use a lot of those. And nails. And those washers you mentioned. But not screwdrivers."

Gamache nodded, but his thoughtful gaze lingered on her.

He's wondering how much I know, she thought. Even as she wondered how much he really knew.

Armand turned to Daniel. "We think Stephen was behind the venture capital you and Monsieur Plessner used to invest in that company."

"No, you're wrong. It came from a fund, from different sources."

"Those different sources were all Stephen. Mrs. McGillicuddy confirmed it."

"Really?" Daniel's surprise was complete and genuine. "But why wouldn't he tell me?"

"To keep you safe," said Reine-Marie.

They explained about Stephen selling his art collection and about the buy orders Mrs. McGillicuddy had found, going back years.

The investments Stephen was quietly making in diverse companies.

And the huge funds transferred into his account with the Banque Privée des Affaires.

"But why?" asked Annie. "What's he doing?"

"We don't know. We hoped you could help," Armand said to Daniel.

"Me?" said Daniel. "You don't think—"

Armand held up his hand. "I believe you. But you know the markets. Know how these things work. What does this sound like to you?"

Just then the concierge arrived and directed a worker to put up the easel and paper, while Armand handed him an envelope.

"Do you know which companies Stephen was buying into?" Daniel asked.

"Here's what Mrs. McGillicuddy found."

Armand picked up a green magic marker and, consulting the email from Mrs. McGillicuddy, he wrote the names of the companies in large letters on one of the sheets of paper.

"Anything look familiar?"

Daniel was scratching his beard and leaning forward. Eyes intense.

"I've heard of some, but there doesn't seem to be any cohesion, any plan. And some are numbered companies. I can't tell from this what they might be doing and why. Or if there's any connection."

"It looks almost like a shotgun approach," said Annie. "Like Stephen didn't really know what he was looking for and was covering as wide a field as possible."

"Or hiding the one important buy among all the others," said Daniel.

"That's what we wondered," said Reine-Marie.

Armand turned to Arbour, who was studying the list.

"No, nothing," she said.

"We need more information on these companies," he said, drawing a streak down the paper next to the names. "Can you do that?"

"Yes, absolutely," said Daniel. "I can go into the bank. Use my access to get information on the companies. The numbered companies will be more difficult, but I can try."

His father gave him a nod of approval, and Daniel felt something stir.

What he saw now wasn't the man who'd made his mother cry. It wasn't even the fellow in the kitchen helping prepare meals, or playing with the grandkids in the garden, or sitting by the fire reading.

What Daniel saw was a senior investigator, with a clear mind and a quiet, but complete, authority.

This was, Daniel thought, someone he could get behind. He had no beef with Chief Inspector Gamache.

It was Dad he had the problem with.

"Could Stephen have been going for a hostile takeover of GHS itself?" asked Annie.

"No," said Daniel. His answer unequivocal. "Even selling everything he owned, he'd never be able to raise enough. And a company that guarded would notice. He'd never get away with it. But if it looks like Stephen was involved in the venture capital, should I tell Commander Fontaine that? It might be important."

"I suspect she already knows," said Armand.

"But how? I didn't tell her."

"Commander Fontaine would know," said Jean-Guy, "because she might be involved."

"What?" demanded Daniel and Annie.

Séverine Arbour raised her hands. "Wait. Are you saying you think the Préfecture de Paris was responsible for the murder of Alexander Plessner?"

"Not the entire Préfecture," said Jean-Guy. "But a select few, yes. It's possible."

"That's ridiculous."

"What makes you think they might be involved?" Annie asked.

"When your mother and father found Plessner's body in Stephen's apartment," said Jean-Guy, "they interrupted someone."

"Yes, I know."

"What you don't know is that what alerted them was a scent. Still hanging in the air. A man's cologne."

"It's a very unusual scent," said Reine-Marie. "Claude Dussault, the Prefect of Police, wears it."

"Ohhhh," Annie moaned. "That can't be good."

"And you suspect this Fontaine woman just because she's his second-in-command?" asked Madame Arbour. "Does that mean every time this guy screws up, I'm also to blame? Just because I'm his number two?" She'd waved toward Beauvoir, who glared at her.

"It's more than that," said Reine-Marie. "We had the Dussaults over for dinner last night. Dr. Dussault told me that the cologne was a gift from his second-in-command, after they'd been to a conference together in Germany. According to Claude's wife, Irena Fontaine bought some for herself, too."

"So it could've been either of them in Stephen's apartment," said Daniel.

"Yes," said Gamache.

"Or neither," Madame Arbour pointed out.

"True," admitted Gamache.

"Or both," said Jean-Guy.

Daniel had gotten to his feet and was standing beside his father, examining the list of companies Stephen had, through Plessner, invested in.

Armand watched him for a moment, knowing he'd have to drop another bombshell.

"There's something else. When we were at your place, for the interview with Commander Fontaine, she wanted to talk privately."

They were all listening, though it was clear that he was speaking directly to Daniel.

"Yes?"

"She had a file on Stephen, information collected at the end of the war. It questioned whether he really worked for the Resistance or was a Nazi sympathizer, even a collaborator."

"Come on. Anyone who knows him would know that's ridiculous," said Daniel.

"But most people don't know him. Not personally. All they'd have to do is raise a suspicion, and the damage is done," said his mother. "We all know how easy it is to commit character assassination."

She glanced at her husband, the target of many such assassination attempts.

"We think Stephen went to the company and told them, or hinted at, what he'd discovered," said Armand. "Demanded they stop whatever it is, and that he get to speak to the board. Whatever it is, it's enough to ruin them. So they had to stop him."

"They thought they could blackmail him into silence," said Reine-Marie. "When that didn't work . . ."

They all knew what happened next.

What Daniel didn't know was why they were staring at him. All except Madame Arbour, who was looking out the window.

"I was at the archives this morning, to check into that old file," said Reine-Marie, her voice ominously gentle. "According to their records, the dossier on Stephen was requested five weeks ago. By you."

"What?" said Daniel, his face going an immediate, and vibrant, red. "I never did that. Why would I do that? I didn't even know there were records on Stephen in the archives."

His voice had risen, loud and high.

"We believe you," said Armand.

"Wait a minute," said Daniel, and they fell silent, allowing him to think it through. "The cop Fontaine had that file. She's the one who showed it to you, right? Is she the one setting me up? Did she put my name on the request, thinking you'd believe I was also involved?"

"She might've been the one who did that," said his father. "But they'd know we'd never believe it, and we don't. They're playing with us. Showing us what they can do, if they want. It's psychological warfare."

Jean-Guy turned to Annie. "In legal jargon that's called a mind-fuck."

"Yet more for Honoré's vocabulary," she said, and Jean-Guy laughed.

Daniel was pale. "They're predicting our every move."

"Not all," said his father.

Just then the doorbell chimed. It was the food and drink.

Plates of finger sandwiches, egg mayonnaise, coronation chicken, smoked salmon, and cucumber were put on the table, along with tea cakes and scones. Clotted cream and jams.

And two large bowls of seasoned frites with mayonnaise.

Armand signed for it and received an envelope from the waiter, which he opened, scanned, then placed in his pocket.

As they helped themselves to the food and drink, Armand brought Stephen's agenda from his breast pocket and turned to the upcoming week. As he did, the scrap of paper he'd tucked into the flap fluttered to the ground.

Séverine Arbour quickly stooped down and picked it up, beating Gamache to it. Though Beauvoir noticed he didn't really try. And wondered if that paper had really fallen by accident.

"*AFP*," she read as she placed it on the table. "Monsieur Horo-witz's writing?"

"Yes," said Gamache.

"Agence France-Presse?"

"Alexander Francis Plessner. We think the dates are when Stephen and Plessner met. He made the same notation, *AFP*, in his agenda this past Friday, the day Plessner arrived in Paris." He handed the slip to Daniel. "Do the dates mean anything to you?"

Daniel studied them and shook his head. "They're not even in chronological order. They go from oldest to most recent, except that final one. It goes back four years."

"Might mean nothing," said Armand, tucking it back under the flap in the agenda. "Now, the GHS Engineering meeting tomorrow," he said, consulting Stephen's notes. "Stephen's not on the board, so how would he get into the meeting?"

"He wouldn't," said Daniel. "Couldn't."

"And yet," said Gamache, "that seems to have been his plan. So how would he do it?"

Daniel was shaking his head. "No, it's impossible. He'd have to get a seat on the board."

"And how would he do that?" asked Armand. "There must be a way."

Daniel was staring into space. Thinking.

So like his father, thought Jean-Guy.

He himself tried so hard to emulate Gamache, it seemed a shame, a waste, that someone who did it naturally didn't value it.

"Board members of corporations are often rewarded with perks," said Daniel, finally. "Luxury trips to meetings, that sort of thing. And sometimes, rarely but sometimes, they'd be enticed with shares in the company. Nonvoting shares, so they'd never be able to band together and get control, but the shares would still be valuable enough to make them all wealthy."

"And loyal," said Annie.

"And blind," said Reine-Marie. "Hard to see wrongdoing over a pile of money."

"So Stephen would have to buy shares off a board member?" asked Jean-Guy.

"Yes."

"Would they know?" asked Reine-Marie.

Daniel thought about it. "The individual board member would have to know, but the chair of the board, the CEO, the majority owner, wouldn't necessarily. Not if the shares remained in the board member's name until the last minute."

"That's interesting," said Armand. "According to Mrs. McGillicuddy,

Stephen transferred a huge amount of money into his account at your bank a few weeks ago. It's unfrozen tomorrow morning."

"Just before the board meeting," said Annie.

Daniel nodded a few times, his brows drawn together in concentration. "It's possible."

"Why would someone agree to sell their shares and give up their seat?" asked Séverine Arbour.

"Money," said Daniel. "Why else? He'd offer to pay twice, five times, ten times what the shares are worth."

"Cash raised by, let's say, the sale of a priceless art collection," said Jean-Guy.

That sat on the gleaming table. They finally seemed to be getting somewhere.

"There is," Daniel began, "another reason a board member might sell."

"What's that?" asked Reine-Marie.

"Stephen might've made it unbelievably attractive to sell, and unbelievably unattractive not to. A push-pull. Suppose he approached a member of the board and told them what he knew. What he was about to reveal. Something so compromising it could not only bring about the collapse of the company, it would ruin anyone connected with it."

"And within days their shares would be worthless anyway," said Armand.

"But how would Stephen know that person wouldn't go directly to Madame Roquebrune?" asked Séverine Arbour.

"He'd have to know the board member personally or have some information that would make him think this person would agree," said Daniel. "The devil you know."

"*Oui,*" said Armand.

"Who's on the board?" Daniel grabbed the annual report and flipped to that section. "Holy shit."

"What?" demanded Annie.

Daniel passed it to his sister and looked at his parents.

"Have you seen? Former Presidents, Prime Ministers. Emirs.

Generals. She's a former Secretary-General of the UN. And this one's a Nobel Peace Prize winner. Two media moguls. It's a who's who. And all respected, or, well, mostly respected."

"All with a great deal to lose if, as you said, it comes out that they've been propping up a corrupt conglomerate," said Armand.

"Collaborators," said Reine-Marie.

"So," said Annie. "Which of them sold his or her stake in the company to Stephen?"

"We don't know that's what really happened," Gamache cautioned.

There was silence. No answer was possible, yet.

"We have news, too," said Beauvoir. "Something I didn't tell you." He turned to Annie. "You're not going to like this. When I left here a couple hours ago, I was pretty sure that man was back, watching us."

"The SecurForte guard? The one you chased last night?"

"Loiselle. Yes."

"And you went after him again?" demanded Annie. "Once was bad enough. You said yourself he's ex–special forces. He could've killed you."

"But he didn't."

"That's not the point." She was shouting now. Balling up all her anger, all her fears, and hurling them at him. "Suppose he had? I can't imagine . . ." She stopped, unable to find the words. "What would we do without you?" She had both hands on her belly. "If something happened? What—"

She dropped her head and started crying. Sobbing. Her mother and father made to go to her, but stopped. It wasn't their role anymore.

Jean-Guy was already there, kneeling down and holding her. Whispering, "I'm sorry. I'm sorry. But I had to know what his orders were. To hurt you? The baby? Honoré? I had to stop him. I'm sorry."

"You can't leave me," Annie whispered. "I can't . . . this child . . . I can't raise her on my own. I need you."

"You won't have to. I promise. I promise."

Annie and Jean-Guy left, returning more composed a few minutes later.

"Okay?" Armand asked his daughter.

When she nodded, he turned to Jean-Guy. "Annie's right. A younger special-forces-trained guard should've been able to take you. He'd take all of us, combined."

"It was stupid, I admit," said Jean-Guy. "The guy must've been told to intimidate me, but not to directly engage. When I confronted him, he disappeared."

Madame Arbour cocked her head. She knew that wasn't the truth. But at a look from Jean-Guy she remained silent. Still, she wondered if she should say something.

This was getting far too complicated.

"That's when I went to see you," Jean-Guy said to her. "To get some answers."

"And what were the questions?" asked Armand.

"Is GHS involved? And if so, what did Stephen find out that was so bad?" said Jean-Guy. "I think now that's why he got me my job there. He knows my strengths aren't in business or engineering. But they are in criminal investigation. In noticing if something's off. And something is off in GHS. Unfortunately"—he turned back to Madame Arbour—"I thought it was you."

"And I thought it was you. I mean, really? Why hire someone obviously unsuited to the job? Why put someone so absolutely in-competent in charge?"

"I wasn't so incompetent," said Beauvoir. But at a stern look from Madame Arbour, he conceded the point.

"Unless," she continued, "because of his vast ignorance, he could be easily manipulated. Or, more likely, you were part of it. There to help them cover up. If you knew crime, presumably you'd also know how to hide it."

"While we're at it," said Beauvoir, "why put a competent engineer—"

"Brilliant engineer."

"—in a department where there's no original engineering done? Unless the idea is that you're there to cover up, to make sure I didn't spot anything."

"No fear of that," said Madame Arbour. "You're perfectly capable of missing it without my help."

"Their office Christmas parties must be fun," said Daniel to his mother.

"I eventually realized my mistake," Jean-Guy admitted. "You weren't covering up, you were digging for something, and I wanted to know what. That's why I went to your home this afternoon. To find out what you knew about the Luxembourg project. But you surprised me."

"How?" Gamache asked.

"Patagonia," said Arbour. "I still think there's something off with Luxembourg, but like we talked about at the Eiffel Tower, I think Patagonia's the key."

"The Eiffel Tower?" asked Annie. "Why go there?"

"I needed someplace where we wouldn't be overheard," said Jean-Guy.

"It's perfect," Armand agreed, though Reine-Marie noticed that just the mention of it had made him, and Daniel, pale. "Now, what about Patagonia?"

"Wait a minute," said Madame Arbour, putting up her hands and looking around. "If we had to go all the way to the top of the Tour to avoid listening devices, what's stopping someone from listening in now?"

"Nothing. I can almost guarantee they are," said Gamache.

"What?" said Daniel. "With all we've talked about? Are you kidding me?"

"They might not be, but we have to assume they are. There's no avoiding it."

"Then shouldn't we be discussing the weather or ice hockey or whatever it is you Canadians talk about," said Madame Arbour.

Gamache got up and walked to the floor-to-ceiling window. "There may be bugs in the room, but more likely high-powered mics from one of the buildings nearby."

He paused to gaze out, then turned to them.

"They've attacked Stephen, first with blackmail and then they tried to kill him. They succeeded with Monsieur Plessner. They've set you up, Daniel. They've done everything they can, over the course of years, it seems, to cover up, to hide. I want them to know"—he raised his voice slightly and turned back to the window—"that they've failed." Then he dropped his voice and whispered, "We're coming for you."

He'd leaned so close to the window that his words fogged up the glass. And on it, he drew what looked like a snowflake before returning to his chair. "Let's continue."

"They'll hear everything we say," said Annie, lowering her voice. "They'll know what we know. And don't know."

"Yes, but—" Jean-Guy began.

At that moment there was a bang and the door to the suite blew open. While the others froze, Armand and Jean-Guy sprang to their feet.

Roslyn and the girls came in. Laughing and talking. Then, seeing their faces, Roslyn stopped.

Armand immediately lowered the knife he'd grabbed from the tray. A spoon clattered out of Jean-Guy's hand.

"What's wrong?" she asked.

"Nothing," said Jean-Guy.

"Nice, Rambo," said Annie, glancing at the spoon.

"Yeah, well, look what you grabbed, Betty Crocker."

Annie looked at the scone, now crushed in her hands. And smiled.

"Okay," said Roslyn, uncertainly. "We're just getting our coats. Sky's clearing, so we thought we'd walk over to the Arc de Triomphe."

Daniel got up, hugged them, and explained that it was probably best if they stayed in the suite. Roslyn was about to protest when she studied his face and nodded.

"Come on, girls. Grab your books. We'll go upstairs, lie on the bed, and read."

It took some convincing, and the promise of time on the iPad, but they finally agreed.

Daniel took them up, then returned to the table. "You'd better be right," he said to his father. "If you're wrong and anyone gets hurt . . ."

He couldn't finish.

"Yes." Armand turned back to Madame Arbour. "Tell us what you know about GHS."

307

She looked frightened and unsure. And she was.

Séverine Arbour was used to flow charts and schematics. To things that made sense. Or, if they didn't, there was a method, a way to find the flaw and correct it.

Engineers were problem solvers.

But this was a problem she couldn't seem to solve. Couldn't even see. Not clearly.

And it was getting muddier by the minute. She could feel the hysteria roiling up inside her.

Composing herself, she took a deep breath and plunged on.

"This all started—"

Gamache's phone buzzed with an incoming text, and he dropped his eyes for a moment, then held up his hand.

"*Désolé.* Just a moment."

He turned his phone around for all to see the message that had just arrived.

Can we meet? Fontaine des Mers, Place de la Concorde. 9 p.m.

It was from Claude Dussault.

He typed, *Oui.*

"Are you insane?" demanded Daniel.

"Maybe," said his father, but without a smile.

"He's listening," said Annie, looking around, as though the Prefect might appear from behind the sofa. "He knows we're getting close. That's why he wants to talk."

Instead of answering, Armand put a finger to his lips and, getting up, he motioned them to follow.

CHAPTER 33

Armand took Annie and Jean-Guy aside. Lowering his voice, he said to his daughter, "You need to stay here."

"No."

"I'm sorry, but Honoré will be awake soon. And there's—" He pointed to the unborn baby. "Please."

"Where're you going?"

"Not far, but I can't say."

She stared at her father, as serious as she'd ever seen him.

Armand turned to Jean-Guy. "Would you like to stay with Annie?"

"I . . ." He wanted to stay. To stand in front of her. And the baby, and Honoré.

But he also wanted to stand beside Armand.

And there were things only he knew. Things he needed to tell them.

"I . . ."

"You need to go with them, *mon beau*," said Annie. "We'll be safe. We have the cop, and no one's going to bother us with such a strong, handsome, manly man protecting us. I bet he has a huge gun."

Jean-Guy narrowed his eyes in mock concern.

"Go," Annie whispered and gave him a long kiss as her father looked away.

Outside the door, Jean-Guy spoke to the cop, letting him know that if anything happened to Annie and Honoré, to Roslyn and the girls, he would come for him.

"*Entendu*," said the flic, and tightened his grip on his automatic rifle. "*Je comprends.*"

"You'd better understand," said Jean-Guy as Armand and Reine-Marie, Daniel and Séverine Arbour waited by the elevator. "And you tell no one we've left."

"*Oui*. I mean, *non*."

The ferocity of Jean-Guy's tone and expression had thrown the cop off a bit.

Once in the elevator, Reine-Marie said quietly to Armand, "You're not really going to meet him, are you?"

He took her hand and squeezed. "We'll talk."

But she had her answer.

Jean-Guy stood in silence, watching the numbers drop. With each floor they passed, there was a chime, meant to be cheerful, but all it did was rattle him further.

"You okay?" Armand asked as they sped past the main floor. And kept going.

"*Oui.*"

Past the basement. Past the subbasement. And as they dropped, so did the color from Jean-Guy's face.

"You can go back up, if you like."

"*Non.*"

When it could go no deeper, the elevator stopped.

They stepped out, and Armand took an envelope from his pocket and removed a slip of paper and a key.

Unlocking a door, he led them down a dim corridor, pausing once to consult the hand-drawn map. Then he headed this way, then that.

Both sweaty and ice-cold, Jean-Guy followed. *Adown Titanic glooms of chasmed fears.*

A fine time, he thought, to remember that quote. But he finally understood what it meant.

Pipes hissed, as though serpents were passing overhead. The walls clanked and groaned.

Finally, Armand stopped in front of a metal door. Consulting the map again, he unlocked it.

When the lights came on, they could see stacks of broken equipment. Vacuum cleaners, trollies, crates.

"How did you know?" Reine-Marie whispered.

Closing the door and locking it, he held up the key and spoke in a normal voice. "Madame Béland."

"The General Manager?" asked Reine-Marie.

"*Oui.* The waiter gave it to me when she brought up the food."

"How did she know you wanted it?" Madame Arbour asked.

"I sent a message down with the concierge—"

"That was the envelope you gave him?" asked Reine-Marie.

"*Oui.* I asked for the use of a room in the lowest level, where there were no cameras. I knew we'd eventually need a place where we couldn't be overheard. Or seen."

Daniel stared at this man, this stranger. Who thought so many steps ahead. Who found a corner of order in chaos.

Was this really the same man who made scrambled eggs in his bathrobe on Sunday mornings?

"Why didn't we come down sooner?" Daniel asked as they pulled crates into a circle.

"Because we wanted them to overhear," said Jean-Guy.

"You knew about the key?" asked Daniel. "The plan to come here?"

"No, but I trust your father."

Daniel stared at Jean-Guy in open and undisguised amazement. Even as his heart sank.

What this man and his father had went so far beyond the bounds of camaraderie and friendship. Beyond even blood.

Daniel now knew he could never, ever compete. Once, maybe, but not now. It was far too late.

He'd ceded his place to Jean-Guy Beauvoir.

"Since they were listening anyway," said Armand, "it made sense to have it work in our favor. Tell them only what we wanted them to hear—"

"—and not tell them everything we know," said Jean-Guy. "Let them think we're further behind than we are."

"Loiselle," said Madame Arbour. "You didn't tell them the truth. I was wondering."

"Thank you for not saying anything," said Jean-Guy.

"Look, I'm just trying to keep my head above water," she said. "I have no idea what's going on."

Armand, from his crate across the circle, wondered if that was true. Another advantage of being down there was that, while no message could get in, neither could messages be sent out.

They were isolated. Which was good.

But they were also trapped. Which was not.

"What's this about Loiselle?" he asked, but before Jean-Guy could answer, Reine-Marie touched his arm.

"If the GHS meeting is tomorrow morning, wouldn't the board members be in Paris already?"

"Yes, probably. Why?"

"Where would they stay? Most don't live here."

Armand looked at his wife in wonderment. How had he missed that?

"A hotel," he said.

"A luxury hotel," she said.

Jean-Guy's eyes opened wide. "Is that why Stephen decided to stay in the George V instead of the Lutetia or another place? He knew that this's where the board members are being put up."

"I bet Stephen arranged to meet that board member here," said Daniel. "To finalize his deal to buy the shares."

"When we leave, I need to speak to the General Manager," said Armand.

"I can go up right now and ask," Jean-Guy volunteered.

"That's not a bad idea," said Armand, then narrowed his eyes. "You will come back?"

"Maybe." But he nodded as he took the key and map from Armand.

Jean-Guy stared at the door. His way out. His way up. Then offered the key and map to Reine-Marie.

"You go. The GM knows you and is more likely to tell you what we want to know."

"You sure?"

He looked anything but. *"Oui."*

"Move quickly to the elevator," said Armand. "If anyone stops you, shout and we'll come."

"D'accord."

Just as she was about to leave, he quietly handed her his phone.

"Take this," he whispered. "Messages will download on the surface."

Reine-Marie slipped out. He closed the door only when it was obvious that she'd made it safely to the elevator.

"Okay now," he said, sitting back down on his crate and leaning toward Beauvoir. "Loiselle? What haven't you told us?"

"He was following me because he wanted to talk."

"Talk?" said Gamache. "You mean threaten?"

"No, I mean talk."

"What did he want to say?" asked Daniel.

Jean-Guy told them everything, with Séverine Arbour jumping in now and then.

"And you believed him," said Gamache when they'd finished. "That he wants to work with us now? Seems pretty abrupt."

At that moment there was a knock on the door. "Armand?"

When he opened it, Reine-Marie quickly slipped through. As she hugged him, she slid his phone back into his pocket.

"That was fast."

It didn't bode well.

"Madame Béland saw me right away. The board members aren't staying here, and the meeting isn't here either."

"Damn," said Jean-Guy. "It was such a good theory."

"But?" said Armand. He could tell by Reine-Marie's bright eyes that there was more.

"But Madame Béland did know where they're staying, and where the meeting's being held. Can you guess?"

"The Lutetia," said Jean-Guy.

"*Oui.*"

They looked at each other. And smiled. Yes. They were moving forward.

Reine-Marie was brought up to speed about Xavier Loiselle, and the SecurForte operative's desire to switch sides and help them.

She listened closely, shooting glances at her husband, and remembering his prediction. That the next thing they'd do was get someone on the inside.

And now there were two potential "someones." Arbour and Loiselle.

"You believe him?" she asked, unknowingly repeating Armand's question.

"Honestly, I've gone back and forth, but yes, eventually I decided he probably meant it."

"Probably?" asked Daniel. "Is that good enough?"

"It's all we've got, so yes, it's pretty damned good." Jean-Guy turned to Gamache. "With Loiselle on board and on the inside, we can finally make a plan."

"Great," said Daniel. "*Everyone has a plan until they get punched in the face.*" On seeing their expressions, he explained. "Mike Tyson said that."

"You're getting advice from Mike Tyson?" said Beauvoir.

"And you're inviting someone who might be a killer to join us? What's worse?"

At that moment, Jean-Guy was tempted to show Daniel what being punched in the face felt like.

And yet, maddeningly, he recognized that Daniel, and Mike, might be right. Only the most disciplined, or the most stubborn, stuck to a plan when the first blow landed.

The key was knowing when to adapt, and when to hold firm.

And he also recognized, somewhat grudgingly, that Daniel had a right to question. He had a lot at stake.

Was Xavier Loiselle an ally, or a spy?

Was he a member of their Resistance, or a collaborator?

"You're right," said Jean-Guy, to Daniel's surprise. "But I think this's a risk we need to take." He turned to Séverine Arbour. "What was your impression of Loiselle?"

She thought about it, then nodded. "I agree. I think he's sincere. He could've turned us in when we went to the office this afternoon, but he didn't. I think he's on our side. Is that a certainty?" She looked at Daniel. "No. As an engineer, I'm not at all comfortable with probabilities. *The bridge will probably stay up. The plane will probably fly.* No. We deal with as close to certainties as we can get. But life isn't a schematic. It's not an engineering project. Sometimes we need to take a risk. And sometimes, I guess, we need to be the one doing the punching."

Beauvoir nodded to Daniel. And Daniel, after a pause, nodded back.

"Did you say you went back to GHS Engineering this afternoon?" asked Armand.

"Yes," said Arbour. "All three of us. Loiselle pretended he was still tailing us."

"Why did you do that?" asked Reine-Marie. "Isn't that like walking right into the rat's nest?"

"We wanted to try to get into Carole Gossette's files," said Madame Arbour. "She oversees both the Patagonia and Luxembourg projects. We thought we might find out what GHS Engineering was really doing."

Armand sat forward. "You mentioned Patagonia earlier. What's that about?"

"Seven years ago the regional government realized that an abandoned mine was poisoning the drinking water of a town downriver," she explained. "GHS Engineering was contracted by the Chilean government to build a water treatment plant. Which they apparently did."

"Apparently?" asked Reine-Marie.

"According to what I was seeing coming across my desk, it was taking a very long time to build. Far too long. I wasn't suspicious of anything at first, except maybe government corruption, payoffs. The usual. Contractors prolonging construction to make more money. I did see that one of the first things GHS did before even beginning the project was to order a water sample taken and analyzed so they'd know what was coming down from the mine."

"That makes sense, doesn't it?" said Reine-Marie.

"Yes. What didn't make sense is that the detailed results of that test were missing. What I did see was that GHS bought the mine and closed it."

"But why buy it?" asked Daniel. "If it was already abandoned and closed?"

"Exactly," said Madame Arbour. "So I began to look closer. What really triggered my suspicions were the containers coming back from Chile. The documentation said they were equipment, but the weights didn't make sense, and the destinations didn't either. They cleared customs in record time, then the containers moved from site to site, eventually ending up in smelters. You don't melt down an excavator."

"The mine had been reopened," said Jean-Guy. "They were shipping back ore."

"And hiding the fact," said Madame Arbour.

"But why? What's in the mine?" asked Daniel. "Gold?"

"Something even more precious."

"Diamonds?" he asked, and when Madame Arbour shook her head, he said, "Uranium?"

Madame Arbour held up her hand to stop the cavalcade of guesses. "Rare earth minerals."

Daniel leaned back on his crate. "Wow. Are you sure?"

"Pretty sure. There was a mention, just in passing, in a report from a Chilean geologist. But it didn't say what sort."

"What's a rare earth mineral?" asked Reine-Marie. "It sounds familiar."

"The market went wild for them a few years ago," Daniel explained, "when scientists realized what they could be used for."

"Like?" asked Armand.

Séverine Arbour ran through some of the uses. Everything from laptops to medical equipment. From nuclear reactors to airplanes.

"And there're experiments with next-generation telecommunications," said Jean-Guy.

"Shit," said Daniel. "If you could get in on the ground floor . . ."

"Yes," said Séverine Arbour. "You could make a fortune. The thing with rare earth minerals is that they tend to be far stronger than other minerals. Last longer, are lighter and easily adaptable. Versatile. Pretty much an engineer's dream."

"What kind did they find?" Daniel asked.

"That's the problem," said Jean-Guy. "And that's why we wanted to find the water test. We don't know."

"So you don't know what it might be used for," said Armand.

"Exactly," said Arbour.

"Is that what they're trying to cover up?" said Reine-Marie. "Not that they found the minerals, but what they're doing with it? And that's what Stephen and Monsieur Plessner found out?"

"I think so," said Jean-Guy. "But when we went to GHS, Loiselle interrupted us."

"But I thought—" began Daniel.

"He had no choice," explained Jean-Guy. "Someone from Secur-Forte was with him. Someone way up the chain. It was clever of Loiselle to be there, too. He appeared to have informed on us, but I think he was playing the only hand he could. Solidifying his position with his superior while also protecting us. But there's something else. I recognized the SecurForte officer. And so would you."

"Me?" asked Gamache. "Who was he?"

"That man we saw on the security tape here at the hotel, having tea with Claude Dussault and Eugénie Roquebrune."

Gamache absorbed that information quickly, then asked, "Did he tell you his name?"

"Yes. Thierry Girard."

Jean-Guy Beauvoir wasn't prepared for Gamache's reaction. Rarely had he seen his former boss and mentor so surprised.

"What is it?" he asked.

"Thierry Girard?" Gamache asked. "Are you sure?"

"Yes," said Madame Arbour. "Why? Do you know him?"

Instead of answering, Gamache was quiet for a moment. Thinking. Slowly leaning back until he rested against the concrete wall. His hand went to his face, and his eyes narrowed in concentration.

"Thierry Girard used to be Claude Dussault's second-in-command. He told us last night that Girard had left the Préfecture for a job in private industry. But I didn't know it was with SecurForte."

He looked at Beauvoir across the storeroom. As he had across so many rooms, across so many crimes, across so many corpses, across the years.

"They were both meeting with Eugénie Roquebrune yesterday," said Jean-Guy. "It looks like he's still Dussault's second-in-command, only now in SecurForte."

His voice was gentle, knowing that Claude Dussault and Gamache went way back. And that his father-in-law considered Dussault a friend.

Though evidence was now nearly overwhelming that that was no longer true.

It looked like Claude Dussault had quietly taken over as head of SecurForte, with Thierry Girard back as his loyal second-in-command. Running the day-to-day operations of the private army, while Dussault remained at the head of the Préfecture.

His power absolute.

Had these two men, individually decent, somehow warped each other? Found, fed, magnified, justified the worst in each other? Until the unthinkable became acceptable became normal?

"Wait a minute," said Daniel. "This Thierry Girard was the second-in-command at the Préfecture de Paris before Fontaine?"

"*Oui,*" said his father. "Irena Fontaine took over eighteen months ago." Armand turned back to Beauvoir and was about to speak, when Daniel interrupted.

"I was in Fontaine's office this afternoon. There're posters around, including one of Copenhagen Harbor. I commented on it. Asked how she liked Copenhagen. But she said she'd never been outside France."

Beauvoir was about to ask what that had to do with anything when he suddenly got it.

"Cologne," he said.

"Cologne," said Armand, nodding, and smiling at his son. "Well done."

"I don't understand," said Séverine Arbour.

"Irena Fontaine couldn't have been the one who bought the cologne for Claude," said Armand.

"Not if she's never been outside France," said Daniel.

"When Monique Dussault told me that Claude's second-in-command gave him the cologne," said Reine-Marie, "I assumed she meant Commander Fontaine. But actually she meant Thierry Girard, who also bought some for himself. Was he the one we interrupted in Stephen's apartment?"

"Perhaps," said Armand.

They were getting closer to the truth, but there was still far too much they didn't know. And time was short. It was now quarter to six. Just a few hours before he was to meet Dussault in Place de la Concorde.

Information would be his only ammunition, and so far he had precious little of that.

He checked for the messages that had downloaded when Reine-Marie took his phone to the surface.

Jean-Guy, the rational man who lived in a near perpetual state of magical thinking, also checked his phone.

Not surprisingly, it was empty of new messages.

Armand's was not.

"What is it?" Reine-Marie asked, noticing Armand's brows drop, then draw together.

"An update from Mrs. McGillicuddy. It looks like Stephen sold all his holdings."

"We know that," she said. "The fake art—"

"*Non.* All his holdings. Everything," said Armand. "All his shares, his investments, even in his own company. He's mortgaged his homes. Liquidated everything."

"But that's not possible," said Daniel, moving to his father's side to read the message.

"He's in the hospital," said Reine-Marie. "How . . . ?"

"It says here he did it late Friday," said Daniel, scanning the message. "Minutes before market close."

"Mrs. McGillicuddy's just discovered it," said Armand. "This was no last-minute whim on Stephen's part. He's obviously spent years putting everything in place. This"—he held up his phone—"was the *coup de grâce*."

"That would come to—" Daniel began.

"Billions," said Armand.

"Wouldn't the markets react?" asked Arbour.

Daniel was shaking his head. "He timed the sell orders so they wouldn't be noticed until the European markets opened tomorrow morning. By then they'd be unstoppable and he'd have the weekend to do whatever else he needed."

"But what was that?" asked Jean-Guy. "Does Mrs. McGillicuddy say?"

Armand shook his head. "She's as shocked as we are."

"Maybe he wasn't the one who sold it all. Maybe someone else did," said Reine-Marie. "Broke into his accounts and did it."

"No, it was Stephen. Mrs. McGillicuddy confirmed it before writing me." Armand looked at Daniel. "What do you think he's up to?"

Daniel returned to his crate and thought, finally shaking his head. "Buying his way onto the board would take maybe a hundred million, maybe more. Not billions. He had something else in mind. But what? It looks like he's going all in on something. If there's a sell order, was there also a buy order?"

"Mrs. McGillicuddy's looking. Is it possible to put in a buy order late on Friday," asked Armand, "to be executed first thing Monday?"

"Yes, for sure. But there'd still be a record. Somewhere. We might be able to track it down," said Daniel, considering. "If I go to the bank, I can at least see if the money is still in his account, and if not, I might be able to trace where it's gone. I can also look into those numbered companies he and Monsieur Plessner were buying into."

Armand brought out his wallet and without hesitation gave the tattered old JSPS card to his son. "This might help."

Reine-Marie watched Daniel put it in his jacket pocket, and she wondered if he understood the magnitude of what his father had just done.

Armand did not particularly value possessions. But there were two that he held precious. One was his wedding ring. The other was that small card, which he hadn't been parted from in half a century.

"We need to find out which board member, if any, Stephen approached," said Armand.

"That's something I can look into," said Reine-Marie. "Research the members, see who might be the most vulnerable. I'll call Madame Lenoir from the hotel reception and see if we can use the terminals at the Archives nationales."

"I'll go with you," said Séverine Arbour. "I can help."

"*Non,*" said Armand. "Jean-Guy, can you go with Reine-Marie?"

"*Absolument.*"

"You come with me," he said to Arbour. "I think we can rattle them a bit more."

"How?" she asked.

"By going to the Hôtel Lutetia."

"A punch in the face?" asked Jean-Guy.

"Let's start with a tap on the shoulder," said Gamache, with a smile. "Sometimes more frightening. Besides"—he turned to Madame Arbour—"I need more information from you about the Patagonia and Luxembourg projects before I see Claude Dussault."

"You're still going to meet him?" asked Reine-Marie.

"Unless something changes, yes. If Claude wants to talk, I want to listen."

"What if he wants to do more than talk?" she asked, trying to keep her tone casual. But the stress was obvious.

"Then he wouldn't have chosen such a public place," said Armand. "A side street. A private home. I'd be worried. But Place de la Concorde? It's far too public to do anything other than stroll and talk." He held her eyes. "Believe me."

Reine-Marie nodded. She believed him. She trusted him. It was Claude Dussault she didn't trust.

"Jean-Guy?" she said, turning to her son-in-law.

"I agree. It's safe. I think Dussault wants to see how much we know without revealing his own position. They're worried."

Armand handed Reine-Marie the scrap of paper from Stephen's agenda after first taking a photo of it.

"You might look up those dates, too. See if anything significant happened." He got to his feet. "We need to go up."

"So soon?" asked Jean-Guy.

CHAPTER 34

⁓

"M onsieur Beauvoir?" asked the concierge, crossing the lobby of the grand hotel.

"*Oui?*"

Up from that crypt, Jean-Guy was breathing in the sweet scent of the fresh flowers in the lobby and almost tearing up at the sight of the fading daylight beyond the doors of the George V.

"A man dropped this off for you."

She handed him an envelope. Beauvoir opened it. On the slip of paper was written one word.

Neodymium.

And below that the letters *XL*.

He showed it to the others. "What does this mean?"

They crowded around.

"Neodymium is a rare earth element," said Séverine Arbour.

"Extra large?" asked Daniel. "Oh, right, it's—"

But a look from his father stopped him.

The message was from Xavier Loiselle. He'd managed to get into Carole Gossette's files and find the water sample results.

"So he is on our side," said Reine-Marie.

Though it looked like it, Armand wasn't totally convinced. He'd used agents to infiltrate organizations, and part of the technique of a spy was to hand over legitimate information as proof they could be trusted.

What he did think was that this information, at least, was correct.

GHS Engineering had discovered neodymium in the abandoned mine.

"What's it used for?" he asked Madame Arbour.

"Magnets."

"Magnets?" repeated Jean-Guy. "Fridge magnets?"

The engineer stared at him.

"Yes," said Madame Arbour. "People are being murdered in an epic battle for control of the fridge magnet empire. Look, magnets are used in all sorts of things, not just to stick hockey logos on your fridge."

"A simple 'no' . . . ," said Beauvoir.

Though it was true. He had several Montréal Canadiens up there.

"What else are they used for?" he asked.

"Computers, I think," she said. "But there must be a lot of other things. I'm no expert."

"We need to find out more about this neodymium," said Armand.

"Shouldn't be hard." Séverine pulled out her phone.

"*Non,*" he said. "We need someplace more private."

"Then I can go to the archives."

Jean-Guy glanced at her. This was the second time she'd suggested that.

Why was she so determined to go there, and why was Gamache so determined she should not?

He thought he knew why.

If Madame Arbour was an infiltrator, she must not be there when they found out which board member sold their spot to Stephen.

They were close. So close. They couldn't take any chances.

"No," Gamache said to Madame Arbour. "I need you with me at the Lutetia, if you don't mind."

There was, as always, courtesy in his words, but their meaning was clear.

Allida Lenoir hung up the phone and turned to her wife. "Back to the mines."

Far from a derogatory way to describe her work, the head archivist considered the miles and miles of files a gold mine. Filled with treasures, with adventure. The unknown waiting to be unearthed.

"I'm coming with you," said Judith de la Granger.

As the Chief Librarian for France, Judith de la Granger knew, better than most, that the documents contained in the glorious old buildings were both fascinating and dangerous.

And this night had the makings of both.

Ten minutes later they were greeting Reine-Marie at the main gate.

"Hope you don't mind my bringing Judith along," said Madame Lenoir.

"God, no," said Reine-Marie.

The Chief Librarian was legendary in Reine-Marie's universe.

From an old aristocratic family, Judith de la Granger's ancestors had owned, almost a millennium ago, the original château where the archives and museum now stood.

Slight, fine-boned, she radiated a fierce energy and intelligence. A lioness stuffed into a gerbil's body.

"I hope you don't mind my bringing my son-in-law," said Reine-Marie, introducing Jean-Guy.

Reine-Marie explained that while he now worked in private industry in Paris, Jean-Guy had been a senior officer in homicide in the Sûreté du Québec.

As they made their way to the reading room, Reine-Marie followed Jean-Guy's eyes out the window and saw what he was staring at.

A dark spot against the sunset. Like an astigmatism in the eye.

A drone.

The Banque Privée des Affaires, for security reasons since the recent terrorist attacks, did not encourage weekend visitors. And the guard was more than a little suspicious of a junior executive who urgently needed to get in at seven on a Sunday evening.

Even when, especially when, Daniel produced the JSPS card.

The guard looked at the card, then made a call.

"Can you come to the front desk please, *patron*. There's someone here who has an ID in the name of Daniel Gamache. But he just gave me a card with someone else's name. Yes, it is suspicious."

"No—" Daniel began, then stopped when the guard put his hand up for him to be quiet.

A door opened and the supervisor came out. Not saying a word, he studied Daniel, then turned his attention to the card on the counter in front of the guard.

Picking it up, he looked at Daniel more closely, then, to the guard's amazement, said, "Come with me."

Séverine Arbour went over to the statue of Gustave Eiffel at the entrance to the Lutetia and was admiring this hero of France. A giant among engineers and innovators.

A man of vision, of courage, and of brute ambition.

While she studied the face of the great engineer, Gamache studied the faces of the hotel guests, to see if he recognized any from the annual reports. Reine-Marie had been right, of course. This was a rat's nest.

At least one, probably more, of the people under that roof had been involved in the murder of Alexander Francis Plessner and the attack on Stephen.

They'd threatened, hounded, pursued, chased his family from their homes. All in an effort to make them go away.

And he wanted them to know it had not worked.

Far from going away, he'd come to them. For them.

"Madame Arbour?" he said, and together they walked down the long corridor, their footsteps echoing off the marble surfaces.

At bar Joséphine, they found a table against the wall and ordered drinks.

While Madame Arbour took a long sip of her red wine, Armand simply swirled his scotch, then put it back on the table.

"Recognize anyone?" he asked.

She looked around at the other patrons. Well-heeled, well-dressed. Mostly white, mostly French. Mostly older. They looked like them.

"No."

But Gamache did. Over there, in a quiet corner, was the former head of the UN Security Council. She now sat on the GHS Engineering board. Joining her was another member of that board.

And there in the center of the room, holding court, was the head of a media conglomerate who also sat on the GHS board.

Loud and laughing, corpulent and confident, the man commanded attention.

Gamache continued to study the room. He'd become, through practice and necessity, very good at faces. He recognized most of the members of the board from news reports over the years. And their photographs in the annual report.

He suspected some, if not most, would have no idea that anything untoward was going on. They'd been flown to Paris on private jets, put up in a luxury hotel, were being pampered in advance of an annual rubber-stamp board meeting.

But some would know what was really happening. The question was, which ones? And which one had Stephen approached with a sackful of money?

As he looked around, not trying to conceal his interest, a few caught his eye and paused. Returning the stare of the distinguished stranger before turning away.

Yes, some in that room definitely knew what was going on.

He just wished he was one of them.

"I've never been to this hotel," Séverine Arbour was saying. "I'd have expected it to feel different. Not so inviting."

"Why do you say that?"

"Well, isn't this where the Nazi interrogations happened?" She fixed him with a hard gaze. "Seems appropriate."

He raised his brows. "You think you're here for an interrogation?"

"Aren't I? Not torture, you're far too civilized for that. But you are trying to work out whose side I'm on, isn't that right?"

Armand smiled and tilted his head slightly.

She was smart. Clever. He'd have to be even more careful than he'd thought.

"My job has made me suspicious," he admitted. "But it's also taught me not to prejudge. I am curious that by your own admission you began to suspect something months ago, but hadn't yet found the results of the water test. Something this Xavier Loiselle found in minutes."

"I wasn't initially looking in that direction," said Madame Arbour. "As I told you, at first I thought it was something to do with building the plant. Contractors dragging it out. It's only recently that I realized the issue isn't the plant, but the mine."

Gamache nodded and opened his hands. "That explains it then."

"Listen—" She dropped her voice. "Beauvoir came to me, remember? Practically dragged me from my home. Believe me, I'd much rather be in my living room drinking wine and watching reruns of *Call My Agent*. I'm an engineer, not"—she waved her hands and looked around—"whatever this is."

"Then why did you agree to help?"

"Honestly? If I'd known it was this bad, I'd never have answered the door. I was curious. I thought GHS was involved in some scam, not"—she dropped her voice still further—"murder."

She was certainly stressed. Afraid. Perhaps because she knew her people were also in bar Joséphine. Watching, listening. And she knew what they were capable of.

Or perhaps because she'd woken up in her nice bed, in a nice neighborhood of Paris, expecting a nice quiet Sunday, and had instead been swept up to the top of the Eiffel Tower, then down into the bowels of the George V. Swept into another world. One where people killed other people. For reasons as yet obscure.

And now, instead of letting her go with the others to the relative safety of the Archives nationales, he'd brought her here. Exposing her to the very people she'd been trying so hard to avoid.

All good reasons to be afraid. But was she afraid of them, or him?

"Well, I am used to this." He didn't bother to drop his voice. "It's what I've done, all day, every day. For decades. You find problems and solve them, I also find problems and solve them. It's what we both do best."

"Yeah, well, your problems kill people."

"So do yours, I expect." His thoughtful eyes held hers. And then he did drop his voice. "You're doing fine."

She lowered her eyes to her wine and took a deep breath in. A deep breath out.

This was making less and less sense. And she wondered if she should tell him. Everything.

"Now," he said, his voice at a normal level again. "Neodymium?"

She hesitated for a moment, clearly considering her options. If she got up and walked out, he couldn't stop her.

But Madame Arbour was smart enough to know there were no options left. She had to see this through.

"All I have is my phone," she said. "Should I look it up? Suppose they've hacked it? That's what you're worried about, isn't it? And aren't they listening now?" She looked around.

"Probably. Don't worry about your phone. If it's all we have, then we have to use it."

"You want them to know, don't you." It was a statement, not a question.

"I see no way around it. Time they felt our warm breath on the back of their necks."

"If we're that close to them," she said, bringing out her phone, "aren't they that close to us?"

"Yes, but they always were. What's changed is our position, not theirs. And they know it. What do you have?"

He put his reading glasses on and leaned close.

She'd entered the name of the rare earth element into a specialized site for engineers. And up popped the information.

"Nothing," said Jean-Guy, throwing himself onto the back of the chair and staring at the screen.

They'd divided up the members of the board and were searching the databases, looking for anything that could point them to the one Stephen might have approached.

"You?" he asked the others.

From their terminals scattered down the long tables of the reading room, he heard mumbled, "*Non*. Nothing yet."

And more tapping.

"I'm going to look up the dates from Stephen's notes," said Jean-Guy. "Maybe there's something there."

"What notes?" Allida Lenoir was sitting across from him and glanced at the piece of paper. "Agence France-Presse stories?"

Beauvoir smiled. "*Non*. AFP are the initials of the dead man. Alexander Francis Plessner."

"Are you sure?" said the head archivist.

"Pretty sure, but if you want to try Agence France-Presse, be my guest."

A few minutes later Madame Lenoir sighed. "Nothing. I put the dates into the wire service site and nothing unusual came up. A protest in Washington. European Union in turmoil. And the usual series of tragedies. Refugees fleeing brutal regimes and being turned back. A plane crash in the Urals. A bridge collapse in Spain. Shootings in two American cities."

"No mention of GHS?" he asked.

"Nothing."

"No stories out of Patagonia or Luxembourg?"

"No."

"Let me see that."

Madame de la Granger had wandered over, and without waiting for him to give it to her, she snatched the scrap from his hand.

Bet she could catch a fly with chopsticks, thought Jean-Guy.

He got up and walked over to his mother-in-law. "Anything?"

"Not yet. No scandals to do with the board members," said Reine-Marie. "No bankruptcies. No obvious need for money. No sudden big purchases. But I haven't finished yet. You?"

But she already knew the answer. Then a thought occurred to her.

"Are there any board members with the initials AFP?" she asked, reaching for the report.

They began putting the names into the searches. Sure enough Annette Poppy, a former British Foreign Secretary, turned out to be Annette Forrester Poppy.

Jean-Guy looked at his watch. It was ten past seven.

"I know this man," came the voice of the Chief Librarian over Jean-Guy's shoulder.

Madame de la Granger was pointing to a member of the GHS Engineering board. "He's the son of an old family friend. We were at the Sorbonne together."

She moved her finger so they could read his name. Alain Pinot.

Alain Flaubert Pinot.

They stared at the photo of the middle-aged man. Thinning hair and fleshy face.

"His father owned newspapers," said Madame de la Granger. "He asked if I'd tutor his son. As a favor, I agreed. What a waste of time."

"Why do you say that?" asked Reine-Marie.

"Because Alain Pinot was as dumb as they come," said the Chief Librarian. "If stupid was sand, he'd be half the Sahara."

They looked at her.

"What? It's true. This guy's father knew I was into research. He hoped I could teach the kid how to track down information. Prepare him for a job at the newspapers. But all he was interested in was partying. And yet . . ."

They waited, as Madame de la Granger cast her mind back.

"I quite liked him. He was a couple of years younger than me, spoiled, entitled, thick but harmless. He had a poor brain but a good heart." She looked again at the photo. "Just before he flunked out of the Sorbonne, his father had him transferred to another university, and I lost track of him."

"Where to?" asked Beauvoir.

"I have no idea. Far away from the distractions of Paris is all I know."

"Université de Montréal?" said Reine-Marie, looking at Jean-Guy. She entered Alain Flaubert Pinot's name into the archive database, and up came his biography. "Yes. Says here he studied in Montréal. But not at UdeM. McGill."

Reine-Marie and Jean-Guy stared at each other.

An unruly young man sent far from home to study? It seemed more than likely his father would contact a friend in Montréal to watch over his idiot son.

Was Stephen Horowitz that family friend? Was this the connection?

They called up more information on this A. F. Pinot.

Married with three children.

Father died of cancer fifteen years ago.

Son took over the company and, against the wishes of his board, immediately expanded into cable, telecom, tech companies.

He'd bought low, after the tech bubble burst, and turned hundreds of millions into billions.

"Jesus, maybe the guy's an idiot savant," said Madame de la Granger. "Though I saw no evidence of the savant part."

"There," said Allida Lenoir, pointing to her screen. "Six years ago. Pinot's company bought a controlling interest in—"

"Agence France-Presse," said Reine-Marie, triumphant. "That must be it."

Jean-Guy was shaking his head. "We still don't have a connection between this guy and Stephen. We don't know whether AFP in his notes means Alain Pinot, or Agence France-Presse, or Plessner, or someone else."

"Something's missing," said Madame de la Granger. "Some link."

"I'm going to write Mrs. McGillicuddy," said Reine-Marie, "and find out if Stephen knew the Pinot family, and especially Alain Pinot."

The four of them sat in individual pools of light, their fingers tap-tap-tapping on the keyboards, like the soft patter of feet, sneaking up on a killer.

* * *

Daniel stared at the screen, jotted some notes. Then he looked up another file. And made more notes.

He'd been at it for almost an hour, exploring avenues and dead ends. Eliminating possibilities, narrowing options. He'd started by trying to track down the numbered companies, with limited success.

Then he went into the sell and buy orders, the ones stored for execution Monday morning. There were thousands. Listed not by investor, but by investment.

He needed to scroll through them all. His eyes were bloodshot, his concentration wavering.

He stopped. Went back. Something he'd passed needed another look.

Daniel stared at the screen.

A buy order had popped up. Placed by Stephen Horowitz late Friday, to be executed first thing Monday morning.

"Holy shit," he whispered.

He'd found out what Stephen was going to do with his billions. But it didn't tell him why.

So absorbed was Daniel that he didn't hear the click of the door behind him.

The rapid tapping of his fingers on the keyboard masked the soft approach of footsteps.

He didn't hear the murmured voice, advising the weekend supervisor to go back to his office. And stay there.

But he did feel the warm breath on his neck.

"Neodymium is fairly common," Madame Arbour read off her phone. "In China. Less so elsewhere. The find in Patagonia would be significant."

"Why?" asked Gamache. Though he believed he knew the answer.

Geopolitics. China was an authoritarian regime that could be as thin-skinned as it was brutal. Agreements were vulnerable to political machinations. Regime change. Subject to trade wars and tariffs. And a Western government that actually put human rights above profit.

"The supply could not be guaranteed," said Madame Arbour. "But a European company owning a rare earth mine in South America would be able to guarantee delivery."

"You mentioned magnets. Is that neodymium's main use?"

"Yes."

"Sounds harmless."

"You're thinking of a normal magnet. But look at this."

She hit play, and Gamache watched as a piece of metal shot through a cantaloupe and slammed into a metal sheet.

"Here's another one."

It showed a grown man—he looked like a weight lifter—trying to separate two steel rods stuck together.

"Can you go back to the other video?" After rewatching it, he said, "A neodymium magnet did that?"

"Yes, and a small one."

"Can it be used as a weapon?" It sure looked like that shard would pass through a human body.

"It doesn't say. In an earlier search I didn't find any reference to rare earth minerals as weapons, but they might've found a new use. Listen to this," Séverine read, "a neodymium magnet can lift a thousand times its own weight."

"But it also says here," Gamache was reading off her phone, "that there's a problem with neodymium."

"More like a caveat. When heated or frozen, it breaks down. And if under stress, it can shatter."

"So it's unstable?"

"Not if it's used properly."

"And what would those uses be?" asked Gamache.

She scrolled down. "Microphones, loudspeakers, computer hard drives. All the things we already know."

"You mentioned cutting-edge telecommunications earlier. That's exactly the sort of investment Stephen would notice."

Gamache leaned back in the comfortable chair, staring at the small screen. It didn't make sense. Nothing they'd discovered was, as far as he could tell, unethical, never mind illegal.

So why the secrecy? What were they hiding?

From what they could tell, GHS was mining the rare earth element, then shipping the raw ore to refineries. And then?

He took off his glasses and narrowed his eyes. "Can you go back to that second video?"

She did, and this time played it all the way through. The strongman finally managed to separate the bars, after a struggle that clearly left him embarrassed.

"The nickels," Gamache said.

"Pardon?" asked Madame Arbour.

His irises were moving, as though he was watching a film no one else could see.

Then he looked at his watch.

Eight ten. Almost time to make his way to Place de la Concorde and his meeting with Claude Dussault. He had one stop to make first.

But what to do with Séverine Arbour?

Take her with him, or leave her here in the Lutetia?

If she came with him and she turned out to be a spy planted in their midst, he'd be putting them all at risk. But if she wasn't a spy and he left her in the bar, something awful might happen to her.

There was, Chief Inspector Gamache knew as he stood up, no decision to be made.

"Come with me, please."

More than one set of eyes watched them leave bar Joséphine.

CHAPTER 35

———

N othing," said Reine-Marie, staring at the screen as though accusing it of willfully withholding information.

While waiting for Mrs. McGillicuddy's reply about Stephen and Pinot, she'd gone back over Agence France-Presse stories on the dates Stephen had jotted down.

She was getting frustrated. This was, after all, her forte. Tracking down information. Finding things hidden in full view but overlooked.

She was, she knew, overlooking something. It was the reflection in the screen she was annoyed at. Not the screen itself.

Then she had an idea. "Suppose the dates are when the thing actually happened?"

"Yes," said Jean-Guy. "Isn't that what we're looking up?"

"No, we're looking up the dates the Agence France-Presse stories ran."

"Wouldn't they be the same thing?"

"Not necessarily," said Reine-Marie. "Sometimes it takes a while for an event to be discovered, or to be reported on. Especially an event in an isolated region like, say, Patagonia. We need to check stories on either side of the dates."

A few minutes later she called Jean-Guy over to her terminal.

"Look at this. An Agence France-Presse reporter disappeared in Patagonia four years ago. It happened on the first date Stephen's written down, but the story didn't run until three days later. That's why we didn't find it the first time."

Overhearing this, Judith and Allida went to look.

"Anik Guardiola. Twenty-four. Stringer for AFP," Judith read. "Disappeared in the mountains of Patagonia while on a hiking trip."

"Alone?" asked Jean-Guy.

"Apparently."

"Who hikes in those mountains alone? Did they find her?" he asked.

"Just a moment," said Reine-Marie as she put the young woman's name in the search engine.

"Agence France-Presse sent representatives to the area," she said, leaning into her screen and reading. "And pressured the local government."

"The police, the *carabineros*, didn't seem to take it seriously," said Allida.

"Her body was eventually found in a gorge," said Judith, from her terminal behind them, where she'd also brought up the story. "If you go a week later you'll find the report. The police ruled her death an accident. Said that she'd fallen, but AFP wasn't satisfied. Their head of news says neither her phone nor her computer were found. But then . . ." There was a pause as Judith scrolled. "It goes quiet. The story dies."

They looked at each other.

"Dies? The cops and the paper just dropped it?" said Allida. "Does that make sense?"

"*Non*," said Jean-Guy, staring at the screen. "Someone was bought off."

"You think she was murdered?" Reine-Marie asked.

"I think she found out something someone really wanted to hide," he said, his fingers hitting the keys, chasing information. "But what?"

More tapping. Tapping. Tapp—

"Got it," said Judith.

The Chief Librarian had let the others follow the Guardiola lead while she took a different tack.

It had struck them as strange that the dates were all in chronological order, except the final entry. The last thing he'd written was, in fact, the earliest date. They'd thought perhaps he'd transposed numbers, but now it seemed not.

It was the last thing he'd discovered. But the first thing that had happened.

"A month before Anik Guardiola disappeared, she wrote a story about the derailment of several train cars in Colombia," said Judith, as the others crowded around. "It was a minor story, so wasn't picked up by Agence France-Presse until a week later and sent out as a brief."

"Colombia? Not Patagonia?" asked Reine-Marie.

"*Non.* See here? Colombia."

"Was anyone killed?" asked Allida.

"*Non,*" said Judith, scanning. "No one died. It was a freight train."

"Carrying ore from the neodymium mine?" asked Jean-Guy.

"*Non.* Grain."

"So why was Anik Guardiola interested?" asked Judith.

"Why was Stephen?" asked Reine-Marie.

Jean-Guy picked up his phone. It was time to call Armand.

"*Oui?*"

"*Patron?* We've found something."

Jean-Guy did not identify himself. While he suspected this precaution was meaningless, it made him feel slightly better about breaking their silence.

Gamache and Madame Arbour were in a taxi moving across Paris. The light turned red, and in the pause he watched patrons in a brasserie, spilling out onto the sidewalk, drinking and eating.

Carefree.

Though he knew very few people were ever really carefree. But there were moments of bliss. He thought of his last moment of bliss. Walking along after dinner Friday night. Before . . .

Like all those locked in a nightmare, he wished he could wind back the clock. Set down the cracked cup.

Then the light changed and the taxi moved on through the night. As he listened to Jean-Guy.

"It looks like Stephen did mean Agence France-Presse when he wrote *AFP.*"

He told Gamache about the derailment in Colombia. The disappearance of the reporter who'd written the story and that her body was eventually found in a gorge in Patagonia.

"Near the mine?"

"We're trying to find out. The local police dismissed it as a hiking accident."

"She was alone?"

"It seems so. AFP sent people to investigate. They discovered that neither her phone nor her laptop were found on her, or in her hotel room."

"She was murdered."

"Looks like it, though the local authorities never agreed and didn't investigate. And eventually the story died."

"Really?"

"The local cops must've been paid off."

"She was on to something," said Gamache. "But what? Might be the derailment, or might not. Have you figured out the other dates?"

"We're working on it." Jean-Guy paused, wondering if he should say more. Knowing their phones were probably being monitored. But it also felt like they'd passed the point of no return. "Do you know an Alain Pinot?"

"The media fellow. Yes. He's on the GHS Engineering board. I saw him just now at the Lutetia. Why?"

"His company owns Agence France-Presse."

There was a pause as Gamache absorbed that news and considered what it could mean.

"But do you know him personally?" Jean-Guy asked.

"*Non.* Should I?"

Jean-Guy told him about McGill, and the possible connection to Stephen. "Reine-Marie's written to Mrs. McGillicuddy to see if Stephen did know him. This would've been thirty years ago or more. Stephen never mentioned him?"

"Not that I remember. If he was looking out for Monsieur Pinot back then, I'd have thought he'd introduce us. We'd be about the same age, *non*?"

"He's a couple of years younger, but yes, that's what I thought, too."

Jean-Guy was obviously a little disappointed. There might not be a connection between Alain Pinot and Stephen Horowitz after all. If there was, Stephen would almost certainly have introduced the wild young man to his more stable godson.

"I might've been away at university," said Armand. "Let me know what you find out."

"Any news your end?"

"Seems neodymium, while a rare earth element, isn't exactly rare. It's a powerful magnet, but that's about it. We're looking into the telecommunications connection. Still, it's puzzling why GHS kept the find a secret."

"Maybe that's just the culture," said Jean-Guy. "They don't exactly like broadcasting their business."

"That's probably it."

Both men knew Jean-Guy's statement was for the benefit of whoever might be listening. The truth was, this wasn't extreme secrecy. It was a cover-up.

"Is Reine-Marie there? Can I have a word?"

"Armand?" he heard her say. "Jean-Guy told you what we found?"

"Yes, much more than we've found. Have you heard from Daniel?"

"Not yet. Do you want me to call him?"

"No, I'll do that. Let me know what Mrs. McGillicuddy says about Stephen and Monsieur Pinot."

"Absolutely. Armand?"

"*Oui?*"

"Everything all right?"

"Yes. We're moving forward. Getting closer and closer." He chose not to tell her where they were getting closer to.

If GHS was good at keeping secrets, they were amateurs compared to the head of homicide.

Though the key was knowing what information to let slip, and what to hold on to.

He called Daniel. Heard it ring. And ring. And then Daniel's recorded voice, deep, cheerful, warm, inviting him to leave a message.

"Daniel? It's Dad. Call me when you can."

Up ahead he could see their apartment. And in it what he'd dashed across Paris to find.

Since silence was already broken, Jean-Guy decided to make one more call.

As soon as he heard Annie's voice, he relaxed. Until that moment, he had no idea how tense he'd become.

"Everything all right?" he asked.

"Just fine. Honoré and the girls have had their dinner and baths, and we're just tucking them in. Did you know Great-Aunt Ruth has taught him a song?"

"Oh, God, what now?"

Their son's very first word hadn't been "Mama" or "Papa," or "milk," or "please."

Thanks to Great-Aunt Ruth and her duck Rosa, Honoré's first word had been "fuck." Which he'd screamed, loud and clear. In the middle of a party. Repeatedly.

Annie and Jean-Guy had tried to explain that he was actually saying "duck," but his enunciation was so perfect no one believed that.

Honoré adored Great-Aunt Ruth and her duck Rosa and absorbed anything they chose to imprint.

"Here, listen," said Annie and held the phone out.

In a clear, high voice, their son was singing, *What do you do with a drunken sailor?"*

"A sea shanty? Jesus," sighed Jean-Guy. "Still, he can hold a tune."

"Yes, that's the thing to focus on."

"You're all right?" he repeated.

"Yes."

A few minutes earlier she'd felt a twinge. It was, she told herself, indigestion. Though in her heart, and slightly further down, she knew it wasn't that.

She could feel panic rising, but she wouldn't say anything to him. Not yet. Not until she was sure.

"I'll tell you more when I see you," Jean-Guy was saying.

"Come home when you can," she said. *Soon. Soon.*

As he said goodbye he heard, in the background, "*Way, hey, and up she rises . . .*"

"No need to take off your coat," said Armand, as they entered the apartment. "We aren't staying long."

"Long enough for me to use the facilities?" Madame Arbour asked, her voice brusque. Clearly not used to being lugged all over the city like a sack of occasionally intelligent potatoes.

"*Oui. Certainement,*" he said. "It's just off the bedroom."

When she left, he went over to the box from the hospital. It was still where they'd left it the night before, sitting beside the armchair in the living room. Taking the top off, he looked in.

And jerked back in surprise.

Something had been added. Even covered in a cloth he knew what it was.

He unwrapped the gun, careful not to get his prints on it. Was this the weapon that had killed Alexander Plessner? Was he being set up now?

He smelled the muzzle. It had not been fired recently, but that meant nothing.

Using a handkerchief, he released the magazine.

It was fully loaded. But . . .

He ejected one of the bullets. It was not standard issue.

Hollow point? Illegal, brutal. Effective, if the effect you wanted was to blow a hole clean through another human being.

No. This was something else entirely.

He stared at the bullet for a moment, his mind whirring.

Replacing it, he looked around. Someone had broken into their apartment between the time he and Reine-Marie had stopped there that afternoon on their way to the Louvre, and now. Was anything else changed? Added? Taken? Without a thorough search, he couldn't tell. And he didn't have time for that.

Who'd done this? Claude Dussault? Irena Fontaine? Thierry Girard? Xavier Loiselle?

And why? He looked at the firearm in his hand. What was the purpose?

The water stopped running, and he knew he had moments to decide what to do.

He slipped the gun into his coat pocket and bent over the box once again. Then, he hesitated. And changed his mind.

Walking quickly over to the bookcase, he pulled a few books out of a high shelf and hid the gun there.

When Séverine Arbour reappeared, she found Gamache going through the box.

"What's that?" she asked, joining him.

"These are the things Stephen had on his desk, and what the hospital gave us after he was hit by the truck. The investigators have kept his laptop and phone, but everything else is here."

"What're you looking for?"

She'd been a bit surprised by the apartment. It was smaller than she'd expected. Most powerful people, men in particular, liked homes that reflected what they saw as their place on the ladder. Which was, in reality, a few rungs lower than their egos believed.

This place was petite, beamed, with bookcases and a fireplace. The floors were parquet, in the classic herringbone pattern.

An old oak dining table shared space with a comfortable sofa and armchairs. The kitchen, through an archway, was compact and dated.

But it was calm, peaceful even. It smelled of coffee and wood. And felt like home.

"Neodymium," he said.

As she watched, he dug into his pocket and dropped a handful of coins into the box.

It was such a bizarre thing to do, for a moment she wondered about his sanity.

But he looked completely, intensely sane.

Stirring the contents with his hand, he picked up the coins along with some screws and the Allen wrench.

"Nothing."

And she understood. If something in there was made of neodymium, it would pull metal to it. And magnetize what it touched.

He sat back in the chair and stared at her. "So what magnetized the nickels?"

"Nickels?"

"Stephen had two Canadian nickels that were stuck together. We thought they were glued, the seal was that strong, but when I saw that video about neodymium, I realized they might've been magnetized."

"Which would mean your friend had a sample of the neodymium," she said. "That's what had magnetized the coins. Is that what you thought was in the box? The neodymium itself?"

"I'd hoped."

It was now clear that his godfather had had suspicions for years. Had spent the last precious years of his life, and any amount of his fortune, to piece together the evidence. Had brought the engineer and his trusted friend Alexander Plessner in to help.

He'd sold everything he owned, mortgaged his home, gone all in.

But what had he found out? Was it corporate espionage? Was it something to do with neodymium?

They knew, he realized, almost nothing.

He checked his watch.

Quarter to nine. Time he left for the rendezvous.

But he wasn't armed, with information or anything else. He glanced at the bookcase. Had he just made a fatal error?

But it was done now.

He called Daniel at the bank again. And again, no answer.

"Something wrong?" Séverine Arbour asked.

"No."

He stared at his phone, then hit the app. Within seconds it showed Daniel's location.

Armand exhaled.

He was at the bank. Probably with his phone on silent.

"I'm going to meet Commissioner Dussault," he said.

"Can I go home now?" she asked.

"I'm afraid not."

"You still don't trust me? What do I have to do?"

"It's not that," he said, though of course it was. "It won't be safe for you at home. The only safety is in numbers. You need to join the others at the archives. You'll be fine there."

"Fucked up, insecure, neurotic, and egotistical?"

When he looked surprised, she explained. "Beauvoir told me about your Québec village. He talks about it a lot. Apparently it's filled with fine people."

They'd left the apartment and were walking quickly through the dark streets of the Marais, trying without success to avoid puddles on their way to the archives.

Armand laughed. "They're certainly fine. And so am I."

He called Reine-Marie, and when they approached the massive gates, he saw her and Jean-Guy waiting for them on the other side.

He was surprised by the wave of emotion that washed over him. And by the gulf that existed between them, the immeasurable distance between in there and out here.

"Let me come with you," said Jean-Guy.

"Claude wants to speak to me alone."

"I can still be there. Watch from a distance."

"And do what?" asked Armand.

Without being more explicit, they both knew if it came to that, Armand would be dead before he hit the ground, and there'd be nothing Jean-Guy could do except get himself killed.

"Stay here," said Armand. "I'll be in touch as soon as I can."

As he left them for his rendezvous, he felt very alone.

CHAPTER 36

M agnificent, isn't it?" said Claude Dussault as he took his place
  beside Gamache. "Almost mesmerizing."

The two men stared at the Fontaine des Mers, on the Place de la
Concorde. It was lit up in the dark, so that what spouted from the
leaping dolphins looked more like quicksilver than water.

"It is," agreed Armand.

He hadn't paused to admire the fountain in years, always passing
right by on his way from the Champs-Élysées to the Tuileries Garden.

But now he stared. And noticed that the center of the huge fountain was supported by mythical figures representing the oceans, each
sitting in the bow of a ship.

The symbol of Paris? The storm-tossed vessel, threatened, but
never foundering.

"When I was growing up," said Dussault, "no one threw coins
in fountains to make wishes. Seems incredible anyone thinks that
works."

The next thing Gamache heard was a plop.

"Then again," said Dussault, who was watching his coin sink to the
bottom, "it probably couldn't hurt. You might want to make a wish,
too."

"What do you want, Claude?"

Far from being put off by the abrupt question, Commissioner

Dussault nodded. Appreciating that there was no longer a need for pretense.

"I thought it was time we talked. Alone."

"Are we alone?" asked Gamache.

"What do you think?" Dussault looked this way, then that, then began strolling around the fountain.

"I think it's time for the truth," said Gamache, falling in beside him. "You're involved in this, aren't you."

They were walking slowly, heads tilted toward each other. A moment of quiet companionship between two old friends.

That would be the perception. The reality was, as it so often is, far different.

"Perhaps," said Dussault.

Gamache was struggling to remain civil when standing so close to a man who'd all but admitted his role in the attempt on Stephen's life. In the cold-blooded murder of Alexander Plessner, an elderly, unarmed man.

Around them, floodlights lit up the magnificent monuments. Vehicles passed by. Distinctive French sirens sounded in the distance. Visitors took selfies in front of the statues.

Armand heard snippets of conversations and bursts of laughter.

But mostly he absorbed the words and subtle movements of the man beside him.

The Prefect stopped in front of the Luxor Obelisk. Etched into the base of the great column were what many mistook for ancient hieroglyphics, but which were actually diagrams describing the engineering involved in bringing the three-thousand-year-old monument from Egypt to Paris. Then erecting it on this site.

"Amazing what engineers can do," said Dussault. "Where would we be without them? They're the real magicians."

"What do you want?"

"Did you know this was where much of the Terror took place?" Dussault looked at his companion. "But of course you do. You're a student of history. You'd know that Madame La Guillotine stood right on this spot. Louis the Sixteenth. Marie Antoinette. So many others lost their lives. Right here." He looked at the people laughing and taking selfies. "Do you think they know? Do you think they care?"

Dussault turned to face him. "You're a smart man, but like them, I don't think you have any idea what you're close to."

"Oh, I have some idea." He stared at Dussault with undisguised disgust. "I saw the security video. You tried to have it erased, but they missed some. You were in the George V Friday afternoon, with Thierry Girard. You met with Eugénie Roquebrune. You're running SecurForte, with Girard once again your second-in-command. You ordered the killing of Stephen and Monsieur Plessner. You're the one who's behind all this."

Dussault nodded, resigned. "I'm sorry you found that video. Sloppy." He tilted his head back, staring at the gold pyramid at the very top of the obelisk. "Did you know the top of the obelisk was stolen in Luxor, in the sixth century B.C.? What's up there now is fairly recent. People mistake it for original. But—"

"Why are we here?"

"I don't know why you came. Seems an awful risk. It's true I took that meeting, but it's a huge leap of logic to go from my having tea with friends to being guilty of murder, don't you think? Don't overreach, Armand. That's when you fall."

"Are you denying it?"

"I'm saying you don't know everything. Far from it. I tried to warn you once, and you didn't listen. Alexander Plessner is dead and Stephen Horowitz is dying." Dussault waited, but Armand didn't argue. "What you're doing will only make things worse."

"You forgot Anik Guardiola."

"You know about her."

"Yes. So did Stephen."

"That's too bad." Claude Dussault lowered his voice. "You and Reine-Marie need to get your family and leave. Get on a plane and go back to Montréal. For God's sake, I'm begging you."

"You know I won't do that, so stop wasting time."

"You're a fool. The only consolation is that it's probably too late anyway. For you. For your son."

Armand froze. "Daniel?"

Dussault turned and began walking toward the Seine. But Armand reached out, grabbed his arm, and swung him around.

"What've you done?" he demanded. "Where is he?"

"He's safe." Dussault held his eyes. "But you know what they can do. And will do. What you don't know is what they've already done. Those three, Plessner, Horowitz, the journalist? They're not even the tip of the iceberg. You have no idea how powerful these people are. And now, thanks to your godfather, how desperate."

"Are you threatening to hurt Daniel?" When Dussault didn't answer, or blink, Armand lowered his voice. "If you touch my son, I'll bring holy hell down on you."

"Too late," said Dussault. "It's already here. The funny thing about Hell is that we assume it's obvious. Fire, brimstone. We'll be plunged into it by some horrific event in our lives. But the truth is, Hell can be as subtle as Heaven." He looked around. "Sometimes we don't recognize we've wandered into Hell until it's too late."

"Where's Daniel?"

Dussault focused on the man in front of him. "Know this, Armand. I tried to help. If something happens to Daniel, or any member of your family, it won't be on me. It'll be your fault."

"Where's Daniel?"

"You bumbled in, you and your little group, like some amateur theater troupe putting on a show." Dussault shook his head. "You think you're so clever, going to the top of the Eiffel Tower. Going to the basement and whispering about Patagonia. You thought you were moving forward, but that's an illusion. You don't even see the truck hurtling toward you. It's two feet away and you can't stop it. You and your family are nothing more than bugs on a windshield to these people."

Gamache grabbed Claude Dussault, lifting him almost off the ground. Bringing the shorter man to eye level. Within millimeters of his face.

"Where's my son?"

"Put me down." Dussault's voice was strangled by his coat. "Or it ends now."

Gamache's grip tightened. Then, against every instinct he possessed, his clenched and cramped fingers released the coat.

Dussault had all but admitted there were snipers aimed at him. If he went down, all was lost.

If Daniel was to have a chance, if any of them were, he had to think clearly. Act rationally.

Gamache took several deep breaths and brought the thudding in his chest under control. "You asked for this meeting before you took Daniel. You want something."

Dussault raised his brows. Gamache had recovered his senses far faster than he'd expected.

"There is one possible way out of this."

Gamache recognized what had just happened. It was a common technique. Scare, threaten, raise the pressure and the stakes until the person was out of their mind with terror.

Then offer them a way out.

Even as he recognized it, he also recognized that it worked. He was terrified and he was desperate. And he was listening.

"How?"

"There's something they want. Something your godfather has."

"What Thierry Girard was looking for in Stephen's apartment. Something to do with the neodymium mine."

Dussault pressed his lips together.

Armand could see that Dussault hadn't expected him to know so much. This was not working out as Dussault had planned. But neither was it going as Armand had hoped.

Both had delivered punches. And now both were reeling.

But Armand knew he was by far the more bruised. Dussault had Daniel. And therefore Dussault had him.

But Claude had said there was a chance.

"You want me to find whatever evidence Stephen's hidden. That's why you've taken Daniel. To make sure I do it."

"Added incentive, yes. It needs to be found before tomorrow morning's board meeting."

"And if I do?"

"I think I can convince them to release your son, and let you all leave Paris."

Armand stared at his feet. Then, looking up, he gave a small nod. As though he believed him. "I'll need to see Daniel."

Dussault brought out his iPhone.

"*Non.* I mean in person. There must be"—the familiar phrase Armand had used so often in hostage negotiations now stuck in his throat, so that for a moment he tasted vomit—"proof of life."

Dussault considered the man in front of him. "Follow me."

He turned and walked briskly away from the ghosts of the Place de la Concorde.

They walked for ten minutes, in silence, Armand Gamache following Dussault along boulevard Saint-Germain. Past the young lovers and elderly men and women arm in arm.

Though one elderly woman caught his eye. And smiled reassuringly. As though she knew. That all would be well.

Daniel's father clung to the look in those clear and kindly eyes long after she was gone. He knew it was an illusion, a delusion, but it comforted him as he walked through the darkness.

When they turned down boulevard Raspail, Armand knew where they were going. Where Daniel had been taken.

It was both cruel and kind. Armand was both sickened and relieved.

They were holding Daniel in Stephen's apartment. A place Daniel had visited many times. Where his son had happy memories and where he might be less afraid.

But it was one more violation for Armand. His own safe place defiled beyond redemption.

When they arrived, Madame Faubourg came out to greet them.

"It's wonderful to see Daniel. I hope you don't mind my letting him and his friends into Monsieur Horowitz's apartment. He did have the JSPS card." She leaned closer to Armand. "Not that he needed it. I'd have let him in anyway."

Light spilled from the open door to her apartment, and with it the scent of ginger and molasses.

"Any more news about Monsieur Horowitz?"

"I'm afraid not. I won't be staying long, but I think Daniel and his friends might stay the night. Sort through things. Best not to disturb them."

"Of course."

She nodded to Dussault and wiped her hands on her apron as she watched them walk through the courtyard.

In the elevator, Gamache turned to Dussault. "How can you be part of this? What happened?"

"Don't be so fucking sanctimonious, Armand. Have you looked around? What's the difference between this and the tobacco companies? The pharmaceuticals that continue to sell drugs they know are killing people? Airlines that fly planes they know are dangerous, elevators that plunge to the ground? How about nuclear power stations coming online? Engineers who continue to use faulty and inferior materials? The governments that drop regulations in favor of profit? They're killing thousands, hundreds of thousands. Don't look at me like that. Don't tell me you haven't knowingly endangered innocent lives, justifying it as for the greater good. Where's the line?"

"That's your justification? I'll tell you where the line is. It's buried under that pile of corpses you helped make."

The elevator jerked to a stop, and Dussault yanked the metal accordion door open.

"You can't win. Since you refused to leave, what you're fighting for now is how badly you're going to lose. How much you're going to lose. If they think you know what Horowitz has and aren't telling them, they'll kill Daniel now. In front of you. And then they'll go to the archives, hunt down everyone there, and kill them. And then they'll go to the George V—"

"Enough!"

"—and they'll kill everyone there. One by one. Until you hand it over."

"You'd do that?" demanded Armand, horrified. "You'd let them do that?"

"I can't stop it even if I wanted to. Fuck, Armand, they're the truck and you're the bug. You and your family are about a millimeter away from that windshield now."

"But I don't know what Stephen found. Maybe nothing." Armand felt himself sliding into panic. "Maybe he just had suspicions and no hard evidence. He might've hoped it would be enough to frighten the board. He might've thought coming from him, that would be enough." He stared at Claude Dussault. Desperate now. "Maybe there's nothing to find."

"You'd better pray there is, and that you find it."

Dussault knocked, then opened the door to Stephen's apartment.

Four men stood up and turned to them. One of them, Gamache saw with near despair, was Xavier Loiselle.

He was holding an assault rifle. On Daniel.

CHAPTER 37

———

Armand pushed past Dussault.

Xavier Loiselle swung his weapon toward him, but Dussault simply gestured and Loiselle stepped back.

Armand grabbed Daniel and held him close, whispering, "I'm sorry, I'm so sorry."

He could feel Daniel trembling as he clutched his father. Then Armand pulled away and, holding Daniel at arm's length, he examined the bruise and blood on his son's face.

Then he turned to the three large men.

"Who did this?"

"I did," came a voice from the dining room. And Thierry Girard appeared. "He wouldn't tell us what he found at the bank. But then"—Girard smiled—"he did."

"Dad, I'm sorry."

"They already knew," said Armand, his voice a snarl. He faced Girard. "You already knew what he found, didn't you? But you beat him anyway, you sadistic shit."

Gamache took a step toward him, then stopped, frozen in place by a familiar sound. The soft, metallic click of a safety coming off.

He turned to his son.

Daniel's eyes were wide with terror as the gun pressed against his temple.

"You're right," said Girard, his voice conversational, almost chatty.

354

"We did know. But you better than most know the advantage of having a cooperative witness. Sometimes people just have to see the full advantage of being helpful. And the disadvantage of not."

Gamache glared at him. "I'll kill you."

"Ah, you just slipped from your favorite spot on the higher ground, Chief Inspector," said Girard. "What does it feel like to be in the dung with the rest of us?"

"You'd better frisk him," said Dussault. "Make sure he's unarmed."

Gamache glared at Loiselle as he frisked him.

"Nothing." Then he gave Gamache a quick jab in the solar plexus with the butt of his machine gun, dropping him to his knees.

"Dad?"

Armand raised a hand, to indicate he was all right, then struggled to his feet. As he did, he looked at Claude Dussault.

The Prefect's brows had risen, very slightly. In surprise. In annoyance. At Loiselle's blow? No.

Claude Dussault had expected Loiselle to find a gun.

Armand knew then that Dussault had planted the weapon in his apartment. In the box of Stephen's things. Where he was bound to find it. And do what?

Use it? Or try to? But if so, why insist he be frisked? Why give it to him, only to have it taken away?

Had Dussault expected Armand to pull it on him in the Place de la Concorde? In a rage when told about Daniel?

If he had, he'd have been immediately gunned down by the heavily armed police who patrolled the place.

Another execution.

Was that what Dussault wanted?

But no, that didn't make complete sense. They didn't want him dead. They needed him alive, to find Stephen's evidence.

So why had Claude Dussault left a gun in his apartment? And did he really expect that the head of homicide for the Sûreté du Québec wouldn't notice what it was loaded with?

"Dad, Stephen—" Daniel began, and once again Loiselle raised his rifle and Daniel cringed.

"Let him tell his father what he found at the bank," said Dussault. "Monsieur Gamache here needs to know if he's going to help us."

Armand's eyes held Daniel's, and he said, softly, gently, "Tell me."

It was the same voice he'd used tucking Daniel into bed: "Tell me about your day."

And the little boy would. It would all come spilling out from a child who found wonder everywhere.

He'd hear about the odd-shaped clouds, the piles of autumn leaves, the snow forts Daniel and his friends had built and defended. The carefree battles waged and won. The first daffodils in the park, and the splashing in the fountain on a sizzling summer's day.

"Tell me," Armand said now.

And Daniel did.

"Stephen put in a buy order late Friday, just as the New York market closed. He was going all in on two of GHS's holdings."

"The numbered companies?"

"*Oui.*"

"What do the companies do?"

"One's a tool and die company. But his main target is a smelter."

Armand's mind raced.

A smelter meant ore. Ore came from mines. Which led to GHS, which led to Patagonia.

Which led to the rare earth elements.

Which led to neodymium.

Armand's eyes flickered to Daniel's pocket.

Oh, God, he thought. *That's where they are.*

The nickels. The ones he'd been looking for earlier, in the box. Magnetized, not glued, together.

Armand saw again Honoré in the garden, and the mighty toss. Saw Jean-Guy's panic, thinking his son had them in his mouth. And he saw Daniel, in the background, stoop and pick up the nickels. Putting them in his jacket pocket for safekeeping. Away from the hands, and mouths, of other children.

And that's where they still were. In the same jacket Daniel was now wearing.

If Dussault put it together and realized what they were . . .

If they found them on Daniel and thought he was deliberately hiding them . . .

Armand quickly considered his options. Bringing out a handkerchief, he looked at Daniel, then over to Dussault.

"Is it all right if I . . . ?"

Dussault nodded.

He approached Daniel, and as he wiped the blood from his son's face, Daniel grabbed his arms and whispered, whimpered, his voice high and strained, "I'm not brave, Dad. I'm so afraid."

Armand pulled him close and held him tight. "I'm here. It's all right. I've got you." He stepped back and looked his son in the eye. "And you are brave. You're still standing. Most would be curled on the floor by now. Remember Superman."

Daniel gave one gruff, unexpected laugh.

It was something he'd explained to his father, at great length, when he was six. That at first Superman was completely invincible. But then his creators—"One was Canadian," Daniel had excitedly said—realized that was a mistake.

"They had to have something that could hurt him," the earnest little boy had explained.

"And do you know why that is?" his father had asked.

Daniel had taken his time to think about it.

Two days later he'd slipped his hand into his dad's as they walked through the park to the playground, and said, "Because you can't be brave if you're not afraid."

"*Oui*," his father agreed, and watched Daniel run off to play with the other kids.

"Please, Dad," Daniel now said. "Tell me you were a commando."

"Better." His father leaned closer and dropped his voice further. "I taught commandos."

Stepping back, he looked at the handkerchief. Reine-Marie had given it to him as a stocking stuffer at Christmas. It was now stained with their son's blood.

Just as he went to put it back in his pocket, Girard reached out and

357

bent Gamache's hand back, almost breaking his fingers. Gamache winced and twisted, opening his hand and dropping the handkerchief.

Girard examined it. Nothing hidden in the folds. Then he tossed it back at Gamache.

He could have just asked to see it, Gamache knew, as he flexed his hand and replaced the handkerchief in his pocket. Or even snatched it away from him.

But instead, Thierry Girard had chosen to hurt. Not much, but even a little seemed to give Girard pleasure.

Here was a sadist with a gun, and Armand Gamache wondered just how much control Claude Dussault really did have over his second-in-command.

"You have until tomorrow morning at seven thirty to find whatever it is Stephen Horowitz has hidden," said Dussault. "The GHS board meeting is at eight. We need it before then."

"You've looked for it for weeks and haven't found anything," Gamache said. "But you want me to find it in hours?"

"I think you can do it," said Dussault. "Given the motivation."

Gamache looked at him with loathing. "If you really want me to succeed, I need more information. What's GHS up to? I have to know what I'm looking for."

"You're smart," said Dussault. "I think you'll know it when you see it." He looked at his watch. "It's now ten fifty-three. You have almost nine hours."

"I'll need help. Someone needs to come with me."

"Did you have someone in mind?" asked Dussault.

"Daniel."

Dussault smiled. "Saw that coming, and no. He stays safe with us."

"Then Beauvoir. Let me bring Beauvoir in. Together we have a chance."

Dussault made a subtle gesture toward Girard, and the two men stepped away, to consult in a corner.

Watching them, Gamache could see that Dussault was definitely in charge, and had complete control over the brute Girard. What should have been a relief was actually even more alarming.

"You have your Beauvoir," said Dussault, returning to them.

Gamache put out his hand for his phone, and as Girard gave it to him, he said, "Put it on speaker."

Armand noticed that several calls and texts had come in from Reine-Marie. He was sorely tempted to read them, but knew he had to place the call first.

It rang only once before he heard Jean-Guy's excited voice.

"Annie's gone into labor. We're heading to the hospital."

The emotions were so strong, so conflicting, that for a moment Armand felt light-headed. As though he'd been spun in a centrifuge.

"*Allô?*" said Jean-Guy. "You still there?"

"*Oui.* Is Annie all right?"

"Hi, Dad," came her voice. "I'm here in the car with Jean-Guy and Maman. You coming?"

"As soon as I can. I'm with Daniel and we're just discussing our next step. Reine-Marie?"

"I'm here," came her voice. "Everything okay with you? Daniel's with you?"

Daniel called out, "*Salut, Maman.* Everything's fine."

Armand heard the cheerful tone coming from his bloodstained son. How could he possibly think he wasn't brave?

"Allida and Judith are still there along with Séverine," said Reine-Marie. "We haven't been able to make any connection between the dates in Stephen's notes and GHS. It's frustrating."

"Not to worry, we'll figure it out. And there are more important things right now. Annie?"

"Yes, Dad."

"We'll be there as soon as we can. I love you."

"I love you, too, Papa," she said, though he could hear her disappointment and slight confusion that her father wasn't also rushing to the hospital, to be there with her.

"Wait a minute," said Jean-Guy. "You called me. Did you want something?"

"Just to check in. Please, please, let me know about the baby and Annie."

"You'll be here long before anything happens." There was a pause. "Are you all right? What did Dussault want?"

"It was a fishing expedition. Trying to figure out what we know."

"So he is involved in all this?"

"I'm not so sure. Look, this will wait. You have far more important things happening. If we're not there before she arrives, tell your daughter that her uncle and grandfather love her."

"You'll tell her yourselves. Armand—"

But Gamache had hung up before Jean-Guy could say more.

"Congratulations," said Girard as he took the phone back. "Happy day."

He read the emails and texts, then handed the phone to Dussault, who also read them.

Reine-Marie had been trying to reach Armand to tell him about Annie.

"Shame Beauvoir can't join you. I suspect your chances of success, never great, have just collapsed." Dussault handed the phone back to Gamache.

"I'll need the JSPS card." Armand walked over to Daniel. "I gave mine to him."

Sliding his hand into Daniel's pocket, he found the card and felt for the coins.

"Let me see," said Girard when Armand withdrew his hand.

It held only the card.

"Should we send one of them with him?" asked Girard, indicating the guards.

"*Non*, no need. What's he going to do? Run away? Go to the police?" Dussault smiled. "All we need are the documents. I don't care how he does it, but he'll be faster, more efficient without one of them tagging along."

Armand turned to Daniel. "I have to leave, but I'll be back in time. I promise."

He pulled Daniel to him, in a bear hug. And whispered, "I'm so proud of you. I love you."

Daniel nodded.

CHAPTER 38

~

Armand unlocked the door to their apartment in the Marais and quickly went over to the bookcase.

The gun was still there.

Slipping it into his coat pocket, he locked up and left.

But where to? He had no idea where Stephen and Plessner had hidden the evidence, if there even was any.

Had Stephen and Plessner uncovered a scam, claiming to use neodymium in next-generation telecommunications where actually it didn't work? Taking investor's money on false pretenses?

Or maybe it was real, and GHS needed to protect a breakthrough that would net them billions.

Was it corporate espionage? Fraud? Money laundering?

What had that young journalist found in the mountains of Patagonia? And how could the derailment of a train in Colombia four years ago have anything to do with it?

There was something. Something terrible enough to murder. And now he had just hours to find it.

Armand stood on the sidewalk outside their door and looked this way, then that.

He honestly had no idea where to go next.

He turned toward the Seine and started walking, his mind racing. Though he tried to slow it down, to marshal his thoughts.

What did they know?

For one thing, Claude Dussault had let slip that he knew that they'd talked about Patagonia in the subbasement of the George V.

Which meant he knew everything they'd discussed. Which meant there was an informant in their midst.

And that could be only one person. Séverine Arbour.

What had Dussault said? That the deaths Gamache knew about weren't even the tip of the iceberg. GHS was responsible for many, many more. On a scale almost unimaginable.

Gamache stopped, realizing he was standing across from the hôpital Hôtel-Dieu. Where Annie was busy giving birth, and Stephen was busy dying.

He took a step off the curb, toward the entrance. Then he stepped back.

No. He couldn't give in to the nearly overwhelming temptation to go in.

In an act so painful he was trembling, Armand Gamache turned his back on them and walked on, sparing a glance at Notre-Dame.

Then he turned his back on that, too, though he allowed his thoughts to linger on the heroics of the men and women who'd run in to save the artifacts. Who'd fought the fire at risk to themselves.

Hell might be empty, but there was evidence of the divine in their midst, too. The trick, as Stephen had taught him in the garden of the Musée Rodin so many years ago, was to see both.

Dreadful deeds were obvious. The divine was often harder to see.

And which, he heard Stephen's voice and still felt the tap on his chest, *would have more weight with you,* garçon?

He was essentially alone now, on the Pont des Coeurs. The Bridge of Hearts.

He stopped to peer over the edge. To cool and calm his thoughts. Reaching out, he felt the old stone, the cold stone, wall and looked down at the dark water.

Claude Dussault had suggested he make a wish. And perhaps he should have also thrown a coin into the Fontaine des Mers. It was ironic, of course. To call a site where the Terror had taken so many lives the Place de la Concorde. The Place of Agreement.

How many wishes, how many fervent prayers, had gone unanswered? Unless the slide of the guillotine was the answer. He wondered now what Dussault had wished for.

Gamache turned toward Place de la Concorde. His mind finally settling. Coming to a halt.

Why had Dussault asked to meet him there, of all places? In front of that fountain? In front of the famous column. That marked the guillotine.

Armand went over what Dussault said. What Dussault did.

Gamache's eyes opened wide. "Oh, my God," he whispered.

He hailed a taxi. He had to get back to the Place de la Concorde, but on the way he stopped at the Hôtel Lutetia.

Alain Pinot was no longer in bar Joséphine. Nor was he in any of the other bars or restaurants of the grand hotel.

The front desk called Pinot's room, but there was no answer.

Gamache approached the concierge. "Has Monsieur Pinot asked for a restaurant reservation for tonight?"

"*Non, monsieur.*"

Armand knew that might not be true. Discretion was a vital part of a concierge's job.

"I'd very much appreciate your help in finding a restaurant for this evening," he said, sliding a hundred-euro note across the marble top.

"Most of our guests belong to private clubs."

"I've always wanted to join one. Any suggestions?"

He walked out of there with a short list. Any the concierge's fingerprint smudging one name.

Cercle de l'Union Interalliée. What General de Gaulle had called the French embassy in Paris.

"May I help you, monsieur?" the well-dressed woman asked in a hushed voice as he entered the private members club.

Gamache had heard about this place but had never been in it.

The Cercle, in the Eighth Arrondissement, was a hub for diplomats, political leaders, industrialists. The elite of Paris.

In other words, the boards of directors of most of the major corporations in Europe.

Armand quickly, instinctively, took in his surroundings.

The high ceilings. The opulent décor unchanged from a century earlier. And yet there was nothing faded about its grandeur.

It whispered power and glory.

Decisions that changed the world, for better or worse, had been made within these walls for a hundred years.

The woman at the door expertly sized up the man in front of her. Well-groomed. Good coat, classic cut. No tie, but crisp white shirt and well-tailored jacket beneath the overcoat.

An elegant man. Clearly used to a certain authority. But then, everyone who came through that door had authority. Or they wouldn't get past her.

"*Oui, merci.* I'm looking for one of your guests. Monsieur Pinot. Alain Pinot."

"Are you a member of a reciprocal club? Perhaps the Mount Royal in Montréal?"

How subtly she's made it clear that she'd placed him as a Québécois.

"*Non.* I'm just a visitor. Is Monsieur Pinot here?"

"I really cannot say."

"I understand. If he were here, could you please give him this?"

Gamache handed her the card and saw her face open in a smile. "*Bienvenue.* This"—she held up the JSPS card—"is your membership. Do you mind?"

Selecting a burgundy-and-dark-blue Pierre Cardin tie, she waited while he did it up, then indicated he should follow her up the wide stairway.

At the top, in a hushed voice, she said, "Wait here, please."

They were at the entrance to a massive room, with groupings of sofas and armchairs.

Gamache watched as she walked over to a gathering of men and women, all of whom he recognized from the GHS board.

The man looked up as the concierge bent over and handed him the card. Then he looked over.

At Gamache.

Alain Pinot rose, saying a few words to his companions, and followed the woman to where Gamache was waiting.

Corpulent and red-faced from too much wine and too much rich food over too many years. And yet, Gamache thought, there was about him a force. Here was an undeniable personality.

Pinot looked at Gamache, then said to the concierge, "Is there a private salon available?"

"Absolutely. Follow me please, gentlemen."

The room she led them to was intimate, the walls lined with bookcases. There were two large leather armchairs with the imprints of bodies, as though the spirits of long-dead members, reluctant to leave this sanctuary, still sat there.

A small fire had been laid in the grate, and before she left, she lit it.

There was a decanter of cognac and bulbous glasses on a sideboard.

"May I bring you anything?" she asked.

"*Non, Marie, merci.* I think we'd like to be alone."

"Of course, Monsieur Pinot."

Pinot locked the door and turned to Gamache. "You were at the Lutetia earlier. Who are you? And"—he handed him back his card—"how do you have this?"

"My name is Armand Gamache."

Pinot's eyes widened and he grinned. "You're Armand. The famous Armand. I've been jealous of you for years. Decades. Stephen's son."

So Pinot and Stephen did know each other, and apparently very well. Armand exhaled, almost a sigh. It was the first time he'd felt relief in what seemed ages. They were finally getting somewhere. He hoped.

"Godson," he said.

"Stephen didn't seem to make the distinction."

He put out his hand, and Armand took it, feeling it both fleshy and strong. A man of immense appetite.

Alain Pinot should have been a king, might have been a king in another lifetime. Gamache could see him wrapped in miles of armor on top of some great staggering warhorse.

Leading the charge, slashing and mutilating anyone who stood between himself and whatever he wanted.

But this was now, and the closest a man like Pinot could get to that sort of power was to ride atop some great corporation. And Agence France-Presse was that. It was the power behind the power. It could make and break politicians, governments, industrialists. Corporations.

And did.

"So you do know Stephen?" said Armand, declining the offer of cognac. "I wasn't sure."

Taking a seat in front of the fire, he glanced at the carriage clock on the mantel.

Eleven thirty.

"He never mentioned me?" asked Pinot. "I guess not." There was no mistaking the disappointment, even hurt. "Still, he talked about you." Pinot leaned forward. "Is he . . . ?"

"In hospital. Critical condition. You know what happened?"

"Yes. Hit-and-run. Terrible. I tried to visit him, but they wouldn't let me get even close." Pinot's eyes, almost buried behind folds of flesh and outcroppings of skin tags, were searching. Shrewd. He examined Gamache. "I'm guessing it was no accident."

"No. I was there. It was a deliberate attempt on his life."

"*Mon Dieu,*" said Pinot, leaning back. "*Merde.* Who'd do such a thing?" He was silent for a moment, studying Gamache. "Do you know something about this? Stephen told me you're now the head of the Sûreté du Québec."

"Used to be. I'm now the head of homicide."

Pinot raised his brows. "That doesn't sound like a promotion."

"It isn't." Gamache left it at that. "Did you hear about the body found yesterday morning in an apartment in the Seventh Arrondissement?"

"No."

No, of course not, thought Gamache. The police hadn't yet released the news.

"The man was murdered. The apartment is Stephen's, and the dead man is Alexander Plessner."

"Oh, shit. I know Monsieur Plessner. Stephen introduced us a few months ago. Jesus, what's going on? What's happening?"

Pinot's face was blossoming from red to purple. Gamache wondered if, before their conversation was over, he'd have to do CPR on him.

How deeply buried was his heart? Wrapped in layers of ambition and foie gras.

"I don't know," said Gamache. "I'm hoping you can help."

"How?" asked Pinot.

"What do you know about GHS Engineering?"

"Ahhh, so that's it."

"What do you mean?" asked Gamache.

"I'm on the board. Stephen approached me about buying my shares, which would get him on the board. I asked why, but he wouldn't tell me."

"How long ago was this?"

Pinot considered. "Six, seven months."

About the time the job at GHS had been offered to Jean-Guy, thought Armand. Stephen was putting his plan in place.

"And did you agree? Without even knowing why?"

"Of course."

"Why?"

"Because he asked. That's all I needed." Pinot studied Gamache. "Would you need more?"

Armand smiled slightly and shook his head.

"I was willing to do it immediately, but Stephen wanted to wait until the last minute, until the morning of the board meeting. He swore me to secrecy. Do you have any idea what he had in mind?"

"No, but I found this in his agenda." Armand showed Pinot the photograph of the slip of paper. "We think the AFP means Agence France-Presse. Do these dates mean anything to you?"

Pinot studied them. "Yes. This one. It's when one of my reporters disappeared."

"Anik Guardiola. In Patagonia."

"You know about her?"

"I know it was called an accident. But almost certainly wasn't. What happened?"

"I don't know. Not for sure. I should've asked more questions, back when her body was found. Should've pushed more. That's how I got on the GHS board, you know."

Armand did not know. But he knew enough to keep quiet and let Pinot talk.

"The police in Patagonia said it was a hiking accident. I sent investigators. They discovered that her laptop and phone and all her notes were missing. But by then her body had been cremated. We pressured the government, but—" He lifted his beefy hands.

"What story was she on?"

"It was about water quality. We traced her steps to meetings with various corporations, including GHS. They were very open, said she'd visited the site of the proposed treatment plant and the mine that they'd closed. They seemed extremely disturbed by her death. That's when they offered me a seat on their board. As a gesture of transparency and goodwill."

He took a sharp breath and a long exhale. "This was four years ago. It seems they knew me better than I knew myself. It appealed to my ego. I was dazzled by the other board members. Completely taken in."

"When did you realize things were not as they seemed?"

"Only when Stephen asked me to give him my seat on the board."

"Give?" asked Gamache. "He was going to pay you hundreds of millions, *non*? Hardly a gift."

"You do know a lot."

"It's what I do," said Gamache, his patience wearing thin. "I get information. Please stop obfuscating. We don't have time."

"Yes, he was paying for the shares, but it wasn't for me. A trust has been set up for victims. Some of that has been set aside for the family of my murdered journalist. You can check."

"Victims. Of what?"

"I don't know. I asked Stephen, and all he'd say is that it would be clear at the board meeting."

Armand nodded, taking this in. It sounded like Stephen, who liked to keep information to himself. "Have you ever heard of neodymium?"

"It's a rare earth element, isn't it? We did a series on them a couple of years ago. They've become a hot commodity. Why?"

"That mine in Patagonia GHS bought and Anik Guardiola investigated hasn't been closed. They've been mining neodymium. I think she found out about it."

Pinot's brows rose. "Huh. If that's true, it's quite a find. GHS hasn't announced this to the board. Why keep it a secret? Why would Anik Guardiola finding out about it be a problem? It's not illegal, is it?"

"I think the issue isn't the mineral, but what they're doing with it. I think your young journalist found out too much and was murdered to keep her quiet. She also did a story, which Stephen noted, about a train derailment in Colombia. Any idea what that was about?"

"No, none. You're going to have to remind me. What's neodymium used for?"

"Batteries. Laptops. Hard drives," said Gamache. "But there's some suggestion a new use has been found. Something in telecommunications. Do you know any engineers, someone not associated with GHS, who might know?"

"My daughter-in-law's an engineer. Works for Lavalin." He made the call.

As far as the daughter-in-law knew, no revolutionary new uses had been found for neodymium.

"Ask her if it could cause a train to derail," said Gamache.

Pinot did. Listening to the answer, he grimaced. Thanked her, then hung up.

"She says it would have to be a cartoon magnet to drag a train off its tracks. I think she thinks I'm nuts."

Gamache looked again at what Stephen had written. "The derailment has something to do with the journalist's murder. And these other dates are significant, too."

Pinot got up. "We need to look them up. The Agence France-Presse morgue keeps all the old stories. We can go there."

Armand also got to his feet. "Can you get access to your files from anywhere?"

"Yes. They have trusted me with the passwords," said the owner of AFP, with a smile.

"*Bon.* Make your excuses to your guests and meet me at the front door."

Pinot joined him a couple of minutes later. "Well, I just left three baffled friends including a former Prime Minister of Italy, though I suspect he's often baffled. I might've suggested I was going to meet a mistress. I just hope they don't see us together."

"You could do worse," said Armand.

"True." Pinot laughed. Then, at a subtle signal, a liveried chauffeur hurried over to a limousine. "We can use my car."

"Best not," said Gamache, and asked the doorman to get them a taxi. Telling him where they wanted to go.

"*La Défense, s'il vous plaît,*" the doorman told the driver.

Pinot opened his mouth, but at a stern look from Gamache, he shut it.

A block along, Gamache leaned forward again and said, "But first, we need to go to Place de la Concorde."

"*Oui, monsieur.*"

"I thought we were going to my offices," said Pinot.

"*Non,*" was all Gamache said.

Pinot settled into the back of the taxi, marveling that it had been years, decades, since he'd used anything other than a limousine or a helicopter to get around Paris.

He did not like this new experience.

Once at Place de la Concorde, Gamache quickly crossed to the Fontaine des Mers. As the driver and Pinot watched, he took off his shoes and socks, rolled up his trousers, and climbed into the fountain.

Shoving up his sleeves, he reached into the freezing-cold water and moved his hands around until he found what he was looking for.

As he got out, a woman approached and gave him a two-euro coin. "Use it for food, monsieur."

"*Merci, mais*—" Gamache began, but she'd walked away, into the night.

"What was that about?" asked Pinot when Gamache returned, shivering, to the taxi. With a look of warning not to actually speak, Armand opened his hand.

Resting in his palm were two Canadian nickels. Stuck firmly together.

CHAPTER 39

⁓

Annie was catching her breath after a labor pain, and Jean-Guy took the opportunity to leave the room to get her more ice water. And to catch his own breath.

Reine-Marie followed him out.

"Armand should be here," she said, lowering her voice. "Why isn't he? Is something wrong?"

"I don't know," admitted Jean-Guy. "I do know he'd be here if he could."

"Something's happened." Reine-Marie looked behind her, at the closed door to the small private room where her daughter was laboring to give birth to her own daughter. "I'm going to call."

The phone rang only once before Armand picked up.

"Is everything all right?" he asked without preamble.

At the sound of his voice, concerned but nothing more, she felt herself relax. "Yes, everything's fine. We're still hours away. Annie's doing well. It's Jean-Guy who's driving us all crazy."

Armand managed a chuckle. "That's what husbands and fathers do. A woman loses her water and a man loses his mind."

Reine-Marie laughed. "You sure did. You were a lunatic. When Daniel was finally born, and they asked if you wanted to cut the cord, you cried. I didn't think you'd ever let him go." There was silence down the line. "Armand?"

"Yes," he said. "I remember it well."

372

"Where are you? I hear noise."

"I'm in a taxi, but I can't come just yet. Call me if anything happens. Give Annie my love. Tell Jean-Guy to take a deep breath in . . ."

"And a deep breath out. Armand?"

"Oui?"

"Are you all right?"

"Yes. I'll be there. I promise."

When he hung up, Pinot asked, "Your wife?"

"Yes. My daughter's in labor. They're at the hospital."

"You should be there."

Armand clutched the coins and made a wish as he watched Paris, beautiful, troubled, luminous Paris, slip by.

Once at the GHS tower in La Défense, he paid the driver, then grabbed Pinot, who was heading toward the building, and guided him away. To the métro.

"Hold on to your wallet," said Gamache, "and don't make eye contact with anyone."

"Huh?"

If Alain Pinot didn't much like the taxi ride, he was about to meet something far worse.

Half an hour later they popped up at the station de métro Hôtel de Ville stop. Gamache hurried through the dark, deserted streets of the Marais. Pinot trudging along behind.

"I thought we were going to AFP," he said. For the tenth time. "This isn't the way."

"Just follow me."

The roundabout journey had eaten precious time Armand couldn't really spare, but he needed to throw off anyone tracking his movements on his phone, which wouldn't work in the depths of the métro.

They'd know where he was now that they'd surfaced, but it would take a few minutes to catch up. Confusion was his friend. As long as he was not the one confused.

"This's the Archives nationales," said Pinot, looking up at the gates. "What're we doing here?"

Armand asked the guard to ring Madame Lenoir, then turned to Pinot. "We're getting help to look up those dates in your morgue and figure out what Stephen and Monsieur Plessner knew."

Allida Lenoir hurried over and vouched for them.

"We haven't found out anything more," she said as she led them back to the reading room.

"Madame Arbour?" asked Gamache.

"Is still with us."

"Good."

She looked behind her at the large man lumbering to keep up. "You're Alain Pinot, aren't you? You run Agence France-Presse."

"I own it," he wheezed. "There's some question as to whether I actually run it." He stopped at the entrance to the reading room. "My God, is it . . ."

"Judith de la—"

"Granger," he said, going forward, his arms out. "I haven't seen you in years. Decades." He kissed her on both cheeks, smiling broadly. "What're you doing here?"

She explained, and he nodded approval, turning to Gamache. "Good. With Judith on board, we might have a chance. Best researcher in the business."

While Allida and Judith got him organized at a terminal, Gamache waved Séverine Arbour over.

"Do you mind if I see your phone?"

Perplexed but not alarmed, she handed it over.

Alain Pinot talked as he logged in to the AFP's own archives. "As you know, we store stories that've already run in the newspaper's morgue. What you might not know is it's where we also archive stories that were filed and never ran, as well as research and reporters' notes."

"My phone, please," Madame Arbour said, holding out her hand. But instead of giving it back, he slipped it into his pocket.

She had, Gamache knew, been feeding Claude Dussault information all day. It would stop now.

All the way there on the métro, while Pinot had muttered expletives, he'd gone around and around what Dussault had said. And done.

What those coins in the Fontaine des Mers could possibly mean.

When he'd embraced Daniel, not the first but subsequent times, he'd slipped his hand into Daniel's pockets. To get the magnetized coins away from his son.

But the nickels weren't there.

He'd tried again, to be sure, when he'd taken the JSPS card. Still, he came away empty-handed.

And then, finally, on the Bridge of Hearts, he'd put it together. What Claude Dussault had thrown into the fountain.

Dussault had obviously found the coins on Daniel, but instead of handing them over, he'd kept them, then thrown them into the fountain.

That's why he wanted to meet there. He needed to get rid of the nickels without being seen. Someplace where he could later retrieve them.

The coins were part of the proof that neodymium was involved.

What was the Prefect up to? Was he double-crossing his employers? Planning to blackmail them by keeping some of the proof himself?

Were the coins insurance, in case GHS turned on him?

Gamache was beginning to suspect that everything Dussault had said that evening, everything he'd done, had been calculated. But what was the sum? What did it add up to?

Armand knew if he came up with the wrong answer, it would be catastrophic.

But one thing he did know. Claude Dussault was the most cunning and therefore the most dangerous person in the picture.

By far.

Alain Pinot was typing away at the terminal. He'd also given Allida and Judith access to the AFP morgue. The three were deep into it now.

The stories and reporters' notes from those dates were wide-ranging and global, from a plane crash in Ukraine to various road accidents to riots sparked by fears of both climate change and the new nuclear power stations coming online to help solve the problem.

There did not seem to be any common thread or theme.

"Give me my phone back," said Séverine Arbour.

"Come with me," Gamache said, leading her away.

When he stopped, he brought out her phone, removed the SIM card, and slipped it into his pocket.

"Why did you do that?" she asked as he handed her phone back. "This's useless without the SIM."

"Is it?" he asked. "What about the tracking app?"

He could have neutralized that, too, but didn't want to alert whoever was monitoring the phone that Arbour had been discovered.

She tried to rally. "What tracking? Has someone tampered with my phone?"

He raised his brows and stared at her.

She paled. "It's not what it seems."

"Really? Because it seems you've been passing information to the very people who've murdered their way across Paris. The very people we've been desperate to avoid. You've given them information that led to my son being picked up, beaten, and now held at gunpoint."

"I didn't know. I didn't mean—" Now she looked both panicked and confused.

"Tell me now, what do you know about GHS? What've you been hiding?"

"Nothing. I don't know anything."

"You're lying."

He took a step toward her and she cringed.

And Armand Gamache, a good, decent man, understood how good, decent people could resort to torture. If time was too short and the stakes too high.

Because he wanted to do that now. To do whatever was necessary to get the information out of her and save Daniel.

He was so shocked by this realization, so horrified by his temptation, that he took a step away. And clutched his hands behind his back, in case . . .

"Tell me what you know. Now."

Séverine Arbour was looking at him, clearly terrified.

She thinks I'm going to beat the information out of her.

And yet, despite her terror, there was resolve. She would not talk. Not easily.

What could be so important that she'd endure torture rather than talk?

"Come with me," he said and, taking her by the arm, they returned to the others.

"I'm sorry," said Pinot. "There's nothing."

"We can't find anything connecting any of these dates and stories," said Judith de la Granger.

Pulling up a chair, Gamache sat down and scanned the pages, going from one date to the next to the . . .

Then he sat back, as though softly shoved. His mouth had dropped open slightly.

"What is it?" asked Madame de la Granger. She'd seen that look before when researchers finally found what they'd spent decades searching for. Usually some apparently trivial line in an obscure text that illuminated everything.

She leaned closer to read the story that had so struck the Chief Inspector.

It was about a plane crash in Ukraine a year and a half ago. She remembered reading about it. The passenger plane had hit the center of a town. Three hundred and thirty killed.

But Gamache was onto the next date and the next series of stories.

Then he turned to Arbour. "What's GHS Engineering building in Luxembourg?" When she didn't answer, he said, "It's a funicular, isn't it."

"But there's no story about a funicular, Armand," said Pinot.

"*Non,*" he said. "Not yet. But there is that."

It was a news brief, about an elevator that had plummeted thirty-two stories, in Chicago, killing the two people inside.

He got up and looked at his watch. Just over three hours left.

Séverine Arbour saw him coming and backed away, but he walked right by her, as though in a trance. And began pacing the reading room. Almost prowling. Like a great cat in captivity. Looking for the way out. Up and back. Up and back.

What did Claude Dussault say?

Think. Think.

Calm. Calm. Think. Think.

With every step forward he threw his mind back. To what the head of the Préfecture de Paris had said as they'd sat in the corridor of the *section d'urgence.*

Then, later, over the body of Alexander Plessner.

In his office at the 36 and in the suite at the Lutetia.

Their dinner the night before.

His conversation at the fountain.

Their exchange in the elevator of Stephen's building as they went up to see Daniel and his captors.

Armand put his hands in his pockets. His right hand felt the gun. It had almost certainly been placed in his apartment by Claude Dussault. Or on Dussault's orders.

In the other he felt the nickels. Stuck together with a magnet more powerful than anything else known to engineers. Known to engineering and design.

They'd been tossed into the fountain. By Dussault.

Everywhere Gamache looked, there was the Prefect.

Despite his efforts not to be manipulated, was that what was happening? In thinking he was carving his own path, was he really only doing their bidding? Dussault's bidding?

He walked on, in the dim room, lit by pools of light at each reading station. Time was short, but he couldn't be rushed. Patience. Patience. With patience comes power.

He needed to think. Think.

Dussault, in what appeared to be a rant against Gamache's arrogance, had demanded to know what was different between the deaths GHS had caused and what other industries did. Killing people by the tens of thousands and getting away with it. In full view.

Airlines that flew planes they knew were dangerous.

Pharmaceuticals that allowed dangerous drugs to remain in circulation.

The entire tobacco industry.

Elevators that plunged to the ground.

Engineers using faulty materials.

He stopped in his tracks and stared into the darkness. Then turned toward the others, sitting in the pools of light. Watching him.

Faulty materials.

That cause elevators to plunge. That cause planes to crash. That cause trains to derail. It wasn't the design that was the problem. It was the material.

Neodymium.

Each of the dates Stephen had noted had some sort of major accident. Including the first one. The train derailment that Anik Guardiola wrote about.

He turned and stared at Arbour.

His face had gone pale. His eyes were wide.

"It's the accidents," he said, striding past Arbour and back to Pinot's terminal. "That's what your journalist was on to, at the very beginning. That's why they killed her. She asked too many questions. I got it the wrong way around. Stephen didn't bring Plessner in. Plessner contacted Stephen. As an engineer, he must've made the connection. He's the one who dictated those dates to Stephen."

Gamache sat down and started going back over the AFP stories.

"That plane crash eighteen months ago," he said. "And there was another, just four months later on the next date." He brought up that page. "Different airlines, different make of plane. Two hundred and thirty killed in the second crash. They'd appear to be unrelated, but suppose that's not true? Look here, cars exploding into flames. Again, different makes. That bridge collapse in the middle of winter in the Alps. The failure of the elevator's safety mechanism.

"The inquiries into every one of the so-called accidents, even the plane crashes, came to no firm conclusion, and the investigations petered out."

"So-called accidents?" asked Madame de la Granger. "You think these were sabotage? Even terrorist attacks?"

"No," said Gamache, staring at the screen. "I think the first one, the derailment in Colombia, really was an accident. And I don't think the others were deliberate. At least, not targeted. But neither were they unavoidable."

"What're you saying?" asked Pinot.

"He's saying that GHS is responsible for all these accidents," said Allida Lenoir. "Or whatever they are."

"I'm saying they've known for years that something was wrong, ever since the train derailment. And they've done nothing to correct it," said Gamache. "I think GHS Engineering is using the neodymium to make something common. So common that it's used in all sorts of things."

He went back to the airline story.

"What happens to aircraft at thirty-five thousand feet? We've all watched the flight maps, and seen the report on speed, altitude, and outside temperature."

"It can get to minus sixty or more," said Judith.

"Everything freezes. A plane is designed to withstand that. But suppose one element is not? Neodymium has many advantages, but one flaw. When overheated or frozen, it can shatter. I think that's what's happening." He turned to Séverine Arbour. "Isn't that right?"

But she didn't speak. Didn't say a word. She, too, was pale.

"Holy shit," said Madame Lenoir. "They knew, and they didn't stop it?"

Gamache turned to Alain Pinot. "What would happen if GHS accepted responsibility?"

"Early on? After the train derailment?" He thought. "Not a lot. No one was killed."

"So why didn't they?" asked Madame de la Granger.

"Denial," suggested Pinot. "They didn't want to see."

"I think it went far beyond denial," said Gamache. "I think by the time the train went off the rails, whatever caused it had already been built into all sorts of things, all over the world. Hundreds, thousands, hundreds of thousands, maybe millions of things. Some would never cause a problem, but some would. And to issue a recall would be ruinous."

"So they turned a blind eye?" said Judith de la Granger. "Knowing what would happen? That thousands would be killed?"

"Not thinking anyone would make the connection back to them," said Pinot. "And no one did. How many planes are taking off right now, with . . ."

"We have to stop it," said Allida Lenoir.

"We don't even know what 'it' is," Judith said. "What're they making?"

They stared at each other, but no one had the answer. At one time, Gamache had thought it had to do with the Allen wrench or the screws Stephen had lying around. But that couldn't be right. They were not made of neodymium.

But something Stephen had was. Something magnetized those Canadian nickels.

"We need proof," he said. "We can't just tell aviation around the world to stop flying. We'd be dismissed as cranks. Oh, my God."

"What is it?" Judith demanded, seeing the look of shock, of horror, on the Chief Inspector's face.

"Something Dussault mentioned. The nuclear power plants coming online. Some already are."

"Oh, fuck," whispered Judith, sitting, collapsing, into a chair.

"Planes freeze," said Allida. "But nuclear reactors superheat. And if there's neodymium—"

Gamache, wide-eyed, was nodding. Seeing the map the newscasts had shown, of the new power plants around the world.

In Colorado. In Arizona. In Ontario and Manitoba. In the UK and France. China. On and on. Next-generation, safer. Safest, they were guaranteed. Brought online to reduce fossil fuel use. Their designs checked and rechecked. Until even the most ardent environmentalists gave their reluctant approval.

But the problem wasn't the design. The catastrophe would be caused by the material. A near-miraculous rare earth element that promised to make everything more efficient.

Safer.

If one or more of those reactors goes . . . ?

"We have to stop it," said Allida.

"We have to find out what it is," said Armand. "We need proof."

"Can't we just tell them it's the neodymium?" demanded Pinot.

"Would you shut down power plants, ground planes, stop elevators in office buildings internationally based on us saying it's neodymium?" asked Gamache. "Of course not. We need to know exactly what it is they've built into those things."

"If Horowitz and Plessner had the proof, why didn't they sound an alarm?" asked Judith. "Go to the authorities?"

"I think they suspected, but it took years and hundreds of millions of dollars to get the evidence," said Gamache. "And it would have to be absolute, undeniable. Something the board members and the authorities, many of whom are in the pocket of GHS, couldn't ignore."

Out in the street they could hear sounds. Paris was stirring. The start of another working week. He checked his watch. It was 4:37 in the morning. Less than three hours now.

Gamache turned to Séverine Arbour. "I think you—"

But she wasn't there. While they'd been focused on the computer, she'd disappeared into the shadows.

"Damn," he said, standing up so quickly his chair fell over. "We have to find her."

"Why?" asked Madame de la Granger. "You think she knows something?"

"She's working with Claude Dussault," said Gamache. "She's been passing him information all day."

"What?" demanded Judith, her face opening in horror.

"We'll find her," said Allida. "I know every inch of this building."

"She can't have gone far," Gamache called after her. "I locked the door when we came in."

Pinot took his arm and pulled him around. "You said Claude Dussault just now. Did you mean the head of the Paris police? That Dussault?"

"*Oui.*"

"Are you saying the head of the whole fucking police force is behind this?"

"The Prefect, yes. Do you know him?"

"Not well. I've met him socially, at the opera and fundraisers. We've done stories on him and his reorganization of the Préfecture after his predecessor died. He seems a good man, a decent man. Why would he be involved in this?"

"Money. Power," said Gamache, staring at Pinot. "You understand those."

Pinot's shrewd face examined Gamache. "If you do find that evidence, what'll you do with it?"

"You know."

"You'll hand it over to them, won't you?"

"To save my son. Yes."

"You know I can't let you do that."

Armand felt the weight of the gun in his pocket. "And you know you can't stop me."

"They'll kill him anyway, Armand. And not just him. You. Me. Them." Alain Pinot nodded toward the Chief Librarian, on her hands and knees now, looking under the tables, and the Chief Archivist appearing from, and disappearing into, dark aisles of books and maps and documents.

"And anyone else who's touched this case," said Armand. "Including my wife, daughter, son-in-law."

"And the 'accidents' will continue."

"Yes."

"Damn," came Allida's voice from out of the darkness, followed milliseconds later by a thud, as Judith de la Granger went to stand up and knocked her head on the bottom of a table.

"What?" she called.

"The door connecting the archives to the museum is open. She must've gone out that way. She's in the museum. But there're guards there and the doors onto the quadrangle are locked. She still can't leave."

"But there are phones," said Gamache. "She can call Dussault and tell him what we know."

"Fuck," said Madame de la Granger.

"I've never heard you swear before," said Madame Lenoir. "You always said it was the refuge of a second-class mind."

"I was wrong," said Madame de la Granger.

"We have to get out of here," said Pinot.

"Not yet," said Gamache. "We have to find whatever proof Stephen and Plessner had."

"Wait a minute," said Judith, turning to Gamache. "You think it's here? In the archives? We're not just looking up references, you think the proof itself is hidden here."

"Where would you hide a book?" Gamache asked her.

"In a library."

"Where would you hide a document?" he asked.

"Here," said Judith. "With other documents."

"But this isn't the only archive collection," said Allida. "There're different archives in buildings all over France. Why would you think Monsieur Horowitz would hide the proof here?"

"Because he'd want us to be able to find it, and this building is around the corner from our home. Reine-Marie knows it well. If he put it in any of the archives, it'd be this one."

"That's a big 'if,'" said Judith.

Allida turned full circle, scanning the endless rows of files. "How do we even begin . . ."

"He'd have hidden them fairly recently," said Armand. "Since they forged Daniel's name. That's in the last five weeks."

Madame Lenoir took them over to the archivist's desk. "The requests are logged here, but there'd be thousands from all over the world. You can't possibly go through them all."

"Can we search by name?"

"Of document?"

"Of the person requesting it."

"Yes." She showed him how.

Armand's fingers hovered over the keyboard. "He wouldn't have used his own name, or Plessner's. Still—" He put them in. "Worth a try."

It came up empty.

"Who else's would he use?" asked Pinot. "Yours?"

Armand tried it. Nothing.

They huddled around and watched him put in names. Reine-Marie's. Daniel's. Annie's. His desperation growing. Showing. In the increasingly unlikely attempts.

Zora. Florence. Honoré. He typed. Pinot.

Nothing.

Then Rodin. Calais. Burghers. Ariel. Ferdinand. Canaris. Lutetia. Eustache de Saint-Pierre. Luxembourg. Rosiers.

He was running out of ideas.

"What, what," he mumbled. "Stephen, what name did you use? What would you use?"

Armand stared at the screen. At the black slash of cursor throbbing.

What name, what word?

Remembering his conversation with Stephen in the garden of the Musée Rodin, and his godfather's apparent mistake. Stephen knew perfectly well that he hadn't proposed to Reine-Marie in the jardin du Luxembourg.

It was in the jardin—

"Joseph Migneret," Armand muttered as he typed.

And up flashed a request.

CHAPTER 40

⁓

J oseph Migneret," read Judith de la Granger. "Who's he?"

"One of the Righteous," said Gamache, as he clicked through.

"The document was taken out at eleven twenty-five a.m., then almost immediately returned," said Madame Lenoir, pointing at the times. "He had it out for only twenty minutes."

"But what's the document?" Judith asked.

They could only see the file number.

The head archivist typed in the reference number and shook her head in amazement and some amusement.

"He managed to request the most obscure of our documents. No one except your friend has asked for it in decades, probably centuries. Maybe ever."

"What is it?" asked Pinot. Bending over, he read, "A survey of the number of hand-forged nails made in Calais in 1523? That's the evidence? Nails in Calais? It doesn't make sense."

Calais, thought Armand and smiled. *The burghers, you old devil.*

"We need to see the file," he said. "Where is it?"

She pointed down. "Purgatory. Where documents are put that can't be thrown out, but neither are they likely to ever see the light of day."

"This one has," said Gamache. "And recently. Can you take us to it?"

Madame Lenoir made a note of the reference number. Then they followed her through another thick door, which Gamache quietly locked behind them, and down, down, down flights of stairs into a subbasement.

Turning on the overhead lights, they saw what looked more like a crypt than an archive. The brick ceilings were vaulted and the floor was dirt. But the temperature and humidity were constant and no daylight could penetrate. It was, in fact, the perfect place to keep very old, frail documents.

Allida Lenoir went looking for the file.

"You really think Stephen hid the evidence here?" Pinot asked, looking around.

"No."

"No?"

"But you said—"

"I know what I said, but on seeing the name of that file, I think he had another idea. I think he'd get the evidence as far from him, as far from Paris, as possible. Wouldn't you?"

"I guess so," said Pinot. "So where is it?"

"Calais. That's why he asked for that file. He's not interested in nails in Calais. Who is? He's telling us, telling me, where he hid the evidence."

"It's somewhere in Calais?" asked Pinot. "But that's a city. How're we supposed to know where to find the stuff, if it's even there?"

Gamache looked down the long subbasement. He could no longer see the Chief Archivist.

"Do those work?" he asked, nodding at the computer terminals.

Madame de la Granger sat down and hit some keys. It sprang to life.

"Can you look up Calais?" said Gamache. "You know Stephen well, Alain. See if there's a place you think he might've gone. We used to talk about the burghers. Maybe one of their homes. A museum there. Something."

"What're you going to do?"

"I'm going to find Madame Lenoir."

Alain Pinot seemed far from convinced, but he sat beside Madame de la Granger and the two began to hunt while Armand went hunting for the Chief Archivist.

He found her down a side aisle, deep in a cabinet.

"It's here," she said, handing a dossier to Gamache.

Putting on his reading glasses, he rapidly went through the pages, once. Then, more slowly, a second time. Finally, he raised his head and caught her anxious eyes.

"Nothing," he said, removing his glasses and rubbing his eyes. "I was hoping this might tell us where in Calais he hid the evidence. That he might've even left a note behind."

He looked at his watch. It was 6:35. Less than an hour. Making up his mind, he closed the folder.

"Can you keep the others here?" He tucked the file under his arm. "While you?"

"Take this to where they're holding my son." Before she could ask, he said, "Time's run out, and I have to take them something."

Allida Lenoir stared at him, then glanced at the thick file. "You know, stealing a document, especially one as valuable as the number of nails in Calais in 1523, is a criminal offense."

"I will await the full force of French law," he said with a smile. "I locked the door behind us. Is there a back way out?"

"Yes. Not used often. It's down this way. Apparently this was originally built by the second duke as a way to sneak out to see the stable boys."

Gamache followed her to what appeared to be a dead end. But on closer examination what looked like paneling was actually a stout door.

"This will let you out onto the second floor of the museum. What was once the duke's bedroom. When you get down to the main level, head to the right. There's a corridor that'll take you to a side door. It'll be locked, but there's a panic bar."

"*Merci.* Lock this behind me. Whatever happens, don't let them out."

"Why not?"

"It's just safer."

She looked at him, then nodded. "Do you still want me to keep up the Calais ruse?"

"Ruse?"

She looked at the dossier he clutched. "There must've been a helluva need for nails in 1523. That file's unexpectedly thick." She paused. "But I am not."

"*Non,*" he said with a smile. "You're not."

He slipped through the door and turned on the flashlight on his phone.

As he took the stairs two at a time, he heard the key turn in the lock.

There was no going back now.

"Where's Gamache?" asked Alain Pinot.

"He's gone."

"Gone? Where?"

"How?" asked Judith de la Granger.

"There's a door at the other end. He found it and went through."

"Then we should leave, too," said Pinot, getting up.

"We can't."

"What do you mean we can't?"

"He locked us in."

"Why would he do that?" demanded Judith de la Granger.

"Oh, shit," said Pinot. "That file he found. It's got the documents, doesn't it? He's going to give it to them."

"Don't be ridiculous," said Madame de la Granger. "He'd never do that."

"No? Then why's he free and we're trapped down here?"

"Not trapped," said Madame Lenoir. "Safe."

"Is that what he told you?" said Pinot, staring at the locked door. "Does this feel safe?"

Gamache knew he was nearing the surface because his phone started vibrating.

And it also, he knew, began transmitting his location.

He looked at the battery level. It had been more than a day since he'd charged it, and it was down to four percent.

Putting it on low-battery mode, he took the final twenty steps and, pausing at the top, he shut off the flashlight.

Every moment counted. Every percent of power on his phone counted. But he took the time, and the power, to look at his messages.

Annie was in the last stages of labor. It looked like they'd have to do a caesarean. It was not uncommon in these sorts of births. They didn't want to put more stress on the baby's heart.

Armand wrote a quick message to Reine-Marie and Jean-Guy. Sending encouragement to Annie and to let them know he was all right.

Love, he wrote, *Dad.*

Then, tucking his phone into his pocket, he peered through the crack and listened.

He couldn't afford to be stopped now. He touched the gun in his pocket.

Nor would he use that on one of the museum guards.

Crouching, he pushed the door open and moved quickly into the bedroom.

He heard a sound and ducked behind the high bedstead.

A guard walked by and paused at the open door. Not a museum guard. This one was in full combat gear and wore the SecurForte insignia.

And carried an automatic rifle.

Gamache backed farther away. And knelt. Placing the dossier on the floor, he opened it and took some photos. Using up precious battery power. Then he sent them to Jean-Guy, Isabelle Lacoste, and himself.

He knew now. Knew what they were hiding. And others needed to know also. In case.

Removing most of the documents, he spread them under the carpet, then checked his phone.

It was now down to three percent power. And the time said five to seven.

He had to get out of there.

He crawled forward to the doorway. The guard had stationed herself at the top of the marble stairs, and now he could see others.

Including one he recognized.

Xavier Loiselle. Cradling his assault rifle. And scanning the area. For him.

Gamache peered into the room next door. It contained large exhibition boards with mariners' maps. Extraordinary hand-drawn charts of the known world six hundred years earlier. The positions of land, and water, and dragons.

He heard boots on stairs. A small army on the march. Coming his way.

He had to act now, or never.

Bringing up a search engine on his phone, he put in *Sûreté, factory raid*. When the vile video on YouTube appeared, he made sure the volume was on high.

Pressing play, he slid his phone along the polished floor, into the next room, and silently blessed winters in his tiny Québec village, shivering on the frozen lake as neighbors tried to teach him the subtle art of curling.

His phone, with one percent battery left, slid to the far end of the room and came to rest under a display case as the sound of shouts and gunfire filled the empty map room.

It reverberated off the marble walls and floors. Echoing, magnifying the sound of a terrible battle being fought amid the sea creatures and dragons, the Sirens and the demons.

The SecurForte guards converged on the room. Assault weapons raised, they entered in combat formation.

He didn't wait to see what happened next. Taking off in the opposite direction, Gamache raced down the stairs, chased by the familiar gunfire. The familiar explosions licked at his heels. The familiar orders given. His orders. The hot breath on his neck was his own. His voice on the recording. Commanding his people forward. Deeper into the factory.

And then the familiar screams of agony. As his own agents were cut down. Like wraiths, they pursued Gamache. As they had, every day, for years.

He flung himself against the metal panic bar of the side door and flew out into the sunshine.

* * *

"Cease fire," the leader commanded. "There's no one here. It's a recording. Bring it to me."

Loiselle, on his belly, retrieved the phone. As he handed it over, he saw a man sprinting down the side of the château.

"There he is," shouted Loiselle and, using the butt of his rifle, he broke the glass and started shooting.

Gamache didn't swerve. Didn't look back. He just kept running, even as the bullets struck the columns and walls and ground around him.

"Fuck, Loiselle, get him," shouted his commander.

Gamache was at the huge wrought iron gates. Loiselle sighted him, but it was too late. Gamache had pushed through and, stumbling, he disappeared down rue des Archives.

"Well, you fucked that up," said the commander, glaring at his foot soldier. "But at least we know where he's headed. Better get there, and do it right this time."

"Yessir."

Loiselle looked down at the video, still playing on the phone in the commander's hand.

He watched the familiar images, of Chief Inspector Gamache dragging his second-in-command across the factory floor to safety. After quickly staunching Beauvoir's abdominal wound, Gamache bent and kissed him on the forehead, whispering to the man he feared was dying, "I love you."

Then the phone died.

Who would rescue him, Xavier Loiselle wondered, if he was badly wounded?

None of them, he knew as he looked around.

Who, he wondered, would whisper to him in his final moments, *I love you*?

CHAPTER 41

———

"You okay, man?" the taxi driver asked, glancing in his rearview mirror.

His passenger was twisted in his seat, staring out the back window and trying to catch his breath.

"Fine, fine," said Gamache, in a sort of gasp, as he turned to the driver. "As fast as you can."

It was 7:19. They'd threatened to kill Daniel at 7:30. Gamache had little doubt they meant it.

Of course, they'd kill them both once they got what they needed.

He clutched the dossier to him and deliberately slowed his breathing.

Hyperventilating and passing out rarely made things better.

Deep breath in. Hold. Long slow breath out.

They were in the narrow streets, clogged with Paris's Monday morning rush hour. They had to get across the Seine, over île de la Cité, from the Third Arrondissement to the Seventh. From the Marais, all the way over to the far side of Saint-Germain-des-Prés.

They were, he could see by the driver's satnav, twelve minutes away. At this rate, it would be too late.

"I'll give you all the money I have if you get me there before seven thirty."

"Rush hour," said the driver, then glanced down at the hand thrust between the seats clutching a fistful of euro notes.

The driver leaned on the horn and sped up.

Armand sat back and reached for his phone to call Reine-Marie, then remembered where it was.

"May I use your phone?"

"What? No. I need it for directions. You want to get there or not?"

Gamache tossed a hundred-euro note at the driver and said, "You have a second one. Give it to me."

He was moments away from pulling the gun out of his coat pocket when the driver handed him his personal phone. "Okay, man, calm down."

Gamache placed the call, but there was no answer. Reine-Marie was either too busy or wasn't picking up a call from a number she didn't recognize.

He tried Jean-Guy. No answer.

Then he tried Reine-Marie again. This time she answered. *"Oui?"*

"It's me."

"Armand, where are you?"

"How's Annie?"

"She and Jean-Guy are in surgery. They've decided on the caesarean."

"Is she all right?"

"I think so. Yes."

"The baby?"

"I don't know." There was a pause as Reine-Marie fought for control. Then repeated, "Where are you?"

He looked to his right and could see the hôpital Hôtel-Dieu. His heart threw itself against his rib cage. Squeezing against it. Pushing toward the hospital. He thought for a moment it might break through.

"I'm in a taxi, on my way to Daniel. We'll be with you as soon as we can."

"Are you all right? Is Daniel? Armand, what's happening? Whose phone are you on?"

"Mine lost power. I'm using the taxi driver's. I love you. I've got to go."

"I love you," she said, and then the line went dead in her hand.

Armand gave the phone to the driver, who handed back the money.

"I have a daughter, too." And turning down an alley, he cut three minutes off the drive.

Armand stared straight ahead, trying to see the way forward and through. The exact sequence of events that had to happen. Had he guessed right?

If not, no amount of planning could possibly work.

They arrived at Stephen's building with just over a minute to spare.

Taking the stairs two at a time, Gamache got to the door of Stephen's apartment and pounded on it.

The door was opened by one of the SecurForte guards. Armand looked past him and saw Daniel on his feet in the middle of the living room. Girard was beside him, pressing a gun to Daniel's temple.

Daniel's eyes were squeezed shut, and he was trembling.

"No," shouted Armand.

Daniel opened crazed eyes. "Dad?"

"Seconds," said Girard, lowering the gun.

"You came back," said Daniel as his legs buckled.

Armand stepped forward and caught his son, lowering him to the floor so that both were kneeling.

"That was probably a mistake, Armand."

Claude Dussault's voice, languid and soft, came across the room. He was sitting on the sofa. Legs crossed. His hand resting on the gun beside him. Perfectly at ease. Apparently not caring if Daniel was executed.

He got up slowly and, walking over to Gamache, picked the file up from where Armand had dropped it. "Let's see what you've found."

"Are you all right?" Armand asked Daniel.

He didn't ask if they'd hurt him. Of course they had. Few knew better than Gamache that the worst wounds were not always visible. Or physical.

Daniel's hands were trembling, and his breathing shallow. His eyes bloodshot and steady, on his father.

"You came back," he whispered.

Armand gripped Daniel to him. Tight.

And whispered, "Always."

Then he leaned back and, looking into Daniel's eyes, he said, "We can do this."

He could see that Daniel understood what "this" now might mean.

It was the tumble down the ice slide. It was the void beyond the balcony. It was the headlong fall over the edge.

But they wouldn't have to face it alone. There was some calm, even comfort, in that.

Armand helped Daniel to his feet and shifted his gaze to Claude Dussault. His nerve endings tingling as he watched Dussault return to the sofa and open the file.

Just then Xavier Loiselle appeared at the door. Without hesitating he strode across the room, lifted his rifle, and hit Gamache across the head with the butt end, dropping him to the floor.

"Dad!" shouted Daniel, but Loiselle turned the weapon on him.

"Come on, kid. Do it." Then he turned back to Gamache. "That's for making me look like an asshole in front of my team."

"Okay," said Girard, reaching out to stop Loiselle from taking it further, while Dussault watched from the sofa, amused. "What happened?"

Loiselle described Gamache's escape from the archives, and heard the Prefect laugh.

"Admit it, Loiselle, he got the better of you."

Gamache, on one knee, struggled to his feet, holding the side of his head. His hair matted with blood. "It wasn't difficult."

"You fucker." Loiselle started forward again.

"All right," said Dussault, like a grandfather calming a child who'd had too many sweets. "More important things now."

He went back to reading. Armand watched Dussault closely. Putting his hand in his pocket, he felt the gun there.

But it wasn't time yet. Almost. Almost. But not quite.

Instead, he brought out his handkerchief and pressed it to his head.

"Did you find the Arbour woman?" Girard asked.

"She was hiding in the museum," reported Loiselle, bringing himself under control. "I took care of her."

"And the others?"

"In the subbasement."

"How many?"

"Three bodies. So far. The commander's there overseeing the wet work."

Three, thought Gamache. Arbour. Two others. Who'd escaped? Lenoir? De la Granger?

Pinot?

"They were unarmed," Gamache said, glaring at Loiselle. "Hiding. No threat to you. Is it just a game to you? Hide-and-seek? Is that it? Like Daniel here used to play? Right here in this apartment. Remember, Daniel?"

Daniel, in a daze, nodded. Not sure why his father shot him such an intense look.

"When you have children of your own, young man," Gamache said to Loiselle, his voice now uncommonly mild, "and they play hide-and-seek with you. Remember this day. Remember what you did."

"Ah, you're back," said Claude Dussault. "Good."

Their eyes shifted to the door.

Alain Pinot walked in. A little rumpled, but not as dead as he might have been.

Seeing his father's expression, Daniel said, "Dad, what's happening? Who is this?"

"Go on," said Dussault. "Tell him."

Gamache was staring at Pinot, glaring at him. "This's the piece of *merde* who betrayed Stephen."

"You know, I'm not sure I've ever heard you swear, Armand," said Dussault. Then he turned to Pinot. "You better hope he's never in a position to get at you. I doubt you'd survive."

"Alain Pinot owns Agence France-Presse, Daniel," said Armand. "He's on the board of GHS Engineering. He's behind all this."

"Well, I had some help," said Pinot. "Including from Stephen himself."

"He came to you with his suspicions," said Gamache.

"He did."

"He trusted you," said Armand. "And you betrayed him. Ordered him and Plessner killed."

"No. I handed those decisions over to my security company." He nodded to Girard. "I had nothing to do with it."

"He's the one Stephen approached?" asked Daniel. "To buy his seat on the board?"

"Yes," said Armand.

"I see the evidence was in that file after all." Pinot nodded toward the dossier.

Dussault held it up. "All here. Memos, emails, notes in the margins of schematics. Reports by accident investigators, suppressed of course. Damning, to say the least."

"And you brought it here, knowing what we'd do with it," said Pinot. "I doubt your godfather would've approved. He was willing to die to protect it, and you just hand it over. If I betrayed him, so did you. Good thing you weren't in the Resistance, Armand. You'd have given them all away."

"What makes you think you won't end up in some Parisian landfill?" Gamache asked him. "Just another piece of toxic waste."

"Because I hold the purse strings. Those hundreds of millions Stephen paid me for the seat on the board." On seeing Gamache's raised brows he smiled. "Yes. He actually gave me the money on the understanding that when we met this morning, I'd sign over the board seat. Like you, he had no idea what was actually happening."

"Are you so sure?" asked Gamache.

"Well, he's dying, and you and your son are standing here at gunpoint. This can't be going according to plan."

"True. But neither is it going according to your plan. I did suspect you, but hoped I was wrong."

"That's bullshit," said Pinot. "You never suspected me."

"I did, you know. Why do you think I asked Madame Lenoir to lock you in the basement?"

"Now this is interesting," said Girard, who clearly had little time for Alain Pinot. "What gave him away?"

"The attack on Stephen Friday night," said Gamache, speaking directly to Pinot. "Someone had to know where he'd be. He was very careful. He knew he'd be targeted, which was why he wasn't staying here, in his own apartment. But someone found out he'd be at Juve-niles. You. You were the one he met for drinks earlier Friday evening. In his agenda he'd written *AFP.* Stands for Agence France-Presse, but they're also your initials. That confused us for a while. We thought AFP stood for Alexander Francis Plessner. And those notes he made, with dates? They were ones he asked you to look up from your files."

"True," said Pinot.

"But of course, you told him you found nothing. And that was your mistake. Stephen knew there was something there. That's when he, too, began to suspect you."

"Impossible," said Pinot. "I'd have known. When we met Friday afternoon, he was his usual self. I'd asked him to bring the evidence with him so that I could see it before committing."

"And did he?"

"Well, no. He said he'd left it here, in his apartment."

Gamache gave him a contemptuous look.

"Just an old man's memory lapse? You really are a fool." Gamache turned to Girard. "Is that when the wheels started coming off your plans? Was he supposed to have an unfortunate accident leaving his meeting with Pinot? But when he didn't bring the evidence, you had to scram-ble." He turned back to Pinot. "Did Stephen tell you about his dinner plans? No, I doubt he'd do that. So how did you know? His agenda?"

"I saw it there," said Pinot.

"What did you do then?" Armand sounded calm, but his mind was whirring. Trying to keep them engaged, trying to stay one step ahead. "Wait, don't tell me. You came to the apartment, thinking Stephen would be here, changing for dinner. You could force the evidence out of him, then kill him. But once again, things didn't go to plan. Instead of Stephen, you ran into Plessner. But . . ." His mind skidded to a halt and changed direction. ". . . No, I have that wrong, don't I?"

He turned to Daniel. "Girard here couldn't have come to the apartment because he was in the George V, having tea with you"—he looked at Dussault—"and the head of GHS Engineering."

Girard's eyes narrowed and his lips compressed. But Dussault looked almost amused.

"I told you it was a mistake to underestimate him."

"Did Madame Roquebrune want to know why your operation was such a dog's breakfast?" Gamache asked.

"No, not that exactly. She didn't want any details, just that it was being handled."

"But it wasn't. In fact, it was about to get even worse," said Gamache. "You didn't find the evidence, one of your operatives shot Plessner, making it impossible to claim accident, and then your attack on Stephen was bungled. Must've been some pretty stressful hours, sitting there with me in the hospital. Is that why you hung around? To see what I knew?"

"And to make sure Horowitz didn't regain consciousness, *oui*," said Dussault. "And to comfort you, of course."

"*Merci.*"

"I came here the next morning, to look for myself," said Dussault. "That's when you and Reine-Marie arrived."

"Then it was you. We weren't sure if it was you or Girard here."

"If it was me, you'd have been dead," said Girard. "It was one of the few mistakes the Prefect has made."

"He's right," said Dussault. "I probably should have killed you then. But then we wouldn't have this"—he tapped the file beside him on the sofa—"would we?"

"I've read the evidence," Gamache said, his voice no longer matter-of-fact. "Thousands were killed in the so-called accidents, over years. You're the head of the Préfecture. You could have stopped it, but you didn't. How does that happen? How could you make that choice?"

He was searching his old friend's face, his sharp eyes flicking over to the file, then back again. Trying to find the answer to a crucial question.

"Me?" Dussault looked up. "Not me. I was still only second-in-command at the Préfecture when all this started. I had nothing to do with it. Not then."

"Then when?"

"Turns out, when Messieurs Plessner and Horowitz had enough

evidence to be suggestive but not enough to be sure, they went to my predecessor in the Préfecture. Clément Prévost. Hoping he'd be able to start an investigation. You met him."

"I did. He wasn't just your predecessor," said Gamache. "He was your mentor."

"True. While he believed Horowitz and Plessner were sincere, he needed proof. There were very powerful people involved. Some were personal friends of his. He began to ask questions. Quietly. Uncomfortable questions. But then there was that accident two years ago. Poor man was hit by a car crossing from a brasserie in broad daylight. And, voilà, I was made Prefect."

"Were you working for them then?" asked Gamache.

"No. I knew none of this at the time."

"So what happened? What changed?"

"I went to Monsieur Prévost's funeral. State funeral. Impressive. You were there, too, I believe."

"I was," said Gamache.

"But you didn't go to the family reception?"

"*Non*. It was private. Only for the closest friends and colleagues. I was neither."

"But I was," said Dussault. "I went back to their apartment. It's a small two-bedroom walk-up in the Eighteenth. Neat, tidy. Orderly, like the man. And I saw my future. All the sacrifices, Armand. My own. My wife's. My children's. What we gave up for people who didn't notice and didn't care. A two-bedroom walk-up."

"Clément Prévost was a good man," said Armand.

That simple statement left Dussault silent for a moment. "He was a dead man."

"He was murdered," said Gamache. "When did you start to work for them?"

"Girard here had left to work for SecurForte, as their second-in-command. We'd get together for drinks, and he'd talk about his day. It sounded interesting. Fascinating, in fact. The international aspect, the businesses, the clients. And, of course, the money."

"So you recruited him?" Gamache asked Girard.

"I didn't have to, he asked me."

Gamache turned back to Dussault. "When did you realize—"

"That part of the job would be to cover up criminal activity?" Dussault thought for a moment. "Fairly early on. I was essentially moonlighting, but then many officers do. They work their shift as a flic, then work nights as a security guard somewhere. This was no different. I had my job as head of the Paris Préfecture, and worked on the side for the largest private security firm in Europe. As a consultant."

"As the head of it," said Gamache.

"That's not what my contract says."

"But what's written and what's reality are often two different things, as you know," Gamache said to Alain Pinot, before returning his attention to Dussault. "So you did as they asked?"

"We have to go, *patron*," said Girard, tapping his wrist.

Dussault shot him an annoyed look, but otherwise ignored him.

"At first the requests were small. Fixing traffic tickets. Getting a wealthy client's spoiled kid off a charge. And then it slowly increased. And I discovered something."

"What?"

"That I didn't care. That money, comfort, security, balances out all the rest."

"They killed Clément Prévost. Your mentor. The head of the Préfecture. They murdered him. What exactly balances that out?" demanded Gamache.

"It was done," said Dussault. "I'm a realist. There was no undoing it."

"You were working for the people who murdered a man you admired," said Gamache, his rage spilling out. "By then you must've known they were involved in other crimes, other killings. How do you justify that? Has the world gone mad?"

Dussault stood up and nodded to the guards, who raised their weapons.

Armand stepped in front of Daniel. "One thing I don't understand. Who's Séverine Arbour in all this? She's working for you, or was. Why kill her?"

Dussault made a small gesture, and Loiselle and the other guards lowered their weapons a few inches.

"You're so smart," said Girard. "Who do you think she was?"

Gamache thought on the fly. Putting the disparate pieces together. "Her job was to kick over any evidence of the neodymium and the accidents. Make sure no one clued in."

Girard was smiling.

I've got something wrong, thought Gamache. *Something doesn't fit.*

He paused. Thinking. Thinking. Watching. Watching. Seeing.

Then his face opened in astonishment.

"Carole Gossette." He could see by Dussault's smile that he had it right. He nodded toward the file. "Those emails and notes are from her. To her. She wasn't in on it. She suspected something was wrong. That's why she agreed when Stephen asked that Beauvoir be hired. That's why she hired Arbour, an accomplished engineer, and put her in the department charged with oversight. She knew if there was anything to find, Séverine Arbour would ferret it out. Madame Arbour wasn't trying to cover up," said Gamache. "She thought she was working for the police, to uncover wrongdoing."

Dussault nodded. "I approached her, warned her about Beauvoir, and asked for her help. She agreed without hesitation. I am the Prefect, after all."

"You've been setting Carole Gossette up," said Gamache. "Should anything go wrong, it'll be laid at her feet."

"Someone has to take the blame, though I suspect she wouldn't want to face that," said Girard. "And might even take her own life."

"In the archives tonight," said Gamache, "when I confronted Arbour, she began to see the truth."

"She called us," said Girard. "That's when we decided not to wait for you to find the documents, but to move in."

"It's almost eight," said Dussault, and tucking the file under his arm, he nodded to the guards, who raised their rifles.

"Dad?" said Daniel.

"Wait," said Gamache. "There's something you're missing. Something you don't know. Stephen and Plessner tracked down one more piece of evidence, hard evidence. The piece of equipment made out of neodymium. The thing causing all the problems."

"He's lying," said Dussault.

"I have proof," said Gamache, trying without success to keep the desperation out of his voice. "They had it in their possession. How else could the nickels have gotten so strongly magnetized?"

"What's a nickel?" demanded Girard. "What's he talking about?"

"Nothing," said Dussault. "He's babbling. Trying to buy time. Kill him. Do it now."

"If you do," said Gamache, holding his hand up in front of him, "you'll never find it."

"There's nothing to find," said Dussault.

"Then why did you throw the coins into the fountain at Place de la Concorde? It's because you wanted to go back and get them later. Keep them for yourself, as blackmail."

"What coins?" asked Girard.

"The ones in my pocket."

Gamache went to put his hand in, but Girard stopped him and gestured to one of the guards.

It was all Gamache needed. As soon as the armed guard lowered his weapon and reached out, Gamache grabbed him. Pulling the gun from his pocket he got off two quick shots.

Blood spread over Claude Dussault's chest as he staggered backward and collapsed.

"Run!" Armand shouted to Daniel.

He heard the door slam just as a burst of gunfire hit the SecurForte guard he was using as a shield. They both fell back. The dead weight of the guard against him dragged Gamache to the floor.

As he fell, the gun bounced from his grip.

Daniel had slammed the door closed. But was still in the apartment.

He knew he could never outrun the guards, or their bullets. And he couldn't leave his father behind. His only hope was to hide.

Hide-and-seek. The game he and Annie had played as children.

The one his father had reminded him of just minutes ago.

The game Grandma Zora had taught them.

Over and over, she'd challenged the children to quickly find some-place to hide. Not under a bed. Not in a closet, or behind a curtain. Too obvious.

She'd made it fun, but there always seemed something intense about it. It was the same intensity his father had just now. When talking about their game.

Then, one day, he and Annie had successfully hidden from everyone. Here in Stephen's apartment. Unaware it was a game, their parents and Stephen had searched for them. Growing from anxious to worried to terrified. The children were missing. Gone.

Once they'd emerged, laughing, their mother and father had, through thin lips, explained that they'd been scared to death.

And now Daniel remembered where that hiding place was. The false cupboard in the armoire in Stephen's bedroom. It looked like drawers, but actually swung open, revealing a large empty space in-side. Large enough for two children.

And now, Daniel, a very grown man, threw open the door and squeezed in. Shutting it behind him. Only just.

There wasn't a centimeter to spare, and hardly any air to breathe. But he was in.

Through the crack, he could see into the living room.

Alain Pinot was cringing behind an armchair.

Claude Dussault's body was on the floor.

And his father was struggling to get out from under the dead guard.

Girard put his own gun back in its holster and picked the weapon off the floor. "Get up."

Daniel's breathing came in sharp jabs as he watched his father get to his feet.

"He got away," said Loiselle, returning to the living room.

"He couldn't have," snapped Girard. "He must still be here. Find

405

him." But just as Loiselle gestured to the other guard to follow him, Girard said, "No, wait. I have a better idea."

He stepped back and aimed the gun at Gamache.

Armand stared Girard straight in the eyes and lifted his chin, in defiance.

But instead of firing, Girard called, "Daniel Gamache. Come out now, or we'll kill your father."

"Daniel, don't."

"Daniel, do," ordered Girard. "Or he dies now."

Daniel stared, frozen.

He knew if he did, Girard would kill them both. If he didn't, his father would be gunned down. In front of him. And then they'd find him. And kill him anyway.

He closed his eyes and stepped off the ledge.

"Okay, okay," he said, and crawled out from his hiding place.

"Oh, Daniel," his father whispered.

"Now that was a mistake, young man," said Girard.

He nodded to the guard, who raised his rifle at Daniel.

"No," screamed Armand, and leaped forward, just as the guard pressed the trigger.

Armand knocked the weapon down so that the shots went into the floor.

At that moment, Girard fired. Point blank. Three shots. *Bang. Bang. Bang.*

"Dad," Daniel shouted.

His heart pounding, his brain exploding, he fell to his knees as his father collapsed.

Girard put two more bullets into him. To be sure.

"Oh, no," whispered Daniel, crawling across the carpet. "Dad?"

"Fuck me," said Alain Pinot, coming out from behind the chair and staring at the bodies.

Girard was bending over Gamache, going through his pockets. When he stood up, he was holding something.

"Huh. So, these are nickels. He was right. They're magnetized. Somewhere along the line they came into contact with the neodymium."

"Then there is hard evidence somewhere," said Pinot. "And you just killed the only person who knows where it is."

"Exactly. No one else will find it." He looked at his watch. "The board meeting's about to start. We have to get you and the documents over there."

"What about him?" Pinot nodded toward Daniel, who was holding his father and crying.

Girard picked the file up off the floor. "Loiselle, you know what to do."

Daniel heard the door close and the now-familiar rattle of a rifle being lifted.

He hugged his father, rocking him gently, and whispered, "I've got you. It's all right. I've got you."

As the scent of sandalwood and rosewater settled around Daniel, he was transported back home.

He lay in bed. Curled in his father's arms. Reading *Babar* together.

One more, one more. Please, Daddy. I don't want to go to sleep. Not yet. Don't leave me.

I will never leave you.

Daniel felt the kiss on his forehead, and heard the deep, soft voice: *Sleep tight. I love you.*

Kissing his father's forehead, Daniel whispered, "I love you, too."

As they walked down the stairs, Girard and Pinot heard a burst of gunfire.

"Here she is."

The nurse handed the pink and crying child, wrapped in a blanket, to Jean-Guy. He held her close against his chest. Cradling her, tears streaming down his cheeks, he kissed his daughter's forehead and whispered, "I love you."

CHAPTER 42

⁓

The GHS board meeting was finally called to order.

There had been twenty minutes or so of chat, of drinking strong coffee and teasing each other about their night out in Paris. Alain Pinot was a particular target since he'd arrived disheveled, in the same clothes he'd been in the night before, and looking slightly ill.

Thierry Girard had placed the file in front of Eugénie Roquebrune.

"Is this . . . ?" she asked, looking at Girard over her reading glasses. Another declaration of power. No contact lenses.

"*Oui.* It's all here." He bent down and whispered, "There was some trouble, but we have it contained."

"Where's Monsieur Dussault?"

"Tragically, there was a series of terrorist attacks overnight, assassinations really, including the Prefect of Police while he was with a Québec colleague and some others. The police will soon be on full alert."

"The Prefect is dead?" Madame Roquebrune asked, her tone abrupt and businesslike.

"*Oui.*"

The CEO simply gave a small nod. "*Fluctuat nec mergitur.* Paris will be in mourning."

"And those responsible will be found."

"Alive?"

"Who can say?" said Girard.

The CEO looked at Girard. They could both say. Then her eyes traveled down the long shiny table. "And him?"

Girard followed her gaze, to Alain Pinot. "As you know, journalists, and the head of media organizations, are often targets, too. Loiselle—"

Madame Roquebrune held up her hand. *"Merci."*

Girard was dismissed, and the board chair, after taking a long sip of fresh-squeezed orange juice and rearranging the papers in front of her, called the meeting to order.

The luminaries took their seats around the table once used by Louis XIV to sign official documents.

"I don't think this will take long," said Madame Roquebrune. "Some of you clearly need to catch up on your sleep."

There was a rumble of amusement as all eyes went to Pinot, who lifted his coffee cup in acknowledgment.

After going through the usual business, the board chair said, "I'm sure you've had time to study the annual report. If you'd like I can read it out loud—"

There was an immediate protest. Not necessary.

"Then we'll need a motion to take it as accepted."

It was motioned, seconded, voted on, and unanimously passed.

There was a tap on the door, and two waiters brought in more refreshments including fresh fruit, croissants, cheeses, and smoked salmon.

If the other board members noticed the slightly stained file in front of the board chair, they didn't mention it.

She'd opened it briefly, but hadn't studied it. Hadn't needed to. Girard's murmured "It's all here" was enough.

The servers left, but the door to the suite remained open.

One of the board members turned and asked politely that it be closed. When there was no response, no soft click of the door closing, first one, then others looked over.

"I believe," said a young man, stepping into the room, "that you're in my seat."

He was talking to Alain Pinot. The other board members turned to the head of AFP, as Pinot's eyes widened.

"Who are you?" the chair demanded.

"My name's Daniel Gamache, and I'm the new member of your board."

"The hell you are," said Madame Roquebrune. "Call security. Get the police if necessary."

"Already here," said Claude Dussault, stepping into the room. He stared at Pinot, who looked like he was having a stroke. While Eugénie Roquebrune, at the head of the table, had turned as gray as her hair.

Then the Prefect surveyed the room.

Not with any triumph, not even with disgust.

With resignation.

This was what modern devils looked like. Not the writhing creatures captured by Rodin, but good, decent, silent people.

Walking over to the CEO, he placed the pages, retrieved from beneath an Aubusson carpet in the Musée des archives, in the dossier.

"Now it's all here," he said.

Her father kissed Annie lightly on the forehead, so as not to wake her up.

But still, she stirred.

"Dad? Have you seen her?"

"She's beautiful, Annie."

As soon as Girard and Pinot had left the apartment, Loiselle had shifted his rifle.

"What the fuck are you doing?" demanded the other SecurForte guard.

"Drop it," said Loiselle.

"What?"

"Now."

Claude Dussault got up. "Fire your weapon," he ordered Loiselle. "They need to hear it."

"Dad?" said Daniel, staring as his father groaned and stirred, his eyes fluttering open as he struggled for consciousness.

Loiselle swung his rifle over to the empty sofa and fired.

Armand opened his eyes wide. "Daniel? Oh, God, Daniel." He grabbed his son to him, and held him tight. Then, releasing him, he ran his hands over Daniel's head and chest. "Are you all right?"

"Are you?" He placed his open palm on his father's bloody chest. His eyes wide with shock.

"Oh, thank God," Armand whispered. "I'm so sorry. I couldn't tell you."

"Tell me what? I don't understand. You're not hurt? Neither of you?"

He looked at Claude Dussault, who'd gone to the guard on the floor and was checking for a pulse. He found none.

"Hurt is relative," said the Prefect as he kicked the guard's rifle away. "We're not dead. You okay?" he said to Gamache, who was now kneeling.

"Not dead," he said, though his voice was strained.

"I thought—" Loiselle began, clearly as confused as Daniel. He looked from Dussault to Gamache. "How?"

Daniel doubled over and threw up.

Armand rubbed Daniel's back, murmuring, "We're safe. It's over. We're safe."

"I thought you were dead. I thought I was about to die." Daniel sobbed, coughing and spitting.

"Shhhh," said his father. Not to stop his tears, but to comfort him.

"How?" Loiselle repeated, staring at the great red stains on Dussault's chest, then over to the stains on Gamache's chest, head, and back. "Dye?"

"No." Dussault shoved up his sleeve and showed the puncture where his blood had been taken. "Girard would know fake blood. I loaded his gun with cartridges filled with real blood."

"Girard's gun?" Loiselle asked.

"No, his." Dussault pointed to Armand, who had struggled to his feet and was bending over in pain. "I left it in your apartment, hoping you'd find it, Armand, and have it with you. When you didn't—"

"When I first met you last night? No," he said, straightening up. "It took me a while to work out what you were doing. Whose side you were on. Did you know about the attacks on Stephen and Monsieur Plessner?"

"*Oui.* But I couldn't stop them." The two men, who'd both had to make horrific choices in their lives, stared at each other. "I'm sorry, Armand."

"You could see why I'd doubt," said Armand.

"When did you know what I was really doing?" Dussault asked.

"When I found the coins in the fountain, I began to suspect you threw them there to get them away from Daniel and to keep them safe, as evidence. I couldn't think of any other reason for you to not only do it, but do it in front of me. So I'd see. But it wasn't really until you started reading the file that I was certain."

"As late as that?" asked Dussault.

"*Oui.* There was almost no evidence in there. I'd taken most of it out and hidden it in the Musée. When you didn't say anything, I knew. All the way over here I'd tried to figure out how this could possibly work. The only way I could see was if Girard frisked me and took the gun. Then used it to shoot me and Daniel. When he didn't, I had to improvise."

"By shooting me," said Dussault.

"By pretending to, yes."

"How did you know he was on our side?" asked Daniel, looking at Loiselle.

"When he hit me in the stomach, he'd obviously pulled the punch. I was pretty sure then. And even this"—he touched the side of his head—"was glancing, designed to draw blood but nothing more. But by then I knew."

"How?" asked Loiselle.

"At the archives, when I was running to the street, you were shooting and missing. Believe me, no special-forces-trained commando would miss. I take it Arbour, Lenoir, and de la Granger are safe?"

"Yes," said Loiselle. "Before I left, I arrested the commander. The others quickly gave up, as I knew they would. Their hearts aren't in the job. There's no loyalty."

"Well," said Dussault, looking at the young man. "There is some."

"Yessir."

"If you knew these two were on our side," Daniel asked his father, "why not just end it then? Why take the risk Girard and the other guards would kill us?"

"They almost did," said Gamache. "I think Girard would've killed me if you hadn't come out. That distracted them. Gave me a chance. You saved my life."

"We couldn't stop them yet," said Dussault. "We had evidence against Girard and Pinot, but not against GHS. They were setting up Carole Gossette to take the blame. We need Girard and Pinot to take the file to the CEO. We need her to accept it. We have to prove it goes much higher, much further. And we need Pinot to sit down at that table. Speaking of which, we have to go. The board meeting's about to start."

"You have to get the evidence first," said Armand, and told them where he'd hidden it.

"Aren't you coming?" Dussault asked.

"No." He turned to Daniel. "You're going in my place."

After he told his son what needed to be done, he said, "Thank God you're a banker. This has to be done exactly right, and you're the one to do it. None better."

Daniel turned a furious red and nodded. "It'll be done."

"What're you going to do? Sit on a bench and sip Pernod?" asked Claude.

"Why do people keep asking me that?" said Armand. "No. I'm going to meet my granddaughter."

Armand had stopped at their apartment for a quick shower, a change of clothing, and two extra-strength aspirin for his splitting headache. In fact, his whole body hurt.

Except his heart.

He'd called Reine-Marie and told her what had happened. She in turn had told Jean-Guy, but Annie had been resting.

"Dad? You've seen her?" Annie now asked, her voice thick. "Idola."

"Idola," her father whispered. "Perfect. She's perfect."

He looked at Jean-Guy. "May I?"

Idola's father got up and carefully handed his daughter to her grandfather, looking him in the eyes. "We're safe?"

"*Oui.*"

Armand cradled her, then reluctantly handed the baby back to her father.

Jean-Guy sat down and, closing his eyes, he rocked his daughter, feeling her heart against his. And her tiny feet resting against the jagged scar across his belly.

Daniel walked around the table to stand behind Alain Pinot. He bent down and whispered, "You're in my seat."

"What's this about?" demanded the CEO.

"He sold his place on the board," said Daniel.

"That's not true," said Pinot. "I have no idea who this man is."

"Of course you do, sir. You tried to have me killed just a few minutes ago."

"That's absurd," said Pinot, appealing to his fellow board members.

"You conspired to murder the Chief Archivist, the Chief Librarian, and one of GHS's own engineers, Madame Séverine Arbour," said Claude Dussault. "And you were party to negligence by GHS Engineering that has led to the deaths of tens of thousands."

There was an immediate uproar in the room amid calls for the chair to do something.

"Quiet," Dussault demanded.

He walked them through what had happened.

The derailment of the train in Colombia. The questions asked by the journalist. Her visit to the water treatment plant, and the old mine. Her subsequent murder in Patagonia. The recent attack on the financier Stephen Horowitz. The murder of Alexander Plessner.

"But why?" asked the former President of France.

Claude Dussault concisely, precisely, told them about the mine. The neodymium. The ore secretly shipped back. And used in planes that crashed.

As he listed the tragedies, the Prefect felt his control slipping. His voice rising. Bridges that collapsed. Trains that derailed and elevators that failed.

Until, at the final example, he lost all composure.

"And nuclear power plants."

Pounding the table with both fists so that the board members startled, he shouted, his voice almost a scream. "For God's sake," he pleaded. "What. Were. You. Thinking?"

Tears had sprung to his eyes, and he had to stop himself. Bring himself back under control.

"You knew. Some of you knew." He looked at Madame Roquebrune, who held his eyes without apology. Then to Alain Pinot. "You piece of shit, you knew. And you'd have let it happen."

He saw the blood drain from the room. And he wondered how many of them were thinking of those who'd died and might still. Or of themselves.

"Stephen Horowitz came to you with his concerns a few years ago, didn't he?" Daniel said to the CEO, giving the Prefect a chance to catch his breath. "You promised to look into it, but instead you covered it up. And when he realized that, and collected evidence himself, you began a campaign against him. Ending with an attempt on his life Friday night."

"That's a lie," said Eugénie Roquebrune. "Slander."

"The truth," said Claude Dussault. "Monsieur Horowitz sold his entire art collection. Raised hundreds of millions of dollars, and with that money he bought Monsieur Pinot's seat on this board."

The CEO was shaking her head and smiling. "You're misinformed. The places on the board are given freely. They're not for sale."

"But the stock options that go with the seat are. They're not supposed to be, there was an understanding that they're never sold. Stephen knew he had to approach someone who was especially greedy."

All eyes turned to Alain Pinot.

He looked at his fellow board members and colored.

"Okay, yes, he approached me. Because we're old friends. He was like a father, a mentor to me. Most of you know that."

There were some nods, but most remained stony-faced.

"He wanted on the board, but I refused, of course," said Pinot. "I'd heard rumors about his Nazi past, and I knew that would tarnish GHS and everyone associated with it."

The mention of "Nazi" had the desired effect. Daniel and Dussault could feel the tide turn. Could see support for Pinot rising. There were murmurs of agreement.

"Well done."

"Quite right."

"*Merci.*"

"Stephen Horowitz was no Nazi," snapped Daniel. "Just the opposite. He worked for the Resistance."

"Right," said one member. "And so did Pétain."

The damage had been done. Doubt had entered the room.

"I have proof," said Pinot, pressing his advantage. "A file on Horowitz you yourself found, Monsieur le Préfet, hidden in the Archives nationales."

"It wasn't proof," said Claude. "Far from it." He looked at the CEO. "You used it to try to blackmail Stephen Horowitz into stopping his investigation."

"He came to me with his wild ideas," said Madame Roquebrune. "Poor man was clearly in the early stages of dementia. I took him for dinner, reassured him, and we parted friends. Or so I thought. But he kept coming back with more and more crazy accusations. I'm sorry you believed, Monsieur le Préfet, what amounts to a sad old man's delusions."

Claude Dussault pressed on. "Stephen Horowitz and Alexander Plessner worked for years, and finally had their proof. It's all there. In that file."

The CEO glanced down at it, then looked around the table. "I'm afraid the Prefect here might also need to be tested. This is a dossier on the number of handmade nails in Calais in 1523."

That was met with laughter, and relief.

"Does it not look a little thick to you," said Dussault. "Must've been a lot of nails. No, that was found this morning where Monsieur Horowitz had hidden it. Inside are the internal GHS memos and emails, schematics. External investigations that were suppressed. Internal reports that were suppressed. As well as the notes of the Agence France-Presse reporter murdered in Patagonia."

"This is ludicrous," said Madame Roquebrune. "If you have any proof, I'll be happy to take a look at it. Make an appointment with my assistant. In the meantime, this is a board meeting and we have important business to go over. Guards," she called. "Remove these people."

There was no movement.

"No one's coming," said Dussault. "And Monsieur Gamache has a perfect right to be here. He now sits on the board."

"He does not. I never sold him my place," Pinot repeated.

"Then what's this?" Daniel put a paper onto the table. "Stephen put this in that file with the rest of the evidence."

Pinot looked at it and felt light-headed.

Stephen had told him it was a customs and excise form, to allow the transfer of that much money out of Canada and into France.

Alain Pinot had trusted Stephen. Alain Pinot had underestimated Stephen.

The old man had tricked him into signing over his seat after all.

"Even if this was legitimate," said Pinot, scrambling, "the shares would belong to Horowitz, not you. And he's in a coma."

"True. And while he is, my father has power of attorney. And he's delegated me to take his place. So if you'll stand up."

"You idiot," snarled the CEO as Pinot blanched.

The Prefect of Police faced the head of Agence France-Presse.

"Alain Pinot, you're under arrest for the murder of Alexander Plessner and the attempted murders of Stephen Horowitz, Allida Lenoir, Judith de la Granger, and Séverine Arbour."

Then he turned to Eugénie Roquebrune. And slowly, carefully, listed the charges against her.

CHAPTER 43

⁓

Armand and Reine-Marie sat on either side of Stephen's bed, each holding one of his thin hands.

The monitors beeped. The ventilator rose and fell with soft whooshes for every breath. Lights blinked with medical messages the Gamaches didn't understand and didn't try to.

They understood only one thing.

It was time.

For all humane reasons, it was time.

"We found the evidence you hid in the file," Armand told him. "Daniel's at the board meeting right now."

Armand paused, as though he expected a reply. Then went on.

"Nails in Calais," he said, with a small laugh. "Very clever. Joseph Migneret. The Agence France-Presse notes by the murdered reporter. The links you and Monsieur Plessner made from the neodymium mine, to GHS's manufacturing plants, to supermagnets and those accidents. It's all there. And the final evidence. The hard evidence. I almost missed it. You were almost too clever for me."

"You have it, Armand?" asked Reine-Marie.

He shook his head. "But I'm pretty sure I know where it is. You got them, Stephen. You and Monsieur Plessner did it."

Finding the truth had cost Stephen his fortune. It had cost him his life. To save the lives of strangers. But it was done. If the seat on the

418

board didn't sink those giants, the hostile takeover of those two GHS subsidiaries would.

It had fallen to Armand to release that torpedo. Which, as Stephen's guardian, he had done just before entering the hospital room.

At the start of trading on the Paris Bourse, Stephen's buyout of the refinery and the tool and die manufacturer would go through. Giving him, or his heirs, the right to examine GHS's books.

And then it would all become public.

Stephen had sunk everything he had into taking over those companies. Knowing in doing that, he himself would be sunk.

The doctor hovered behind Reine-Marie and caught Armand's eye.

"Monsieur Gamache?"

"Just another minute, please," said Armand. "We're waiting for someone. Oh, here she is."

Jean-Guy entered, holding the baby.

"This is your great-granddaughter," said Armand.

Jean-Guy stood beside Armand. His mentor. In many ways, his own father. And wondered if he'd be able to do what Armand was about to.

Armand stood up, still holding Stephen's hand, and said, "It's time. Let him go."

Then he sat back down, his legs weak.

If this was the right thing to do, why did it feel so wrong?

But no, it didn't feel wrong. It felt wretched. Horrific. A nightmare.

But sometimes "right" felt like that.

When the ventilator was removed, and all the IVs and tubing and equipment taken away, the room grew very quiet.

What remained was Stephen.

Jean-Guy bent down and placed the child in the crook of Stephen's arm.

"Her name's Idola," Armand whispered. "Named after Idola Saint-Jean, who fought for equal rights. She never gave up. She never gave in."

"Her name means 'inner truth,'" said Jean-Guy.

He looked into the irregular eyes and the flat facial features of their daughter with Down syndrome.

They'd known since early in the pregnancy. And had made a choice. For life. Just as Armand had just made a choice. To end a life.

There was, at that moment across Paris, a chorus of pings as, one after the other, board members received urgent messages.

Daniel looked at Claude Dussault, who nodded.

It was done.

The buy order Daniel had discovered at the bank had gone through.

The pings were the sound of a torpedo rapidly approaching the great conglomerate.

Armand brought out Stephen's favorite book of poetry and began reading.

> I just sit where I'm put, composed
> of stone and wishful thinking . . .

In order to save their skins, if not their souls, the board members voted to kill GHS Engineering themselves.

They had to be seen to be on the side of right. The side of the angels.

It would have to be made clear, to the regulators, to the public, that as soon as they found out what GHS Engineering had been doing— the murders, the cover-up, the thousands of people killed in accidents that could have been prevented—the board members had themselves acted swiftly and decisively.

They voted to contact the authorities and regulators.

To shut down the nuclear power plants.

To ground affected aircraft and stop affected trains.

To inspect bridges and elevators.

While the CEO, Eugénie Roquebrune, was led away, they voted to set up a genuine compensation fund for the victims and their families.

And to make Carole Gossette the acting head of GHS, to oversee its demise.

"That in the midst of your nightmare," Armand read, softly. *"The final one, a kind lion will come with bandages in her mouth—"*

Outside the boardroom, Xavier Loiselle approached Daniel.

"That was incredibly brave of you, to come out of hiding for your father."

"Brave? I was scared shitless."

"But you did it."

"I can't believe my father let me think he was dead."

"He wasn't playing dead. Being hit at close range, even by cartridges, is no joke. He was knocked out. I know the difference between someone pretending and someone who's actually out cold. And just so you know, he couldn't have known Girard had picked up his gun. When he jumped in to save you, he had no idea the bullets were the fake ones. He expected to die."

Loiselle shifted his gaze to the Prefect, supervising the arrests, before returning to Daniel. "Don't shy away from the truth. It's an amazing thing, to be willing to die for each other."

Claude Dussault came over and, patting Loiselle on his arm, said, "Come see me later in the week. We can discuss your future."

"*Oui, patron.*"

"—And lick you clean of fever," said Armand. No longer reading. He'd memorized the poem, by their neighbor Ruth, long ago. One of his favorites, too.

Stephen was still and silent.

Armand leaned close to his godfather, reciting so softly no one else heard, *"And pick your soul up gently by the nape of the neck, and caress you into darkness and paradise."*

He kissed him on the forehead and whispered, "Thank you. Safe travels, dear man. I love you."

"Excusez-moi," said the doctor and, bending over Stephen, he used his stethoscope to listen for a heartbeat.

Then he straightened up.

CHAPTER 44

⁓

I t did seem appropriate that a garden named for a man who hid Jews in the war should itself be almost hidden.

But the Gamaches knew how to find it, just off rue des Rosiers.

The jardin Joseph-Migneret was quiet this Thursday morning in mid-October, and they had it almost all to themselves.

The girls ate crêpes, bought from Omar, and now ran like dervishes between the trees and benches, chasing each other and shrieking with laughter.

Annie rocked Idola in her arms, while Honoré tugged at his father's hand, trying to break free. Eventually, Jean-Guy let go and watched him race into the walled garden, to play with his cousins.

The adults had paused in the passageway, between the busy street and the garden. Standing in a semicircle before the plaque, they read each name. Noting the ages of those Monsieur Migneret had not managed to save.

The children of the Marais, sent away. Who never came home.

Then the Gamaches joined their children.

Armand and Reine-Marie stopped, by habit, at the exact spot where he'd proposed, and she'd accepted, more than thirty years earlier. And watched their grandchildren play.

There was a chill in the air this October morning, and Armand adjusted the blanket around the knees of the elderly man in the wheelchair and got a "Fuck off, I'm fine" from Stephen for his trouble.

Smiling, Armand straightened up in time to see a woman, about his own age, approach.

"*Excusez-moi,*" she said, pulling a sweater tighter around her. "I live in that apartment"—she pointed to a series of tall windows on the second floor—"and saw you here."

"*Désolé,*" said Daniel. "Are the children disturbing you?"

"Oh, no. Not at all. Just the opposite. This garden was created with children in mind."

She knelt down and, bringing a photograph from her pocket, she placed it on Stephen's knees.

After examining it, Stephen lowered it to his lap and looked into the woman's eyes.

"Arlette?"

"Arlette's daughter. She died four years ago, but kept this by her bed. My father never minded. He knew he owed all he had to the man in the photo. And so do I."

The cracked and faded picture showed a young woman, in coat and slacks, smiling. But her eyes were grave. And beside her was a young man. Arm across her shoulder.

"That's you, isn't it?" said the woman. "You're Armand?"

"*Non,*" Annie began, but Stephen interrupted her.

"*Oui.* That was the name I used in the war."

Reine-Marie looked at her Armand, who was staring at Stephen, dumbfounded. He never knew that he'd been named after him.

"My mother told me that 'Armand' means 'warrior,'" said the woman. "And she said you were."

"We both were. My real name is Stephen. And your mother? I only knew her as Arlette."

"Hélène," she said. "She looked for you after the war, but you'd gone."

"*Oui.* To Canada. This's my family."

"Your son?" she asked, turning to Armand.

Stephen began to explain, but this time Armand cut him off and said, "*Oui.* And these are his grandchildren, and great-grandchildren."

"You've done well with the life you were given," she said and, kissing his cheek, she left them.

The next day they boarded the flight to Canada.

Daniel and Roslyn's furnishings were being shipped back to Montréal.

They were going home.

As was Stephen. But his home was now with Armand and Reine-Marie, by choice but also necessity. He'd lost everything.

Stephen was ruined. Stephen was happy.

After the doctor had removed the life support, Armand had sat with him for hours as color returned to the old man's face and his breathing became deeper and steadier.

Then he and Reine-Marie had gone to Stephen's apartment, where Irena Fontaine was directing the forensics.

"My God," she said on seeing him. "What a mess. The Prefect's gone home to change, but he told me what's been going on. It's going to take months, maybe years, to sort it all out."

She looked around. The body of the guard had been taken away and the scene-of-crime team was again doing its job.

"I'm sorry, Chief Inspector," she said. "For not believing you."

"Did you know what the Prefect was doing?"

"Not at all. He kept it close to his chest. Had to, I guess. I just wish he'd trusted me."

"Oh, I trust you, Irena," said the Prefect, just arriving back. "But I couldn't bring anyone in. Just as my predecessor couldn't bring me in." He turned to Gamache. "Monsieur Horowitz?"

"We removed the life support."

"Armand, I'm sorry," Claude began.

"He's alive," said Armand. "The doctors say he seems to actually be gaining strength."

"My God," said Dussault. "He's indestructible."

"Maybe even inhuman," said Reine-Marie, and Armand laughed.

"Come to get some of his things?" asked Fontaine.

"*Non,*" said Armand. "I've come to give you the final proof."

"You mean you weren't bullshitting?" asked Dussault. "It exists?"

"It not only exists, it's been here all along."

Armand walked over to the wall and took down the small watercolor, handing it to Reine-Marie. Then, getting a screwdriver from the toolbox, he removed the screw from the wall and held it in his closed fist.

"Stand back, please," he said, and the agents in the room stopped and looked over.

Turning to a lamp across the room, he opened his fist. The screw flew like a bullet and hit the lamp, knocking it over.

"Holy shit," said one of the investigators. "What was that thing?"

Claude Dussault went over and looked down at the screw attached to the metal lamp.

"Proof."

"Plessner had come back here Friday to retrieve it," said Armand. "But was interrupted and killed. They thought they were looking for papers, but the most damning evidence was just feet from them all the time. One small screw."

"How did you know?" Reine-Marie asked.

"Took me a while. I'd thought it strange that Stephen would have screws with him. So I thought it might be that. But the ones in Stephen's box weren't made from neodymium. I now think he and Plessner had a collection of normal screws, and invested in Daniel's venture capital company—"

"Screw-U," said Reine-Marie as Commander Fontaine shot her a confused look.

"—in order to cover up their interest in the real hardware," said Gamache. "I dismissed the screws because they weren't magnetized. But Stephen, thanks to Plessner, had another one."

He walked over to one of the large oil paintings and removed it.

"See here?" he pointed to the wall. "A picture hook."

"So?" said Fontaine. "I have them hanging my pictures. What's so strange about that?"

"Nothing," Gamache said, replacing the work. "What is strange is that he'd use a screw to hang a tiny, inconsequential painting. Why was that? Normally, if you were going to use a screw at all, it'd be for the largest, heaviest paintings. Why use it for the tiniest? And then there was what it's hung by."

Reine-Marie turned the painting around. "It's a nylon string, not a wire. And the little eye hooks are plastic."

"Exactly. I thought it was because the painting was obviously inexpensive. But then I began to think the reason was far different. Stephen hung this painting from the most valuable thing he now owned."

"And it was within feet of them, inches, all the time?" said Fontaine. "What would've happened if they'd found it?"

Armand and Reine-Marie returned to the hospital where, twelve hours later, Stephen regained consciousness.

The first thing he saw was Armand and Reine-Marie and, behind them on the wall, the peaceful little painting.

"You found it," he rasped.

CHAPTER 45

⁓

It was dusk when they got into cars at the Montréal airport and headed south across the St. Lawrence River toward, but not quite to, the Vermont border.

Once off the autoroute, the small procession took smaller and smaller roads until finally turning onto a dirt road.

There were no signs pointing the way. The GPS showed that they'd left the known routes and were now wandering in a sort of wilderness. But they knew they weren't lost.

Just the opposite.

At the crest of the hill, Armand stopped the car, and by mutual and unspoken consent, he and Reine-Marie got out. And helped Stephen out.

The three of them stood in the cold October evening. A light snow was falling, and they could just make out the forests and the rolling hills stretching to the horizon. While below them in the valley, as though in the palm of some great hand, was a small village.

Buttery light shone from the fieldstone, brick, and clapboard homes that surrounded the green, turned white with freshly fallen snow. The crisp night air held a hint of maple smoke, from the chimneys.

And in the very center of the village, three great pines swayed in the breeze.

Reine-Marie touched Armand's arm and pointed.

Someone had put the lights on in their home so that their wide front verandah was illuminated.

Getting back in the car, they drove slowly around the village green, passing Monsieur Beliveau's general store, the boulangerie, the bistro.

They could see Olivier and Gabri chatting with patrons. At the sight of their headlights Gabri turned and, nudging Olivier, they waved.

Myrna's bookstore was dark, but there were lights in her loft above.

Roslyn and Daniel pulled up behind his parents, and Jean-Guy and Annie behind them. Together they unloaded the vehicles of luggage and children.

One by one, villagers came over to lend a hand.

Clara Morrow opened her front door, and across the green came bounding Henri. His huge satellite ears forward, his tail wagging furiously, the shepherd raced across the snow-covered grass and plowed straight into Armand, almost knocking him off his feet.

Fred came next, trotting as fast as his old legs would take him, and Gracie, frantic to reach them, brought up the rear.

Stephen, with Reine-Marie on one side and Ruth on the other steadying him, said, "A chipmunk just ran into your house."

"That's not a chipmunk, you senile old man," said Ruth. "That's a badger. My God, you look awful. Are you sure you didn't die?"

"If I did, and you're here, this must be Hell."

Ruth laughed while Rosa, waddling beside them, muttered, "Fuck, fuck, fuck."

Annie and Jean-Guy got Honoré and Idola settled while Roslyn and Daniel had the girls bathed, then changed into their flannel pajamas.

By the time the children came back down, the fire was lit, and the home was filled with the aroma of the cottage pies Gabri and Olivier had brought over.

The old pine table in the kitchen held a huge bouquet of fall flowers and foliage from Myrna. As well as her signature butter tarts.

Drinks were poured as Clara, Ruth, Myrna, Gabri, and Olivier brought everyone up to speed on the events in the village since the Gamaches had been gone.

Honoré fell asleep against Ruth, with Rosa nestled on his lap, while the girls sat with Myrna and Clara.

Gabri held Idola, gently rocking her in his arms.

"I want one," he said quietly to Olivier.

"You are one," said Olivier.

Claude Dussault put down their suitcases as Monique drew back the curtains and threw open a window.

Their small stone home in Saint-Paul-de-Vence hadn't been lived in for months.

Dussault had been busy in Paris with the investigations into GHS. And answering questions into his own behavior.

Finally it was decided that he should, for the good of the Préfecture, step aside. Step down. Step back. Way back.

"Retire, Claude," the Minister of the Interior had said. "Go plant roses. Enjoy your life."

It was framed as a reward for decades of service. Though everyone knew it was a punishment. A consequence.

Still, neither Claude nor his wife regretted his actions. Though he did deeply regret that he couldn't prevent the murder of Alexander Plessner or the attack on Stephen Horowitz.

"Here's a postcard from Xavier Loiselle," said Monique, checking the mail their housekeeper had put on the dining table. "He's accepted the job you found him, but not the one in Paris."

"*Non?*" said Claude as he opened more curtains and windows to air out the place.

Their home looked across the rolling hills of the Côte d'Azur, toward the Mediterranean, not quite visible in the distance.

"No. He's with the Commissariat de Police in Nice. Just a few kilometers from us."

"Huh. I wonder why."

Monique looked at her husband and smiled. "I don't." She went back to the postcard. "Get this. He's started saxophone lessons. And sounds like he's smitten."

"With the sax?"

Claude had opened the French doors to their stone *terrasse* and stepped out. He felt the sun on his face and breathed in the fresh air, scented with lemons from the grove just below them.

"With his teacher," said Monique. "He'd like to bring her by one Sunday. Oh."

"What is it?"

"A letter from the bank." She ripped it open. "That's strange."

"What? Are they calling our mortgage? That's all we need."

"No." She stepped onto the *terrasse* and showed him the paper. "This says the mortgage had been paid."

Sure enough, the balance owing was zero.

"I wonder who did that?" he said.

Armand put on his coat and hat and, opening the door, he called to the dogs. And Gracie. Who might, or might not, have been a ferret. Though it didn't matter. She was family.

The animals ran out the door, skidding slightly on the snow-covered porch.

The children had been fed and put to bed. Stories were read to them as they drifted off to sleep, snug and warm under their duvets as a cool breeze puffed out the curtains.

Daniel stood beside his daughters' beds in the dark, and looked through the window at his father walking around the village green.

Then he put his hand in the pocket of his cardigan and brought out a scuffed envelope. On it, in his father's hand, was written, *For Daniel.*

It was what his father had slipped him that day, years ago, on Mount Royal. Daniel, assuming it was money, and a not-very-subtle message that he couldn't provide for his own family, hadn't opened it.

He'd told his father he'd thrown it away, but had actually shoved it to the back of a drawer, and only found it again when they were packing up.

Now he tore it open. There was a short note inside, and something else.

Tipping the envelope up, out slid a thin silver chain, and a tiny crucifix.

> Dearest Daniel. This was what your grandfather, my father,
> wore throughout the war. He always said it protected him. He
> gave it to me on my ninth birthday. The last, and most precious,
> gift he gave me, besides, of course, the gift of his love. He said it
> would keep me safe. I've worn it since. And now, I want you to
> have it.
> Love, Dad

Closing his fist around it, Daniel watched as Jean-Guy sprinted across the snow to join his father. Then, after kissing his sleeping children and whispering that he loved them, Daniel went downstairs to join Stephen, who was nodding by the fire.

"What've you got there?" Stephen asked.

"You're ninety-three and were run over by a truck, shouldn't you be blind or demented by now?"

Stephen laughed. "Unfortunately for you, that truck seems to have knocked some sense into me."

He nodded toward the chain in Daniel's hand. And Daniel told him.

"May I see it?"

When Daniel gave it to him, Stephen gestured for Daniel to turn around. As he fixed it around Daniel's neck, he whispered, "See this for what it is."

"A good-luck charm?"

"The truth."

"Mind some company?" Jean-Guy asked as he fell into step beside Armand.

"Not at all," said Armand.

Their feet crunched on the snow and their faces tingled as large, wet flakes landed softly and melted.

"I spoke to Isabelle today," said Jean-Guy, his words coming out in puffs. "She brought me up to speed."

"Good."

"I can start on Monday, if that works for you. It won't be awkward, will it? My coming back to homicide and sharing second-in-command duties with her?"

"If she can stand you, so can I," said Armand. He stopped and looked at Jean-Guy. "Are you sure Annie's all right with you coming back?"

"From Paris? There was no question. This's where we belong. This's where we want to raise our children. Here, in Québec."

"I meant with you coming back to the Sûreté," Armand clarified. "To homicide."

Jean-Guy smiled. "Do you think I'd be doing it if Annie didn't agree? It was her idea. She said we were meant to be together. You and me. She says it's fate."

"Do you believe that?"

"In fate?" Jean-Guy considered, then nodded.

Though he couldn't quite bring himself to say it out loud, his actions had spoken.

"I was thinking about the Tremblay case . . ."

They continued their stroll around the village green, talking about murder, while the dogs, and Gracie, romped and rolled in the fresh snow.

Annie, holding Idola, along with Roslyn and Reine-Marie, had gone over to the bistro, and were visible through the window, sitting with Clara, Myrna, and Ruth by the roaring fire.

Wedges of lemon meringue pie sat in front of each of them.

"Before you go," said Stephen as Daniel put his coat on. "Can you help me with something?"

Stephen gripped Daniel's hand as they walked slowly down the hall to his bedroom on the main floor. His suitcases were there, partially unpacked. Digging through one, he brought out a bulky sweater. Unwrapping it, he revealed the small watercolor.

"There, please." Stephen pointed.

Daniel hammered a picture hook into the wall, then picked up the painting.

"No," said Stephen, taking it from him. "I'll hang it. You go outside."

After Daniel left, he turned the painting around and saw Arlette's writing.

For Armand, with love.

Bringing out a pen he carefully added two words, so that it now read, *For Armand, my son, with love.*

Then Stephen Horowitz hung the watercolor where he could see it first thing in the morning and at the end of the day. The end of his days.

And know that, while he'd taken the long way, he was finally home.

"Want to go in?" Jean-Guy asked as they looked through the bistro window.

"*Non*, I'm heading home," said Armand. "We left Daniel alone with Stephen."

"And his cane," said Jean-Guy, who'd received more than one whack.

Armand watched his son-in-law join the others around the bistro fire. He could read Ruth's lips as she greeted him: "Hello, numbnuts."

Reine-Marie put her head back and laughed.

Armand smiled, then turned full circle.

His gaze took in the dark forests and luminous homes, the three huge pines and the soft snow falling from the sky, as though the Heavens had opened, and all the angels were joining them. Here. Here.

"Dad."

Armand turned.

ACKNOWLEDGMENTS

Michael took me to Paris for the first time back in 1995. I was thirty-six years old and we'd been seeing each other for five months. He was invited to give a talk on childhood leukemia to a conference in Toulouse, and asked if I'd like to go along. When I regained consciousness I said, yes, yes, yes please!

We flew out of Montréal in a snowstorm, almost missing the flight. Michael was, to be honest, a little vague on details, like departure times of planes, trains, buses. In fact, almost all appointments. This was the trip where I realized we each had strengths. Mine seemed to be actually getting us to places. His was making it fun once there.

On our first night in Paris we went to a wonderful restaurant, then for a walk. At some stage he said, "I'd like to show you something. Look at this."

He was pointing to the trunk of a tree.

Now, I'd actually seen trees before, but I thought there must be something extraordinary about this one.

"Get up close," he said. "Look at where I'm pointing."

It was dark, so my nose was practically touching his finger, lucky man.

Then, slowly, slowly, his finger began moving, scraping along the bark. I was cross-eyed, following it. And then it left the tree trunk. And pointed into the air.

I followed it.

And there was the Eiffel Tower. Lit up in the night sky.

As long as I live, I will never forget that moment. Seeing the Eiffel Tower with Michael. And the dear man, knowing the magic of it for a woman who never thought she'd see Paris, made it even more magical by making it a surprise.

C. S. Lewis wrote that we can create situations in which we are happy, but we cannot create joy. It just happens.

That moment I was surprised by complete and utter joy.

A little more than a year earlier I knew that the best of life was behind me. I could not have been more wrong. In that year I'd gotten sober, met and fell in love with Michael, and was now in Paris.

We just don't know. The key is to keep going. Joy might be just around the corner.

I've tried to bring that wonderment. That awe. That love of place because of the place, but also because of the memories a place holds, to this book.

That love of Paris that I discovered with Michael. And that the Gamaches have.

This is a book about love, about belonging. About family and friendship. It's about how lives are shaped by our perceptions, by not just our memories, but how we remember things.

It's about choices. And courage.

Michael and I returned to Paris several times after that. But since his death, I had not been back. Too chicken.

But I knew in my heart it was time. It was time for Armand and Reine-Marie to visit Daniel and Roslyn. Annie and Jean-Guy. And the grandchildren. In Paris.

It was time for me to return.

It was time to leave the safety and security of Three Pines, and face whatever was waiting.

The first time I returned, to research *All the Devils Are Here*, I knew I couldn't go alone. I asked my good friend Guy Coté if he'd come with me, guide me, show me places in Paris I'd never normally see.

Places the Gamaches would know about, but that I did not.

So we rented an apartment in the Marais, where Armand's grandmother once lived and where they've inherited her home. Then I asked if Kirk and Walter, great friends of ours, would join. They did.

Then my Québec publisher, Louise Loiselle, said she was going to be in Paris at the same time. So she joined our little troupe.

Suddenly, what had been fraught with emotional turmoil felt safe. And fun. I was not alone.

I am deeply, deeply grateful to Guy. For all his research, for the lunches and coffees we had together in Knowlton in preparation. For the books and maps he bought me and that we pored over together.

And, once there, for the fun we all had, exploring that extraordinary, luminous city.

Thank you to Kirk and Walter, for coming along and making it all the more meaningful and fun. And for always being, over the years, so supportive. Michael thought of them as sons. And they reciprocated his love.

Thank you to Louise Loiselle, of Flammarion Québec, for all her help, including setting up meetings in Paris with Eric Yung, a former undercover cop in Paris and now a crime writer, and with Claude Cancès, the former head of the Police Judiciare de Paris.

Guy, Louise, and I sat in the Hôtel Lutetia, as Claude and Eric recounted stories of investigations in Paris. Of crimes. Or criminals. Of events both horrific and hilarious. Of how the Préfecture de Paris is organized.

Claude became the inspiration, though clearly fictionalized, for the Prefect of Police in the book.

Something else quite amazing happened during that first Paris research trip (I returned several times for more research). Through a mutual friend, I was introduced to Dorie Greenspan, the cookbook author and columnist for *The New York Times Magazine*.

She and her husband, Michael, live in the U.S. and have an apartment in Paris. They invited us over for drinks one night, and then out to dinner to one of their favorite little restaurants.

Juveniles.

None of us had met Dorie or Michael before. As we walked through

Paris to the restaurant, Dorie and I fell into step. And by the time we arrived we'd fallen into a deep friendship.

Through her I've discovered a Paris I would never, ever have found on my own. And I found a kindred spirit.

Someone else I met there is Eric Zenouda. Who walked me around the Marais and talked about the little-known history. He too has become a friend.

I hope you've finished the book before you read on, because there are going to be some spoilers now.

A huge thank-you to Stephen Jarislowsky, the inspiration for Stephen Horowitz. I want to make it clear that Horowitz is fictional, especially the descriptions of his family in the war. A dramatic decision on my part that has absolutely no connection to the real Stephen.

I do need to point out that in a previous book Horowitz has children. In this book he does not. I'm afraid I made a mistake in that first mention of Horowitz, in being far more specific than I needed to be.

Lesson learned. Children erased.

As always, a huge thanks goes to my assistant, Lise Desrosiers. A colleague and great friend. There's no way I could do what I do without her help, and her unfailing support. What a gift to love a person you work with.

Thank you to my U.S. publishers at Minotaur Books and St. Martin's Press. My wonderful new editor, Kelley Ragland, one of Hope's protégées. Publicist Sarah Melnyk. Paul Hochman, the father of the virtual bistro and so much more. David Rotstein, who has designed this marvelous cover. Andy Martin, the publisher. And Jennifer Enderlin, Sally Richardson, and Don Weisberg of SMP.

Thank you to Jamie Broadhurst and the entire team at Raincoast Books in Vancouver.

Thank you so much to Linda Lyall, in Scotland.

Thanks to Danny and Lucy who run the bookstore, Brome Lake Books, in my village and organize the annual prelaunch event.

Thank you to my longtime agent, Teresa Chris, for all her help over the years, and to my new literary agent, David Gernert.

Thank you to Rocky and Steve, to Oscar and Brendan, to Allida and Judy, to Hardye and Don, Hillary and Bill, Chelsea and Marc, Jon, Shelagh Rogers, Ann Cleeves. Rhys Bowen, and Will Schwalbe.

And to my family, Rob, Audi, Doug, Mary, and the nieces and nephews who, while amazed and shocked by my success, never fail to cheer.

This book is dedicated, as you might have noticed, to Hope Dellon. Hope edited the Gamache books, from *The Cruelest Month* onward. She became ill and went on sick leave a couple of years ago, but continued to edit my books, from home.

As special as the word "friend" is, as powerful a concept and reality, it doesn't come close to what Hope and I had. It was an intellectual and emotional intimacy that comes from working so closely together on something we both cared deeply about.

Hope realized she couldn't continue, and so she announced her retirement this year. But, over lunch in New York, she agreed to become my First Reader. To take over the role Michael always held.

So she read *All the Devils Are Here* before anyone else, even Lise. And she gave me her thoughts. Always incisive. Thoughtful. Kind even. But clear. What she liked. And what she did not.

We were all to gather at the home of her close friend Sally Richardson, the longtime publisher of St. Martin's Press, to celebrate Hope's retirement. But two weeks before that, Hope suffered a heart attack, and passed away. Her beloved Charlie and daughters Rebecca and Emma at her side.

The loss is incalculable. As is her contribution to literature. The books she edited and improved, including mine. The writers she worked with and improved, including me. The young editors she mentored.

Hope was a passionate supporter of all things literary, from libraries to bookstores, from theatre to books of all genres.

It breaks my heart that Hope is no longer with us, but I take comfort in imagining her sitting with Michael by the fireplace in the bistro. Waiting for us.

As I write this, I'm looking at one of the many gifts she sent. It's a pillow and on it is written:

Goodness Exists.